Monty

Monty

A Novel by Philip U. Effiong

ISBN: 0-75960-873-3

This book is printed on acid free paper.

1stBooks – rev. 05/03/01

Monty is for—

Amaeka, my second daughter, too precious for words;

Philip Effiong, Snr., my dad, a people's General without a doubt, whose self-sacrifice has brought the hope of renewal and sanity to so many;

And not least—

Valentine, my big brother, whose superior art continues to confound and bring life to the unliving.

Life at the Camp 1
Laughter 9
Conception 11
Delivery 15
Birth of Monty 17
Rescue 19
Born Again 21
Passage 23
A Whole New World 27
Alone 31
The Other Side 35
America 39
The Joneses 45
Cold 49
Warmth 61
Escape 65
Songs 71
Not the Joneses Again! 79
Dorothy 83
The Kennedys 87
The Flute 95
New Ground 99
Other Walls 101
Special People 107
Dreams 113
Rivalry 121
Uncertainty 139
Outside 147
Independence 151
Saint Peter 157
Myra 173
Lamentation 185
Talk Show 189

Still Sobbing 201
Dorothy Again! 205
War Songs 211
Crossroads 223
The Ribbon 235
Flight 243
Monty 251
Trapped 253
Descent 257
Where All Roads Meet 259
One More Bridge 273
Sunray On Glass 279
Fragments 281
Memories 295
Homecoming 301
Baptism 311
Divination 319
Wayfarer 323

Life at the Camp

Monty was born some two hundred yards from the refugee camp. He wasn't born within its cracked and dented walls. Not too long ago, they stood tall and strong. Now they chipped away, unwillingly and with little cause. He wasn't born within those gray and black and brown and ashy walls. They used to be bright white, the once proud walls of a small town's first colonial primary school. Once proud and full of praise, bringing honor to a town probing the twentieth century.

The War had doled out a crumbling sensation to the people. Within their walls they felt the sensation, and in their spirits too. As their lives crumbled, so did their walls. Like the once proud walls of the school--they weren't yet lying in complete ruins, but they were plastered with ugly scars and holes in no particular order. In those holes were a frenzied competition for space by spirited rats and sophisticated roaches. Those walls, painted with blood and pus and vomit and forgotten grime. Those walls, stained with laughter gone dry.

Because the filth had pierced their world so freely, they were desensitized to it. Monty wasn't born among the sick who were wrapped around each other; their misery shared in embraces cold and hard. He wasn't born among the dying who generously exchanged, in ignorance, the fruits of death. No, Monty wasn't born within those walls.

He was born away from the hunger that forced stillness. The refugees lay on their rags for hours, sometimes on naked concrete, sometimes naked, and stared. Even when mist formed over their eyes, the red broke through, along with thin lines of tear. But the lines dried up too quickly because their frail bodies carried little or no water. The stillness encircled them; it was one thick grip, and movement was either stifled or slowed. Even when measly ration found its way in, usually once a week, sometimes not at all, and the mad war for a bite raged, the stillness didn't die. There were those who just lay there in their nakedness and half nakedness, their dried-up, thin skins stretched frightfully by their tired bones. They just stared, sometimes out of their sockets it seemed, their sunken eyes almost lost in two widening hollows.

And even when a proud, daring warrior returned from a successful hunt, a dead puppy, cat, or snake hanging by a fiber cord from one of his shoulders, the stillness was overbearing. A beastly orgy often resulted from such kill, especially after the privileged meal was roasted over flames forced from dry wood, dry rock, and dry leaves. Excitement and impatience never allowed the complete preparation of such sacred feasts. And soon the refugees, those who could invoke a minuscule of reserved energy, or what passed for energy, were tearing at each other and the half done feast. Human and animal flesh was torn, and the blood that oozed forth mixed in nicely to confirm the bizarre marriage between man and beast. Whenever there had been a failed attempt at creating a flame, they refused to abandon their feast to frustration. The orgy still took place and since the meat was raw the blood flowed in thicker streams and louder spurts, and the tearing and gorging completed what the War had begun, draining away the remnants of humanity. But those who embraced the stillness lay impervious to such revelry, staring from those hollows as if lifeless, sometimes lifeless.

Little ones with no understanding of shortage, and no patience with endurance, wrestled furiously with flat, wrinkled breasts that dangled from the chest of an apathetic mother. The inability to squeeze anything out of resistant breasts brought their own brand of frustration, and not only for the little ones. When they tugged and bit and scratched and twisted, the mother fidgeted, but too often it was slight and not easily visible because, for the sake of the infant, she preferred to swallow her pain as best she could. She swallowed hard, with willpower summoned from somewhere. It was hard to tell what hurt more, the physical pain or the mental pain that came with the truth that nothing could be produced, at best a transparent imitation of what should have been. And when the imitation did come, it did so in weak, infrequent drops, tasteless.

Monty wasn't born within those walls where death was a collective story waiting to be heard or told. The refugees died so often, it was as if they did so at will. A peculiar stench usually rose above the rest as clue that death had taken place. The way they lay in one spot for eternity, and because they emaciated at the same speed, you couldn't easily separate the alive from the lifeless. You had to wait for the clue, the unique stench. When the stench was obvious, the probe began. Those who hungered for activity sniffed at the bodies, hit them, even spilled on them rain water gathered in twisted, rusty buckets from what was left of twisted zinc roofs. Finally the body was identified. Sometimes it was more than one body. If it was a child who still boasted a parent or two, the parent or parents summed up remarkable energy to let out a piercing howl or two, but such howls soon faded away. Either the parents lacked the strength to continue, or suddenly realized that death was merciful and snatched a child's life out of compassion. Otherwise there was seldom any lamentation.

It never took long for shallow graves to be dug out with any object that half served the purpose. It was tough to identify one of those graves trapped among the mounds of human excrement that dotted the rear of the buildings. One wonders how people who ate so little, if anything, had the ability to clear their systems so generously. And the corpse, always stark naked, was flung in more from a desire to escape the stench than to perform a humanitarian service. It was a masochistic ritual that added an aura of numbness to the stillness. An ambitious refugee always stripped the corpse; all articles of what passed for clothing were highly prized. As shallow as the graves were, all it took was a slight drizzle or the scratches of hungry chickens to unearth a decaying limb or head, the bones often eaten through by nomadic dogs and rodents.

Monty wasn't born within those walls where the walking dead pretended to be alive. Their pencil necks carried their

3

oversized heads precariously. Their bloated stomachs drooped over their contorted, pencil legs. Some of them began to swell in odd places. It was always a mystery how lack of food caused this peculiar fattening in spurts. A colorless liquid flowed from the limbs of those who suffered from the fattening virus. And they developed a subconscious act of scooping the liquid and wiping it on other parts of their bodies, or on the rags that barely covered anything. Their thinning, even decaying flesh caused a sudden transformation from full human to skeletal human. Accentuated by the cavities beneath, their protruding cheekbones pushed desperately against their near-transparent face skin. Or, at the other extreme, the skin bunched up tightly, as if in hopeless desperation to self-protect, taking on a reptilian look and feel. So cracked and hardened, it only falsified the frailty that lay underneath.

...

To say nothing of those who had once fought on frontlines, now too useless to do for themselves, let alone fight a war for reasons not quite known. A leg cut in half, maybe contorted beyond recognition, or a loud, dark void where an eye once sat proudly. Perhaps a mind that ran freely without hesitation or restraints that were routine, or joints that froze and caused an overall paralysis of body and spirit. Merely signs that enemy fire, deliberate and casual, had found its mark. Sometimes as the owner slept or daydreamed, a child patiently peered--maybe stuck a finger--into a cavity once filled with flesh, as if sure that some indication of life would spring forth. Sometimes a battleground was not responsible for the loss of limb or some other generous chunk of flesh. There was always the possibility, even when you quarreled with no one, of being in the way when the enemy suddenly broke through, or when bombs were tossed from a plane that swooped down without hesitation, a gift from Great Britain. Incomplete and so misshapen, their movements defied any particular order, and like crabs and chameleons it was hard to tell in what directions they were headed. Incomplete and so asymmetrical, it was a mystery how their frames were able to store their souls.

But Monty was born outside of those walls.

•••

The stench. The stench was always there, determined and mixed. The stench from sores that sprouted without warning, even on their tongues. The stench from colorless liquids that oozed from their limbs. The stench from black and yellow teeth, mostly cracked and shaky, begging for attention. And even from those gums that had since lost their every teeth to neglect, the stench was unbelievable. The stench from pus that trickled from orange boils that grew on their heads, causing the quick loss of red hair that used to be dark.

More from lack of activity than from a desire to heal, a compassionate mother would squash the boils between her thumbs. The ritual was unbearable for the victim, a child whose head was clamped between two knees as the mother, the surgeon, sat on the floor or a low stool. His or her struggle and protests climaxed in a loud yelp when a boil was successfully burst open, then fell to a constant whimper. It was victory for a weary mother who was fatigued by the least exertion, and the juice, yellow, red, dirty brown, or in-between, splattered in every direction, sometimes in the face of the mother. The aftermath was rarely therapeutic and the resulting sores, larger and fresh, invited flies to a more luscious feast. The stench.

The stench from the boils and sores, even when they crusted over. The stench from their excrement behind the buildings. The stench from their excrement splattered in other places not made for that purpose.

•••

Monty wasn't born within those walls where laws were broken before they were made. Wrapped around their wasp waists, the luckiest infants carried damp rags already defiled, emergency diapers also used for other things. Though they discharged too little, it added up and soon the rags could not protect like they were expected to. Weak, fecal spurts marked places that were thought to be unusual, a mother's body or threadbare loincloth perhaps. The older they got, the more widely and freely the children were inclined to spread the waste they hated to carry on the inside. But age did not necessarily come with respect for etiquette and privacy. Without warning, they could offload anywhere--beside a wall as people went about their daily, mundane habits, or within a wall on the middle of the floor; anywhere where there was room to squat. Done, they usually pulled themselves up calmly and with some effort, and then walked away without wiping what should have been wiped diligently. Those who knew better at best held their nostrils and looked the other way, unimpressed. Either they lacked the inspiration to do more, or they resigned themselves to a standard, which, within those walls, was actually high. The flies buzzed constantly; for them the bacchanalia saw no end and they had no excuse to fall asleep. But when the culprit wore a tuft of thick, uneven beard, sometimes gray, or boasted wiry breasts that stretched to her stomach, it caused some attention, maybe a little havoc. Clearly, knowledge of decency had been dulled by the morbidity that lingered, or by some other absurdity of war. When they squatted beside a building, sometimes within, sometimes humming a rhythm-less tune that they alone could understand, they flaunted a state of regression that couldn't go any deeper. And when they exposed body parts that were as undesirable and as unsightly as what they let loose, the repugnance was hard to bear, even for the inhabitants of those walls. It was not enough to just look away or grab one's nostrils; you had to leave the scene or, as some did, send away the culprit whose mind had been lost to the promises of war. Sticks and stones often did the job, even if they were rarely hurled with power or precision. When the assault was successful, the grownup fled with little speed, but with hallucinations of actually running. Between his or her butt cheeks were sandwiched repulsive hints of unfinished business. Ambitious flies followed eagerly, having waited long and impatiently for a feast no less appealing. The chase and the escape left a fetid trail that was easily traced by a starving dog or wild chicken.

For people who ate so little, they released a lot. And the stench cuddled up so closely until they were immune to it. The stench of feces delivered at the right places and at places that were convenient, not right. The stench from greasy rags that tripled up as clothing, as towels, as beds. Sometimes they more than tripled up and came in handy when the monthly bleeding struck an experienced woman or an unsuspecting girl at the corridors of womanhood. If the rags were all taken, they either stole or sought the protection of leaves that sometime itched or stung, and sometimes left sores or rashes. For those who were not that daring, they knew not to trouble themselves against such odds and they let the blood flow generously, making no effort to hide it from those who should not have known, let alone see. And the flies danced some more.

The stench.

Philip U. Effiong

Laughter

Monty wasn't born in the midst of defiance that wasn't necessarily intelligent, just amazing. The yearning to live on-- when all else either failed or was used up--was expressed in nighttime folktales rendered in voices so feeble they were not easily heard or understood. With the great effort at storytelling came a search for consolation in related genres. Banging the floors and walls, or hammering out a beat on twisted, rusty, corrugated cans and buckets with sticks, stones, or withering, bare fingers, created the best music that the situation would allow. When a voice rose to lead others in ancient folk songs, or recently created songs that confronted and accommodated the War, it was never difficult to recognize the struggle brought on by starvation and exhaustion. The words that came out were commonly faint, and even when they were clear they didn't stay that way for too long. They easily evolved into a howl that was as dirge-like as it was supposed to be empowering, but the songs never went to waste. Whether the words were heard, unheard, understood, or misunderstood, they were known and so were the tunes that gave them meaning and beauty. For people to whom song and dance were an intrinsic part of existence, it was hard to remain still. They forced themselves up and performed what came across as a ritual chant and march of drunken zombies; they were like sagging silhouettes, fractured and without direction or form. In their wasted state their efforts were breathtaking, like they would slowly crumble and go to pieces, engulfed in their own courage and distress. But they held on, sometimes by sheer determination that may have been best discarded, sometimes by leaning on or holding on to one another, sometimes with the aid of a stick. For those who couldn't muster enough energy to stand, they squirmed or twitched where they lay or sat. To the outsider, it would have all been absurd, even gothic, but to them it was the type of diversion that could

9

preserve, renew, and reinvent laughter. Whatever it was, Monty was born away from it all.

Conception

Monty was born outside of those ominous walls; walls hunched over as if weeping in silence. He was born outside, outdoors. It all began within those walls, believe it or not, with the strange effort to be consumed in fleshly passion. It tore the refugees between the terror that they meant to appease every day, and the urge to feel human. And so when darkness fell, and with the aid of no substitute for natural light, they groped. They groped, with the aid of an unwritten code relayed without words. They squirmed, like worms headed in no particular direction, relying faithfully on their near-numb sense of touch. Refugees who were strangers at daytime became emergency lovers under the camouflage of darkness, and without any real desire to love. They squirmed and groped in the dark, they rolled over, undaunted by the cold pain of the hard concrete that was stretched to near unbearable by their deep and thick sores. They stretched their arms, their fingers transformed into trusted proboscis, touching and testing with mysterious skill. The women and girls sometimes gave in with the hesitant belief that satisfaction might just be reached, something to temper their misery and a reason to wave off death one more time. But their bodies, tested to the maximum, and their skins, wasted and fragile, mostly suffered a relentless pain, no matter how wide they spread their legs and no matter how desperately they tried to ignore the fierce lacerations and the torture. When they were so torn open, they wasted the little blood that their bodies still held, dark red, almost black. The early morning light filtering through cracks and gaping holes, unsuccessfully plugged with decaying banana leaves, exposed the dark stains, still fresh, even wet. For those women and girls who tried to refuse, theirs was a battle that was always lost. With nowhere to borrow spare energy, they had to lie there as their bodies were drilled into, terrorized and helpless. Feeble thrusts drew blood and screams that soon died out as the women and girls lost the strength and motivation to protest or beg or weep or stay conscious.

For most of the men the excitement was also too much to bear, and in their rickety state they too agonized. An erection didn't always come easy as a willing spirit hardly ever enjoyed the cooperation of depleted flesh. The battle to attain and maintain an erection, and the strain of plunging down a congested passage, brought fear and torment and bruises. Because the act depreciated the mind and body much faster than it satisfied, contentment was forced, joy restrained. But joy, no matter how little, was still etched and sustained in the knowledge that the Civil War hadn't snatched away all levels of masculinity.

Morning always showed the fresh stains, telltale signs of the previous night's hysteria. But there was never any absolute knowledge of who had mounted who, freely or forcefully. Speculations usually sufficed as none of the women really wanted to know who her rapist or depraved lover had been the night before. And none of the men really wanted to know who owned the withering, sore-infested legs between which they had sought solace the night before. It was an orgiastic ritual, as sickening as it was healing, as sadistic as it was selfish.

No one spoke about the frequent night drama, not even after it gave birth to another miracle when an occasional pregnancy, way too heavy to carry, showed prominently. They usually terminated in merciful miscarriages, the loss of blood always too great to handle, and many mothers accompanied their unborn children in death. When a pregnancy was carried through its cycle, and it was very seldom even for wartime, the story wasn't different. Either the child emerged hard and cold, a nine-month-old rock, or the mother lay there forever, hard and cold too, or both mother and child lay wrapped in each other forever, still hard and cold. But Monty lived.

Monty was born outside those walls. His mother met sunlight several mornings while resting in her blood and in the anguish and madness of the previous night. Within her, not too far inside, putrid spurts of sperm would have dried up. And even when a lump showed on the front of her wrinkled stomach, the strange men, unknown and persistent shadows, still crept on her in the dark until they found the lump too inconveniencing. She had long come to the realization that her best weapon was to lay still and bury the anguish deep within the insanity that it came with.

Delivery

They said the man came from one of the health centers set up by the Catholic Church. No one could ascertain his training or skills in the field. And no one cared. He looked like he was in serious need of medical attention himself, the way his bent over, depleted body was almost drowned out by his threadbare, white overall. The once-red cross, a sanctimonious emblem hurriedly sewn on the rear, looked awkward as it had lost its right limb and a lot of its red.

Her water must have broken though you had to peer closely to see any water. The man didn't look too confident about the prospect of delivering anything from the comatose refugee woman that early morning. She had prayed fervently for death to rescue her; that was months ago. But her body had been merciless and survived the impossible. It was one of those mind games that confounded any logic. Her body had spurned nourishment; it wasn't there anyway, and yet life had refused to release her to death. The child, independent and unmoved by the piercing horror, sapped its mother mercilessly, leaving very little, if anything, to just sustain her consciousness. As she shuddered in great disjointed bursts, the sweat flowed profusely, then dried up. And then even the shudders ceased and the only hint of life was expressed in occasional heaves that soon dwindled to barely noticeable breaths. They were far between, but the way her eyes were shut tight you knew that it didn't matter. A few of the women had gathered. It was more from a sense of customary duty than with real faith in their ability to be of any help.

And then there was the sudden commotion. It was either caused by an air raid or by the unexpected outcry announcing the arrival and seizure of the small town by enemy troops. Whatever caused it, its impact was swift. The spectacular rush of energy was beyond comprehension and in no time everyone was gone.

Birth of Monty

Within the bare walls, the bare space was deserted, silent and creepy. Filling a tiny area of the solitude, except for one or two near-dead or totally dead bodies, was the refugee woman, her legs still spread wide apart. Her subconscious desire to relieve herself of the load had not been totally lost. Before the panic that took everyone away, the infant head had already began to show, hairless, almost transparent, white, and covered in thin, red veins. The child was more dead than alive when it emerged in full, and yet it was much closer to life than its mother. It had dropped out within those walls, but it wasn't born within those walls. Whether it was by divine intervention or by that indomitable human spirit that is divine anyway, the use-up of all that energy, gleaned from who-knows-where, had taken what seemed like its final toll on the woman. And yet she moved. Somehow she inched her way, crawling, rolling, but never once lifting herself up. The infant, all bloodied, was entwined with her all the way and still attached to the umbilical cord. His cry, an inconsistent whimper, was constant but too faint, and even if it were louder it would not likely have drawn any attention from the delirious crowd that ran to no particular destination. Together mother and child gradually transformed into little more than a red orb, the mother's instinct half forcing her to grab her baby, mostly weakly and unsuccessfully. But it was the umbilical cord that kept them together, and it was by its string that she half dragged the newborn. For hours they made snail-paced progress, leaving behind a trail of blood which one mongrel traced and partially lapped up. It wasn't until about two hundred yards from those walls that she stopped. All around her there was a handful of corpses and maimed people on the red, dusty road and by the roadside. There was an occasional distant explosion or sound of gunfire. There was an occasional scream. There were a number of federal troops who marched by, their rifles at the ready and their black boots eating into short shrubs and the sandy road. If they noticed the human carnage that lay all around them, they showed no interest. Not even for the mother and child that lay wrapped in each other and soaked in the mother's blood, bonded by a now half-torn umbilical cord.

The child twitched every now and then, and ever so lightly, his little cries drowned out by the pervasive havoc. Its birth had only begun. Mother wasn't moving or making any sounds. But her eyes were wide open, showing a ghostly white upon which flies buzzed, settled, and fed freely. Her prayers had been answered at last.

Rescue

Her instinct suspected that the infant still held on to life. Which was quite a feat, considering that she was desperately making her getaway. It was early evening and nature, unperturbed by the madness of war, sent an orange sun to gradually sink behind graying clouds. It was calm compared to the chaos earlier that day. The grinding noise made by her badly beaten Volkswagen Beetle interrupted the relative calm. Patched over and over in several places, you couldn't tell the original color of the car. This was made even more difficult by the amount of smoke that escaped from its exhaust, engulfing it almost completely.

Her very white, chubby face exposed what might have otherwise been masked. The Irish reverend sister was petrified. But the silver cross that hung around her neck, reaching down to her chest, still maintained its shine. Once the news hit the Catholic Medical Center, everyone was on his or her own. It was not worth waiting to find out if indeed the enemy was running over the small town. Before any gunshot or explosion was heard, the Center was abandoned and so were its sick, maimed, dead, and insane tenants. Like other deserters, she fled into the bush behind the Center, holding her robe above her knees in the process, and showing tremendous speed for a woman her age and size. Even after her glasses fell from her pointed nose she continued to run until she found what looked like the perfect undergrowth within which to lay low until things calmed down.

The reverend sister emerged from the undergrowth when a sense of normalcy seemed to return to the outside world, oblivious of the long hours that had transformed morning to evening. When fear rules, of what use is time anyway? Like the others, she had made the right decision in fleeing and hiding. The federal troops were especially piqued by the Center because of the medical and relief supplies it provided their insolent enemy. The two whitewashed buildings that housed its resources, workers, and inmates were among the first few buildings that they leveled with rockets. Both buildings came down in two large heaps, providing immediate, unceremonious tombs for those inmates who were either dead, almost dead, or calling on death. If they weren't in a big hurry to tear down the town and everything it contained, maybe the federal troops would have discovered the ancient vehicle camouflaged underneath dry palm frond leaves. It sat quietly behind the Center, in the bush and not too far from where the reverend sister sought protection.

In a crouching position too uncomfortable, and with stealth inspired by anxiety, she came within yards of the palm frond shelter that had housed her Beetle for many months. Only then did she believe that her treasure had been undiscovered and untouched. But the bigger miracle was yet to come. After carefully picking the palm fronds apart and entering the jalopy, she forced the rusty key in the ignition and turned it back and forth several times, pumping the accelerator fervently. The car didn't let out its rattling sound immediately, but when it did her hopes more than tripled. After a few more persistent tries, and after a few clattering protests from the car, it came to life. She didn't waste time revving it. After making a huge sign of the cross and raising her arms in the air to acknowledge a God who now proved to exist, she made her sneaky exit.

Born Again

Sister Eileen Doherty was accustomed to the horror and cruelty of war, but this was like nothing she had ever dealt with or witnessed. A dog tearing at one of the refugee woman's shriveled breasts quickly sauntered off as the Sister instinctively swerved her car to the side of the road, pumping the breaks furiously to get the car to a complete halt, and raising a huge smoke of red dust.

The way those flies fought each other in a frenzy to have access to the refugee woman's eyeballs, her ears, her mouth, her sores. The way they swarmed all over her battered vagina, their buzzes sounding like a deliberate hum of gratification. The way they danced around and in the decaying patches of blood. The way they settled on the half-torn umbilical cord. Sister Eileen observed how they didn't show as much interest in the infant. Its inconsistent twitches, far between and barely noticeable, showed that the child was fighting hard to cry out and live. But it was incapable of producing sound. Using an old razor that sat on her cracked dashboard, Sister Eileen sliced the umbilical cord, finally separating child from mother. She was scared to pick up the mouse-sized infant, almost premature and transparent, streaks of green and red vein showing through its skin. She carefully wrapped it in a small greasy towel that sucked the blood almost immediately, and placed it on the seat beside her. She drove off and the car creaked, as if resentful, staggering up a slight incline with much effort.

Just before the car made it to the top of the incline, a shot rang out. The bullet struck below Sister Doherty's left breast and lodged near her heart. The impact and sting threw her off momentarily and she almost ran into the side bush with its tall mahogany trees. After swerving wildly from side-to-side, she managed to steady the overused car and simply continued like nothing had happened. Exhausted by this insanity to which she had sacrificed her career and life for some three or so years, perhaps she should have abandoned control of the car and her fate to some opportune soldier. But she looked at the little red parcel that lay beside her and she was urged on by a sense of sublime duty. She wasn't the one who mattered, even if her ghost-white face spoke of fear, and even if the growing patch of red beneath her breast spoke of excruciating pain. She confronted the challenge, slowly and head-on, as her life slowly ebbed away. And she continued to drive.

Passage

As they plunged deeper into the bush, the Beetle slammed into miniature rocks and potholes, tossing its occupants carelessly. It caused a sickly feeling. The winding road was hardly any wider than a footpath, and had been used as a secret pathway to the secret airstrip. From there, the Catholic Mission arranged delivery of relief supplies and airlifts for fortunate refugees, mostly children who were always whisked off in the dark. They were offered renewed hope in France, Ireland, Gabon, the Ivory-Coast, or the United States, even if they were almost always separated from their parents. There simply wasn't enough room for parents and children, not on the mini cargo planes or in the countries that offered refuge. For those countries, their logic was all too simple. What political and economic gain would their compassion bring after all?

Almost the entire front of Sister Doherty's robe was soaked in a map of red. But she continued, throwing up once or twice during the trip, and barely staying conscious. In the distance her vision, quite blurred at this point, and without the aid of her glasses, picked up dots of what remained of the tar that once coated the road. Black and uneven, they looked like old cow shit. The real Sister Doherty had given up, but her other persona was energized by the thought of the little red bundle and the possibility of actually saving it; a thought she had very little faith in. But she continued, blanking out the echoes of death that hovered all around and within her. Once she made it to the side road and plunged in, her hopes were rekindled and held there by intuition.

The sniper's overzealous shot, above from a tree where he perched, had been surprisingly accurate though hasty. The bullet still lodged near her heart but each second seemed to guide it closer and closer. Yet she kept going, evoking power from somewhere and for the sake of the red parcel. It was getting dark and she turned on the one headlight that was working. Its narrow, weak streak caught the shapes of thousands of insects doing an uncontrollable war or food dance. If only her windows could be wound up, that is exactly what she would have done. But while the rear ones were eternally wound up and stuck, the front ones were halfway up and stuck too, propped up that way so many months ago. After several agonizing and sapping efforts to return free motion to the windows, Sister Eileen gave up and so did the few helpers at the Mission who had honestly done their best. But they did so only after the window winders were either broken from incredible pressures applied, or twisted beyond recognition. And so mosquitoes poured in from both windows, stinging the semi-conscious Sister and the red parcel that she was struggling to deliver. Black, jobless flies followed suit, and why not, settling on the parcel and the huge patch of red on the front of her otherwise white rob, sucking playfully. Some ventured further down to devour from the shallow mounds of vomit, now solid and shapeless, that smelled of stale food and drink, and stuck to the lower ends of her robe.

She had long created an imaginary wall around her, blanking out the sounds of war and the echoes of death. She continued, implanting in the little that remained of her conscious self, the belief that as long as she moved, death could be eluded. It didn't matter, therefore, that they barely ambled along. And it didn't matter when that annoying, whining sound began to escape the engine. It was the same sound it had produced over a year before, just before the car had to be grounded for three or so months. Then a local mechanic showed up and performed some mystery repair trick. She pretended as if she didn't hear the sound, and she struggled on, feeling no less abused than the car.

It was impossible to calculate how long she had been on that stretch of road, if indeed it could be called a road. But when the exhausted car and its cargo finally burst into the remote clearing, she received a sudden boost of life that lasted a very short time. A narrow runway, riddled with more potholes than were necessary, stretched across the middle of the clearing with each end disappearing into ancient palm-trees. In the background a two-propeller cargo plane stood still, partially camouflaged by dry palm fronds. Even in the growing darkness you could tell that it was quite outdated and flew at the mercy of God. Further away, and more immersed in the bush was a thatched-roof building that held relief supplies secretly flown in from Ireland, the Ivory Coast, Gabon, sometimes France.

Activities at the airstrip went round the clock. Irish priests, reverend sisters, and a lot of local help were always milling around, talking in low tones, looking around furtively, running in and out of the low building, and bumping into one another. Once every two or three weeks a one or two-propeller cargo plane flew in with supplies, momentarily breaking the attempt at silence. Fear reigned whenever an expected flight didn't arrive. Sometimes it was the result of delays caused by bad weather or very common mechanical problems. But sometimes it was the worst. A relief plane was periodically shot down by enemy fire.

As if the car had been in synch with her all along, it spluttered a few times, jerked a few more times, and ceased. But even after its engine stopped complaining, it rolled a couple of yards before a low banana tree finally halted it. A clanging noise indicated that a tire rim had also hit a small rock. The tire had been shredded many miles back, but she had not noticed or pretended not to know. The scenario drew immediate attention. As a reverend father and two or three of his acolytes wandered immediately, though cautiously, toward the car, Sister Eileen used up her last bit of spare energy to point repeatedly at the silent parcel that lay beside her, taking in huge gulps of air in the process. She recognized, hazy though it was, Father Brendan's tired face. Beneath his eyes the bags were becoming more obvious. She also recognized the outline of a dark hand reaching through the passenger window for the parcel. And then she jerked violently before going into a deep, peaceful sleep, her thin lips wide apart, and her eyes wide open, frozen and aimed beseechingly at the tall Irish priest. She went to sleep forever, taking in her last gulp of air. Father Brendan and the others understood what, for them, was habitual. They headed back to the building with the parcel, its mutilated umbilical cord dangling like a long, bloodied earthworm. Taking care of the living took precedence over decisions concerning the dead. The one headlight on Sister Doherty's car continued to show the insects doing their demonic dance.

A Whole New World

He was three, and far as he was concerned, that is when life began. He couldn't remember all that had happened to him before now. Past years were subsumed in a maze perhaps better left alone and forgotten. The robes that wafted by came in different sizes, shades, and colors. From gray, to blue to immaculate white. They were the different robes of different sisters, nuns, fathers, mothers, brothers, and seminarians at different stages of their spiritual and academic growth in the Catholic ministry. One of them, a tiny lady almost lost in her robe, and with an everlasting smile, stopped by his crib and leaned over him for a number of seconds. The beam was not lost from her face as she hovered there, her cross caressing his chest lightly, her hood almost hiding both their faces. And then she stroked him fondly on one cheek before raising her little frame back up straight. Only then did the weapon show in her other hand, the mighty syringe and the needle it carried. First she pushed the bottom of the syringe until a drop or two of some liquid trickled from the needle. And then she flipped him over, pulled down his shorts and diaper, and dabbed his right buttock with something cool and soothing. But the cool was brief and deceptive. She fired and though it stung, it was more from shock than pain that he shrieked. He couldn't understand how pacification and aggravation could be so intimately connected.

...

That night, three years before, after Sister Doherty and her Beetle passed on, Father Brendan received the red parcel from the man and they returned to the only building on the airfield. There they lay it on a thin mattress on the floor and set out to return it to life. Doubling up as physician, Father Brendan stuck a number of needles and tubes into the limbs that were hardly larger than the tubes. That way he was able to reinvigorate it

27

with liquids that were slowly passed into what veins it had. The presence of life in that body was as strange as the arrival of Sister Doherty in her Beetle. She still sat there with her head slumped against the driver's seat, stiff and at peace, her mouth wide open, and her eyes, open too, showing a fading white where insects and dust had long gathered.

For two weeks the infant lay on the mattress. Using a wet rag, they carefully dabbed its delicate body each day, giving it its first baths. Wiping away the red, they were able to slowly transform it to human, even if it still looked more like a rodent than anything else, and even if its pink and white skin was still near transparent. Its cries, no more a simple whimper, grew a little louder, though they were still faint squeaks. But they came with a desperate, passionate plea that pierced the soul more than they did the ear. And then there were those intermittent twitches, a matter of subconscious intuition, which evolved into more intelligible motion. The bundle had come to life.

When they loaded it on to the little cargo plane that night, at least it wasn't red anymore. It had been packaged in a white towel that stayed white. Thin stains of light brown had begun to show on parts of its skin, slowly replacing the dull pink and white. And while they couldn't quite get the cloth diaper to wrap snug around its needle waist and thighs, the diaper did elevate it to full baby status. If the infant passed anything from its bowels, there was more than enough room for everything to escape. But it didn't really matter; after all, its body didn't quite have the capacity to release anything substantial.

The aircraft was loaded by way of a ladder that was placed against its side. Just before Father Brendan handed the white parcel to the man who carried it into the plane, he looked one last loving time at the sleeping infant and, with tears in his eyes, said a short prayer.

"May your trip be safe, Monty. I'll really miss you. May you enjoy new life. You will grow up to be a great man. I know you will. Stay healthy and strong, Monty. I will always love you. And I know we will meet again. God bless you my child."

As dangerous as it seemed, the priest gave the bundle one final careful squeeze before he handed it over. Why he called it Monty, nobody knows, but the name stuck forever. Maybe it had something to do with the infant's unexpected arrival on a Monday.

In the cargo plane the man made room among the bits and pieces of luggage, all different shapes, sizes, and colors, awkward and strange, even for he who had been a part of such trips several times before. He placed their traveling bag and the infant on a blanket and slumped down beside them, leaning against a section of the fuselage. There were no seats in the plane. He had to carefully watch Monty throughout the trip. All around them were wobbly trunks, boxes, and cartons that sometimes tumbled over during the rocky flight. Though they were empty and to be refilled, they were still dangerous. In their traveling bag, among other things, were cans of relief powdered milk, Monty's food. Too harsh for the bowels of a normal child, let alone an infant born under such punishing circumstances, there was no other option. Monty had received it with great courage when they initially tested it on him. Perhaps his little spirit already understood the importance of making the best of whatever was available. In years to come he would desperately need that type of stubborn spirit.

The flight was unusual, and must have been rushed, as Monty was the only refugee passenger aboard. The plane soon sped down the narrow strip, its fate in God's hands. It careened and vibrated wildly as it finally lifted off, but the man stayed calm, one palm resting lightly on Monty. He was used to the plane's unpredictable antics and didn't expect anything less than an erratic and bumpy ride. Down below, in the dark, the priest and his workers watched and waved more from habit than anything else, as the craft slowly disappeared through dense, dark clouds and into the starless night. Tears still welled up in Father Brendan's eyes.

Not too far from them, the Beetle sat alone, leaning quietly against the banana tree. A few days earlier, Sister Doherty's partially decaying body had been laid to rest in a shallow grave dug out by a nearby bush.

Alone

Save for a few crazy but unintentional stunts, the flight was without incident. If enemy fire had attempted to cut short its trip, obviously that had failed. The cargo plane made it to the Ivory Coast, its final stop. Sometimes the Ivory Coast was also the final stop for rescued refugees. But not this time. Monty was considered a problem too big for the Ivory Coast. Soon he was transferred, this time into a two-engine jet, and one in which the passengers were seated on actual seats. He also changed hands, and from here until their arrival in Ireland, was placed in the care of an elderly and wizened Mother Josephine, a veteran of the Catholic tradition of charity.

When she boarded the jet with the white bundle, they drew quite a few curious stares. But in the hours that it took to arrive Dublin, curiosity was gradually replaced by apathy as the other passengers either got used to the bundle or simply got too engrossed in ensuring their own comfort and safety.

...

Monty spent his early years in Dublin's All Saints Orphanage. He grew up without the standard concept of mom or dad and formed his perceptions of nourishment around the things he saw every day. The robes that floated or rushed by, the smiling faces, mostly white and pink but sometimes brown or yellow, even an occasional black. His notion of life and existence were trapped in the white walls that enveloped him, and in the few paintings of holy personages that were nailed to them. It was a world of continuous, even if repeated activity, filled with double-bunk beds on which other infants and children of every shape, size and color lay for a great part of the day. It was a closed world that brought with it children and infants with every possible emotional and physical demand.

Monty took in his world, step-by-step, until the daily routine of being bathed, clothed, diaper-changed, and fed became the essence of real living. Until the ritual of daily mass, supervised games, being stuck with needles, or being forced to swallow pink and purple liquids squeezed down by way of small tubes became unwanted but accepted prerequisites for recognition and acceptance. And yet, with all the sights, the sounds, and activities that crowded him in, he still mostly felt alone.

From the time he was transferred to the jet, everything improved around him, but not necessarily in him. He was almost immediately introduced to milk and, later, a variety of baby foods that suited his constitution perfectly. He was soon clothed, not just in disposable diapers, but in flowery baby clothing, mostly donations to the Orphanage. But like so many of the other orphans, the feeling of aloneness crept in on him.

At three he took his first steps. As he wobbled from one end of the room to the other, and to the cheers of the reverend men and women, he rejoiced instinctively too. And so did the other children who cared anything about a child walking at three. But this was Monty's world, and, as far as he was concerned, to walk at three was an incredible feat. He rejoiced and clapped vigorously, losing his balance in the process and tumbling over a few times. But he would almost be four when he finally mastered the art of walking. For now, he still spent close to half his day in bed. It was the only space where he truly felt free and at peace, away from the people and events that crammed him. From here he took in the world around him, hoping that the interruptions would not be as frequent.

In later years the physical effects of his birth would leave a series of marks that would further set to distinguish and isolate him. And it was too late for the best Irish nutritional and medical talent to restructure him back to what was usually accepted as normal. He didn't care though, since he wasn't yet aware of these peculiarities and, so far, no one had made him self-conscious of them.

He was short and rarely added inches. His feet were extra flat and his toes spread far apart like they were at war with each other. His legs, thin and disproportionate from the bulging tummy that leaned over from immediately above, were so bow that they gave the impression of a hoopla dance when he walked. The way his arms hung by his side, like he was ready to draw a pistol, caused a shadow that was ape-like. His nose was so flat and broad, you could hardly see his nostrils, and it clashed seriously with his thick, protruding lips and small brown eyes. His ears, large and wide, curved in as if they suddenly froze while flapping in mid flight. He didn't receive a full set of teeth until he was four. They were curiously small with large spaces in-between, and looked like grains of poorly developed corn afflicted with a new age disease. No matter how hard they were scrubbed, they held tight to their yellow tinge. Even when he smiled, his benign gaze displayed an impression of curiosity and uncertainty, more than it did delight. On top of it all, he was crowned with a fine patch of thick, curly black hair.

The Other Side

When the children were old enough or simply considered fit, they were taken, under strict supervision, on bus rides into Dublin. Even though they saw stars, birds, clouds, and the sun from their remote spot at the Orphanage, they noticed how on the outside these same dependents of nature seemed to reach out and claim huge amounts of space without boundaries. Because the sounds, things, and moods on this side of the world were intensely different, the children often ended up more confused than enlightened. And while some of them might have been thrilled by the color and magnificence of tall buildings, crowds of anxious-looking people, and vehicles that fought for space on the roads, others felt dwarfed and irritated by the chaos.

There were those moments of calm and compensation when the children were escorted into theaters to either watch drama staged by school children, or children's movies. In the midst of their excitement were secret questions that they held on to. Unasked, the questions sank down and remained there, giving the children things to ponder over even if they never figured them out. They never ceased to wonder at those other children, the ones whose hands were held by one or two adults as they walked down a curb or as they crossed a street. The ones who were never drowned in a specially organized group of too many people. The ones who rode in cars with a lot of room, not in buses packed to the brim. The ones who appeared on stage and in movies, mostly wearing bold, broad smiles and bright, color-filled costumes. Costumes unlike the same drab, white-upon-white uniforms, day-in, day-out, that the orphans wore to church, to class, and on outings. The admixture of incompatible thoughts created an exuberance that left the children both happy and demure.

It was the same sensitive struggle that accompanied them when they were taken to any of Dublin's modest, fast food restaurants. It was the same when they visited the small amusement park in Kildare. If they were taken to one of the larger parks, like Disney World, control would have been a problem. So, they were never taken to such elaborate places. But each time they drove past Disney World, whether it was during the day or at night when firecrackers and an assortment of lights in any color lit the sky, they marveled at the spectacle and strained their eyes until they lost sight of it. Here, too, they quickly noticed the children who strolled matter-of-factly into this world of secrecy and glamour, not in large groups, but in small groups, sometimes as small as two or three. They would learn that such groups often comprise a unit called *family*. And while they had heard the term *family* used to define their collective survival, they came to perceive and assess the *outside families* differently.

Another thing, Monty began to notice how most people on the outside carried similar features and how he didn't share in most of them. From a young age he learned to observe himself in the mirror and to study those minor and major details that were the exception, not the rule, especially on the outside. In the Orphanage there was a greater range of features, of anomalies, of hair texture and skin tone. No one had ever confronted Monty with this truth, but as he grew older he became increasingly aware of it, of the different features that he and the children did or didn't share, and of the realization that on the outside the variations were not as prevalent. A feeling of security was sustained by the wide physical attributes that resided within the Orphanage, albeit some attributes were more prevalent than others. For this reason, Monty resented the outside a little bit more. He had never been attacked on account of his dark skin and short, curly hair, but even before his mind began to process emotions and observations, in his subconscious he foresaw difference as basis for concern, for curiosity, maybe malice and conflict. The thought became more vivid when he reflected on such arenas, as the outside, where difference was the exception, and where one or two traits ruled arrogantly.

An excitement always preceded their outings, the anticipation of something else beyond the dreary monotony of love, Catholic rituals, and activities repeated until they were done without much thinking. But on the outside they were reminded even more blatantly that they were from the outside too. The stares, the sudden drop in voices, the fingers that pointed, the smirks, even outright chuckles, usually done with a failed attempt at subtlety, easily separated them. For those who did not have the heart to pretend, their rude remarks, taunts, and parodies left a deep imprint too hard to erase. There was always something to pick out and laugh at when the children went on an outing. If it wasn't their uniform, it was the awkward walk of a child, sometimes one who needed help to maintain balance, or it was some other ailment that cited a child as an anomaly, if anything else. If the abnormality wasn't physical or mental, chances are it corrupted one of the five senses. Sometimes attention was caused by the regimented handling of the children in long lines of twos that maintained order as much as it imposed restriction.

And then there were those like Monty who, even though they were *normal*, displayed a peculiar look that drew attention and the behavior patterns that accompany attention. The way his shirt protruded under the strain of his belly, the way his feet seemed to steer apart even though his bowlegs initially brought them together. That ape-like stance, those eyes, that nose, those lips, those teeth, his ears. His dark skin and short curly hair.

Eager anticipations of an outdoor trip were almost always succeeded by mixed feelings laced with confusion and dismay. And then there was the ironic yearning to return to the other outside, the Orphanage. For them it was a return to their inside. Here they resigned to the caring though bland lifestyle that at least preserved dignity and respect. And when they remembered the uncertainties and discomforts of the outside, they were always able to rediscover or, at least, invent happiness here.

America

At nine he graduated from kindergarten. All Saints boasted educational facilities that offered training up to pre-high school level. Monty dwarfed most of the little graduands. But then one or two of them in turn dwarfed him. It didn't matter. They lived on the inside, what, to outsiders, was the outside.

On the inside very few things were considered wrong or outrageous. Like that early morning when Brother Francis and Mother Margaret were found half-naked, exploring each other's bodies behind a low shrub. Being that Mother Margaret was at least twice as old as Brother Francis, their daring liaison was extra scandalous. But it also introduced the type of vicious humor that the Orphanage lacked. The discovery sent a shock wave, real or feigned, through the Orphanage, after which both lovers were separated and re-assigned to different Catholic missions at different ends of the country. Even then it was mostly the reverends that were shocked and dismayed, and they expressed their feelings openly as rage, but privately as ridicule, laughing their hearts away. Most of the children either didn't know or didn't care or didn't understand the scandal, and therefore didn't think twice about the stories that drifted, unwelcome and unannounced, into their ears. Except, of course, for those very few who grew at a fairly regular pace, and who either showed signs of facial hair or of extra chest growth.

But for the most part it was uncommon to define any event in the Orphanage as unusual. Not the fact that Monty and a good number of the other children wet the bed daily. Not the spectacle of a nine-year-old boy wearing a cone-shaped paper hat and hanging a white, hand-sewn cape by a string tied loosely around his neck. Monty adorned his graduation gown and hat with much pride. Rehearsed over and over again, he knew what to do when his name was called. In his now famous or infamous wobbly strides, he headed to the makeshift podium where Bishop Roland of all people handed him a tightly wrapped cylindrical object, dazzling white, except for the red ribbon that decorated it. He was in complete awe, even though he had no clue as to what was in the object. But he did have the understanding that the object validated his learning at that level. It confirmed his knowledge of simple addition and subtraction, of reciting the alphabets, of spelling a few words, of tracing and drawing simple objects, of copying writings from learn-to-write books, and of memorizing and reciting well-known children's nursery rhymes. Because he was so immersed in the moment, he could never have guessed how his strong features distinguished him. And because he didn't know or care to know, he savored the moment, gladly receiving many hugs and kisses, and later enjoying the colorful party filled with cake, candy, food, soft drinks, dancing, and games. While his birthdays had been celebrated each year with modest gifts and parties, this party was different as it was stirred by a sense of personal accomplishment. For the first time in his life he was very content and happy to be on the inside.

...

Careful deliberation preceded the decision to send him to America. He was healthy but he didn't look healthy; that was a concern. While there was some debate over his real state of physical health, there was no doubt about his mental needs.

He was potty-trained at five and even though he was allowed to brush his teeth at seven, it still took tremendous effort on his part. It was as if he had a hard time finding his teeth, and as he scrubbed every area in and around his mouth, including his nostrils, he spattered the toothpaste all over himself, the sink, and the floor, and slobbered large amounts of paste mixed with spit. The thick liquid found its way down his chin and into the sink or on to the floor. He had learned his colors quite well, but still confused blue with purple which wasn't considered unusual. It was a little unusual, though, that he confused red with yellow, and brown with pink. He still mistook left for right and right for left, which often showed in the funny looking angles his shoes pointed, otherwise he had done well with dressing himself. And it was hoped that one day he would figure out how to tie his laces properly. For now, he balled them up into thick knots that were almost impossible to loosen. He also did fairly well with feeding himself except that too often he lost a spoonful before the food made it to his mouth. For that reason it was decided that learning to use a knife and fork would have to come later. First, he had to master using a spoon. For that reason, too, he had still not received his first Holy Communion. The Church wasn't convinced that transferring anything to his mouth would come with the ease that it was supposed to come with. And he still wet the bed nearly every day.

America, renowned for her possession of special schools, was the place for him. Since he had graduated from kindergarten and shown signs of progress, the time was ripe.

The day Father McCarthy broke the news to Monty, the boy, now almost ten, was visibly disturbed. The Orphanage was all he had known, and while it wasn't a perfect world, he had grown to understand and accept it. The feeling of aloneness that sometimes plagued him and the other kids were easily interrupted by the aura of love, simplicity, and serenity that prevailed. Initially irked by the numerous social and religious activities at the home, once he got used to them he plunged into the routine without much thought. He kept pace in the manner of a great dancer keeping rhythm with a strange song. Since he was obedient and quite reserved, he was hardly scolded for going against home rules, and he seldom got into altercations with other kids, as mean as kids are. He had found a home in the home, and a family too. For him, the world held nothing more meaningful than what he found in the Orphanage. No, he didn't want to leave. Especially since the outside world, with all its fanfare and color, had left the permanent impression of being cold, carefree, too different, and therefore impossible to adjust to.

During the final weeks leading to up to his departure, he withdrew into his shell and remained there. He went about daily rituals in the most stiff and formal manner, hardly uttering a word. He wasn't necessarily irritable, just uncertain, sad, and distant. At his sendoff party he strained to feign joy, but behind his laughter and smiles, and even when he ate, drank, danced, and played games, his despondence was naked. For a child who loved food, he ate and drank far less than usual, and even his unique monkey-strut dance was displaced by a simple move that was hardly more than marking time. The strut had been a sensation here; outside he would have been laughed at. And when the reverend men and women hugged him, he held on tight like he sought their protection, like he was pleading that they not let him go.

On the day of his departure he wept for hours, loud and hard. Since the day of his birth when he had cried for hours with an exertion that produced little or no sound, he hadn't cried this hard or this long. It soon had a contagious effect and some of the other children wept along. Aside from empathizing with Monty, they realized that some day, they, too, would also face a future unknown, and it frightened them. Even some of the men and women of God let out a teardrop or two, sniffing hard to hold them back and thus display strength. But the only way they could completely hide their tears was by wiping them. Monty received a lot of hugs and kisses on his cheeks, even on his lips, both from the reverends and the other children. He responded to each hug as he had done during his sendoff party, with tight grips that subconsciously expressed his yearning to be held back.

On the drive to the airport, he wept through the highways and streets of Dublin. It was loud enough to invite indiscreet stares from a few pedestrians. He wept extra loud at the airport as he was handed to a complete stranger, a freckled-face elderly lady who beamed constantly and who was excited about something that Monty couldn't figure out. She tried hard, and in vain, to calm him down, still beaming and showing excitement. If only she knew how her disposition enraged him. *What was she happy about after all? What was there to be happy about?* To make things worse, she had a powerful grip, as if to prevent his escape. When the escorts from the Orphanage began to leave, the lady had to lift Monty with both hands in order not to let him run after them. He wailed, and with no regards for the prying eyes that were fixed in his direction. When they disappeared, he practically swooned and went limp, briefly losing the ability to scream and thus making it easier for the lady who, after spending only so short a time with him, was almost breathless.

After they boarded the huge Boeing 747 and the aircraft began to move, the sobs began again until they built up into a high-pitched wail. Monty had regained some crying power. Most children would have been distracted by the majestic vibrations and motion of the huge machine, or overwhelmed by anxiety. But not Monty. His fears centered on his extraction from the only world he embraced, and his being launched into one that, for now, carried images too convoluted to unravel. He cried and cried, drowning out the efforts of a flight attendant to provide pre-liftoff safety instructions. And even after the plane sped down the magnificent runway and lifted off, he continued. He continued until it found the right altitude and remained there as if motionless in mid air. He continued until he cried himself to sleep, still holding his passport in his right hand. His name was spelled out as Monty Monty since it would never be possible to ascertain his real last name. The elderly lady calmly sat beside the boy, staring out of the window. As they pierced the window, the sun's rays gave her wrinkled, freckled face the impression of a historic gold carving, stolen and vandalized.

The Joneses

When they arrived, he could barely walk. After he partially lost the ability to cry and partially resigned himself to cruel fate, he sat there staring at emptiness. Either that or he slept. He must have slept about seventy percent of the time. After a couple of failed attempts to pick conversation with him when he was not sleeping, the smiling old lady decided to leave him in peace.

They made two major stops, changing planes during one, and adding extra exhausting hours to an already exhausting trip. He ate very little, and though this bothered the lady, she soon gave up here too, convincing herself that at least she would deliver him alive. At that point it was the best she could do anyway. She was more bothered by the fact that he didn't use the bathroom often. Aware that he was different in some ways, she didn't put it past him to relieve himself right where he sat, and cleaning up after him wasn't in her contract. But Monty was a good traveler, even if he was out of the ordinary. And when it seemed like they would never arrive, they did.

She needn't have grabbed him the way she did back at Dublin. He had no intentions of escaping here. If anything, he wanted to grab her and hold on tight. Chicago's O'Hare Airport, with its unending hubbub and intimidating space, didn't offer the type of solace he hoped for. After a series of formalities, they walked for what seemed like eternity, until they came to a moving staircase. Monty was glad to give his legs a break as he began to take in what seemed like a heavy mechanical presence that surpassed what he had known in Dublin. The monitors mounted high for all to retrieve relevant information about flights, restaurants, hotels, and rental cars; the variety of computers, the lighting, and everything else that was machine-like or controlled by a devise other than human.

At the foot of the moving stairs he recognized his name spelt out in large, thick, black letters on a large cardboard sheet, and held up high for the world to see. At first he didn't conclude that

45

the **MONTY** on the cardboard sheet had any connection to him, not until his escort carefully turned her focus on the small group. A thin girl, about twelve, held the sign as high over her head as she could; to her right was a short, pudgy woman carrying a child no more than nine months old. And to her left was a man, tall and thin like her, whose face was expressionless. The freckle-faced woman inched her way to the group, taking Monty with her, on her face a fixed look of calculated inquiry.

"Are you the Joneses?" she asked very politely and with her usual smile as they came close to the group.

"Yes," Mr. Jones replied with unexpected agility, as if he had just been awakened from half sleep.

"And you must be Monty." He held out his hand for the tired and puzzled lad. But it was the elderly lady who guided Monty's little palm into Mr. Jones's.

Monty was compelled to shake hands with Mrs. Jones and Betty in like manner, after which his escort also shook hands with the Joneses, except for baby Dave whom she rubbed lightly on the cheeks.

"This is going to be your new family here in America, Monty, isn't that nice?"

In spite of his escort's attempts at warming him up to the Joneses, Monty just stood there, stiff and speechless, carefully taking in each member of the family and almost immediately forming thoughts about each one. But his on-the-spot opinions were interrupted and agitated by a thousand other things that crawled through his mind, revisiting his immediate past, contemplating his present, and anticipating his future filled with shadows that couldn't be decoded. It was good that his mind was so occupied, that way he was diverted from the mortification and apprehension that would otherwise have been caused by their long, hard stares and fabricated smiles.

He didn't miss the elderly lady when she walked off. She had tried so hard to be nice to him, but she hadn't succeeded in providing him the sense of deliverance he had claimed at the Orphanage. And he suspected that he wouldn't find that deliverance among the Joneses.   An overall detached and uncertain feeling stayed with him until they boarded the Datsun Station Wagon. They hadn't gotten out of the airport when Mr. and Mrs. Jones broke the silence, firing him with a series of, perhaps, pre-planned questions.

"Did you like life in Ireland?"

"Was it tough leaving your friends behind?"

"Do you think you'll like the United States?"

"What have you heard about the United Sates?"

"Are there a lot of lions in your native land?"

"Any good news about your relatives? Your people?"

"Is this the first time you'll be living with a family?"

"You miss your parents? I bet you do."

"Did you belong to a cult back home? We hear initiation is done at a young age."

But he just sat there with his head slumped against his seat. If he barely had the energy to stay alive, he didn't have enough with which to answer bland, irritating questions. Some of the questions may have grabbed his attention if he wasn't terrified, half asleep, and in a state of disorientation. Like the ones about his *native land* and his *parents*. But then, maybe not. Just maybe. After all, he may have been too young and too mentally unformed to tune into or to be concerned about such issues. Besides, the Orphanage had indoctrinated him, like other children, to refocus on other strict family concepts, concepts that didn't emphasize the things that caused him to be an orphan in the first place. Things that may have been permanently lost. As far as he cared to know, and at least up until this point, Ireland was his *native land* and those who had played supervisory and parental roles at the Orphanage must have been his *parents*, his *people*. He returned to his twilight zone where he looked straight ahead, seeing a void that now seemed to explain his life.

"Come on Monty, be a good sport and say something." As calm as she sounded, a bit of frustration, even anger, could be detected in Mrs. Jones's voice. The Joneses gave up when they heard Monty snoring.

Philip U. Effiong

Cold

Madison, Wisconsin, in early February, is not pleasant, not even if you are impressed by snow and cold. Monty learned and accepted this lesson shortly after he arrived. Before stepping out of the airport that day, Mr. Jones handed him a bright orange coat that reached to his knees, and helped him climb into it. In spite of the coat, the cold still stung and burnt. In Ireland he had experienced some cold and snow, and may have been a little fascinated but never impressed. For a greater part of the winters, he had been consoled by the decision to confine them within the walls of the Orphanage. Compared to Ireland, Madison was evil.

The Catholic Consulate, through a subsidiary office in Madison, made arrangements with families, mainly Catholic families, that were willing to take in foreign, deprived children for periods ranging from one month to five years. Their reward was a humble monthly stipend as well as recognition, in the form of a plaque, from the Consulate for their selfless service and benevolence.

Consulate policy insisted on cutting off its wards, particularly children, from their traumatic pasts. It was fairly easy to implement the policy when the ward, like Monty, was an orphan or oblivious of his or her past. The logic was that to provide a child with renewed life and fresh hope, the poignant details of his or her initial world be totally severed and replaced with another. While there were those who knew about his story from when he was smuggled into the airstrip that fateful night, the story would be kept from him in as scrupulous a manner as possible.

Even the Joneses didn't know those details. They had been given enough information about the boy who, if they accepted, would be staying with them for a period that would later be determined, pending how they got along with and felt about him. A few pictures had also been sent to them. They had been furnished with what was thought to be important aspects of his history, and all that was known about his health and state of mind. Whatever they told, asked, or discussed with him, they were to avoid topics that probed his past. They were not to talk about them to him in particular, but they were also required to keep them from others. With their barrage of questions, they very nearly broke their vow that first day.

If they knew all these things in advance, it wasn't clear why they spent so much time gaping at him. Maybe the reality of actually having his presence became a trial that could not have been imagined through information and pictures. Soon Monty recognized and felt the intensity of their stares, even when they stared from behind. Initially he was thoroughly weighed down, even frightened by the stares, and would just sit there, his head bowed in agony. Sometimes he sobbed, and even though it was barely audible, he always shuddered violently, a clear indication that, aside from his sobbing, he was overwhelmed. But one day he stared back and noticed the sudden impact of his bold decision. He learned that he could influence the habit considerably and began staring back whenever he was stared at, putting his new discovery to full use. From that day, the stares gradually slowed down, though they didn't cease completely.

Conversation was little, at least verbal communication was, having been replaced by the hints and suggestions that eye communication supplied. Aside from the questions he threw on the day Monty arrived, Mr. Jones said very little to the lad and his attitude was casual. His words centered mostly on greetings and advice, and were far between.

"Hi there, Monty."

"Welcome home."

"And good morning to you too."

"Remember to dress warm."

Sometimes he acknowledged Monty by simply nodding his head at him.

With Mrs. Jones it was different. She was regimental in her interaction with Monty, guiding, advising, ordering, rebuking, and barking. As early as his first morning at the Joneses, Monty sensed that such a relationship was imminent. The night before, soon after their arrival from the airport and after Monty was settled in his quaint, modest room, they had a light dinner before going to bed. His room let in a trickle of natural sunlight at a time, and sustained a shadowy sensation even when the one shaded lamp was turned on.

The next morning, at the breakfast table, Monty lunged for the same chair where he had sat for dinner the previous night. At the Orphanage each child was assigned a single chair at a single position at each table. It was a rigid rule. Monty brought the same expectation to the Jones home. Mrs. Jones's reaction was swift and to the point, almost jolting Monty out of the chair. Wagging a stumpy finger that carried long, sharp nails in his face, she erupted.

"How dare you! In this house we are free to sit wherever we want. D'you hear? No special seats for no special people. Okay? My house will not be treated like a hotel!"

Puzzled, Monty wept and lowered his head as he swallowed large amounts of air in an attempt to stifle the sounds. He cried because he was puzzled. He though the attack was unnecessary.

"Now, will you eat your oatmeal like a good boy?" Her flippant attempt at forcing normalcy failed. Monty, his head still lowered, even if the sobs were receding, sat still and stared at the bowl carrying oatmeal that had now hardened into a lump. Mr. Jones had begun to tear at his bacon like nothing was the matter. Betty, somewhat mystified by the scenario, followed suit almost immediately. Monty knew that his stay with the Joneses was going to be very long. His demeanor remained deceptively sober, but mentally he began to warm up for things to come.

Mrs. Jones's commandments and condemnations were common and predictable.

"Will you stop standing there and go look for something to do!"

"This is how you run hot and cold water in the bath; I won't repeat this so listen and watch carefully."

"Did you tidy your room today?"

"This is how you tie your laces; I won't repeat this so listen and watch carefully."

"I know you just used the bathroom; did you wash your hands?"

"Always your underwear before your shorts, always. Now, start all over again until you get it right!"

"Would you put down that spoon until we say grace!"

"This is how you dress your bed; always tuck the sheets in nicely, okay? I won't repeat this so listen and watch carefully."

"Make sure you finish your food. For someone with such wretched background, you should know better than to waste food. There are many like you who would die to have half of what you get in this house!"

"No, Monty, your left foot in the left shoe, and your right foot in the right shoe."

"This is how you run hot and cold water in the bath; I won't repeat this so listen and watch carefully."

"Whew, what a stench! I know you didn't flush that toilet. If you did, then you need to go spray some air freshener; it's in the cupboard to your left."

"I don't blame you for ignoring my questions, after all you never had any home training. How could you when you never had a home? I really shouldn't expect anything better from you, should I?!"

It was most difficult for Monty to bear the consequences of wetting the bed too often. Each night he had to sleep on a special rubber sheet concealed beneath his bedspread. Whenever he wet the bed, he knew to carry the sheet to the back of the house. Mrs. Jones gave strict, elaborate instructions after he first did it. If the mattress had been touched by urine, he carried it to the back of the house too. There, he hung the sheet on a clothesline and lay the small mattress against the stem of a tree. And that was not all. He had to take his bedspread and comforter, if the latter had been defiled too, to the laundry room where he washed and dried them. Later, he had to return each item back to his room. It was an exhausting task for a nine or ten-year-old who, in many ways, still bore the mind of a five-year-old. It was good, though, that he bore the heart of an older person.

None of the Joneses would touch Monty's rubber sheet, bedspread, or comforter, not when they were wet or dry. Throughout his stay at their home, he was allowed only two different bedspread and pillowcase sets, and one comforter. They must have all been thrashed with the rubber sheet and mattress when he left. Perhaps the bed frame was tossed too. At the Orphanage bedwetting was so normal that it could have been stylish. So, Monty lacked the understanding that it was not okay. It all changed at the Joneses. He was assaulted with reproaches that called him crude and perverted. More than any other criticism, this one shamed him the most and caused him far more grief and regret.

"Just look at you," Mrs Jones would begin, wagging her knobby finger in his face. "You should be ashamed of yourself, do you hear me!? Ashamed! At your age. Even David manages to keep his pampers dry sometimes. I don't know why people like you are not paraded in the streets with signs hanging down your necks. I thought they said your problem was upstairs. I guess it's downstairs too, huh!"

She must have been a powerful woman, the way she went about her daily military routine carrying baby Dave in one hand. Half the time one of her massive breasts hung out of her bra and the baby tugged and wrestled with it as if it resisted him. And he sucked voraciously. Each time she repeated her orders and disapproval, wrinkles formed on her bloodshot forehead and sweat began to build up there too. If Mr. Jones was concerned about her blood pressure, he didn't show it. She seldom admonished Betty or baby Dave, but sometimes Monty overheard her screaming at Mr. Jones, always in their bedroom and always behind closed doors. Over the years, perhaps, Mr. Jones had gotten used to the onslaught and realized that his most effective tool was silence and calm. If that was the case, it explained his usual disposition.

At first, Monty responded to the blows like any ten-year old, whether they were delivered by sight or by word of mouth. He withdrew as far as he could inside himself, and yearned for those moments when he was alone. He rejoiced when it was time for his daily siesta, and at bedtime too. His room became his sanctuary and he spent hours in there consoling himself with tears, reflections, and anticipations that momentarily transported him faraway from the truth. In spite of the wintry cold, in his sanctuary he discovered a feeling of warmth that the living room, with its fireplace, could not offer. Here he conjured a world much like the Orphanage, where calm and affection came naturally. But reality always interrupted his intimate reverie and brutally forced him back to his solitude and the events that created it.

When he wasn't alone, he was responding to Mrs. Jones's directives and admonitions, or Mr. Jones's mimetic hints at what his feelings held. Monty responded, mostly in silence, and when he spoke the words where minimal and came in little more than whispers. "Speak up boy!" soon became one of Mrs. Jones's favorite, albeit forced lines.

And then he began to adjust, what ultimately became a revolt. Instead of holding his head down when she ranted, he began to hold it up. Sometimes he stared right back at her with his brown, cat-like eyes. The first time he did it, she was taken aback and fumbled her words, stuttering and making little sense, not even to herself. At other times he held his head up but looked away with deliberate disdain as if she didn't exist. "Look at me when I'm talking to you!" soon became another of her favorite, albeit forced, lines. Ignoring her or staring right into her off-blue eyes caused a frustration that made the veins stand up in her neck. When this happened and her face turned extra red, dotted with patches of white, it meant that she was approaching the peak of helpless rage.

It took a little longer to conquer the degradation he suffered for bedwetting, but he finally built up resistance even against that. Mrs. Jones was tortured by his apparent indifference when she fumed over the innocent habit. Her frustration was all the proof he needed to know that he had scored one against her. And he knew that he didn't have to look to his sanctuary alone for solace.

She was in the habit of creeping up behind him whenever he was standing in front of any doorway or the stairway, and lifting him up and out of the way. Sometimes she took on the task while carrying Dave in one hand. For Monty, it meant that she was getting crazier.

"Why must you block the doorways? Can't you stay out of the way? Must I always have to pick you like discarded junk?"

Then she would put him down, away from the doorway or stairway. One day as he stood looking for the thousandth time at a Second World War picture hanging at the top of the staircase, she attacked. As she lifted him, he reacted spontaneously, grabbing the railing and holding on tight. She couldn't move, but she didn't want to be the loser so she didn't give up. She continued to tug as hard as she could, but each time she seemed to make progress, he held tighter and she was thrown forward. The tug-of-war continued and she continued to lurch back and forth until her face saw several changes--from white to more white to pink to red to more red. The knot that her hair was tied in loosened and her red hair was tossed all over her face. Finally, still determined not to give in to the insolent brat, she fell back in one heap and he landed on her. Completely mortified and feeling more slighted than was necessary, she quickly got up and piled all kinds of curses and venom on him. As she did, she unconsciously straightened her hair and dress. Undaunted, it seemed, he got up too, looked up at her for one brief second, and turned to inspect the painting some more. Perhaps more exasperated than she had ever been in her entire life, she shook her fists at him, gritted her teeth and blurted out "why you, why you" before storming off, cursing some more until her words faded away with her foot stomps. The incident was another reminder that Monty didn't have to look only to his sanctuary for solace.

Betty didn't say much to Monty when her parents were around. But whenever she was alone with him, she let loose. Her words mostly centered on his looks and they weren't gracious.

"Don't your feet hurt when you wear shoes? I imagine they would have to."

"Man, if your tummy should drop any further they'd be touching your knees."

"Hmm, hmm, hmm. Ever thought about acting in a Tarzan movie? As one of the chimps, that is. Ha, ha, ha. Just kidding, Monty. Don't you have a sense of humor? Come on, loosen up man."

"Now where the hell are your nostrils? It's a miracle that you can breath."

During his first and only participation in Halloween's trick-or-treating, he was made to wear a gorilla mask, a pair of oversized brown jeans, brown boots, and a brown coat. That night it was cool, but not as typically cold as it could get, so he didn't need gloves. Besides, there were no brown gloves to go with his costume. It was safe for he and Betty to walk around the neighborhood, not beyond, and not past a certain time. Once outside, she turned on him.

"I don't know why mom gave you the mask, you don't need it. Hee, hee, hee. You don't need a costume, period. You're a natural one. Hee, hee, hee. Just kidding!"

At several lighted doorsteps, because his palms were uncovered, candy givers were apt to throw related comments and questions about them.

"Oh, it must be the negro-looking lad living with the Joneses."

"Why, what a tan. Are you the colored refugee in the neighborhood?"

"Honey, I'm sure it's the Australian aborigine boy. Or is he African aborigine?"

The Joneses, including Betty, must have been talking too much. While a lot of what they whispered in gossip was imagined, the tales were spiced up some more as they traveled from one neighborhood storyteller to the next. A common theory was that Monty was found in some jungle living among wolves that had rescued him after his parents were killed in war. American Peace Keeping troops separated him from the wolves though it was tough. He had, after all, become one with them and fought fiercely to be left that way. Only recently had he begun to speak like a human child, the result of tremendous work by psycholinguists. Another theory held that he was delivered from his own parents who were going to eat him because war had caused too much starvation.

He wasn't aware of the enigma that careless talk had turned him into, but the comments and questions that Halloween night were enough to aggravate his self-conscious feelings. Worse still, Betty still threw in her erratic, sarcastic remarks about how inconsequential his costume was. He was relieved when his neighborhood tour with Betty was over and prayed that he would never ever have to go trick-or-treating again. His prayers were answered. Except for in-house costume parties at the future training facility where he would board, he never trick-or-treated again in his life. But that night, between Betty and the candy givers, he was reminded all over again that he was from the outside, solitary and different. He withdrew further inside, downcast, more sensitive and more defensive.

Perhaps he would have been able to build some type of conversation with one who in many ways was a child. But because Betty's talk always made him conscious of what he may have looked like, something he otherwise never gave much thought to, they couldn't talk innocently.

Prior to staying with the Joneses, he had caught people gaping at him, but what was there to worry about? After all, they gaped at every other child from the Orphanage? But now, with the eccentricity of the stares, the fact that they were too personal, and with Betty's tactless suggestions, he began to question his appearance. After taking a bath, he would stand for a long time in front of the mirror scrutinizing himself from head to toe, but he never found anything wrong and so he didn't understand. Sometimes he was there so long, Mrs. Jones would yell, "What are you doing in there Monty? Will you get out this minute, or else...." It was the same when he dressed himself up for school in the morning. He patiently examined himself in front of the mirror, and Mrs. Jones, always impatient, would find some foul way to call his attention.

It became worse on those few occasions when he ventured outside with Betty to play with the other kids. They let him play improvised football and basketball, but they also taunted him.

"Pass the ball ape-man."

"Bow-legs, bow-legs, your mama walk like that and your papa walk like that."

"Sorry I kicked you in the gut man, I thought it was the ball."

"Hey Monty, can't you wait for Halloween before you put the mask on?"

Several times they ended their taunts, like Betty, with "just kidding man, come on, don't you have a sense of humor, loosen up."

But Monty didn't loosen up because he couldn't. While he didn't see anything wrong with his looks, he couldn't ignore the smart remarks and their unmistakable implications. He believed it was spite, not his looks, that was the culprit, and thus exonerated his appearance of any unique flaws. Soon he discarded the notion that maybe there was some hope to be found outdoors. Outdoors he was only reminded that he was on the outside and from the outside. He retraced his steps and hopes indoors, having come to the belief that he had better chances of surviving here.

The outdoors was even more unappealing when an old suspicion, first evoked when he was in Dublin, was re-evoked. It was one that would conceal loathing in cynicism. One day it surfaced with a sincere, even if tactless, observation.

"Hey Monty, why you have a permanent tan? Look just like the devil at church. He has a tan too."

The observation triggered a pattern, as if the kids were looking for that one opportunity to release what they had patiently held within.

"Are you dark all over? You know, between your legs, is that dark too? Hee, hee, hee."

"How come you don't live with other darkies?"

"My mom and dad say we shouldn't play with people whose skin is black or yellow or brown. I won't tell them I play with you, okay?"

"You and chimps is the same. You colored like them and you talk like them."

"You're weird Monty. Your teeth and palms is white. How come they ain't brown too?"

"Hey darky, you still chase after your meals? That's what they say."

Warmth

The Special Training Center offered more solace, in addition to his sanctuary and increasing recalcitrance at home. Mr. Jones took him to the school on his first two days. He deliberately took Monty on the bus to teach him how to use it. It was, after all, going to be his main form of transportation to and from school.

"Always wait for the bus at this stop. This is also where you'll get off when you get home. It's a little over a block from the house, not far at all."

"Always use the C bus, no matter what. Okay?"

"Always come down in front of your school. See? There's a Bus Stop right in front."

"Remember, it's twenty-five cents for kids, no more, no less. We'll give you fifty cents each day. Hang on tight to the money. It's all you'll be getting. If you lose any of it, you'll be doing a long, long walk. Okay?"

After his first week at the Center, Monty mastered using the bus to and from school. Summer made things much easier. He couldn't imagine waiting for and using the bus in all those layers of clothing, including the thick scarf they made him wrap around his neck. It was like being strangled in a friendly way. He dreaded going anywhere with the Joneses during winter, whether it was church, a restaurant, or out shopping. Hiding his body in all those layers of clothing only provoked the misery of spending time with them.

Whenever he climbed the bus, he held tight to his twenty-five cent coin, squeezing it tight between his fingers as if to choke it until it died. He remembered Mr. Jones's warning. There was the one instance, though, when he lost his going-home twenty-five cents because of a hole in his pocket. At first it was too little for a coin to pass through, but with all the fun and games at break time, the hole expanded. As Monty set out to courageously do the five-mile walk home, a red Toyota pulled up beside him and stopped. It was Dorothy's father's car. The semi-dumb girl had recognized Monty and indicated to her father that he was one of the children from school. She sensed that something was wrong. It was either by the way he walked or by the fact that the Bus Stop was some four blocks behind. Monty graciously accepted the ride and even remembered to say, "thanks sir, thanks Dorothy" when he was dropped off.

Since that day, images of Dorothy refused to go away. There was something remarkably selfless and effortless about her desire to help. She who needed help and who must have suffered the impatience of outsiders all her life. She refused to go and he warmed up to her. Each break time he would look for her and offer to play a simple card game or checkers, though he didn't fully grasp the rules of either game. She always obliged very politely. Sometimes he even offered her his glass of milk or orange juice. She didn't always accept food, but whenever she refused it was with a courtesy that didn't hurt him.

It didn't bother him that she half communicated with sign language and incomplete words forced out with a lot of effort. He still cherished her company and even learned the meaning of a few hand signals.

He never told the Joneses about the ride he had been given by Dorothy's dad. Neither did he tell them about Dorothy. He wanted to leave both worlds apart and exist in both independently, making adjustments where necessary. As far as he was concerned, even if it was a subliminal thought, home life, if allowed, would interfere with and possibly ruin the contentment of school life. He was never late for the bus to school, but sometimes he was late for the bus going home. Unlike that time when the hole in his pocket could be blamed, now it usually happened when he decided to keep Dorothy company until her dad arrived. But the buses were efficient and about twenty to thirty minutes apart, so such delays didn't cause any problems. Besides, the Joneses didn't seem to have a problem with Monty coming home late. He didn't have a problem with their indifference.

His new school wasn't All Saints Orphanage at Dublin, but it reminded him of it in some ways, and helped him escape from the unpredictable torments he faced at home and outdoors. The children, all in want of distinct emotional and physical needs, occupied a world with him where very few things, if any, were considered strange or alarming. They felt protected within its gray walls, and formed an inside liaison that spontaneously defined the outside world as different and, thus, odd. Their diversity, not just determined by the range of ailments they carried, but by their physical traits, also provided an outlet by which the isolation and hostility caused by dominance was avoided.

Like Monty, those who did not board agonized at different levels when, at the end of the school day, they had to venture outside. They envied those who remained inside and who would not have to adjust to the insensitivity, the fixation, and demands on the outside. They envied those who would remain free and normal, and would not be pressured to alter anything.

There was that one instance, though, when a skinny near-bald lad who drooled when he talked, and hobbled because his left leg was longer than his right, charged Monty unexpectedly during one lunch break, and started doing a weird dance around him. Several times he almost toppled over.

"Chocolate face, chocolate face" he began to chant in a raspy, monotonous drone that was barely audible. "Chocolate face, do me a tribe dance, chocolate face."

But the drama didn't last. Another boy launched at him from nowhere. He looked healthier than most of the students.

"How dare you? With your baldhead and bony ice-cream face. As ugly as you are, maybe you shouldn't be making fun of anyone."

"No Michael, back to your seat. You should know better." It was Mabel, one of the clinical psychologists at the Center. In his head Michael had sincere intentions and believed that he was specially appointed to enforce justice. Which explains why he was restless and easily prone to overreaction, a fact that was

63

common knowledge. The dancing boy had already stopped dancing and quickly walked to a nearby window where he cowered. He peeked outside for no particular reason, holding his hands to his chest. The solemn, distant look on his face was a far cry from the grin he wore when he did his impromptu dance. Soon Mabel was leading him through a doorway and away from the cafeteria. Though the incident was exceptional, other students watched with a calm that was almost sinister. They either suppressed their surprise or had none to express. It was the only time that Monty's appearance was a source of confrontation at the Center.

Escape

For almost a year Monty and the Joneses survived each other. As unsettling as the entire thing was, it rebuilt Monty. He was reborn in a sick, masochistic way, and he learned to invent contentment where it didn't exist, looking to his room--his sanctuary--and to Dorothy. Each step of the way as he discovered a fresh counter weapon, usually a modification in behavior, he learned the value of risk-taking and insolence. Initially he worried about looking like an ingrate. The Joneses had provided him a home and some good things after all. With the acquisition of new wisdom, he discarded his sensitivity without ceremony. The generosity of the Joneses had steadily played out more as self-first hypocrisy than as anything else. If his elementary mind had discerned it, it had to be true. He knew nothing about the monthly stipend they received from the Catholic Consulate. Otherwise, his original sense of appreciation would never have been. He wasn't happy with or at the Joneses, but the more stoical he became, the stronger he became too, refusing to stay down. At school he gained new knowledge, but it was small compared to the lessons of courage and endurance that were forced on him at the Joneses. As he receded further and further away from them, which they were happy about, their mandatory encounters were matched by his mounting stubbornness. It was a stubbornness that didn't fit the profile of a child with the type of problems he was supposed to be plagued by, and so, they, especially Mrs. Jones, were disturbed way beyond his imagination. He had become more at peace in the home than they, but they didn't know it and neither did he.

...

One day Mrs. Jones broke the news without ceremony.

"You will be moving somewhere else soon." She spoke on behalf of her family.

"Okay." He nodded his head, looking straight into her eyes. Without saying more, she walked off in one direction and he in a different direction.

They both resigned to the impending separation, but they weren't as solemn as they looked. They were both delighted and each knew this truth about the other. They remained as detached as they possibly could, except for those unavoidable meetings where Mr. Jones was aloof as usual, and where Mrs. Jones insisted on being the commander-in-chief. But it was Betty who left Monty with an image so foul that he never quite purged himself of it during the rest of his life. She walked into his room, about two or three days before his departure, something she rarely did since she had picked up that he didn't welcome her company.

"So you'll soon be leaving for good?"

"Yes."

"Tell me, Monty, since your people hunt a lot, are you going to be a hunter?"

He didn't know what she meant by "your people," let alone know that they, whoever they were, hunted a lot. For a second the idea struck him then disappeared as quickly as it had shown up. He couldn't make out the basis for her question, but he responded anyway.

"No."

"Why? Don't you like meat?"

"Sometimes." He began to wonder what she was getting at.

"Have you ever eaten white meat?" As she asked, she grabbed his left arm and directed his fingers to her crotch where she led them into a brief rubbing and thrusting motion. Monty's first reaction was to watch and allow her guide his hands freely; and then, as if awakened by a block of ice rubbing against his spine, he recoiled and snatched his arm, taking a few backward steps away from her.

"Uuuhhh! I see you haven't yet eaten white meat. It's the sweetest meat you'll ever taste." She giggled sardonically, loud and long, before skipping out of the room as if she had accomplished a life-long mission at last.

Monty had never been this confused. Odd things were expected at the Training Center, and even at the Joneses. But for him nothing unexpected was this unexpected. Riding way above the unexpected, Betty's actions reflected a bestiality that set itself apart. Monty had never given much thought to what he or anyone else carried between their legs, but he had long perceived that area as very personal and, in some ways, sacred and forbidden. It wasn't to be referred to freely, revealed freely, or touched freely. Betty had broken these unwritten laws and left him perplexed, shamed, defiled, and a little scared. The detachment he felt from her now matured into a feeling of revulsion. For the first time in his life he had the urge to hit and draw blood, though it was only for a brief moment. Betty's actions fueled his longing to leave. He was glad that the day had almost come.

In time, and when he reflected in private, Monty would try unsuccessfully to unravel Betty's purpose that afternoon.

...

The Joneses set things up nicely for the arrival of the man from the Catholic Consulate. He was the Consulate counselor newly assigned to Monty. By way of irregular visits and of information culled from parents or authorized school officials, he would monitor the refugee boy's progress at school and at the homes that took him in. Mr. Ranjid was probably a third generation Indian and wore small round glasses that didn't match his long, bushy beard.

Mrs. Jones carried Monty on her laps while Mr. Jones carried Dave on his and fed the chubby baby--now almost a toddler--bottled milk. Betty sat on a flowery beanbag beside her mother. Monty had seriously avoided her since that unholy visit to his room. They were all dressed formally.

Mr. Jones answered the door and let Mr. Ranjid in.

"Welcome Mr. Ranjid. Do come in, please."

"Thank you. Oh, what a handsome baby." He shook hands with Mr. Jones.

"This is my wife, Yvette. And that's our daughter, Betty. And that's the little man himself, Monty. And of course you've already met little David." It was the most Monty had ever heard Mr. Jones speak all at once. They all rose and shook hands with Mr. Ranjid. Then Betty helped her mother serve orange juice, coffee, cookies, and hors d'oeuvres.

"We are really sorry to let Monty go," Mrs. Jones began.

"Oh yes," Mr. Jones jumped in as if that was his queue. "We'll miss him so much, what a fine and promising lad."

"We had so much fun together," Mrs. Jones continued. "But what a pity that Betty will soon be going away to junior high school. If only she wasn't going to board. But, like you know, it's the best if she's going to grow into a decent Catholic girl."

"And when she's away Monty will be bored to death, all by himself with no one to play with. He and Betty really got along. We'd hate to put him through that."

Mr. Jones's words capped what was really the well-rehearsed dialogue between he and his wife. Mr. Ranjid simply nodded his head throughout the performance, nibbling on one thing or the other.

"Our main goal is to cater to the children's interest," Mr. Ranjid pointed out. "We are glad that you have Monty's interest at heart. Thank you. Thank you very much for taking good care of him."

"Oh it was nothing," Mrs. Jones cut in, "if only we could do more."

Monty saw through the façade of the entire setup and he was disgusted. If he knew the whole truth, he would have been much more incensed. The fact that the skit had been well played out because the Joneses didn't want to lose their commendation plaque. Once they received it, they would proudly hang it on the wall right above the special low table where their *Catholic Family Bible* rested in the living room.

Monty was disgusted but he didn't say anything; he hadn't attained that level of boldness. Instead he negated the voices and faces around him, quickly devising a no-man's-land where they were absent. But it wasn't until a raspy sound escaped his throat that they realized that he was fast asleep though he still sat up straight.

...

"For now you'll be staying at the Special Training Center. Sorry but we haven't yet been able to find a suitable family to replace the Joneses. Once we do, we'll send you there. Okay?"

"Okay."

Monty masked his excitement. Mr. Ranjid would never have guessed that he would rather board at the Center than live with any family. At least not just yet. With his recent battle and the weight of endurance at the Joneses, he lost the zeal to move in with any family. He wasn't ready to deal with the rigors of uncertainty just yet.

"The Joneses gave us very short notice about having to hand you back to us. I'm sorry, but your stay at the Center shouldn't be that long. Okay?"

Monty nodded. He didn't know that the Joneses stretched his stay in order to secure their plaque. He couldn't therefore understand why they didn't invite the Consulate to remove him much earlier. Mr. Ranjid's apologies were irrelevant. As far as Monty was concerned, things couldn't be better. He was glad to leave, but even more appropriate, he was ecstatic about going to the Center. It wasn't obvious as he wore the expressionless look that had too often frustrated Mrs. Jones. For the second time in his life he yearned for the inside, away from the inconsistencies and fallacy that existed on the enticing and colorful outside. If he was going to exist among outsiders, it was obvious that he required a preparedness that he was unaware of, and that would have to come before confidence could be reached. No, Mr. Ranjid owed him no apologies. If anything, the counselor spoke words that were sweet music in Monty's ears.

He steered his Honda hatchback through the gates and into the compound enclosed by sturdy gray walls. It was getting dark and the security lights were turned on, revealing lush, well-kept gardens and several concrete pathways. Mr. Ranjid would help Monty with his suitcase and backpack, first to the registration desk and then to a building about a block away, where, on the third floor, Monty would share a large room with nine other students.

Songs

At eleven, and compared to the other students, Monty was an average second grade student. He couldn't be cited as exceptional, at least not in regular reading and writing subjects. The story was different with music.

Monty performed magic with the flute. From the day he was introduced to the instrument in music class, he displayed a knack that caught Sister Tracy's attention. The way he stared at the golden rod, the twinkle in his eyes, and the beam that covered his face, fixed and determined. The way he stroked the rod as he examined it, peering down its thin, long hollow and the dark holes that lined it, each time with one eye shut. The moment he produced sound with a light blow through the main, top opening, he was hooked. Because of his love-at-first-sight with the instrument, the sounds he initially created were meaningful, even if haphazard and not understood, and this was before he mastered any tune. They were meaningful because they promised him companionship that he didn't know to be humanly possible, and they exposed him to a frontier of inner contentment that he could have never invented.

He learned much faster than any of the other students and hung on to the instrument like it was his blood and soul. Of course, like other students, he was taught to play other instruments, but the effort became a required ritual in obedience to prerequisites. With the flute it was different. Monty was captivated by it and, naturally, bonded with it. In turn, he demonstrated a flair that was captivating to witness. That first day, and on others when he had to hand back the flute at the end of music class, he was visibly downcast. He longed for the day he would own his own flute and take it to and from wherever liked.

Monty was an average student, but not with the flute. It was uncanny, as the source of his passion could not be explained. His ability to play by ear defied logic too. Sister Tracy could not understand. If he was going to stay with the flute, non-dependence on reading music was an advantage. Maybe it wouldn't simplify the art, but it would the process. Soon word went round among teachers, counselors, reverends, and students alike, about this mysterious skill demonstrated by one of the students. It was mysterious because it came from a student who still struggled with the easiest additions and subtractions, with spelling the simplest words, with speaking fluently, and with doing some of the expected things expected of a boy his age.

Those who watched and listened to him play a tune he had learned, or especially one he had fabricated, were always awe struck. They tried hard to make sense of the scenario, but always failed. Monty was, after all, a ten-year old child, believed to be mentally deprived, practically dejected and rejected most of his life, and having just held a flute for the first time in his life. It was unreal. For some, even though they didn't say it out loud, the physical make-up of the boy didn't agree with this elegant gift either. Barely two months after he was introduced to the flute, Monty was invited to play "Happy Birthday" and any other popular children's song during one of the parties that honored all kids born in a particular month.

It was the first time he was going to perform before an audience other than his classmates. Sister Tracy had informed him about two weeks earlier. He was anxious but for the first time in his life looked forward to confronting a situation of uncertainty. He found courage in the flute. Together they could do anything. Sister Tracy coached him meticulously, making sure that he understood his queue each step of the way.

...

The celebration was modest but colorful. All students born in July were distinguished by the special, blue, glittering cone-shaped hats they wore. As center of attraction, they were favored, eating, drinking, and taking the dance floor before anyone else. They played games and had fun, all under the watchful flowery decorations that covered the walls of the hall, and the careful supervision of counselors, teachers, and Catholic reverends.

Parents had been invited and a significant number of them were there. Most of the students who boarded were orphans, in some cases even rejects; abandoned, first, by their parents, and then society. Like the pork colored albino with yellow hair, whose parents were of African descent. Portions of his skin were dark orange and coarse because the lack of pigmentation weakened his resistance to the sun and other elements. For this reason, he was susceptible to skin cancer and other such notorious diseases. They called him "Yellow," but it was with affection, and only because he had come to accept the term as a mark of distinction. "Yellow" distinguished and, therefore, identified in him laudable qualities. That was what the Center did; it restructured stereotypes and defects, even curses, redefining them as ordinary, if not praiseworthy. "Yellow," now in his early teens, had taken what in his formative years was one among several scornful references and, with a fresh vision supplied by the Center, reformulated it into a source of renewal. Each time he received a hug at the Center, "Yellow" recalled the contrary that took place in recent years when his neighborhood treated him like an untouchable. His brain couldn't take it when he learned that his grandmother and grandfather were not really his mother and father, and that his own parents' intolerance had led the trend that ridiculed and marginalized him. The awareness tormented him. When his grandparents couldn't bear with the resulting imbalance, they gave him up to foster parents. But the foster parents couldn't handle him for too long either, so they in turn gave him up to an orphanage. As he grew older, the Center was considered more appropriate than the orphanage.

It helped that "Yellow" sang with the Center's choir, and especially that he did an occasional solo. It was an honor to belong to the choir; the blue, flowing robes gave the impression of majestic cherubs, not of children neglected and suppressed. A rich myriad of lights on the altar produced an aesthetic that was transcendent yet real. It caused the choristers to be idolized. When he sang, the effects of the lights on his skin made him glow and transformed him into something immortal from another world unknown, deifying him some more. Admired as a soloist, a relative star, his place in the Center was fortified and he was forced to be more at home than ever. It was a feeling that reinforced his loathing for nearly everything outside those walls.

But most children who were not orphans still lived with their parents, and most didn't board. This fact showed another striking difference between the Orphanage at Dublin and the Center, and another basis for categorization. In Dublin there was a stronger sense of equality. Here, the concept of some being more equal than others was partly confirmed by either the possession or lack thereof of parents. And for some, like Monty, it engendered the solitude occasionally brought on by their few moments of reflection.

Children who couldn't boast of a parent or guardian, and who were sensitive, quickly picked up on the extra attention that some of the other children received from outside adults. They weren't necessarily sad or jealous, but they felt a vacuum somewhere, somewhere not easily recognizable. In spite of all the attention and care the Center provided, they knew that they missed out on certain emotions though they couldn't tell what those emotions were. They didn't hold the Center responsible; in fact they appreciated its efforts, but for those who pondered more deeply than was expected, they began to understand that completion on the inside was attainable only if the inside and outside fed off of each other unselfishly. And yet it was an ambiguous conclusion since most of them had little desire to enter the outside and conquer the anxieties it invoked. It didn't matter that those anxieties were sometimes steeped in fanfare and brilliance.

After the July celebrants were made to squeeze on to a low platform during which everyone else sang "Happy Birthday to You," it was time for Monty to perform. For the first time the limelight shifted from the celebrants to another Center celebrity.

He was nervous and trembled visibly. Yes, he had anticipated this moment and the fears he would battle with, always finding reassurance in the flute, but reality proved to be far more intense than imagination. The extent to which he was terrified was something he could never have foreseen. When he rose to take the stage, Sister Tracy observed how he hesitated. She also saw how his steps were a little wobbly, even though his bowlegs generally gave the impression of wobbly motion. Smiling broadly, she walked up to him, grabbed his right hand and whispered emphatically in his ears, "you can do it Monty; you're the best flute player in the world."

In spite of her encouragement, she had to half-drag him to the stage. Once they made it there, she released him and returned to her seat. He was now alone and very self-conscious. Slowly he looked down at the magic object that he now held in both hands. He was alone except for it--the flute--, his companion. They were together and inseparable. It meant that he wasn't quite alone after all, and recalled the instances when he tried to predict this day, gathering strength from the flute each time uncertainty crept in. He couldn't guess the future anymore. It was here. Now was the time to tap from the flute just as it would tap from him. Now was the time to exploit power from what was, perhaps along with Dorothy, his best friend. The thoughts filtered through his mind at great speed, and yet they still allowed room for him to instantly recall the Joneses and the impact of staring back in their stabbing eyes. The group expected him to eventually face them, but they didn't expect it to happen that dramatically. In an instance Monty raised his head, eyes wide open, and looked at his audience. It was almost a glare, as if he was challenging them to a duel. Some were impressed, most were surprised, but Sister Tracy was a little worried. She couldn't decipher the implications of Monty's sudden and unexpected stance.

All eyes were on him. He was still short. His thin legs were still bow and his stomach still drooped over his waistline. His nose was still flat, as if it had been stamped to his face and rolled over again and again. His ears had not lost their stuck-in-mid-flight impression, and they were still large, flat, and wide. And it was good that he didn't smile because if he did his aim at encouraging relaxation and good spirits might not have been understood clearly, and might have been mistaken for something else. His outfit did little to camouflage his looks. He was made to wear a white shirt with a bow tie that may have been fitted too tight, and a square-shaped jacket to match. His black jacket also matched his black shorts that reached past his knees, which they caressed lightly. He had worn his black shoes on the right feet and laced them up close-to properly. His white socks, pulled up efficiently, almost met with the base of his shorts. But nothing was unusual in the Center, and he was motivated by this knowledge.

Like Sister Tracy had instructed him, Monty bowed, then, after taking a deep breath, he began. At first it was slow but it built up fast and as it did, so did his confidence. He put a lot of emotion into the well-known "Happy Birthday" tune, embellishing it with an ambience that nearly changed the original. To the celebrants, it just wasn't the rendition of an old song; it was a salutation that came from the heart. They were touched, even those who couldn't quite interpret the beauty of the art form and the way it was rendered. They too were touched by Monty's sincerity and innocence, and by his sheer skill. Everyone in the hall was touched.

When he was done playing "Happy Birthday" twice and "Puff the Magic Dragon," he received a standing ovation. Some couldn't help the flow of tears, including Sister Tracy. But the cheering was cut short when another tune filled the air, piercing every other sound and drowning them out. The people were surprised but interested; their applause steadily died out and they tuned in again, taking their seats. Sister Tracy was concerned as this episode had not been pre-planned. But she, too, sat down, puzzled and biting her nails in expectation.

It was not a particular song or tune; just a hybrid of mellow sounds that came directly from the soul of a naive boy who longed to live life without inhibitions and undue pressures. They were formed on the spur of the moment and he breathed life into what would otherwise have been harsh and meaningless. Somehow he blended the sounds, creating harmony between the slow and the fast, the loud and the soft, and told an enchanting story without words. While each person decoded the story differently, there was a prevailing release of serenity that was received at all levels. He continued for about twenty minutes and time stood still. From Monty's audience the awe, the silence, and the focus were overpowering. When he was done, he bowed again. About two seconds of silence followed and then the place erupted. Sister Tracy rushed on the stage and grabbed him in an everlasting hug, and wept. He couldn't understand why she wept, seeing from the response of his audience that his presentation had been extremely successful. With time he would learn that tears didn't always express pain. In the background the applause and eulogies continued.

Not the Joneses Again!

Mr. Ranjid must have been an angel. When Monty was sent down to the lobby to meet him that afternoon, the twelve-year-old boy prepared for the worst. He was sure that he was about to be sent outside, to be hosted by another family. As far as he was concerned, every American family was like the Joneses. He wasn't prepared for another ordeal of that nature, and he didn't want to believe that another family would show more compassion and patience than the Joneses. Maybe the outside was an arena he would eventually have to enter and explore in order to find completion, but he didn't feel ready just yet.

He loved the authenticity and simplicity of the things that mattered at the Center--the learning, the love, the friendships, the calm, the diversity, and the tolerance. Its culture was reminiscent of All Saints at Dublin, but adjusting was the least of his worries. He had, after all, succeeded years earlier. Besides, the pattern had become, for him, normal, equipping him with the tools, more mental than tangible, that were needed to overlook and overcome the strain. And if he left the center now, he would leave without his flute, his hope for assurance and redemption.

"Hi there, Monty."

Mr. Ranjid rubbed his curly hair fondly as he greeted the growing boy. Monty had added a lot since their first meeting about a year before, except some height. Mr. Ranjid hadn't changed much and still boasted his little round glasses and rich, frumpy, facial hair.

"I'm fine" Monty responded, forcing an unusual smile that was supposed to hide his worries.

"Congratulations. We've heard a lot about your skills at playing the flute. We are so proud of you. Listen. Because the Center is helping you master the flute, we have thought it best that you should stay here a little longer. Now, I don't want you to get upset because it will only be for a while. Is that okay?"

Mr. Ranjid wasn't telling the truth; the fact that it had been difficult to find a family willing to take on the full task of harboring a foreign, refugee child for periods ranging from six months to five years. There were such sterile seasons, and they were dreaded though they were infrequent, when finding a charitable family was difficult and frustrating.

Monty wasn't at all upset. Again, in disappointing him Mr. Ranjid only brought him relief. Monty nodded as he looked up at the counselor. But he didn't scowl or smile, as he didn't want his expressions to be misunderstood. This was good because the Consulate preferred to have children spend quality time with host families. The idea was to expose them to a larger world that would promptly acculturate them into basic American and human mores and values. If they suspected that a child favored the Center over the homes of host families, they immediately set out to deprogram the child and ship him or her off to a willing family, even if it meant relocation. Any hint of unhappiness at staying at the Center produced the same results; it was an indication that the child was in dire need of new space. Monty was expressionless but, in secret, he rejoiced.

"Okay, sir," he replied, avoiding much eye contact.

"For now you will spend holidays and some weekends with another nice family, the Kennedys. They will be very happy to take care of you on these days. They also know how well you play the flute and can't wait for you to play something for them. I'm sure you'll love the Kennedys like they love you. Okay?"

Rather than commit to the full risk of taking in a child for at least six months, all things being equal, the Kennedys were more comfortable with periodic visits from Monty.

"Okay, sir," Monty accepted.

"Is everything else going well?"

"Yes sir."

"Well, I'm sure, I've heard what a good boy you are."

Mr. Ranjid rubbed Monty's hair again before leaving. Monty watched as he disappeared behind the door, and then he turned and made his way to the stairs leading up to his room.

Yes, Mr. Ranjid was an angel in brown skin.

.

Dorothy

Calm, simplicity, and sincerity reigned at the boarding Center. For an outsider, it would have been impossible to grasp the intricacy of the problems handled in there. And it helped that nothing was treated as unusual, even if it was. A break from this pattern was uncommon, yet expected. The attainment of perfection was impossible because, after all, people ran and occupied the place. But there was no digression that was considered threatening. There were still those spectacular moments when people like the thin, near-bald lad came up with an unpredictable act, or when the likes of Michael, feisty and obsessed with setting things right, had to be soothed with specially trained hands or words. And even when the unexpected came at the most ridiculous hour, annoying and desperate, the Center was prepared. There were always experts to return it to its peace, albeit peace sometimes wrapped in seclusion and the bizarre.

...

Dorothy was still Monty's best human friend and her presence, like the flute, reinforced the calm that he cherished. In music class he always made sure he was on the same team with her whenever supervised group activities were announced. And when he got to the fifth grade where students were sometimes required to form two-member, on-the-spur-of-the-moment bands as part of class exercises, he always rushed toward her shamelessly. It happened too often and too eagerly that at a point no one else even dared to pair up with Dorothy. Her favorite instrument was the piano, but her skills weren't above ordinary. Monty didn't seek her because of her piano-playing talent anyway; it was an opportunity to get close to someone among very few, whom he had come to trust without reservations. It was also an opportunity to play a song for her, anything she requested as long as he was familiar with it, and an opportunity to display his ingenuity some more. But he advertised only for her. In reality he was very humble about his gift with the flute. She always said very little, combining hand signals with words and sounds, but the sparkle in her eyes said a lot and told Monty in great detail what he craved to hear. She was delighted whenever he played for her and her appreciation slowly transcended his flute-playing skill and began to embrace the character behind the skill. She grew fond of Monty in spite of his flute, and when she commended him for "a job well done" after he got done playing a few tunes, she would reach out and squeeze his forearm for a few seconds. It was a habit that steadily increased with time.

His looks didn't seem to determine the manner in which she reached out to him. If the other kids noticed the growing affection between Monty and Dorothy, they didn't show it, and neither did Sister Tracy. Band improvisation was usually a fairly active and loud period when only complete lack of focus would allow anyone to get into anyone else's business, musical or social.

One day, after using the bathroom, Monty, a fourteen-year-old fifth grader, was walking down the hallway back to his math class. He hated the class with such intensity. As if to soothe his lackluster desire to return to class, Dorothy showed up at the other end of the hallway heading in Monty's direction. They smiled, each happy with the unexpected surprise, until they met and stopped. They usually had time to interact only during lunch or music class, so this was not typical. For that reason they needed a little time to decide what to say and how to say it.

"Hai Mo-nte," she broke the brief silence.

"Hi. Where are you going?"

"Batrum" she responded rather coyly.

"I just came from there."

"Oh, o-kay…well…I guess I…be go-ing. See you…la-ter."

"Okay."

Though they said farewell to each other, neither one of them budged. They stared in each other's eyes and, again, it was she who broke the stillness. He took a step back when she leaned forward, and then he stopped, unable to move and hardly able to breathe. At first he wasn't sure what she touched his right cheek with, but it felt soft and a little moist. Then he realized what it was when she did it again, this time bringing her lips to his and giving him a quick peck. And then she stood back up straight and looked into his eyes one more time, on her face a look of contentment that blended with a bashful half smile. Though she let out a spontaneous giggle that was both unnerving and disconnected before sauntering off to the ladies room, she was still content.

With Monty it was a feeling of incomprehension, but he was elated; in his heart he was. It was only after he summed up the courage and power to trigger movement that his mind regained the ability to think. But the surprise didn't all go at once, and it showed in his stagger back to class, making his legs appear more bow than they really were. He had just received his first kiss, not the affectionate kiss of an elderly person, but the sensuous kiss of a friend for whom he had more than ordinary feelings. Instantly he had a flashback to the Joneses some four or so years ago, and the episode where Betty talked about white meat. But though both encounters were comparable in the intimacy that underlined them, with Dorothy it was real, not forced, and though he was scared, it was the fear that comes with regeneration, not the type, as with Betty, that threatens degeneration. With Dorothy, too, he felt a longing for what he feared and didn't quite understand, because it was flavored with sincere passion tapped from deep within the heart. It wasn't the type of revolting fascination that comes from imposing one's erotic delusions on a person unappreciated, even despised. Monty was therefore happy, even though he almost tipped over in fright.

The Kennedys

And yet he still had those moments when loneliness overcame him. In spite of the affections he shared with Dorothy, and in spite of the recognition his flute brought him. There were those times when he was by himself, mostly after saying his personal prayers before dozing off at night, when his mind went on an excursion.

At twelve he began to question who he was. If there were people his age that lived with their parents, why didn't he? And while their allusions to a faraway place that first day was vague and didn't register in any substantial way, the Joneses' had begun, by chance, to inscribe in his subconscious the possibility of leaning on more than what was apparent. Beyond the aspirations of standard childhood growth, his slow maturation was achieved with the hazy, sometimes doubtful, knowledge that a part of him was missing. It was a part attached to somewhere too remote to bother about just yet.

He periodically flashed back to the Joneses, as much as he didn't want to, and compared the kinetic phases of his growing up to what must have been a more stable pattern for Betty and baby Dave. He hadn't been relaxed in their home, but he knew that the situation would have been different if he was a blood son of the family. He tried, not too successfully, to imagine conditions at the Center within the context of outside families. It wasn't necessarily a better life that he envisioned, but it was less formal with far more doors opening up. He imagined Christmas and New Year celebrations, and birthday celebrations. He imagined seasonal Catholic rites, rules, and daily routines, and he transplanted them from within the walls of the Center to within the walls of what he had come to construct in his mind, from what he heard and knew, as the standard nuclear family. In the latter the space was always smaller and held fewer people, but seemed to offer larger options and choices than the larger domain that was the Center. But he never could come up with a definite picture of all the factors that distinguished both worlds. The thoughts began to stimulate a desire, not necessarily to abscond to that world on the outside, but to meet with and examine it some more, and to exploit some of the more reliable resources it held. Surely, for most people to reside there, it had to contain something good.

Even though he now tied his laces well and clearly understood the difference between his left and right feet, he still felt an emptiness that wasn't always easily decoded. And though he now brushed his teeth without staining the walls, mirror, and floor, and ate without dropping things on himself, the floor, and table, he still couldn't feel quite complete. It didn't matter either, that he seldom wet the bed anymore. Monty received an ego and confidence boost when he was finally allowed to receive his first and subsequent holy communions, but the emptiness, still deep and unfilled, remained and nagged him.

...

The Kennedys helped him find a glitter. It was faint but it began to slice through the murk he associated with the outside. They accidentally filled some of the emptiness that he felt, rebuilding in him the notion that family, whether inside the gray walls of the Center, or within the less rigid walls of a standard home, was nourished and shaped by the characters that resided there. It did not always depend on whether the structure was constructed on the inside or on the outside.

The Kennedy house was much larger than the Jones's and contained a much larger crowd. It was a huge, red, brick mansion located in the heart of Sherwood Forest, a wealthy section of Madison. The first day Mr. Ranjid, the brown angel, dropped him off there on a sunny Veterans Day, Monty was overwhelmed by its sheer grandeur. Inside the mansion, he was subdued by the glamour of the domineering reddish hue, the silver that lined the borders of the huge painting and picture frames, the pale, yet charming, marble floors, and the splendor of the mahogany wood furnishing. On occasion he found it difficult to breathe freely.

At the dinner table it took him a while to get used to the sparkling, lavish china and cutlery, and for a while he was truly scared to touch them, let alone put them to his mouth. He had never been offered so much food at a sitting, and when he was tired of eating he didn't know how to politely refuse. As each course was delivered, one almost immediately after another, by a butler and maid, each smartly dressed in starched black attires, he indulged until he felt the mounting pressure in his lower stomach. Already extended too far, it extended and drooped even further over his belt. Later that night, just before he went to bed, he put the toilet to great use, freeing himself of all that gas and all that extra load. He wondered if they heard the many, loud motorbike and musical sounds he let loose, and he was mortified.

Throughout that first visit and the next few, he was intimidated by the Kennedy home. When he first walked into the guestroom, he wondered why anyone would trust him with a bedroom of such regal elegance. It was a mini home in itself and contained its own full bathe, embellished by the customary reddish hue, even though its tile floors, walls, and tub were bright white. As with the china and cutlery, he hesitated before he touched the fluffy, ruby towel that was much taller than him, but once he built up the courage he didn't want to let go and almost used it as a blanket that first night. Then he concluded that the comforter that concealed the bed and overflowed on to the thick rug could serve that purpose. The room had its own little living room, complete with a phone, television, side and center mahogany tables, and couches which, like the bed and flowery blinds, retained a tender satin feel that almost contrasted with the intended reddish effect.

It made sense that the house was mighty. There was Great-Grandma Kennedy, Grandma and Grandpa Kennedy, Mr. and Mrs. Kennedy, Mr. Kennedy's brother Centaur Kennedy, who delighted in the bottle, Centaur Kennedy's son Fritz, whose mom was somewhere far away, Mrs. Kennedy's niece Dianne, whose craving to be an ice-skater was threatened by an attack of polio that forced her into a wheelchair for the time being. There were the Kennedy children, all eight of them, Sylvia, Michael, John, Abel, Myra, Roman, Eva, and Trisha, and a sixteen-year difference between Sylvia, twenty-five, and Trisha, nine.

It was a lively home. If Mr. Kennedy wasn't settling disputes between his children or relatives, Mrs. Kennedy was trying to convince Grandma Kennedy that her constant urge to redecorate the main living room was pointless. Else Mr. and Mrs. Kennedy frequently turned emergency counselors, trying to convince Mr. Centaur that his boozing habits were a poor example for the children, especially Fritz, only eleven. But the confrontations and conflicts were really the exception, not the rule, and they were of a mild type in spite of how they came across on the surface. They never created that category of malice that ran deep and lasted, the type that sought to destroy.

For the most part, the spirited nature of the home was realized in the numerous indoor games that they had, from board and card games to pool and ping-pong tables in the basement. There was also the swimming pool where they spent a lot of time during the summer. No matter how much they tried to convince him that the pool had a shallow end where he could start learning, and that it was very safe since they were all there to watch over him, Monty absolutely refused to venture into the clear water. In spite of its inviting, light green effect. It was the same back at the Center. No matter how tight the supervision was at the swimming pool, he avoided the water like he was salt. He just loved to sit back and watch, maybe eat a bowl of ice cream or sip on a tall glass of coke that always held too much ice that left little room for the coke.

Except that a unique feeling crept over him each time he watched Myra in her swimsuit. It was warm and traveled slowly from his stomach to his chest, causing him to be coy and anxious. He struggled to look away each time, but it was half-hearted and he stole sly side-glances at her. The fascination was barely there when she was fully dressed. It was something about her that he couldn't easily place, something triggered by a number of factors--her walk, her voice, her poise, her shape, her long legs, her brown hair stretching almost to her waist and glittering in the sun. Each time Monty indulged in this manner, images of Dorothy, for some strange reason, interrupted his secret scrutiny, and he always felt guilty. Up until the Kennedys, he had been content to regard only Dorothy with an admiration greater than ordinary. Now another person had squeezed into the picture and shared that privilege with Dorothy, and he had no sincere intentions of pushing her out, though he pretended to try. He felt guilty each time. Not only because of Dorothy, but because at Sunday School they had been taught to resist such fleshly desires with a fury. He couldn't fully understand the feeling that flared up whenever Myra showed up in her swimsuit, and he didn't try hard enough to understand. He felt better keeping it deep inside and simulating its non-existence.

They, too, looked at him. But they were more diplomatic than the Joneses and therefore subtler. Long before he was ever presented to them, they had been sent his pictures and told his story with as much detail as could be provided. They had also been cautioned about the need not to discuss particular areas of his past with him. But, as with the Joneses, stories and photos did not have the power to capture reality in its entirety. So, when Monty first arrived, they reidentified him and drew fresh deductions about his appearance and the possible habits that accompanied such appearance. And they stared. But since they were refined, they concealed their stares. Monty must have felt something because many eyes carry energy when they penetrate anything. But since the stares and analyses were not obvious, and therefore suggestive of some regard for him, they didn't bother him. Like their stares and analyses, he picked up on their whispers and private gossip; but they, too, were veiled and didn't cause him unease. They were extremely courteous to him that it sometimes came across as pretentious and counterfeit. But it was really not pretentious or counterfeit, just exaggerated, for they meant to treat him with all civility.

There were very few times when gracious behavior suffered, like such occasions as Thanksgiving when Centaur chugged down bottle after bottle of Heineken at the dinning table, much to Mr. and Mrs. Kennedy's embarrassment. They mightn't have been that irritated if Monty wasn't there; after all, they were all used to Centaur's occasional, petty debauchery. When his resounding and smelly belches became regular, it was a signal that he was getting tipsy. At this stage, all too familiar with the signal, Mr. and Mrs. Kennedy glared furiously in his direction without saying anything. They didn't have to; their glares admonished far more than any words could. But if Centaur was already far along, there was little that admonitions, voiced or unvoiced, could do. He would laugh loud at almost anything he or anyone else said, his speech would become slurred, his eyes would turn red and teary, and he would continue to chug down, belching and hiccuping. He would foul up the air around him when he talked, burped, or let an inadvertent fart, and when he attempted to walk he would stagger precariously. When Centaur was this far, Mr. and Mrs. Kennedy could only wait until he regained some sanity, and then they would go over with him the lectures they had repeated too many times already. If the children were concerned you couldn't tell because they casually minded their business. But whenever his father soaked up too much, the despair and fear in Fritz's eyes were unmistakable.

Mr. and Mrs. Kennedy ensured Monty's comfort and gave him directions in that regard. But their concern for him was genuine and lacked Mr. Jones's elusive posture or the military-type maintenance of order demonstrated by his wife. Meals were prepared in accordance with what casual discussions had established as his favorite meals, and the same was true of the channels they watched on the huge television in the main living room. Of course when he retired to his room at bedtime he could surf through the channels and watch whatever he liked until sleep ended his search. Mr. and Mrs. Kennedy saw to it that the maid and butler kept his room neat and updated his bathroom needs on time.

The children invited him to learn and play every game they had. Except for a few card games at the Center, and maybe checkers, monopoly, and jenga, he had never played anything close to the variety of board games they had. He was slow at chess and scrabble, but they drove him to use his mind and imagination in ways not exploited by the Center. For every successful move he made in either game, his confidence was raised and he beamed excitedly while they clapped and cheered ceremoniously like a cultured audience. His new set of teeth were more naturally shaped than the former, and they were more white than brown, but they were also larger than usual and added to the peculiarity of his smile. In their ritualistic manner the Kennedys observed and wondered, but came through like they really didn't notice anything.

At the dining table, and when they played board games, the girls, like decent ladies, avoided sitting beside him except in very few instances, and they avoided contact with him, except, perhaps, a formal handshake. It was the boys who introduced him to ping-pong and pool, and, when the weather was right, basketball and tennis. The Center didn't have tennis facilities, and he had never had the urge to try out basketball there. There were those times when he was elated by an outdoor picnic and decided to take part in volleyball, but it was more out of a need to demonstrate his excitement than to compete or master something new.

The Kennedys roused in him a fervor to compete, to discover any neglected prowess, and to dare to win. Sometimes the girls played with the boys, and when they did they avoided playing with Monty. Otherwise they mostly played with each other or watched and applauded the boys. As with scrabble and chess, Monty's reflexes and decisions in the more elaborate games were hardly average, and recurrently below. But for each unexpected, proficient move he made, his confidence climbed, the cheers followed, and so did the subtle glances aimed at his exotic smile.

He liked the Kennedy home.

The Flute

They had him over on his fifteenth birthday.   If he had not
gotten used to their extravagant habits, the spread would have
terrorized him.   Still, it was enough to make him speechless.
The dinning area had been specially rearranged and decorated
with flowers and balloons of every color.   Even the butler and
maid wore their special white, super starched uniforms.   The
assortment of candies, snacks, drinks, food, practically lined up
in heaps, was simply too much.   Even with a few extra mouths--
some of the neighbors' children had been invited--the display
was still excessive.   Care was taken not to have alcohol.   With the
number of visiting children, they couldn't risk having Centaur
put up a show.

They all ate, drank, danced, and played games to their
hearts' content.   Monty even proved that he hadn't forgotten his
monkey-strut and he couldn't care less about who gaped at his
eccentric appearance or eccentric dance.   He was having a great
time and wouldn't allow his joy to be stolen by anything, real or
imagined.   After he blew out the candles on his giant two-layered
cake, and then sliced once through the bottom layer, they sang a
resounding "Happy Birthday" for him.   He stood there sweating
from the thrill and exertion of the evening, and after his mind
sped back over some of his recent trials, he couldn't believe this
was happening.   A line of tears streamed down the corner of his
left eye.   He now understood why Sister Tracy had wept that first
time some years back when he played his flute in honor of those
July birthday celebrants at the Center.   Indeed tears were not
necessarily synonymous with pain.

The cake-cutting rite should have crowned the celebration.
But it didn't.

"Would you like to play something for us? " It was Mr.
Kennedy.

"Yes," Mrs. Kennedy followed up, "that would really be nice. We've heard so much about your special talent with a flute. Come on Monty, don't be shy."

As if rehearsed, the crowd showed their approval and goaded him on, and the way they clapped suggested total faith in his ability.

"But I don't have my flute," Monty responded shyly. He felt bad that he would have to disappoint such a pleasant group of people.

"That's okay. You don't need yours. You can use this one."

To Monty's surprise, it was Centaur. Dressed smartly in a white cardigan, black shirt and black pants, he had been uncharacteristically quiet throughout the evening. He held out a dazzling, silver, cylindrical box. Almost shivering in anticipation, Monty carefully received the box.

"Go ahead, open it," Centaur instructed.

Monty was temporarily paralyzed when he opened the lid. The flute fit snuggly, priceless and stunning. He loved the one he had used at the Center in the past few years, but this one was of another class and seemed to introduce a new era and outlook. Reminiscent of his initial introduction to a flute, he gazed at it; he gazed at its radiance for a few seconds, touched it, and then caressed it gently. He felt each hollow, taking his time, until he came to the main hollow at the tip, encased in black, solid plastic. Engrossed in his fleeting miniature world of music, everything and everyone stood still, and there was silence, perhaps not by design. It was the contagious effect of the stillness. Finally he reached in and began to lift it out. This time his fingers trembled visibly.

"Play whatever you feel like, Monty." Mr. Kennedy briefly broke the silence. But he didn't have to. Monty had already decided to do just that, to play the vision that came from within, and without much thought. He wasn't daunted by uncertainty, but by the sheer reality of his being at the center of such ostentation. After all, he had been playing for birthday crowds over the past few years at the Center.

Unsure of what to expect, there was some tension in the crowd when he bowed and lifted the instrument to his thick lips. Suddenly they didn't seem so sure. When he began, the shift in mood to one of relative ease was obvious. He took them on a journey, one that thrust them into several reveries where they met with different emotional motifs and levels, and where they were urged to ponder them. He kept the momentum somber and mellow, playing well known tunes, secular and Christian, and merging them, in quick succession, with improvisations and tunes not-so-well-known. He enchanted them for about twenty minutes without a break, showing a phenomenal ability to switch between seemingly inconsistent speeds, tunes, rhythms, and keys, yet sustaining an accord that was enviable. He reached and searched deep into his heart, and when it seemed he had used up everything in there, he received from his soul. As he exposed his audience to a series of sentiments, touching and briefly transforming them with each new layer, he went through transformations too. It was impossible to ignore because he changed often, mentally and physically, for he was lost in the moment, and he sweat profusely even though it was fairly cool. His face lightened up and his eyes remained shot most of the time. Something was revived in each of their spirits; something otherwise put aside and not revisited recently.

When he finished, he bowed, and there were the two or so archetypal seconds of silence before the screams and applause. For those who also shed a few teardrops, there was no effort to hold them back. Monty stood there, rigid; his smile was half real and half polite. His joy was always more for his success at not failing himself or his flute, but, of course, he loved to satisfy his listeners. In spite of his sweat, they touched him in several ways, kissing his cheeks, hugging him, shaking his hands, and patting his curly hair. After what seemed like a very long time, the touches and commendations ceased and peace returned. Monty carefully returned the silver flute to its box.

"Thank you Mr. Centaur," he blurted out respectfully, as he held the box out. Very grateful for the opportunity to play that flute, he tried hard to hide his sadness at giving it back. His consolation was that there was, after all, the flute that music class allowed him to use back at the Center.

"You're welcome, my man Monty, and I've told you, you don't have to call me Mr. Centaur. Just Centaur. Besides, you don't have to give it back, it's yours."

The words almost knocked him over and he instinctively looked in the direction of Mr. and Mrs. Kennedy. They nodded their approval, smiling broadly and proudly.

"It's your birthday gift. We hope you like it" Mrs. Kennedy added.

"Thank you, thank you so much. Thank you everybody."

He lost control for a moment, and then rushed and hugged, first, Mrs. Kennedy with one hand, in the other hand was the magic box, and then he did the same to Mr. Kennedy. For the next minute or two he just embraced the box, occasionally fixing his eyes on it. He was lost in the moment and could barely hear the fresh clapping and cheers; the power of his feelings blocked them out. From now on, after he played he would keep the flute, not return it to Music Department. It was all too unbelievable. When the tears came again, he didn't try to hold them back. They were, after all, another reminder that tears didn't necessarily suggest hurt.

Yes, he liked the Kennedy home.

New Ground

He had played at virtually all birthday parties after that first time, except for when he was down in health or, perhaps, visiting with the Kennedys. Each time, he played happily and lifted everyone with him. Even after his fifteenth birthday party at the Kennedys, later that month he attended the party for all November celebrants, and he played again. This time, it was with his own flute, his new flute, and attention shifted constantly from him to the dazzling instrument.

Earlier, he had done the right thing and informed Mr. Ranjid, Sister Tracy, and his floor manager, Brother Joseph, about the gift, and they had all been marveled by it.

"Congratulations, good for you," Mr. Ranjid had said.

"Oh, this will take you places," Sister Tracy had screamed, almost in tears.

"Thank God for his blessings," Brother Joseph had remarked with a lot of emotion.

In past years, but not too often, Sister Tracy had hinted at the possibility of Monty playing with the choir or Center band, or both. He recognized them, but he was content and felt adequate about playing during monthly birthday celebrations. And since he wasn't prepared to commit to any other formality beyond the formality of daily Center and Catholic rules, he avoided the band. It was a rule not to push the kids too hard, and to allow them the freedom to choose what they were comfortable with. And so Sister Tracy did not push Monty too hard or too often. She was as surprised as she was delighted when he walked up to her a few days after revealing his most valued birthday gift, and volunteered for the choir.

"Oh, praise God" was her immediate response. She gave him an all too familiar hug and then quickly reached for a handkerchief well positioned in her side pocket. With it she wiped her eyes using rapid, light dabs.

Performing with the choir wasn't just a question of showing off his new flute to the Center, but it had everything to do with the flute. It empowered him some more and convinced him that he was now qualified to address a new and wider world, not simply one of birthday celebrants. He was now blessed with a resource that generated reserved willpower and talent, enough to serve an unlimited audience and to sufficiently evoke the potency of sacred songs. Sunday services at the Center's cathedral attracted churchgoers from all over the city of Madison.

He played his flute among other choir instrument players, but there were times when he was required to lead songs or to do a solo. At such times he walked to the front of the choir, equipped with the confidence of experience and the loyalty of the flute. In addition to their words, and sometimes even more meaningful, hc always unveiled the utmost richness of the hymns. That way they penetrated a little deeper whenever he played, inspiring a reflective quality and some in the congregation had no choice but to slowly shake their heads or weep. Now like one of the cherubs, his flowing robe and flute, against the splendid lighting, turned him into a divine messenger, invaluable and greatly sought after. For the first time in his life, attention didn't rest on his raw looks.

Other Walls

The periodic loneliness persisted. In spite of his flute-playing rise to restricted fame at the Center. In spite of the fresh sense of security, honor, love, and power meted out to him at the Kennedys'. In spite of the undeniable truth that he belonged to Dorothy and she belonged to him. Their affection for each other was in depth and real, and had risen from subtle to glaring. After their first kiss in the hallway, they did it habitually whenever they were alone, and she wasn't necessarily the instigator anymore. It was never anything like a French kiss where masses of spit and phlegm were exchanged generously, and where daring tongues prodded eagerly and deeply, searching every nook of the mouth and even the depths of a willing or unwilling throat. No, it was always more restrained and replicated the gentility and honesty of their affections. Their hugs were neither fierce nor tight, as if they were conscious of not hurting each other. They were innocent and pecked each other's cheeks and lips without pressing too hard and without lasting too long. Sometimes it was an area other than the lip or cheek, but never below the neck; their innocence didn't allow them such freedom.

There was one disappointment in their relationship and it came with a confession from Dorothy. She didn't have to tell Monty but she did, a decision compelled by the torment of guilt and true love.

"Monte, perhaps yu wonda why I ... neva invited yu to ma ... home," she began.

Not true. He had never wondered because he had come to associate his private visits anywhere with the involvement and approval of the Catholic Consulate. As far as he was concerned they were separate, the world of the Center where their love blossomed and the unreliable, outside world, and he kept them that way. He was content with visiting the Kennedys, going out on group trips and outings, and spending time with Dorothy.

The joys or lack thereof of visiting her home had never crossed his mind. Now it did, but only because she raised it.

"Ac-tualle," she continued, "it's ma parents…."

She halted as if she had said too much, tightening her lips as they twitched nervously, and it wasn't because of her speech problems. Monty knew it. Her eyes turned glassy and slightly red before one or two teardrops escaped, and then she lunged forward and grabbed him around his neck and shoulders, then released the hug before it became too tight and before it lasted too long.

He didn't react immediately because he didn't understand and, therefore, couldn't summon the right verbal or dramatic emotions. It was after she left that he began to think and to speculate the reasons for, and implications of her unexpected behavior. During those periods of intimate contemplation, the incident merely added another topic of concern to his list of unanswered questions. What was it about Dorothy's parents? Would they rather have kept him at a distance because of those traits that drew the gaze of outsiders from as long as he could remember? Or was it mistrust; did they suspect that he had coveted their daughter like the Holy Book forbade? In that case, it meant they disapproved of the friendship. Surely it had nothing to do with his distinct features and the vague background they came with. The thoughts did little to clarify this and other concerns that visited him frequently, and that came to life when he was alone. After the questions, evaluations, and guesses came the sad truth that all he could do was deliberate without unraveling.

The aloneness didn't quite go away, in spite of the commendable strides he made, and in spite of the insecurities he discarded. It didn't all go away.

...

Like they used to do in Dublin, the Center organized rides and trips around Wisconsin, but mostly around Madison and mostly on weekends. The University of Wisconsin, huge and attractive, brought variety and unending activity, culture, and color to the city. They were taken to sporting events at the Field House on campus, theatrical shows on and off campus, and on walks down the exotic yet trendy State Street with its numerous shops that sold anything from African masks to Victorian costumes. They attended various cultural events on and off campus, were taken to the malls, and, during the summer, were taken to the banks of the lake behind the famous Students Center, also called the Memorial Union. Here, they lounged around in the sun, played games, and ate hot dogs, popcorn, and chips which they washed down with all kinds of sodas, juices, and lemonades. They weren't all taken out to the same destination at once, but were bussed to different locations and events in long, white luxurious buses with *Special Training Center* painted on their sides in thick burgundy.

The division of students into mixed groups was determined by factors like age, nature of physical or emotional ailment, and class. On each trip, Monty missed Dorothy and wished she came along. But, like others who lived with their parents, she didn't have to. Her absence reopened thoughts and perplexities concerning life outside of the Center walls. Not life as he knew it from living with the Joneses or visiting with the Kennedys, but life completely disconnected from the Center and the visions and modes of existence fashioned in such a different locale. And again, as when he was in Dublin years before, the excitement of the outings was checked by observations of other young people who belonged to smaller groups and who weren't subjected to the type of attention and restraint that they were subjected to. They saw these other young people wherever they went, and they consciously and subconsciously longed for what they perceived as a variety of liberties that the Center could not afford. They saw them by the lake, in the malls, on State Street, at the Field House, in the theaters, and on stage. It was not like seeing them on television because they had inadvertently come to associate television with fantasy and invention. But it was

103

hard to see a living child at a mall or on a street and determine that he or she was counterfeit.

Nothing swayed Monty more than the image of that young Apache girl who had to be about his age. As part of a variety cultural show on campus, she charmed and humbled the audience with her flute, playing solemn tunes that derived from the soul of her heritage. The flute was wooden, not silver and stylish, but it warmed the heart and evoked feelings that were both sad and happy, and told a story from which several themes were taken. She forced Monty to look around the theater and, for the first time, realize its vastness and the number and category of people it held. His was not an old, wooden flute probably handed down through generations. There was no reason why he couldn't reach and impinge on as great and diverse an audience, if not a greater one. A little envy for the Apache girl, perhaps, but he was also grateful to her for the incentive to reject limitation and intimidation.

Madison attracted a wide mixture of human types, partly because of its declared liberalism, and partly because it welcomed a rich, albeit romanticized, array of cultural events. Monty noticed, and so did other children who also observed and assessed elaborately. It was a source of relaxation, for they, too, could imagine themselves as an addition to the human types, not an exception or unfamiliar novelty. They saw people dressed in garbs that couldn't quite be explained, they saw hairstyles that defied logic, they saw behavior patterns that stretched from the comical to the deranged, and they saw people eat what, in their eyes, didn't look edible or swallowable. Sometimes they noticed how a man carried another man on his laps and stroked his hair fondly. They enjoyed but also wondered at some of the plays, dances, music, and costumes they heard and saw on stage, for while they were mostly entertaining, they were sometimes puzzling and too incredible, even scary. They saw a plurality of human attributes that some of them had never seen before. The color spectrum was limitless and included pecan, pink, white, pale, yellow, red, brown, black, and every possible thing in-between. It was hard to feel like an outsider, at least around certain parts of Madison, especially the campus area.

Monty wondered about Sherwood Forest because it was inhabited by people who didn't exhibit the array of types concentrated mostly in the campus area. He was yet to see anything other than a certain social and physical category. It was the one phenomenon that had caused him a little discomfort whenever he visited the Kennedys, but he wouldn't allow it to becloud the satisfaction that came with those visits.

Because Madison flaunted a liberal attitude that claimed to respect every unique human practice and presence, the tendency to be ridiculed or condemned was slim. There was great effort, therefore, to suppress true feelings of resentment against anything that wasn't normal in the traditional sense. Maybe that explains why the children didn't attract great and reckless attention that pitied, mocked, or hated The attention was there, but it was cautious and elusive, and came in the form of disguised glances and brief cynical expressions. But because the stares were too few, too hidden, and didn't last too long, they were easily ignored and didn't arouse feelings of excitement ultimately subsumed in confusion, intimidation, and dislike for things outside the Center walls. It was their return to within the Center walls that awakened emotions too intricate to handle, for the thrill of an outing always clashed with the satisfaction and comfort of the Center. Right after they returned, and lasting up to a few hours, sometimes days, some of them were happy and sad, content yet carrying an emptiness somewhere, grateful as well as indignant. Each time the white bus rode through the Center gates back into the Center, the children were immediately reminded that no matter how much the world outside shared in common with theirs, they didn't belong there. The realization caused a sensation that was as sober as it was pervasive and contagious.

Special People

At graduation, and reminiscent of kindergarten, the age and height range varied considerably. So did the range in chest size for the female graduands, and the range in facial hair for the male. At sixteen Monty hadn't yet grown any noticeable moustache or beard. His legs and chest were bare too, not like some of the other boys who had started to shave or who chose not to, and rather displayed their abundant and not-so-abundant, sometimes even comical, patches of hair. But nothing was surprising at the Center. So, Monty and the other sixth grade graduands, with a lot of sincere pride, paraded themselves with delight and a generally modest sense of achievement. Their white robes and gray caps gave the impression of three-dimensional sketches floating with utmost caution The Center band did its job, providing constant, soft, background music.

This was one of those occasions when guests were not restricted to parents and special church dignitaries. The Catholic Consulate did the honor of inviting guests on behalf of Monty, and then sent him a short note to inform and prepare him. The Joneses didn't show up, but Mr. Ranjid and all the Kennedys did. Monty couldn't believe his eyes. He had been informed in advance, but he didn't imagine that all the Kennedys would show up. Myra looked great in her black jeans and T-shirt, but she wasn't wearing a swimsuit and this contained the extent to which she distracted Monty. They all hugged and gave him quick pecks on his cheeks, even the girls who had normally avoided such close, maybe incriminating, contact. It was a special occasion after all, and came once in a lifetime, especially for people like Monty. When he was called to receive his certificate, a white cylindrical object around which a bright red ribbon was knotted, the Kennedys went wild, clapping and screaming with all the power they could muster, and letting loose a bunch of colorful balloons. They soared gently until they reached and stuck to the high, cathedral-type ceiling, or mingled with other balloons or sound and lighting equipment up there. The hall reverberated instantly, if only for a moment, drawing immediate attention to themselves and the special graduand. Their presence and actions crowned the vision of self-worth and conviction that they had sporadically instilled in Monty over the years. They were special people. He was honored and wished he could adequately demonstrate his gratitude.

The soft-spoken valedictorian, a shy, almost blind girl, was graceful even though she was tall and bony. In her flowing robe and thick glasses, she looked like an obedient messenger from heaven. She inspired and softened the hearts of her audience, but her poise and dauntless approach dissuaded pity and sentimental reactions. Her words of wisdom revealed, analyzed, urged, promised, and thanked. When she was done, she received a standing ovation as she was awarded a plaque before being guided back to her seat.

Monty wasn't the valedictorian and he didn't receive a plaque, but he was one of the highlights of the afternoon. It hadn't taken much for Sister Tracy to convince him to play his flute at the ceremony. It would, after all, be the final ceremony he attended at the Center, and the final opportunity to play before a Center audience. He had come a long way from when he played for those July celebrants, and took the podium with apparent composure when his name was announced. He did what he did best, practically stealing the show, though he limited himself, as was required, to one popular tune and one improvisational. Until he was done, he successfully transformed the mood in the hall from one of merriment and carefree to mellow and pensive. It reverted back when he was done, but not before he was also given a standing ovation.

...

Monty had noticed Dorothy and her parents just before things had begun formally, and though it crossed his mind, he didn't want to believe that she was carefully avoiding him. After the formalities, and after the Kennedys showered him with more compliments, kisses, and hugs, they took pictures. Mr. Ranjid emerged from the crowd, shook his hand, and took one or two pictures with him, courtesy of Centaur. The brown angel then set out to chitchat with the Kennedys and acknowledge the good job they had done with Monty.

Monty noticed Dorothy again, still glued to her parents it seemed. It was the opportunity he hoped for and boldly made his way toward them, conscious of her parents' presence.

"Congratulations, Dorothy. Good day, sir, ma'am," he greeted when he reached their spot.

"Congrat ... Monte" she responded rather officially, and offered her hand.

They shook like they were meeting for the first time. He expected a simple, cordial hug at least. Her parents beamed briefly and nodded at him. As if under obligation to do so, her father then managed to say, "good job with the flute." That was all. They turned and walked off, the parents first, with Dorothy following closely. She stole one quick look at him and continued briskly and somewhat furtively. Monty half expected the reaction, what with Dorothy's earlier indication that her parents were skeptical of their friendship. For that reason, and because his mind carried him back to his method of handling pressure from the Joneses years earlier, he retuned his focus, inviting the day's glamour to block out distracting sentiments. The intricacy and disappointment of Dorothy's actions were suppressed for now, and would be exhumed and addressed later, during those moments of private meditation. He was surprised at how controlled and composed his reaction was. It must have come from his conclusion that the real culprit was more likely to be her parents, not Dorothy. When he sauntered back to the Kennedys, their conversation with Mr. Ranjid was about over. Mr. Ranjid praised Monty one more time and rubbed his hair fondly before leaving. Refreshments were served in another hall that the rest of them found easily. The succeeding entertainment was light and involved mild music and inexpensive snacks.

Before the kind Kennedys left, Mrs. Kennedy handed a bunch of flowers and a small, red parcel to Monty. The parcel held a gold-framed picture of the entire Kennedy family and a simple picture book that told a story about all types of fascinating and outlandish flutes from different parts of the world. He cherished the gifts because he loved them, but more so because the Kennedys had given them to him. Before he left the hall, he caught one last glimpse of Dorothy and her parents at the other end. It was the last time he set eyes on Dorothy, until then his very best and closest human friend.

...

From analyses of Monty's progress, acquired and natural abilities, and emotional state, the Consulate concluded that High School was not the best thing for him. They decided to send him to the Institute for Specialized Learning and Skill Enhancement located in White Water, about an hour's drive from Madison. The Institute was specially designed to cater to the needs of students who demonstrated phenomenal potentials in acting, writing, areas of music, and scientific invention, but who weren't necessarily good in anything else. However one looked at them, they were each special in a way that was not typical. Although they were guided through four years of in depth studies that sought to develop each unique talent, they were also required to take general, required classes in English, Math, and Bible Knowledge. Jointly owned by the Catholic Church and State of Wisconsin, the Institute retained strong Catholic traditions.

The ability to excel in one major area didn't imply an inevitable mental challenge. About eighty percent of the students were from fairly stable homes, assessed to be normal and functional by the State, and therefore in need of no special attention. The other twenty-percent who were assessed with any of several handicaps, received extra, prescribed attention as determined by the nature of the problem. Two dormitories, gray and gothic, were assigned all such students with special needs.

The intentions were good, but the separation produced certain boundaries and relationships that were condescending if not outright spiteful. But that was Monty's second concern. His first was Mr. Ranjid's transfer to another state. Little did he know at his graduation ceremony that he was seeing the brown angel for the last time.

His new counselor was different in many ways. He was a very large man who had a surprisingly small voice and seemed to speak through his nose, also seemingly too small for his size. While he didn't keep any facial hair, the hair on his head was enough to give him an indefinite bad hair day. He breathed very hard and sweated even when there wasn't quite a reason to.

Unlike Mr. Ranjid, Brother Smith was in training for the priesthood in addition to being a counselor, and came from the city of Milwaukee, not too far off. Unlike Mr. Ranjid, too, he smiled little, which actually contrasted, ironically, with the truth that he was jolly by nature. But no matter how jolly he was, Monty had gotten too used to Mr. Ranjid.

That early September evening when Brother Smith dropped Monty off at the Institute, it was colder than usual. Two days earlier they had come to register him and go through a number of standard preliminaries, including a hasty orientation. Brother Smith helped him to the room he would be sharing with five other boys and young men. It was on the third floor.

The room had a phone that the students could use. It was the first time Monty boarded a room in which he could use the phone, albeit only for internal and local calls. At the Orphanage in Dublin he was either too little or too undeveloped, and at the Center at Madison permission had to be taken from a strict supervisor who timed you and breathed down your throat when you made your call. The room was also less crowded than the previous rooms he had shared.

Yet, when Brother Smith left after giving him a loving hug, Monty felt like the entire world came crashing down on him. He had never felt this lonely. The gray walls, as gray as the walls on the outside, closed in on him. They cast an ashen quality that

111

was menacing. Even the paintings of nature and Catholic saints were tainted by the pervading dullness, and they, too, seemed to hold gray where there was no gray. Two students had made it there before him. One was fast asleep and snored with his mouth wide open, a long line of spit oozing down the side. The other, spotting a goatee, sat on his bed and stared in space. Monty had no idea how long he had been in that spot and position, or why. Whoever dropped him off must have known him well enough to abandon him by himself, sure that it was okay. His look of utter loss and despondence only enlarged the overall state of gloom. At first Monty thought to speak to him, but one look at the young man's face and he changed his mind.

It wasn't long before a supervisor came to welcome and direct the students, but before then Monty lay on his bed and got lost in one of his deep thoughts. This time it wasn't only about who he was and where he came from and Betty and Dorothy and his flute and the outside world. For once he also tried to find and predict his future. Up until when he fell into a light sleep, the picture was enormous and empty.

Dreams

They were not only handled with care on account of their gifts, or the efforts to develop, explore, maybe exploit them, they were also treated like adults. The Institute may have been technically equal to a quality high school that comprised honors students alone, but it preserved a tradition of superior achievement and seriousness. It also held a statistically older group of students than was commonly found in high schools. On the inside it ultimately felt more like a mini college, and on the outside was perceived as having as much clout.

Room laws were few. They were not only few, they were not strict. Noise was controlled and all room lights had to be turned off after midnight. No problem. Monty and his roommates were usually asleep before eleven. They said little to one another and none of them owned a radio, so the room was essentially quiet, sometimes too quiet. It helped, too, that there was no television in the room; there was one in the main lounge. For people who said very little, there was also no problem keeping to the twenty-minute phone time limit. As introverted as he could be, Monty still wished for more interaction between he and them.

They didn't have to march in twos to the chapel or dining room. They were simply provided information about cafeteria operations, as well as daily morning and evening services. Of course they were encouraged to attend mass and benediction regularly, especially on Sundays, but whether they did or not was a personal thing. The same was true of their classes, though there were those instructors who penalized you if you missed a certain number of classes in a semester.

For the first time Monty was directly sent part of his stipend money to use as pocket money. The liberty to spend money as he pleased was new to him, though the amount demanded frugal spending. He savored the privilege. It was the closest he had come to being independent.

Monty saw the Institute as a reliable pathway to searching and discovering a sequence, a new social existence that digressed from the fixed pattern he knew. It would possibly magnify the power of his flute, taking both he and the instrument to heights that surpassed carefully chosen audiences and expectations. So, while they weren't pressured into a lot of things, he regulated himself. Every Sunday morning and evening he attended mass and benediction on time, and always sat in one of the first three rows. He also attended Wednesday evening service and at least one Bible study session a week.

...

His problems came, not with thoughts of daily routines, but of the other world that stood not too far off--the walls that housed the *normal* students. For the first time, Monty faced a boarding situation where peculiar things, looks, behaviors, and events were judged as abnormal. It was either a different walk on account of one limb being longer than the other, a speech defect, or any other defect that applied to any of the senses. It was either a level of thinking deemed too low for a certain age, a rare physical build, albinism, or any type of mental imbalance or what appeared to be mental imbalance. If it was an aberration in relation to what was meant to be healthy and proper, it drew attention.

Sometimes the attention was mere observation. But mostly it was observation tainted with a stuck-up quality that sought to define the observer as supreme. It led to a feeling of indignation, for why should superior and inferior have been made to interact freely? Sometimes the attention was a sneer or plain mockery, carefully disguised, not so carefully disguised, or outright blatant.

In the cafeteria the lines were drawn and they were quite rigid. *Normal kids* sat together except in very few cases. Sometimes Monty found himself sitting alone while a *normal* student walked around, even past him, searching for a table with *normal kids*, and eventually squeezing in where there was virtually no room.

The boundaries were maintained everywhere else--at the theaters, in church, and at the field house and stadium during sporting events. Such detachment wasn't necessarily brazen or confrontational, but it was clear and noticeable. The deriding remarks were usually kept low, except for an occasional one-line or one-word outburst. Either way, they were heard.

"God must have hit you in the face with a shovel after creating you."

"Duh, eating salad with a spoon? How creative!"

"Is hard to tell whether you're a crip or whether you're just walking cool."

"With those cross eyes how d'you look your girl in the eyes?"

"Uh-uh, ah-ah, oh-oh, mi-mi-mi-mi, couldn't understand a damn thing you said. Could you speak in English?"

"With those bowlegs please don't be a goal tender."

"What's your race, pork skin?"

"Oops! He is a girl. Was wondering why he went into the lady's room. My bad."

Sometimes attention came in the form of a roaring or simple laugh, but mostly in muffled giggles that lasted too long. But more than the smart, largely subtle, remarks or the giggles, the stares were most prevalent. They were usually deliberate and unmistakable; at other times they were not that obvious. Either way, they were discomforting, especially when they were unfriendly and not just about the human tendency to be easily distracted. They came in degrees--hard and cold, malicious, scornful, pitiful, inquisitive, observational.

At seventeen, Monty received a surge in hair growth. They sprouted unevenly at the top of his upper lip, at the sides of his mouth, on his back and chest, in his armpit, on his legs--especially his calf, and under his chin. They were short and thick, but visible, and didn't fit his height. He hadn't added an inch since he was thirteen, except around his gut. Monty was a sight. He overheard some of the remarks and he felt the stares in their various degrees. At first they cut right through to his soul, each time wounding him deeply. But thoughts of the power of his flute, and memories of his survival over numerous past pressures--these consoled him and recharged his resolve. He had no reason to confront anyone as he was never confronted directly. He also had no need to exchange words with anyone since, even with the obvious remarks thrown his way, no one ever faced him square. But he remembered the Joneses and the fact that his victories against them were attained without words. So, whenever the stares were a little too direct for him, he fired right back, and he never lost a staring match. The so-called *normal* students, natural cowards, always retreated whenever he fired back. And though they would have rather concealed them, their uncertainty and concerns were apparent. It was extra tormenting when a *normal* student gave up and looked away, only to look back up and find Monty still glaring; faithfully, motionless, and firm.

And more than looking back, sometimes he deliberately joined a *normal* student or group at a dining table. When he did, he kept to himself and didn't say a thing, but he made it very clear that he was there and that he enjoyed his meal. Since he was too close for comfort, and could be violently wacky for all they cared, they buried their words and feelings and struggled to ignore him. Whenever Monty, the uninvited guest, arrived and imposed himself, they prayed fervently in their hearts that he would hurry up and leave. Only then could they regain their freedom. But he always took his time, picking his food very slowly and meticulously, and relishing each bite. He was always the last to leave, and some of them were still hungry when they decided to hurriedly abandon their meals and the table. His counter attacks were effective but they isolated him some more.

...

Groups and subgroups also set up boundaries. The Institute lacked the balanced diversity of Madison, especially the campus area. Smaller groups, intimidated by the dominant group of *normal*, mostly white students, whether for valid or delusional reasons, set out to protect themselves. In the process they manufactured more boundaries. There were black, Latino, Asian, Jewish, and others not easily definable. Some were mixed and re-mixed and either chose to side with an aspect of themselves, otherwise remain neutral. And then there were foreign students who fit into every category. More subcategories were established based on gender, religion, political inclination, and sexual practice.

It wasn't certain why anyone who was against a particular religion or denomination sought education in an institution practically run by such religion or denomination. But there were those students who campaigned against the Catholic mass and held mini rallies where they carried placards that demanded the use of the chapel by practitioners of other denominations and religions. They all found time to share their individual agendas, disseminate their complaints, make brash demands, and even issue a warning or threat. Muslims, Protestants, Satanists, Buddhists, proclaimed Voodoo priests and priestesses, and witches alike, they all found time to push for recognition.

Each group and subgroup declared special qualities and demanded special needs. They held individual meetings, created individual constitutions, and put out individual newsletters. Central to each of their demands was a call for better representation in student government, admission of more people like them, justice, protection, and the right to exist freely without any threats. But each one was scared to enter the other one's space, and this contradicted their declared search for security. Their bid to conquer segregation and invisibility led to an ironic self-imposed segregation and restriction where freedom was lost. Their adversary and reason for existing--the predominantly, *normal*, white students--remained most self-assured, silent, and contented. But, if nothing else, the group and sub-group drama added color to the Institute and countered the monotony of standard student life. Monty was glad to stay by himself.

If there was a group that had legitimate reasons to cry out, it was the group that occupied the two gray dormitories that stood a distance off, apart and in many ways shunned. But it didn't complain, demand, or protest. If it was dissatisfied about anything, it didn't show.

...

For the most part, the problem students lacked the ability and, therefore, the zeal for sports. Those who had an interest in that area had to encounter the *normal* students close up. Monty ventured there, having been inspired by the Kennedys. He tried, a few times, to play basketball, tennis, and ping-pong. But he also faced the extra task of competing with direct and indirect stares, and cynical comments that were supposed to count as humor.

"Play with some energy man, you know, like you play with the monkeys."

"Did you grow up playing basketball with coconuts?"

"Move man, don't let that gut get in the way."

"What speed man, what speed! Unbelievable speed with those legs you got."

"Hit the ball, but please don't eat it. Ha, ha, ha. Just kidding."

And, as when he was with the Joneses, they tried to play down their sarcasm with "just kidding man, just kidding, have a sense of humor." Playing with the *normal kids* only nurtured existing feelings of alienation. He didn't experience the motivation to compete and to believe in victory, virtues that had been brought to life at the Kennedys. He withdrew from playing any sport as eagerly as he had gotten involved in the first place.

He didn't regret his increasing aloneness because, after all, it was tranquil and, more so, it provided him time to explore and know his flute some more. In the end it was in his flute, not in sports, groups, and subgroups, that he envisaged expansion and breakthroughs. During his spare time he found a place away from crowds, like one of the empty classes, or outdoors when the weather was good, usually a remote spot. When he played, he was transported to another plane; he sank into it and yet he was lifted. It was not a simple trance state; it was a higher plane where he dreamed dreams that enlarged him. He had begun to understand the science of reading music, but he still relied more on playing by ear. Among popular songs and tunes, anything from the blues to jazz to gospel, and even some pop, he found opportunities to imitate, expand, and reinvent. But more than ever, he created originals, and without much thought. It was uncanny. He would start when the emotions filled him and then go on a journey that ended with music at different, though connected layers of intensity, pitch, energy, tone, and rhythm. It was music that created an ambiance easily felt but not easily recognized. And once he created anything, he stored it and exhumed it whenever he needed to.

Alone, he played his flute. But he also pondered things he still didn't know. His thoughts now came in stages. One stage was his reflections on Betty, Dorothy, and Myra. With Betty it was always brief; he spurned her image and lost it easily. With Myra it was the same old feeling because she always showed up in her swimsuit. Previously the feeling grew from his stomach and traveled to his heart. Now it warmed his heart and moved slowly down to his stomach, leaving him tickled and confused, excited and shy. And then he was hit by Bible class teachings, especially the ones that warned, "flee from sexual immorality" and "there must not even be a hint," and then he would quickly push her aside, but not discard her like he did Betty. He predicted a future where, to obey the warnings, he would have to defy and conquer an army of determined forces, most of which were yet to come.

With Dorothy his reflections began as deep thoughts that recaptured his sincere love for her and the truth that he missed her a lot. Then they evolved to dreams, real dreams when he

119

went to sleep. They were always one of two dreams. Dorothy would grab him by the hand and they would fly high; then, without warning as they soared, she would let go and he would fall and fall and fall, screaming out her name. Once he landed he opened his eyes to find that he had soaked his bed with sweat. In the other episode he would grab her and they would fly into the vastness, their goal the stars that glittered in the distance. And then, again, she would let go and he would plead for her return. But she always ignored him and fell further and further away. Unable to bear seeing her fall, he would go after her, falling and falling and falling, but to no avail. He never reached her. When he hit earth his eyes would open, and again he would find himself soaked in sweat and breathing hard.

Rivalry

Since every student displayed a striking talent, no one really stood out. Not until a special event distinguished you. The event didn't have to be a noble one although a noble one was more highly valued. It did have its detriments though, as jealousy was always admixed with your recognition and veneration. The quiet roommate with a goatee who spent hours staring in space had always stood out, but not beyond Monty's room. One day his recognition spread far beyond the room, and it wasn't for a noble reason, except, of course, you perceived it that way because you were some type of psychopath.

They were all quiet but Theo was exceptionally so. He didn't necessarily break any rules. An occasional question was inevitably thrown his way.

"Have you seen my keys by any chance? I've been looking for them all day."

Sometimes Theo's customary response was to look at the inquirer for a moment; it must have been his method of acknowledging the speaker. Then he sauntered off quietly and back into his personal world. At other times he didn't as much as look at the speaker.

While Monty and the other students quickly adapted to Theo, it wasn't that easy for the supervisor. He was the supervisor after all and had to run things. Running things also meant organizing periodic meetings.

"I'd like to have a short meeting with you guys at three o'clock on Saturday if that's okay."

They would all respond in different ways to indicate that they understood. Not Theo. He either just sat or lay there in his illusionary world. To worsen things, he wouldn't attend the meeting even though it always took place in the room around the general reading table. He would be right there in the room sometimes, but he wouldn't attend. He preferred the freedom of his intimate daydreams, usually attained on his bed, whether sitting or lying. No matter how stern the supervisor tried to be, and no matter how red he turned, he was never able to move Theo. He took his frustrations, first, to Institute authorities, and second, to Theo's parents. When they didn't give him the support he hoped for, essentially telling him to simply ignore Theo, he gave up. Ignoring Theo worked to some extent, but the frustration didn't go away completely. The supervisor realized he couldn't completely ignore students that occupied a room he supervised. As annoying as it was, he found himself confronting Theo now and then, most times wishing he didn't have to.

"I know it's a common error, but you forgot to turn the lights off before you left this morning. And you were the last to leave."

No response from Theo. Not even a look.

"Remember guys, this room will be fumigated tomorrow at noon. Please be out by 11:30, and put all your belongings away. Okay?"

They all nodded their heads or blurted out words that indicated understanding and a willingness to comply. Not Theo. It was bad enough that he acted as if the supervisor was a figment of someone else's imagination. But worse, he wouldn't leave the room for the fumigators to get to work. He crossed a line that time and security officers had to come to the room and escort him out. He followed them peacefully and without incident. The news reached portions of the Institute but those who heard didn't consider it a major occurrence. Soon it faded away and was gradually forgotten.

When it came to his schoolwork, Theo gave his all. He was a phenomenal writer and his short stories had appeared in several periodicals before he was admitted to the Institute. One of his novels had already been accepted for publication and he was working on two more simultaneously. He didn't think the Institute was of any use to him. While this was his main problem, he didn't tell anyone.

...

For one who lived within himself, detached from everything except his passion for writing, Theo's actions that late Tuesday afternoon didn't make sense. He may have been weird, but his was mostly a deviance relayed in silence and with little exertion. After class that day, Monty headed for the cafeteria, then back to his room. Two of his roommates were there when he arrived. He called out a general greeting that was either too soft to hear, or ignored without malice.

Theo was lying on his bed, quite still, his eyes fixed on the light gray ceiling. The other student, Ray, was studying at the main table. For him to have already unwound and settled down to some work, his classes must have ended earlier in the day. The warmth of the room was welcome and Monty set out to relax. He placed his black backpack and its contents on the desk right next to his bed. Putting on his favorite afternoon nap outfit, a white T-shirt and gray sweatpants, he lay down on his bed, fully content. But his decision to take a quick nap was rudely interrupted when Theo, swiftly and with great precision, suddenly sat up on his bed. It was the unique move that drew attention as it was achieved with little sound. The result was infectious and Monty, startled, but not alarmed, sat up too. He observed for a moment then went back to lying down. Theo's incredible behavior, after all, was nothing new. But Monty hadn't stretched out for more than three minutes when the growls began. Even for Theo they were abnormal and caused some concern and discomfort. Ray also paused from his studies and looked up. He, too, thought Theo's behavior was cause for concern. The growls transformed quickly. First, to moans, then to howls, and then to outright shrieks. Then the words followed in quick succession. They unfolded in the manner of a stream of consciousness, maybe unconsciousness, noisy and persistent. To Theo they may have made sense, but to his unwilling listeners they were meaningless.

"Oh! Oh! Oooooohhhhhhh! Mmmmm! Why? Why? Why? WHY! Yes, yes, I say YES! I didn't say no, I said YES! Let me go now, high up and away. Let me go! What is this, huh? How good to fly away, away. How good to fly so very far away. Ah! Aaahhhhhhh! It's of no use, when the time comes I'll just have to be there, I'll just have to fly, okay? But why don't they want me to be there? Why not! Isn't it home? What is this! What is this! How good to just up and fly away, fly away, far, far away home. Come on, come on, I want it NOW! This minute! I have said yes, so why the delay? Do you not hear me, huh? Do you not hear…you, you, you, you evil ones, I say do you not hear, huh? I say NOW! I say YES!"

As he rambled, sweat tore through his skin and his veins seemed to swell. Ordinarily fair-skinned, he blushed profusely and his eyes, bloodshot, took on a unique glow because of the tears that built up in them and which soon began to run. Right after he thundered his final "YES," he jumped off his bed with such athleticism that Monty's discomfort turned to raw panic. Ray, now completely distracted from his books, was also afraid and his body language said so. He had gotten up from his chair and impulsively shoved his books and the chair aside. Then he backed up into a wall, taking in every detail of the spectacle. Monty, too, had instantly hopped out of his bed and moved cautiously and as far away as he could from Theo, not taking his eyes off of him, not for one second.

Once out of his bed, Theo again returned to growling, and sporadically mixed it up with short, sharp shrieks. Monty and Ray's worries were replaced by outright terror when Theo started hurling things around the room. He overturned two beds, then flung books, shoes, clothing, clothe irons, bags, and suitcases in every direction. Anything he could lay his hands on, he picked up and tossed. Things were all over the place, broken, shattered, half-broken, torn, and disheveled. He broke into closets and emptied their contents, all the while building momentum with his growls and shrieks. The tears had stopped flowing but his eyes were still red and glossy, and he sweated much more so that his shirt stuck to his body. When he began to foam at the mouth his evolution from human to ogre was complete and he looked more dreadful than ever.

All the while Monty and Ray ran, jumped, dived for cover, ducked, and hid; their gallant efforts at avoiding flying objects paid off. Struck once or twice, neither one of them was seriously hurt and came off with slight bruises.

The supervisor heard the commotion from his office down the hall and rushed to the scene. Ray was speeding out the doorway at the time and they met there. Perhaps it was because the supervisor lacked the speed of the student, but bumping into each other didn't cause any major damage. They were briefly stunned, picked themselves up from the floor, looked each other in the eyes as if the other person was demented, and in a flash disappeared in opposite directions. Monty shared exactly the same plan as Ray, but just as he was about to follow suit, and though he was terribly shaken, he noticed as Theo headed for the conspicuous silver box that stuck out of the side of his backpack. His immediate impulse urged him to rush in that direction and rescue the box before the ogre got to it, even if it meant exchanging blows with him in the process. But his intelligence didn't fail him and he thought again. Theo looked extra large, extra strong, and extra evil. He didn't look like he could be hurt or overpowered by anything, especially Monty, and he didn't look like he cared a bit about anything, property or human life. He also didn't look like he would require much effort to smash Monty's large head against the nearest hard object. Monty was actually ready to die for his flute, but, well, maybe not yet. So he watched as the ogre grabbed the box and hurled it across the room like a javelin. He held his breath and froze as he watched it fly as if in slow motion and as if for all eternity. Half way across the room, it opened and the flute tumbled out. He clenched his teeth, shut his eyes, and tightened his fists as both box and flute landed. He couldn't bear to look. The clattering sound reverberated through his entire frame and he went to pieces like he thought the flute had.

The supervisor had rushed in and instantly went into shock. Eyes and mouth wide open, he took in what was the most grisly sight of his eight-year supervisory career. The room had been practically overturned and the rampaging Theo acted like he hadn't even started. But he was the supervisor; it was his job to prevent or stop such unacceptable madness. It was either he seized his authority then or never. Yes, Theo was a tough character to supervise, and sometimes he had been allowed to get away with the outrageous, but this time he had simply gone too, too far.

"Stop this minute," the supervisor barked. "I say stop, or else...."

"Or else what?"

It was the first meaningful statement Theo had uttered since he lost control that late afternoon. On this day he was a man of action and obviously relied more on doing than talking. Because Theo's response caught him off guard, the short, hefty supervisor searched desperately for a suitable and immediate course of action, or, at least, an effective verbal counter response. But time was against him. He wasn't done searching when Theo sprang at him. In his younger days the supervisor must have been a superb athlete. It took seconds for him to disappear from the room and down the hallway, and as he tore down the staircase he baffled people he bumped into and those who simply noticed him. It wasn't certain what baffled them more, the fact that he ran or the fact that his short legs moved with such determined speed. For the first time that late afternoon, Theo conceded defeat and gave up on chasing the supervisor. As unpredictably as his actions had been, they came to an abrupt end. He halted at the doorway, staring down the hallway as if hoping that the supervisor would change his mind and return. Slowly he walked back to his bed, the only bed untouched, and calmly lay down. His calm was unreal. He lay there and returned to his reverie, gazing once again at the ceiling, now dented and scratched in several places, and at a world that he alone could make sense of.

Monty struggled to build up the faith that convinced him it was all over. Only then did he regain mobility. Very judiciously, and carrying a lot of suspicion, he made his way to the box and flute that lay almost side-by-side. He feared the worst. His long trip took him past the ogre's bed. When the ogre didn't budge, in his heart Monty sincerely thanked Jesus Christ for his care and protection. The box was slightly dented at one end and its lock was broken. These were problems that could easily be lived with, maybe fixed. Then came the very hard part. He reached for the flute and picked it up gently, almost too scared to look at it. But he found the courage and looked. Then he examined it. He examined it again, more closely. It was in perfect condition. When he thanked Jesus this second time, the words came out loud.

Outside the room, a puzzled crowd had begun to assemble. But it was a while before anyone of them would sum up the courage and strength to venture inside.

The incident had been explosive enough to be explained as remarkable, even if scandalous. And so, Theo became popular, but the popularity was short lived. The Institute had had enough of him. The supervisor too. He was threatening a lawsuit against the Institute for emotional distress caused by panic and humiliation, and for its failure to guarantee him unconditional protection. Theo was expelled. His departure was swift and before Security Department could ensure that he complied, he disappeared without a trace. He must have been glad to leave. Rumors held that he was returned to the mental facility where he had spent most of his adult life. The supervisor was relieved and actually began to smile again. A small group of student activists, who claimed to defend the right to free expression, spent the rest of the semester campaigning for Theo's return. His actions, they contended, were not simply a frenzied and dangerous outburst that had steadily built up with months of inner frustration, but the singular and harmless expression of a young man's dissatisfaction with a seriously flawed system. The group's thesis was never fully understood by anyone, not even its members. They abandoned their quest at the end of the semester. It had been as entertaining as it had been futile.

Other less politically correct groups, one or two in fact, intermittently made it clear that they were worried about their safety in the midst of people who were not so stable or reliable. For them, it was a valid excuse to be nastier toward those students on the other side. But majority of the students were amused by the story and laughed loud when they discussed and analyzed it. Those who had sincere pity for Theo kept it to themselves. Like Monty.

The news reached the Catholic Consulate and Brother Smith paid Monty a special visit to make sure he was okay. The Consulate also sent the Institute a strongly worded letter, reminding it of its responsibility to protect its students and insisting it to do a better job in that regard.

...

It was more fashionable to seek popularity of a different kind. Sports provided one outlet, especially for the men who played football, basketball, and baseball. They were all believed to own a collection of women who were awestruck by their great bodies, skills, and the likelihood that with time they would be very wealthy. Love scandals usually centered on the exploits of male athletes, with themes of unrequited love, multiple partners, being dumped, being swapped, and being raped. The more prominent the athlete was, the larger his harem and the juicer the erotic tales that surrounded him.

There was a popularity that was prized though, one that was forged on an arena where barriers of every kind were desecrated. For *normal* and *abnormal* students, and students that were customarily demarcated by any conceivable social or physical definition, this was a level ground where the only factor that counted was the ability to excel beyond verbal proclamations and mental fabrications. Here, victory came with pride almost too much to handle, opened up doors, and attracted as much jealousy as it did praise. It came with the end-of-year talent show that was open to all sophomores, the Annual Arts and Science Talent Show.

The demonstration of talent was many and varied. Books covering all areas of literature were entered, and so were scientific discoveries, updates, and imitations. Competitors read excerpts from their experimental works, works that sometimes combined a multiplicity of genres that crisscrossed. One student made a mini space rocket, one tripled the speed of his computer with a gadget made from copper and lead, while another replaced his car's alternator with an unknown devise that was thought to extend the life of the battery. A television was designed with materials that were mostly natural, in fact taken from surrounding woods, and a microwave oven was created out of an abandoned computer.

There were solo and group performances of well known, not-so-well-known, and unknown dramas and musicals, most of which were either written or recreated by students. Songs, familiar, not-so-familiar, and unfamiliar, were sung solo and in groups, either acappella or with the aid of background music. As with the musical and dramatic shows, students wrote a lot of the songs, including accompanying music. Groups and individuals played musical instruments of every kind and from every corner of the globe. They came in all forms, colors, and sizes and were made of every substance--wood, clay, metal, gold, silver, plastic, and blends. From fifteen-foot Swiss trumpets to two-foot wooden guitars from northern Nigeria.

Performances were largely done in attempts to stretch their styles to postmodern limits. One actress really stretched something when, with pulleys and cables, and tall pins that pierced areas of her skin, she hung from the ceiling of the stage, stark naked. With a brilliant yet harsh background lighting effect and stage design and props that tormented the mind and imagination, she remained elevated for about thirty minutes. What sacrifice and torture, just to achieve originality and to prove loyalty to an art form.

There were art exhibitions of every kind--paintings, drawings, carvings, sculptor, quilting, and pottery. They ranged in aesthetic appeal and so were easily understood, not-so-easily-understood, challenging, thought-provoking, stupefying, and plain mystifying.

The competition, lively and vibrant, lasted all Saturday and turned the Institute, though for a day, into White Water's center of attraction and a bevy of activity. Makeshift food and drink stands were hurriedly erected at every corner, and crowds streamed into the campus from White Water, surrounding towns, and places not close by. Friends and family members constantly trooped in. Security Department had a tough time dealing with the number of people and parking problems. But the hustle and stress were well worth it for the contestants, the visitors, and even Security. It was all worth some tension and worry, the glamour, zeal, anticipations, anxieties, hopes, disappointments, and victories.

Monty had entered the competition. A horn segment that featured trumpets, pipes, bagpipes, flutes, whistles, clarinets, and horns, constituted the sub-category of musical display under which he would compete. He had conquered a small variety of audiences ever since his love for the flute was evident, but this was by far his greatest challenge. He wondered if, this time, his companion, the flute, would succeed in stimulating and empowering him. In battling debasement from the Joneses till now, he had disposed of some of his self-consciousness, but not all of it. He thought about what lay ahead but he refused to be prophetic. Stealing the show as the only flute player was one thing, but trying to do so with great competition was something else. Your competition was ingenious too, aside from being ruthless and greedy. It hated its adversaries, those who threatened its hunger for the prize--the first, not second or third-- and was set to eliminate them without mercy. Thus far, there was no opposition in his life that had been this fierce.

It was good that the Kennedys would be there. Anticipating their presence built his faith and reinforced the courage he found

130

in the flute. He was honored and, again, would have loved to show them his gratitude beyond a few hugs and smiles, and a mere "thank you for coming."

...

He had spent about a year at the Institute, receiving few visits from Brother Smith and fewer correspondences from the Consulate. The visits and letters were designed to encourage him and to remind him that they cared for him. During one of his visits, Brother Smith relayed the good news. The Kennedys wanted him to continue to visit their home during breaks and on special days like his birthday or the birthday of a family member, or on occasions when Confirmation in the Church or a first Holy Communion called for celebration. The Consulate was glad to extend the periodic interaction between a family and refugee or orphan, if both parties were in agreement. That way, he or she was rescued from the ordeal of readjustment as brought on by constant relocation. The offer also came in the form of a letter, complete with letterhead, from the Consulate. When Brother Smith asked if he would accept the offer, Monty knew the question was more formal than real, and it sounded like a joke. He suppressed his joy, a strategy he was used to, when he accepted with all humility. When he departed Monty's dormitory that evening, Brother Smith could not have guessed that the refugee had upgraded him to an angel. Not a brown one like Mr. Ranjid, but an angel nonetheless.

His subsequent visits to the Kennedy home echoed elements and qualities of past visits. Except that Myra had grown and matured in obvious ways too hard to ignore. To complicate things, the warm feeling that traveled from his heart to his stomach was no longer induced only when she wore a swimsuit. Almost anything she wore awakened the feeling, especially if it wasn't loose or if it was a pair of pants. It became more disturbing and problematic when the feeling dared to drift a little below his hanging belly. The warning from Bible study, "flee…"

always harassed and checked him. He would wrestle the feeling and look away, but the lure was too magnetic, and as he wrestled uneasily, he couldn't control the convenience of well-concealed, random, rapid glances.

It was a sharp contrast, the gray walls of his dormitory room and the splendor of the Kennedy home. But each time he returned to the Institute from there, the reminder that he didn't truly belong there was cruel. The truth aggravated his feelings of aloneness.

···

When he stepped out on stage that evening, he was immediately subdued by what lay in front of him, the sea of heads that bobbed continuously just to stay afloat. Any spectator who observed closely would have noticed his legs trembling, even though they did so under the cover of baggy pants. The white pants paired nicely with his white jacket and white pair of shoes. Only his bow tie was black, though his shirt was of a creamier white than the rest of what he wore. His strong features were mostly hidden by the magnificent lighting and sheer aura of the theatre, but he was still recognized as different. Dark, notoriously short, and crowned with a fine layer of thick, curly hair that shone extra because of too much grease, he stood out. For those who sat close to the stage, they also saw how his tattered facial hair, despite diligent efforts to maintain a smooth trim and shave, subtracted some of the beauty of his outfit and striking dark hair. He was the atypical expectation for a music student, let alone one who dared to participate in an event as huge as this one. It was, after all, an event that terrorized its participants, and even those in the audience who had favorites among the participants.

Monty had never faced an audience, theatre, or stage of this magnitude. They swallowed him whole. The lights hit him square in the face without pity, and just as the Master of Ceremonies announced his name over a public address system,

"MONTY MONTY," introducing him as the next performer. The impact forced him to take two steps backwards before recovering. He fought to comport himself and hoped that his anxiety wasn't as apparent on the outside as it was on the inside. He bowed and lifted his flute up, seeing it always reassured and spurred him on. But this time the heads, like a million obscure balls floating on disorderly waves, disarmed him for a moment and snatched his confidence. Then he summoned thoughts of the Kennedys and of the opportunity to impress Myra. It dawned on him that he was equipped to express sufficient gratitude for their presence after all. All it took was giving his best, maybe winning too. Yet his principal motivation did not come from them but from the blind valedictorian at his primary school graduation, and the fleeting image of that Apache girl who had stolen the hearts of a campus audience not too long ago. Her strength had been forged by a sincerity and dedication that came from the depths of her heart and an ancient flute. Monty took in a deep breath and began.

Initially, the flow was quite commonplace. Monty worked his way from known tunes that he spiced to the point of rediscovery, to improvisations that were either unknown or not previously heard by many. Sometimes he embellished an old song with an aesthetic that altered it beyond recognition. The more he played, the more he relaxed, and the more he got lost in the hypnosis of the moment. The more he became one with his music, the more he separated from the obscure, floating heads, and the more his spirit reached inside and grabbed from the inexhaustible repertoire that lay within. Maybe it had been one of his goals when he started, but his prime concern wasn't to please anyone anymore. He was satisfying a hunger to exploit his flute so that it transported him far away, to a place where nothing tangible could reach, to a place where nothing mattered because the mundane met intimately with the celestial. If others came with him, fine. If not, fine too. More than before, he was able to weave hymns and gospel tunes into his act, preserving a unified tempo nonetheless, and redefining their archetypal form.

So, while their Christian motifs were not lost, they traversed the rigid stipulations that could come with such music, attaining a scope that cut across religious values and beliefs.

The heads, now solemn, were barely moving, having been drawn in by Monty's original style and the temporary relief that it brought. Their reactions went through phases, from the solemn to the sentimental, and some tears were shed, mixed in with tender sighs and hums. When the pace suddenly gathered speed, the result was a dramatic turn that wasn't expected. It wasn't the type of speed that razed an otherwise gentle flow, or attained a height that assaulted the mind. Not too fast, it inspired a mood that could easily have been a cross between an opera and disco party. A fresh audience reaction was imminent. The grayish heads began to nod, but it wasn't as before when their movement was scattered. It was more uniform and steady, and built with the speed and energy of the flute. From nodding heads to clapping hands and wiggling bodies, the temperamental changes were spontaneous. The contests had a reputation for being lively, but an audience-performer interaction of this scale was as yet unknown. It was above lively; it was eerie, unbelievable. Monty strayed away from assumptions linked to fine musical performances; and yet, even in defiance he was graceful in the eyes of his audience.

Unknown to him, he had, in some sinister way, drawn from the magnetic resources of a musical legacy. That evening there was an incantational appeal that he dared to use rather than resist. And, of course, his ability to play by ear was well known. Regardless of his macabre birth, his original background, it seemed, had implanted in him a musical tradition that had remained. Now it was coming to life in a way that it never had, and engendered a participatory effect that would otherwise have been inexplicable.

After about thirty minutes, he returned to the stage, in spirit that is. He was drenched in sweat. The heads had gotten too absorbed in the routine, they were not happy that it came to an end. But Monty had to stay within a time frame and they seemed to understand. For when he faded to a superb finish and bowed, the place exploded. The standing ovation was literally deafening. He started to weep even before he walked off the stage, and continued long after he left.

A post-ceremonial announcement of winners was capped by the handing out of trophies and cash prizes. It was no less intense and nerve-racking than the main competition. The sentimental reactions that followed came in several shades. While some of the contests were not held in the main theatre, all prizes were awarded there. So many cried; you couldn't always tell who cried from joy and who cried from agony. People screamed, cheered, booed, clapped, hugged, and wept. Some hid their disappointments behind counterfeit smiles while some didn't care to and scowled openly, even throwing an occasional curse at the judges and organizers who couldn't be easily pinpointed. But this extreme was the exception, not the rule. There were those who collapsed under the weight of too much emotion but soon picked themselves up. Some collapsed and didn't pick themselves up. They were carried out once it was obvious that they had passed out. The Institute was ready for the emergencies that were replicated every year. About five ambulances stood outside the theatre building, their engines running constantly.

First, second, and third winners received trophies and money. The first, $1,500, the second, $800, and the third, $400. Second and third winners were soon forgotten and they knew it. For that reason, a good number of them were unhappy and raged silently at what, to them, was a close, if not unfair call. More than any of the other contestants, they received the highest number of condolences.

When Monty's sub-musical category was invited on stage for the awards, as with previous awards that night, the theatre went dead silent. The anticipation was so thick; you could reach out and grab it, maybe cut it with a knife. The third position was announced and a chubby student stepped forward. He was received with a combination of noises, whistles, and claps that acknowledged his effort. It was basically the same pattern when another student, this time a lanky contrast to the first, stepped forward and received the second prize. This group comprised phenomenal talent that had been too difficult to judge. Second place was thus awarded to two students. The other was a timid lady who looked down throughout. It was a miracle that she had summoned the courage to contest in the first place, let alone do so well.

And now the moment of truth had come. Dead silence filled the theatre again. When Monty's name was announced, the crowd almost brought the place down. More like mayhem than an applause, it lasted for a long time too. Maybe it was the noise, maybe it was exhilaration, or maybe it was a combination of both, but Monty stumbled and almost tripped over when he stepped forward to receive his prize. His hopes of winning were one thing; the reality of winning was another. No matter how much he longed for this moment, he could never have prepared himself for it. He was weak, helpless, and in a near-numb state that didn't go away altogether until the following day. Fellow contestants shook his hands and hugged him, whether sincerely or as a courteous ritual. Two of his musical instructors also appeared on stage from nowhere to commend him with their hugs. They were all smiles and teary eyed, and without any shame. Though the envelope that contained the cash was gold-rimmed, it looked ordinary compared to the trophy. The trophy's magnificence was not lost in its small size. A silver figure blowing on a cigarette-shaped object was mounted on a thick block of fine wood. Inscribed on the block of wood in fine prints were the words: *First Prize, 20ᵗʰ Annual Arts & Science Talent Show, Horn Segment.*

It was out in the lobby that the Kennedys met him.

"We are so, so proud of you Monty. Wow, what can I say?" It was Mrs. Kennedy. When she hugged him tight he didn't mind that the rough hair stubs on her face rubbed hard against his neck.

The rest of them expressed their compliments in the form of hugs, handshakes, or light pecks on his cheeks. There were the usual tears and the usual words.

"Great job."

"Wow, that was amazing, man, amazing."

"So proud of you Monty."

"You know, you are going places. I swear."

The climax came with the mighty bouquet of flowers that Myra handed him on behalf of her family. Was there any meaning to her representing the family this way? He imagined Mr. or Mrs. Kennedy playing this role, maybe Centaur, but not Myra. She thrilled him some more when she planted a big peck on his right cheek. He managed a timid smile that gave away the truth that he was shy, even a little scared, and his dark skin concealed the blush that was running within. Ordinarily, the Kennedy girls never got that close to him. It must have been the special occasion; as with the Center graduation ceremony it brought its own unique privileges. Even though she had on a pair of tight jeans, he was able to stop the feeling before it gained power. He had to, what with all the people hovering around him. They left soon after handing him the flowers and he returned to his room, alone.

In the distance the final, fading stages of the contest continued to echo.

Philip U. Effiong

Uncertainty

At 20 and going on 21, he still grew. Not in height but in almost every other area. He still hadn't added an inch since he was thirteen. But it was hard to keep pace with the hair that covered his face, almost hiding his lips. When it was apparent that a close shave would always produce hefty pus-filled bumps, and on the advice of a doctor at the Student Health Center, he stopped shaving close. Since the hair had begun to sprout evenly, not as in the past when it was scattered, it made things easier. He could at least maintain a decent, uniform trim. A lot of his growth was horizontal, and his stomach stretched some more, putting a strain on his shirt buttons. His arms, legs, backside, and head all expanded too, until he looked like a weight-lifter-turned-politician. On his head he still carried short, dark, curly hair that shone because of grease. He looked older than his age.

He hadn't made new friends, at best throwing or receiving a greeting from fellow students or roommates, or getting into a conversation at the Cafeteria, in class, or in his dorm. The conversations never lasted and they were more civil than they were intimate.

He did remain something of an intriguing icon after winning first prize at the talent competition two years earlier. The Consulate, first, had sent him a special congratulatory letter. Then Brother Smith paid him a visit, accompanied by a Ghanaian bishop who was on special assignment at the Consulate. Bishop Henry Akyea, in his red robe, lined with pale white, and the silver cross that dangled from his throat, was tall and muscular, flaunting a solid form. He smiled little from one corner of his mouth, but because it was sincere, it was effective. Compared to the holy men and women of the church Monty was used to, the Bishop was something of an anomaly. It was ironic since, of all the Catholic reverends that had ever been in close proximity to Monty, this one shared features that came closest to

139

his. That is, when you take away the signature strokes his birth had dealt him.

Monty enjoyed the visit from Brother Smith and Bishop Akyea. Sending down a man of Bishop Akyea's caliber was the Consulate's way of according recognition, simple yet eminent, on Monty. He was, after all, used to witnessing, at close quarters, the likes of reverends with lower ranks. Their company, influenced by the Bishop's presence, was marked by a light-hearted quality filled with stories, questions, hugs, and humor. Brother Smith, jolly in his own way, was not always that playful. Monty took in the Bishop's simplicity because it was not one he expected of a man with his profile, and he admired him for it. He knew that it was conscious, if it wasn't in his nature, and done to make him feel at ease and undistracted by authority. He was honored yet composed. The Bishop's goal was achieved. After they gave him dinner at a posh, downtown restaurant, they handed him the framed plaque. Inside the frame, the certificate fit snugly with the words, written in bold Italics,

*The Board of Directors, Catholic Consulate, New York is proud to award this certificate to **MONTY MONTY** In recognition of outstanding talent and dedication to hard work.*

The certificate was titled, in bold, ***CERTIFICATE OF ACHIEVEMENT***, and signed by a consul, a cardinal, and a bishop. It was also dated. Monty embraced the frame and thanked them over and over again. He missed them when they left, and returned to his room where he placed the frame beside the trophy that already stood on the desk next to his bed. And then he went into one of his numerous daydreams.

Up until he left the Institute, he was hailed, waved at, and congratulated repeatedly. Sometimes he was stopped as he strolled to some place, and engaged in a brief conversation. It was almost always an intellectual dialogue as it either inquired after his inspiration or extolled him graciously. The attention slowed down after a few months but didn't cease completely. Monty had to adjust considerably since his lifestyle at the Center, and means to finding sanity, bordered on reclusive. He found himself standing much closer to people than he wished to, exchanging much more words than he wished to, and even touching or being touched when and where he didn't care to touch or be touched. He soon learned that handshakes, a fond pat on the shoulder, a despised conversation, no matter how brief, were unavoidable, whether he welcomed them or not. He had to adjust. It was a process that took time, and that became a regular battle made obvious by the discomfort he was trying to hide. The discomfort manifested in a number of ways. In a stutter perhaps, a weak smile that couldn't deceive anyone, or a demeanor that announced loudly, "I'd like to leave, please." When he eventually mastered the art of dealing with more people than he cared to, he invited in another persona and for the time suppressed the real him. Once the interaction was over, he returned and retook himself, reimplanting the real him and sending the persona away until such a time as he would be needed.

Some admiration came from the *normal* students too, and from across racial, ethnic, gender, sexual, and ideological barriers. Monty must have affected a significant number, much more than he would ever know.

Sometimes it was hard to tell what really drove those people whose recognition he had won--jealousy or admiration. Familiar with the subtleties of body language, Monty was often able to read into things that were not stated verbally. Even if it was with sincere appreciation that some approached him, he recognized when close proximity engendered panic and then the potential praise-singer degenerated into a state of near paralysis. He or she wouldn't be able to release words easily or at all, or would string together words that didn't make a lot of sense. Either that or the person would stand there stiff, as if unsure about how to use the simple gift of motion. He knew that it had something to do with his looks; stage lights had apparently reconstructed or veiled some of him that evening. Those who had not ever come close to him, and who concentrated on him for the first time that night, were taken aback when they found the opportunity to express personal eulogies right before him. To them, he didn't display the physical attributes and sophisticated poise one associated with a standard music maker. And the way he was built departed further from that ideal.

When it came to his looks, his build, he had been confused from as far back as his days with the Joneses. He received derisive references to it from Betty and other kids, but it was in the same manner that he received other unpleasantness. He shielded himself from the comments in the manner that he shielded himself from the Joneses, believing that they were malicious, not true, and redefined himself as a normal boy with average, if not handsome, looks. But the hints continued past the Joneses and followed him wherever he went. On group outings when he was at the Center, and then at the Institute, the hints came from too many people to ignore, about his stomach, his legs, his eyes, his lips, his smile, his walk, and other things that could qualify as special. They came in different shades, as jokes, as simple, sincere observations, and as contempt. And, as he had done at the Joneses, he found private time to size himself up before a mirror, never seeing anything wrong. But there had to be something awkward about him, or, maybe everyone else, at some time or another, was assaulted the same way. Maybe it just wasn't him. Yes, that had to be it. But as much as he soothed himself with notions that countered the obvious, the torments didn't go away. It was painful to conclude that perhaps he was more unsightly than your average person. No, unsightly was too strong a word. Maybe he was different. And not just plain different, different in an impressive way, just as he was different but impressive in his flute playing styles. There were, after all, those who hated him for that too. So why wouldn't they hate his looks for the same reason?

He was confused by the love Dorothy had shown him and his grand desire to have Myra care for him. He was confused by the adulation he had been accorded time and again when he performed before a variety of audiences. How could he be so loved and valued if he wasn't good to look at? He was confused.

There were those who loved him selflessly just as there were those who revered his talent, but they didn't bring him complete comfort. His gallant efforts at reidentifying himself as normal brought consolation, but it wasn't sufficient. Speculations on his appearance haunted him and made him restless. They also forced him to be suspicious, and to question the extent to which those who encountered him did so without consideration for his looks. When it came to total trust and the potential for complete comfort, the only thing he could look to without hesitation was his flute. And he spent more time with it than anything or anyone else.

Monty also received another kind of attention for his victory that night. It also cut across all recognizable barriers and came from *normal* and *abnormal* students alike. It was envy, intense envy, and the package it often comes with. It came in different shapes too, was obvious and not so obvious, and was relayed in glares, sarcastic comments, usually muffled, gossip that he was not supposed to hear, and even in smiles. Monty could tell when envy lurked behind a broad smile or word of praise. If it was not too apparent, or if it was disguised behind kind words or kind smiles, he didn't let it get to him. But if it came in the shape of a bold statement that was too honest and louder than intended, or a glare that was deliberate and direct, he fired back in his usual manner. He glared back, unwavering and stubborn, and since he never gave up, he always won. The adversary, usually a coward and always stunned by his counter attack, would flee, its tail between its legs.

...

Graduation couldn't have come at a better time. He had had enough of the Institute and it had served him well. He learned all he needed to learn as it applied to music and his love for the flute.

His only disappointment with graduation was Myra's absence. For the first time, not all the Kennedys showed up at an event on his behalf. It didn't bother him, except that Myra was one of the ones who didn't show up. He noticed then swallowed his dismay.

Graduation followed the archetypal pattern, with processions, monotonous speeches, awards, and the distribution of certificates. He didn't play any spectacular role. Playing the school anthem with the school band, ninety percent of which was made up of Music Department students, was not considered spectacular. It was a role expected of the school band every year. In a sense he was done a favor when Chairwoman of the Graduation Committee approached him by way of a letter, and requested that he play with the band. There may have been a good number of people who recognized him in the band; otherwise, he was lost, like other band members, in the banal position the band occupied that afternoon, and in other colorful and dreary graduation activities.

He received customary, post-graduation praises and well wishes. He appreciated the bouquet of flowers Mrs. Kennedy handed him on behalf of her family. But it didn't look or smell half as good as the flowers that Myra had handed him that night when he won the Annual Arts and Science Talent Show.

After graduation, he retreated to his room and into himself, and to his world of dreams. Almost on a daily basis, he meditated on the same things that had stalked him most of his life--his looks, Myra, Betty, Dorothy, Dorothy's parents, his future, his past, who he was, and more. The meditations came when he was awake or asleep, or at some obscure region when he was neither awake nor asleep.

Recently, deliberations on who he was began to dominate his rituals of isolation and deep thinking. And the more he focused on the subject, the more he delved into the more disturbing matter of who his parents were and who exactly he was. It had actually come to life long before, but was carefully suppressed. Of all the motifs that visited and revisited his mind, for which all kinds of images materialized, this one stood out and, he believed, was best left alone. Because it carried a huge sensitive strain, he had no clue as to how to address it. And because it was more psychologically intricate than anything else he had ever wrestled with, he avoided it. But as his intelligence and perception level matured, the matter cornered him each time he tried to escape it. It sneaked in, interrupting his other thoughts, and until he confronted it, those other thoughts were increasingly jumbled.

Wondering about his parents initially came in the form of a few questions. Then they expanded into a myriad of questions, speculations, and concerns that evolved into a labyrinth of immense, gothic, though fuzzy, images. What did his parents look like? Did he look like one of them? Or did he, in some greedy fashion, borrow from both and end up with an appearance that was warped? Were they alive? If so, why was he taken away from them? If they were not alive, then.... And where did he come from since most people didn't look like him? He concocted answers to his questions, but they were always inadequate.

It was with this barrage of uncertainty that he waited for word from the Consulate about their next move on his behalf.

Outside

It was time to put Monty to the test. When its dependents were thought to attain a level of stability and maturity, the Consulate put them to the test. If a dependent failed the test, he or she was put to a different line of test.

Monty had made worthy progress. No one could say for sure what his reasoning capacity was. But a parallel was drawn between his ability to play the flute and his ability to use his brain. It was a parallel that equated his creativity with cognition. Counselors were careful to warn that the comparison could prove inaccurate. But the best was hoped for.

For the first time he was going to be independent. At least more independent than he had ever been. He was going to be returned to Madison. There, he would be staying in St. Mary's Cooperative Society, located on Main Street on the outskirts of the University. It was Catholic-owned and popularly called the Catholic Co-op. Fifteen people could be housed there at a time. All fifteen, male and female, were, for a number of reasons, wards of the Church. Each one coped with a peculiar challenge that was anything from psychological to physical and even spiritual.

There were those wards, mostly orphans, who were assessed as *normal*. Instead of putting them up in a co-op, they were assisted to find and rent subsidized studios and efficiencies. If they climbed economically and socially, they were encourage and helped to rent more standard apartments. Things being equal, their growth continued until they attained complete independence away from the guidance and protection of the Church. When this happened, the individual was often in his or her late 20's, 30's, or 40's. Many times it never happened. There were those instances when growth was shaken, twisted, or halted for any of a number of reasons. Maybe a ward committed a crime, or his or her ability to function normally at work or in school was open to suspicion. Sometimes his or her lifestyle, after careful assessment, was deemed too crazy even for Madison.

Like the *normal* wards, Monty and other members of the Co-op were expected to make progress too. If it was smooth, it increased the amount of independence they enjoyed. There was no guarantee that such progress would be achieved.

Running the Co-op was straightforward. Each member was given a room furnished simply with a bed, phone, table and chair, and a trashcan. Bathroom, laundry, dining, and kitchen facilities were shared. Five members were assigned two specific days when they were in charge of cooking for the entire house. This entailed serving breakfast and dinner, and washing dishes. Lunch was not a part of the arrangement as members were typically out of the building during that period. On Sundays members were given a special treat and fed by caterers provided by the Consulate's subsidiary office. Cleaners were hired to clean everywhere except individual rooms, which were the responsibility of members.

A supervisor had an office at a corner of the first floor. None of the members could easily ascertain his job. Every now and then Mr. McPherson could be seen parading the halls and basement, or peeking into bathrooms and the central lounge. Otherwise he was generally disconnected from the members.

For the first time in his life, Monty was going to work and earn money. It was one of the requirements for all occupants of the Co-op. They would work and pay a fixed monthly amount to the Consulate, which would help offset the cost of running the home. From a list of three banks they were each given the option of selecting one. The Consulate opened their accounts under strict guidance and scrutiny. Knowledge of the use of a bank was in Monty's best interest. For two years the $1,500 check he had won at the Talent Show lay at the bottom of his suitcase beneath a pile of books and clothing. Not long after he had stood his trophy and certificate on the desk by his bed, he came to the conclusion that only regular furniture ought to be displayed in that manner. So, he placed them there too, at the bottom of his suitcase, so that all three prizes kept each other company throughout the rest of his stay at the Institute. When he paid the check into his account, it was crumpled and some of the edges were slightly torn. But it was still good enough and accepted gladly.

...

Brother Smith, now Reverend Father Smith, informed Monty of the decision to send him to the Co-op, and explained what a co-op was and what living there amounted to. When he was done, he offered to answer questions if Monty had any. Monty's inquiry deviated from anything concerning the Co-op. Father Smith was caught unawares. He could never have expected the question. Even Monty was a little startled by his own question, as he hadn't meant to ask it. It sprung from his unconscious and fell out of his mouth, carefree and blunt. When he asked, he avoided Father Smith's eyes.

"Who-who-who are my mo-mo-mom and dad? Whe-where are they? When wi-wi-will I s-s-s-see them?" It wasn't a heavy stutter, but since he had never stuttered before, it was strange. He used the words *mom* and *dad* because there was something musical, something endearing about them. He had learned that *father* and *mother* headed the home; they were *parents* and ruled, guided, and organized. But he had also observed how children, the Jones and Kennedy children in particular, used *mom* and *dad* when their goal was not merely formal communication between parent and child. They came with a mannerism, an inflection that showed warmth that wasn't always visible. It was affection, inherent and sublime, made possible only by blood.

Tightening his face in surprise, Father Smith's attempts at treating the question as ordinary didn't work. What could have been a smile was overshadowed by an obvious dilemma that wasn't prepared for.

"Well, Monty," he began, "don't forget we are all one big family. Don't forget."

As he spoke he lowered his already gentle voice. He leaned forward and over Monty in order to get closer to him, as if he was telling him a great secret. His large frame towered over the refugee and he began to breathe hard and sweat more than was necessary. Either he was fatigued or he was anxious. He placed both his meaty palms on Monty and removed them only when he was done. He continued.

"Don't forget. All your teachers, everyone at the Consulate, all the priests and sisters, including me. We are all your dads and moms. You have more than enough of us. You have nothing to worry about. Okay?"

But that was the problem. Monty didn't want many obscure dads and moms. He wanted only one dad and one mom, and, more specifically, only those who had brought him to life. From simple observations, and from being with the Joneses and Kennedys, he deduced that you didn't need more than one of each. He appreciated Father Smith's response and effort at consolation, but he was far from satisfied.

Independence

His job was Church and music related, the perfect job. He received a stipend for playing during every service at Our Lady of Lourdes Cathedral on Badger Road. He either performed solos or played with a choir. Every service meant morning mass on Mondays and Fridays, and evening worship on Wednesdays. It also meant High Mass on Sunday mornings and Benediction on Sunday evenings. And when there was a special event at the Cathedral, like a wedding or funeral service, he played.

Monty's ingenuity had reached a height that was hard to describe. He wielded his silver flute with a flair that could perhaps best be captured by the dreamlike rendering of an impressionistic poet. From the surreal to the joyful to the sad to the pensive, he wove in and out of a series of moods and sub-moods, and moved his listeners to different reactions. Each time, he drifted off into a trance state and was soon dragging his listeners in with him. He now played with authority, the last vestiges of his self-doubt having been erased by his victory at the Institute's Talent Show. He controlled each performance as well as the people, no matter how many, who were there to bear witness. At no time was his audience impassive. If the people weren't gradually swept by an overflow of solemnity, or by the other extreme, an overflow of ecstasy, they wept. And if it was an occasion when weeping was certain, like a Requiem Mass, the weeping tripled.

News of the dark, young man, who could wield a flute with supernatural grace, spread fast. He had already made a slight impact in Madison before he attended the Institute. After he won the competition, the news re-spread, not just back to Madison, but to other areas of Wisconsin and beyond. Before he returned to Madison, he was known, or, at least, heard of. Part of his promotion came from his physical makeup. The more people saw or heard about him, the more they were eager to observe the immigrant who didn't fit their idea of a champion flute player.

When rumors described him as the victim of a brain deficiency, it roused their curiosity some more. Many, who had given up on church long before, began to attend again. But to worship God wasn't their prime motivation; it was to see the phenomenon that Monty was turning into.

It was a sure sign that he was becoming very popular, perhaps too popular, when bands and theatrical troupes began to invite him to provide supplemental or participatory music at their shows. It all began when a fellow Church worker recommended him to a friend who was directing a play on campus, titled *Song of the Nightingale.* He ended up supporting a drummer during a small segment of the play. It was an invigorating and colorful scene, a fine imitation of an ancient Greek dance. The Consulate learned about the show and, through Father Smith, sent an important message to Monty. In future, all such bands, and troupes, and shows that were interested in borrowing Monty had to go through the Consulate. Even though it was Madison, some of those shows were considered too sinful and, therefore, too inappropriate for a good Catholic man. Monty could keep the extra money he made, but he had to report all earnings to the Consulate. The Consulate didn't always grant Monty permission to play with the troupes and bands, but the few times it did was all it took for his popularity to grow.

...

There was something about the Church environment, though it was outside, that gave him peace. Since most people in that space were, or at least claimed, to abide by standards that were not entirely in tune with the liberty of the outside, he was more relaxed there. The contents and structure of his life had compelled him to be outside of the usual, even *outside* of the outside. So, he favored any circumstance that hinted at a digression, even a slight one. The more the unusual was accepted or ignored, the more he fit in. And, yes, Madison, especially its campus and campus area, was flooded with the unusual, a trend that tied into knots the intestines of its conservatives. But a lot of the strange and extreme were chosen, not imposed. Whether a hairstyle was colored red and blue, or a fashion statement was too loud and heavy that it burned the eyes, it was a choice. And whether a woman decided to date, simultaneously, another woman and the woman's boyfriend, or a gay man who was once a woman decided to play music from a boom box and dance in front of the University's Memorial Library, it was a choice.

Monty had had no say in the process that had molded him, and that interfered with what would otherwise have been *normal* growth and *normal* life. It didn't take long for him to understand that even with the unusual, there were categories. His *unusual* was not the vibrant type that was a welcome escape from the pressures of everyday things, or the entertaining type that served as a distraction from things like homework, bills, or a failed love relationship. His was not the type that brought comic relief and prolonged excitement, sometimes in ways that were not always benign, ways that were easily sadistic or masochistic. His was the type that raised questions and caused wonder. It was the type that led to conjecture, concern, and sometimes a loathing that was often hidden.

Among the unusual he was *unusual*, and there were not too many like him. But because it was Madison and political correctness was as much a fad as it was a farce, it didn't get to him though he noticed. He noticed the side looks and the whispers in his direction. Efforts were made to be politically correct, even if it didn't always come from the heart, and not to stare too long, point too directly, giggle too loud, or speak too loud. He noticed but he was not bothered because of the amount of pretext required by political correctness. As long as the attention was not bold and clear, he erected a wall between he and them, a wall that years of resentment and mockery had taught him to raise. Sometimes it had to be raised without warning. In the event that attention wasn't restrained, and it was the exception, not the rule, he fired back in his typical manner, and he never lost the impending battle.

Around the world of the Church, and within its walls, tolerance of him and anything not ordinary, whether feigned or real, was different as it was backed by a fear of the divine. It was also backed by a pledge to "love thy neighbor" for His sake, no matter who *thy* neighbor was, and no matter what he or she looked like. When you merged this sacred correctness with political correctness, it prompted another degree of acceptance that outdid what the free outside promised. Attention on him was even more suppressed here and when it did take place even he found it tough to detect. But he felt it and he knew that even here he was an attraction. And, yes, they looked for different reasons, even if they were discreet about it. They were human and they felt sorry, but then there were those who were afraid and even a little resentful.

But the sentiments at the Church were too infrequent and too formless, so he reached for what was apparent, grabbed it, and held on tight to it. He embraced the smiles and hugs, and the friendly lunch breaks when sitting with him at the same table was not a bitter challenge. He embraced the spontaneous birthday parties, complete with a modest gift, balloons, and a grocery store cake. And he was delighted to cap off each one with a special tune or two. He yearned for each preparation for mass because it always involved a collective familiarity and union that he had never experienced before. He cherished the bazaars, the picnics, and the dinners that celebrated special Christian holidays. And, even though he was immediately hit with the truth that he was alone every time he was dropped off, when he received an occasional ride back to the Co-op he enjoyed the extra opportunity for company.

He situated himself deep inside the Church, the world that he now called his first home. Other than his job, he volunteered himself for other things. He helped when sections of the Cathedral needed repainting. He helped rebuild the ceiling of the main lounge when it began to show cracks. And when potlucks or picnics were planned, he helped to carry and arrange things, from plates to furniture. He also helped to clean after, always the most annoying part of any get-together.

Two years after his return to Madison, he informed Father Kevin Murphy that he wanted to be confirmed. In a regal ceremony during one morning service, he and nine others received confirmation. Up until that point, it was the only service where he didn't play his flute. Though it was only Mr. and Mrs. Kennedy who attended on behalf of their family, he wasn't disappointed. It would have been a nice surprise if Myra showed up too. But he knew that even the two that showed up must have pushed themselves hard, and after a lot of consideration. They attended a smaller church up in Sherwood Forest. It suited them well as it kept attendance to a small, selected group. They could bear with large crowds once in a while, but once every week they had to be a little more discriminating.

That same year he trained to be a mass server. Even though it was a skill he wouldn't be using at the Cathedral, it was believed that some day, maybe in some other place, it could be useful. It was a skill that could never go to waste.

Unlike most of his earlier life, he obeyed Church rules because he liked Church life, not because he had to. He even followed directives that were realized in private, not just the public ones that were sometimes obeyed so that a priest could say, "well done my child." Before he went to bed at night and first thing when he woke up, he read a passage from the Bible, just like Father Murphy had instructed them, and then followed suit with a prayer.

The readings began to conjure a fresh set of visions. They contested pictures that commonly filtered through his mind when he pondered in private, providing a victorious solution each time a situation presented itself as hopeless or too intricate. Even the erstwhile domineering thoughts of who he was and the circumstances that gave him life; they waned slowly as they were increasingly displaced by Biblical readings that proclaimed the right not to lean on any single dream, but to dream new dreams, infinite and absolute.

Saint Peter

He had been an orphan most of his life. His real name was Raul and his grandparents were originally from Argentina. But no one called him Raul. They all called him Saint Peter because at every Bible class he raved about Saint Peter and proclaimed him his favorite and patron Saint. Saint Peter was the rock, his rock, the backbone and pillar of the Catholic Church. As far as Raul was concerned, Saint Peter was Christ's right-hand man. He may have betrayed the Messiah three times, but that was only a minor setback, and one to be expected under the circumstances. Was there anyone who had never given in to fear at one point or the other? If there was, he or she should cast the first stone.

Raul, Saint Peter, lived in the Co-op too, and did house maintenance jobs at the church. He also served mass. How he managed his job was a little bit of a puzzle since he walked with a conspicuous limp. It was the result of his left leg being shorter and thinner than his right, while his right foot curved inwards slightly. His left arm was also bent as if he had a handbag perpetually hanging from the elbow. He was admired because in spite of his birth defects he used his limbs extensively. And he taught everyone a lesson in gratitude. "It could always be worse" and "there are those who'd give anything to have what I have" where among his favorite lines. Eternally full of life and high spirits, he was a lively young man who infused laughter into everything. Even when doctors told him that his kidney was slowly shriveling because of some rare disease, he reminded everyone that he was Saint Peter, the rock. If some inconsequential kidney thought it was going to demoralize and kill him before he "built his church," it had to be delusional. Everyone else tried to feel sorry for him and share a word of encouragement or two. But he would rebuff them playfully and guarantee them that his problems paled in comparison to theirs. Soon they gave up.

Monty and Saint Peter saw each other a lot at the Cathedral. Saint Peter admired the passion with which Monty played the flute and slowly drew closer to him. He asked Monty a lot of questions. The questions Monty couldn't answer, he brushed aside, admitting that he didn't want to address them. He was careful not to confess that he didn't have answers for them. They were questions about his background, his family, and his parents. But the decision to elude specific questions only increased Saint Peter's interest in him.

They began to spend significant time together and chatted about everything, from the Co-op to Madison to church to flute playing and to home repairs. During lunch breaks they sat at the same table in the modest cafeteria at the Cathedral, or strolled out to a fast food place.

Back at the Co-op they started to visit each other's rooms though it was not often. They talked some more and though he was still curious about the questions Monty never answered, Saint Peter had learned not to ask them anymore. With indoor games they became more than acquaintances. Saint Peter brought over his games whenever he visited Monty. Or they played when Monty visited him. Monty had been introduced to indoor games through the Kennedys. Over the years they were his only access to such competition. With Saint Peter he found competition somewhere other than at the Kennedy's.

Since he met Dorothy at the age of ten, he hadn't been this close to anyone. Neither had he been this trusting of anyone. That was some 13 years ago.

Saint Peter was raised in Kenosha, not too far from Madison. But most of his growing up was in Madison. He became a little more than a friend of Monty's. He was an asset too and helped acquaint Monty with Madison. When Monty first lived in the city, it was under the strict protection and supervision of others. Now he had the option of searching the city more. Saint Peter showed him around, taking him to malls, grocery stores, movies, and theatrical shows off campus.

Because he liked an occasional beer, Saint Peter introduced Monty to the bar scene too. Monty didn't see anything wrong with it. Bible class had taught him long before now that it was excess, not the act of drinking itself, that was a sin. And yet he had no desire to drink alcohol or to spend quality time at bars. He hated Saint Peter's breath after his first bottle. A few more bottles caused him to belch a lot and the odor stung Monty's nose until he felt like his nose hairs were singed. After more than a few bottles, Saint Peter's quaint behavior always made Monty uneasy. His limp became much more pronounced and, thus, precarious, and he began every statement with "man" and ended each with "man." But this wasn't the only mutation in his choice of words. Vulgarities became prevalent and he prefixed most statements and phrases, which were quite inexplicable at that point, with "s_it" "f_ck," and "b__ch."

Monty noticed, too, and with some concern and compassion, how Saint Peter would drift off into the same story about his melancholy life. He had been the butt of many crude jokes on account of his deformity, and there were too many things he craved to do but never did and never would. He wanted to play all kinds of sport, run races, do morning jogs, swim, dance; the list was endless. Too many times while growing up, he had been beaten up by other kids, including girls. And all he could do was howl, more from rage than pain, or, if he could, would look for an object to use as a weapon. It seldom worked because his balance was erratic and agitation caused him to be extra erratic. He wasn't a coward and would have loved to fight back, but he couldn't.

And, yes, he liked women too but over the years had lost the courage to walk up to them without a sense of hopelessness. In high school especially, and even after, he had been looked at with disdain when he summed up enough courage to approach a young lady. It wasn't always just a condescending look; the reaction also came in the form of words that burned.

"Excuse me!"

"Imagine the nerve."

"Are you serious, cave boy?"

"I don't think so, funny man."

"Who's to say your thing isn't twisted like the rest of you!"

"You have to be kidding, I know you are kidding."

The stories, told again and again, puzzled Monty. Saint Peter had built a reputation, after all, of being sprightly and optimistic. Alcohol truly had strange powers.

The more Saint Peter took him out, the more they visited new scenes. One Saturday night they went to The Museum, a nightclub that, for whatever reasons, plastered its walls with Civil War pictures and paintings. Monty observed for the first time how a man walked up to a woman and said something to her, after which they walked to an open floor and began to wriggle their bodies with total abandon. He remembered the parties at the Training Center in years gone by, and the dances they used to do. Back then there was an imaginary wall that separated the guys from the girls, and they kept their dance steps to simple, monotonous, back and forth strides that lacked imagination. Monty's monkey-strut had to be one of the more brazen moves at the time. Now he observed how some of the nightclub music caused men and women to come to tight grips as if they would never let go. The wrestling matches roused thoughts of Myra, and then the feeling came. Warm and persistent, it surged from his heart down to his stomach, but when it ventured further, he rebuked it in his all too familiar way. "There must not even be a hint...."

In spite of the theatre on the dance floor, he hated the place. It was overcrowded and rowdy. People cursed for no apparent reason and for every curse he inhaled a whiff of stale alcohol and cigarette smoke. The curses were sometimes playful in an odd way. But there were those instances when they were nasty and almost led to blows. When the drinkers didn't curse, the smell still hung there, thick and stubborn. They had to raise their voices because of the loud music and with this came some more of the smell. A belch resounded more often than Monty could stand, and, again, it added to the smell. Saint Peter watched too;

160

after all, he had no intentions of attempting to dance. But at least he drank. And while he didn't smoke in real life, in the make-believe world of The Museum he smoked. Sitting right across from Monty who sipped from a glass of sprite, he soon transmitted the smell. Monty couldn't take it anymore. The atmosphere of smoke, bad breaths, noise, and cursing was bad enough. But to have Saint Peter replicating the entire scene up close was unbearable.

When Monty made it clear that he was ready to leave, Saint Peter feigned alarm. It was only 11:00 p.m. after all, and things had just begun to heat up. What was the point in staying this late if they were not going to be a part of the real fun? Monty was unimpressed by his drama and Saint Peter knew it. He had learned not to argue with Monty and finally gave in. In the near past he would have stayed back by himself. After all, he used to come here alone before he got to know Monty. But since they began hanging out together, he had gotten used to the cushioning that companionship brought. It was the fortitude to endure cruel attention because focus could be taken away from the stares and redirected at the companion. He drained his gin and lime in one tremendous gulp and stumbled on out with Monty.

Monty refused to go to any more nightclubs with Saint Peter. Bars were manageable, but not the madness of nightclubs. Tough as it was, Saint Peter continued to go by himself. Monty couldn't understand his attraction to that scene.

...

One day Saint Peter cajoled him into looking at yet another form of recreation. The Museum had stretched Monty's tolerance level to breaking point. But since nowhere else had done that to him, nowhere that he had been to by himself or with Saint Peter, he believed that the chances of its happening again were slim. So, and in spite of The Museum, he didn't totally mistrust Saint Peter or his choice of leisure spots. He agreed to go. But first he wanted to know where they were going. A second time that evening, Saint Peter convinced him.

"Hey man, why don't we keep it a secret? Let it be a nice surprise. You'll like it, I know you will."

The glitter in Saint Peter's eyes came with a fervor that spelt mischief. Monty felt some of his trust ebb, but, unsure, he still went along with his friend.

The building was located at a corner of State Street. Coated in dull white, during the day it was almost hidden and lifeless. But at night it suddenly came to life though it still stood silent. A huge sign was lit by red light that declared the words, "Red Red News." Although you couldn't see inside, the tinted windows also had a red glow, an indication that indoors was lit with the same color.

When they walked in, it took a second for the illustrations to hit him hard and Monty's demeanor was instantly transformed. The way he went into immediate paralysis, and though he squinted his eyes, he looked like an abandoned corpse. In front of him, videotapes, hundreds of them, lined the shelves that were bunched together. They carried gaudy and flagrant pictures of men and women, women and women, men and men, and an admixture of all, in explicit acts of sex. Their shapes and sizes varied considerably, as did their backgrounds. To the left a man stood behind a counter with a look of indifference on his face. Behind him on the wall and in the glass cabinet that formed the base of the counter were plastic and rubber doll imitations of mature male and female genitals, complete with pubic hair. In the cabinet and hanging on the wall, too, were packaged and life-sized rubber imitations of naked women. To their right were a few bookshelves that contained every imaginable pornographic magazine and book. Further down was an array of what looked like mini cubicles.

At his age Monty was still a stranger to anything that had to do with private parts and sexual acts. Over the years he had gained some insight into that subject. He had also known or come to know sensations that qualified as the sensuality that grownups sometimes experience. Most of his information about the subject was culled from either discussions that he wasn't a part of, his short education, or what he saw on TV. He wasn't a big reader otherwise he may have gotten some information from books too. While his knowledge was relatively little, he had long come to the conclusion that matters concerning things between the legs and what they were used for were very private.

It took little more than one powerful gaze for him to take in everything. He turned and walked out of the store, more from shame than disappointment with Saint Peter. Saint Peter, far from ready to leave, chased after Monty anyway. He spent the walk back to the Co-op trying to convince Monty that there was nothing wrong with visiting Red Red News. They had denied themselves the possibility of a great time and for no good reason at all. His contention that the Bible didn't condemn pornography was very passionate and he challenged Monty to prove the contrary. Doing *it* in the privacy of your mind's bedroom was sinful, Saint Peter admitted, but Red Red News didn't have to conjure those foul thoughts. The store marketed what could be looked at as art, an exploration of the limits of the human body that God had endowed with so much creativity. It could be looked at as a form of education, an extension of, and a different approach to the subject of biology. How could that be wrong?

Saint Peter didn't believe his own philosophy. Frustrated, he gave up because Monty ignored him. He couldn't have guessed that somewhere on the inside Monty's hysteria had begun to subside. Either Saint Peter's words had affected him somewhat, or, in some ironic way, Red Red News had sparked an interest that wasn't altogether distasteful. Either way, he would never go back there. Such adventure was a little too heavy for his introverted lifestyle.

...

After Red Red News, Monty had sworn that with Saint Peter he would only play indoor games and go to food places. He still enjoyed his company but there were to be no more escapades. And yet, one more time he went out with Saint Peter to another place of obscure entertainment, breaking his own promise.

It was Saint Peter's birthday and he wanted a special treat. Monty was suspicious when he suggested a place of nighttime pleasure. He was especially hesitant when Saint Peter explained that the place was classy and boasted great music and dancing. When he observed the look of cynicism on Monty's face, he pressed harder.

"Come on, man, this is not a wild place. In fact, it isn't even a nightclub though it sounds like it is. This place has class and only a selected few go there. The music is mostly soft and people don't dance on a crowded floor. Trained dancers dance on stage and entertain us that way. Only fine people go there and the women are gorgeous."

He said the latter with a look of lustful mischief. Then he continued.

"The place has special areas for smokers. If you smoke anywhere else, you get thrown out. They also throw you out if you get rowdy or drunk, or if you get into a fight. It's a neat place, Monty, honest it is. You've even got to dress formally to get in there. Think about it. No jeans, no T-shirts, no tennis shoes. I know you'll like it. No, I know you'll love it. And you won't have to pay for anything. I'll pay for everything. Forget that it's my birthday."

He took in a deep breath before rendering his final plea. It was with a gentle voice as if he was trying to put Monty to sleep.

"Man, I wouldn't ask this favor if it wasn't my birthday. It's that special day that comes only once a year. I know I deserve a special treat on this day, I know I do. Let's go just this once. I promise I'll never ask you again. Come on man, what do you say? Remember, you're the only friend I have man."

As he ended, he slowly put an unsteady arm around Monty's shoulder. Tears welled up in his eyes; that's how good his act had been.

Monty didn't believe most of Saint Peter's claims about the place. But out of pity more than anything else, he caved in. The moment he did, his heartbeat gained speed then lost a few beats, a sure warning sign. But he went along. In the near future he would learn to trust his heart, even if it meant breaking another heart.

...

Booby Trap was on Johnson Street, not too far from the campus. Before they walked through the door, Monty felt what came across as the decency of the place. Compared to The Museum it was like a Catholic Church when Latin and organ music was the norm. True, the music was soft and the place was exceptionally tidy and spotless. Some of the music even displayed a dominant flute quality that stirred Monty's heart. There was no thick smoke that almost clouded your vision, no obscene or loud exchanges, and since the noise and belches were kept down, the smell was contained too. A potpourri of lightly spiced, Oriental-type aromas that wafted in from unseen vents checked the little that might have been a nuisance.

Because the place looked so decent, Monty disregarded the fact that only young, attractive women served drinks and snacks. It was easier said than done since they all wore tight, black, leather shorts that were really, really short. Across their chests they strapped measly bras that didn't cover much. A special mechanism must have been used to choose each one since they were all of about the same height and slim build. The effect was an artistic exhibition of Barbie-type dolls brought to life. But Booby Trap was neat and classy, and the women were mere waitresses after all, nothing more. Once or twice he had to spurn the same feeling that overcame him whenever he thought about or saw Myra. But he was always successful, and isn't that what really mattered? Not the allure, but the willpower to arrest and raze it. And even when a few young women, also dressed like the waitresses, went on stage and performed dances that came too close to licentious, he allowed the satin drapes, the marble floor, and the brilliant cherry oak furniture to steal his concentration. But his heart had begun to beat faster.

Since he was determined to embrace the beauty of the place in spite of any unholy distraction, he blocked out other things too. Even the obvious truth that at least 99 percent of the clientele were men--young, not so young, old, and very old.

And then the Arab-looking man came on stage with a cordless microphone after the ladies were done. He was short and round, and, the way he huffed and puffed he must have been struggling to breathe. It was hard to tell where his abdomen ended and where his waist began. His vest was dotted with hundreds of tiny, round, metal-type objects that shimmered with red, green, yellow, and blue colors. They looked like misdirected stars. He had no neck and this, together with the way his chin and neck quivered, was an indication that he ate well. Around what should have been his neck, and on all his stunted fingers, were a chain and rings that amplified the shimmer already radiating from his vest.

"Now ladies and gentlemen," he began, "this is what you've been waiting for."

Monty couldn't understand. He thought he had seen all that there was to see in Booby Trap. The MC, breathing even harder because of his mounting excitement, went straight to the point.

"And now, here they come, the beautiful and luscious Trisha, Annetta, and Jo-Jo."

He was hardly done when soft, yet zesty music filled the club. The song, almost delivered in whispers, said something about sizzling fingers crawling all over tender flesh. As the MC made his way off the stage, he was almost remodeled by the flashes of incandescent lights that attacked and mystified the stage. They were of every color and ushered in the three ladies.

Monty held his breath for a few seconds when they emerged. The waitresses were dressed conservatively in comparison to the three dancers. Each one had on terribly skimpy bikinis and bras, mostly flowery, which exposed more than they concealed. There was one who stood out. Her attire looked like it was made of leopard skin. She had a tail to match. They each performed a personal dance routine that became more carnal as it progressed. The more carnal, the more Monty's eyes and mouth opened, the more he was disturbed, and the more he felt like a fool. He should have known. The ladies were athletic and performed splits that caused Monty to instinctively grab his crutch in imaginary pain. They swung their legs high in the air, rolled on the stage floor in what looked like total bliss, sucked their fingers, threw kisses and hip thrusts at the audience, and lost control.

Except with Monty, everyone seemed to degenerate into carefree insanity. It intensified with each passing moment and they screamed like little kids at a puppet show. For the first time Monty broke with his captivation and observed his friend. Saint Peter was in heaven. He was on his feet and almost tumbled over with each delirious gesture of approval. Either he or one of the other wolves had hit their table and tipped over his bottle of Heineken. The liquid found its level at one end of the table and began to drip onto the floor. But at this time Saint Peter was not interested in the fate of a bottle of beer. He foamed at the mouth and constantly yelled what sounded like an invitation to the ladies to come get and violate him. Monty couldn't understand why he held out a five-dollar bill. But then he noticed that almost all the men were frantically waving bills at the dancers who ignored them for now.

And then they began to strip. A numb feeling overcame Monty and he went limp with shock. Somehow he stayed from falling over and looked away. But he couldn't look away completely. Still wide-eyed and wide-mouthed, he discovered that he had no power over his own fleeting glances. They were more like peeks at an ice-cream cart from a dejected kid whose parents upheld rigorous rules against sweets. All around him there was an upheaval that began to dwarf the initial beauty of the place. The yells, the whistles, the sweat, the obscene signals at the dancers; they slowly drowned out what Monty saw as its unusual elegance. Each time the gyrating women tossed their bras and bikinis in the crowd, the mob, like bloodthirsty hyenas, lunged for them, shoving, squabbling, even punching and biting. In the middle of it all, and able to temporarily overcome any disabilities, was Saint Peter. Monty had never seen him this drunk, though it was not only from alcohol. He felt something hit him across the shoulder; it was slightly heavy but tender. The leopard tail hung across his shoulder and once he turned and recognized it, he shrugged it off frantically like it was a viper. It had been tossed and, in contesting for it, the frenzied mob had somehow diverted it in the direction of the helpless Monty. Once he got rid of it, they swarmed the floor area where it lay.

There must have been a strict rule of conduct that deterred the hungry men when the women danced down from the stage. That none of the men touched, let alone grabbed any of them was incomprehensible, to say the least. There must have been a rule because the women flirted generously and lured carelessly. Once down from the stage and in the midst of the mob, they contorted their bodies even more, raised their legs higher, and spread them wider apart. The men showered them hundreds of dollar bills, and this is where contact between performer and audience stopped. Monty couldn't understand why they went extra wild when the strippers stuck out their tongues or licked their own fingers. What poor manners.

The music died out slowly and with it the flashing lights. The naked ladies walked off, shaking everything they owned vigorously. It was the MC's queue and he remounted the stage. All along he had been in the midst of the fierce pack and its stubborn pursuit of erotic relief. Monty wanted to leave but had to sum up enough strength to rise and walk across the room and out the door. But his mind hadn't yet started to function normally when the MC, sweaty and out of breath, distracted him.

"Whew! Another round of applause for those angels."

They cheered and clapped.

"Do you want more?"

They cheered even louder.

"Without further ado, here's the gorgeous Beverly, the succulent Sylvia, and the stunning Betty."

The lights began to flash again as he left the stage, and another song of lust filled the place. The screams began before the ladies appeared, and got much louder when they did. Their performance didn't seem much different from the first, except that one of the three ladies was black even though she had dyed her hair blond. And the reaction of the delirious mob was predictable. But, for Monty, the performance took on an exceptional twist when the ladies invaded the crowd.

He wasn't sure that she was the one, so he blinked and wiped his eyes a couple of times. Yes, she was the one. She had added some height and her hair was thicker and longer than it used to be. She had also filled out and put on more flesh in key areas. But her face hadn't changed much. Betty Jones. What a place to see her again! What a way to see her again! She charmed him, as if after all these years she still exerted power over him. When she got close to his table, she had already removed and thrown her bra and bikini away. An orgiastic squabble developed around where they landed. Why was she making her way toward his table? Perhaps she had recognized him and saw the opportunity to taunt him again like she had always done? Their eyes met and he could have sworn that her lips formed the word, "Monty." She smiled, grabbed a pole that stretched from the floor to the ceiling, wrapped herself around it and squirmed like the pole could give her a child. In spite of the bestial crowd all around her and him, he could only see her and hear nothing else. Without warning she let go of the pole and took a few, long, seductive strides in his direction. But just when it seemed as if she was going to collide with his table, she stopped, smiled with glazed eyes, winked, and raised her legs high in the air. She was very supple. In the process she sucked her forefinger like a toddler tasting its first lollipop. Her proximity crowded him in more than the madness all around him, and for a moment she alone was visible.

He couldn't resist his sudden transportation back in time, and returned to the room in her parents' home where she had visited him for the last time. There, he replayed the drama in which she jolted him with rash references to "white meat." Now she not only presented her theme again, but also underscored it with raw clarification of the authority of white meat, her meat. And, again, he was more terrified than he was stunned. It was not clear why, since years of pressure had taught him to be daring and impervious, even cold. This time the manipulation of thoughts of Dorothy and Myra couldn't guarantee cheap escape. Dealing with images was obviously not as challenging as encountering a naked stripper. When Monty's spirit returned to Booby Trap, Betty was about to search out more lucrative sections of the room. Just as quickly as she had come, she turned and walked off with the same, long, seductive strides. The wolves drooled and surged after her like flies on week-old garbage.

Monty had to leave. First, he had to conquer his intimidation, even if temporarily. He didn't know when Saint Peter had left their table area, and scanned the room for him. He found him not too far off, completely lost in the neurosis of the moment, and in his own neurosis. It could not be explained from where he tapped his energy, and from where he found the ability to keep his balance. Like all the other wolves, he was drenched, partly from sweat and partly from alcohol that had spilled from his and other bottles. He still foamed at the mouth and his eyes had become redder. In one hand he held his Heineken, in the other he waved a number of bills as a beckoning call to the strippers. Like the other wolves, he had gained immeasurable pleasure from sticking them up all kinds of places. He spent a lot of money that night.

In one swift move that defied all inhibition, Monty pressed through the chaos and grabbed Saint Peter by the arm. It took Saint Peter a while to realize that the grip was not from one of the other men, and when he turned the look on his face was one of irritation. Monty hesitated for a second then regained his composure.

"I'm leaving this minute!"

"That's fine, see you later, hope you had fun."

Saint Peter's response was his most polite way of saying, "do whatever you want to do, just leave me alone." He knew that his bid to initiate Monty into his world of perversion had failed again. After Red Red News, he had hoped that a different approach would soften Monty and bring down his defenses. Booby Trap was supposed to kill two birds with one risky stone. Saint Peter would celebrate his birthday in the most incredible fashion, and indoctrinate Monty into a pastime where he sought an accomplice. Red Red News may have been too sudden since Monty wasn't hinted at what to expect there. It was also easy to resist because it contained an array of inanimate sex icons and experimentation. With Booby Trap he would be encountering a phenomenon that wasn't entirely new to him, having already been to Red Red News. Besides, resistance would be tough since he would be witnessing a larger, more real, play out of perversion.

His plan had failed and Saint Peter knew it. If he left with Monty, it wouldn't lessen Monty's resentment. Instead Saint Peter decided to stay on and get, for all it was worth, the best that Booby Trap could serve. At least he would still be killing one bird with one risky stone.

Monty waded through the crowd and out the door that safeguarded Booby Trap's secrets. He was disappointed with Saint Peter and he knew that their friendship had changed forever. But he still liked him. And he had come to the realization that he hadn't even begun to understand the outside.

Philip U. Effiong

Myra

He still visited with the Kennedys. Their friendship was the longest Monty had kept with anyone. They continued to have him over and he continued to weaken at the sight of Myra. Now that he was on his own, at least more than he had ever been, they didn't invite him as they once did. They could easily encroach in his space and become a nuisance, and they were aware of the fact. He discerned their thoughtfulness and respected them for it. To investigate Madison some more, he preferred privacy.

As always he enjoyed spending time with the Kennedys, but in their home profound changes had taken place. Now when he visited there was an air of formality that was a little more apparent than it once was. Myra, at 25, was a medical student at the University. She didn't find it necessary to show up on vacations, especially the short ones, since she rented her own apartment. She had more than enough friends to kill extra time with. Great-Grandma Kennedy was still at the house, and still spent most of her time in her room in the basement. It looked more like a glamorous suite than a basement, and had everything, including a kitchen, two bedrooms and two bathrooms that contained elegant spas. There, in her room, Great-Grandma spent a lot of private hours. She must have been musing over her life. With all the years she had lived, there was more than enough to muse over.

Grandma Kennedy occupied the other basement room. Her husband, Grandpa Kennedy, had died when Monty was still at the Institute. It was the first and only time he attended their church in Sherwood Forest. Aside from mourning Grandpa, he was also invited to provide flute accompaniment when a large man sang "Amazing Voice" in the raspiest voice he had ever heard.

When they were done, the sobs, even those initially stifled, were let loose.

Most of the children were either out or halfway out of the house. Those who weren't quite out, like Trisha and Dianne, spent more time out. Dianne still depended on her wheelchair and found, in the house, the type of relief her condition demanded. She worked as a Physical Therapist and co-owned a newly opened ice rink on Whitney Road, but she loved to spend time at home.

Monty adjusted to the changes fairly easily, though he missed Myra whenever she was not there on any of his visits. It was in a more sensitive way that he missed Centaur who had left a few years earlier with his son, Fritz. Monty understood the concept of children leaving home as they matured. But he sensed that Centaur's leaving had little to do with maturity and more to do with conflict. He never asked and never knew the truth. Centaur carried too much in his heart and head, and confronted them in ways that showed up as socially awkward, especially when they involved the bottle. Monty had seen through to his heart anyway. And he knew that deep down Centaur was strong-willed and caring. He pitied and missed him dearly.

...

When he heard a knock on his door at around five or six that Wednesday evening, he wasn't surprised. Maintenance people were known to knock at stranger hours, and, after all, Saint Peter still stopped by. Sometimes he stopped by at strange hours too. Monty kept their friendship with utmost caution, leaving it frail and uncertain. But Monty hadn't rebuffed him. While he had to limit interaction to few indoor games and fewer fast-food lunches, he still admired Saint Peter. It wasn't a maintenance person or Saint Peter who knocked on his door that evening though. It was Myra.

Monty knew that she was a medical student on campus, and that she lived somewhere in the area. She, along with her family, knew about his new life at the Co-op and that he no longer played his flute for free. Sometimes on State Street or some other place near campus, he saw her and they waved at each other. Otherwise they chitchatted briefly for the sake of chitchatting, and almost always about the same thing.

"How are you Monty?"

"Fine. And you?"

"Oh, I can't complain."

"How's your family."

"They're okay. Same old same old. Well, got to be going. Take care."

"Bye."

Then they went their separate ways. When there was contact, it came in the form of a handshake, nothing more.

He still nurtured thoughts of her and they were still very intimate. Before he graduated from the Institute, he concluded that his thoughts would have to remain thoughts. He gave up on hoping for something more tangible and even found it amusing that he once dared to have such hopes. Maybe he wouldn't have her like he would have loved to, but he wouldn't give up on the false satisfaction that came with thoughts of her. He kept the thoughts pure. His refusal to cross certain boundaries was, in part, done out of deference to Myra. They hadn't mutually agreed on a relationship and he didn't know that she would want one with him anyway. In fact he doubted that she would. For that reason he refused to think up what she probably wouldn't want to do. That way, he kept from *offending* her. And even if he crossed those boundaries, he wouldn't know what to do next.

Nothing could have prepared him for any visit from Myra, let alone one that was unannounced. Of all his fantasies, none anticipated a visit from her. His heart skipped a number of beats when he opened the door and found her standing there, a broad smile on her face. He was transfixed. Her leather coat wasn't heavy since winter wouldn't set in for another two or so months, but it was of a stylish brown shade and reached to her thighs. It didn't hide the beauty of her shape though, and even if it did there were portions of her beauty that lay bare. Like her rich,

175

brown hair that still stretched to her waist, and her legs which were supposed to be hidden behind a pair of tight, black jeans. The jeans merely assumed the shape of the legs.

Though his lips quivered, he couldn't utter a sound. Perhaps Myra noticed and broke the silence herself.

"I'm so sorry to show up like this. I didn't mean to. I was passing by and realized that this is where you stay, so I thought I'd take a chance and pay a surprise visit. Is that okay? If it's not, I'll be glad to leave, honest."

Her voice, more than her words, was consoling and it gave Monty the courage to speak too.

"Oh, it's okay. I got back from work not long ago and was just watching TV. Please come in."

The Small TV rested on a low table at a corner of the room. He had bought it from Goodwill, the secondhand store on one end of State Street. It puzzled him that people shopped elsewhere. Why would he buy the same TV from another major store at three or more times the price, when it worked as well? He couldn't understand. A good percentage of his extra furniture and clothing came from Goodwill. It was a store that lived up to its name. He had considered placing his certificate and trophy on top of the TV but changed his mind. He still held on to the notion that they didn't qualify as regular furniture, and returned them to the bottom of his suitcase.

She walked in, initiated a handshake, and carefully sat on the chair at the main table, still smiling. He sat down on his bed. Actually, the way he went down weakly, still in shock, it was more like he slumped down. Because he stared intently at his TV in order to avoid her eyes, she stared at the TV too. Neither one of them watched it though. It was the news anyway and held nothing appealing since it was either boring or depressing, or recounted the mediocre perspectives and personal accusations of con artists disguised as politicians. It helped when she accepted the can of Coke he offered. He was not only honored but also loosened up. Not that his controlled panic went away completely. He had never been this close and this alone with her, and yet the feeling that crept in when she was not near was subdued by apprehension. Communication was formal, irregular, and scanty.

"So how is everyone in your family?"

"Oh, you know how they are. They're doing quite good. Did you hear that Grandma was admitted in the hospital again?"

"No. Sorry to hear that. What is wrong with her?"

"Not sure. One of those things old people get."

Pause.

"How is school?"

"I'll be happy when it's all over. Can't complain though."

Pause.

"And how is your job? I'm sure you enjoy doing what you do best."

"It's fine."

Long pause. They kept staring at the TV without watching anything in there. Then she broke the pause again.

"I'll have to be leaving soon Monty. Me and my boyfriend are supposed to be going to a movie tonight."

He didn't know she had a boyfriend and would have really preferred not knowing. For the first time that evening he looked directly at her; it was a look of plea and in his eyes was a yearning. It was the type a dog gave a master chewing on a piece of thick, juicy steak, though the dog understood that the master would absolutely not share. And yet it didn't imply that the master didn't care. Myra might have noticed the look as she looked away.

"But you will have dinner with us, right?"

Monty wasn't sure how or why he made the invitation. The words had simply fallen out and he had refused to hold them back. It could have been his intuition, but words that he alone could hear had begun to drum the truth that this is as close as he would ever get to Myra. To take advantage was his only consolation. It would be best to keep her as long as he could. Her response was discouraging though.

"I don't know, Monty. Like I said, we are going to a movie and I do need to get ready. I just stopped by to see where you stay. It's a nice place."

Her effort at a polite "no" wasn't altogether effective. He didn't have the nerve to press on and diverted his disillusion to the TV. She wasn't supposed to notice. But inside his stare and false smile was an intensity that was all too obvious. It was therefore foolish to think she wouldn't notice. She noticed and she felt sorry for him. She was also concerned, as she couldn't understand what was really going on. And yet, hesitant and still somewhat puzzled, she gave in. What came across as his dejection had touched and swayed her. He had, after all, been a faithful friend of the family for a number of years. She could afford to spend a little more time at the Co-op than she planned to. It wouldn't necessarily spoil her evening plans. A moment of uncomfortable silence sped by. It was enough for Myra to muse over what was becoming an incredible visit. She had to find the strength to speak.

"But, well, now that I think of it, I guess I could stay a little longer. Not too long though. Okay? I'll stay for dinner. That way I could even get to see some more of the place."

From when Myra showed up that evening, she had brought with her a series of strange surprises. While this was another one of them, Monty was still unprepared for it. In his bid to be polite and look at her when he responded, he had to contend with the truth that he really couldn't. So, he kept his words very few, and hoped that she wouldn't notice the euphoria he held inside. His heartbeat had tripled and his breathing became heavier. She didn't notice.

...

The kitchen and dinning area occupied the lower level. In spite of its neatness, it was quaint and confirmed the old age of the building. The stove, huge, black, and slightly twisted, seemed to have a domineering personality of its own. Situated somewhere behind it and extending through the ceiling was a chimney. Another metal, a chimney-like object that looked like it had been patched a number of times, also extended from the floor at a corner of the room, and right through the ceiling. At its base was an opening where wood was lit during the dead of winter, making the room cozy and warm. In the middle of the room two large tables were joined together to serve as dinning table. The tables and surrounding chairs were plain and not of expensive wood, but they were strong and had lasted decades. The mood was dull even though two long fluorescent bulbs shone bright. And yet it sustained a heavenly serenity that blocked out what may have otherwise been melancholic.

Either she adjusted with humility that she was not used to, or she did a perfect job of camouflaging her discomfort at the lack of sophistication. But Myra settled in nicely and either nodded at or shook hands with the ten members who were present as Monty introduced each one. When he fumbled with their names, they came to his rescue in lighthearted fashion, restating their names out loud. Throughout the introduction, she kept her gracious smile.

All went smoothly until Saint Peter greeted her and for the first time some of her smile was lost. His handshake threw her off because he squeezed more than was necessary. And then he threw wanton glances at Monty that clearly declared, "wow, what a catch, where did you find this one?" Throughout dinner, he made a spectacle of himself that must have been picked up by most, if not everyone. Sitting right across from Monty and Myra, his expression was diabolic when it didn't show an impish smile. The wanton glances were quite frequent and occasionally flavored with a wink that wasn't subtle if it was meant to be. More irritated than he was embarrassed, Monty strove to ignore him. Normally he would have stared Saint Peter to submission, but, for Myra's sake, he didn't want to engage in anything that implied conflict. It didn't help that he had too little to say to her.

"I hope you like the food"

"Oh yes, it's nice."

"Good."

Monty spent most of the time gazing at his food even if he wasn't necessarily looking at it. Myra must have observed Saint Peter since she, too, spent a lot of time looking downward. Otherwise, the few times he spoke to her or she spoke to him, she peeked at Monty in a manner that was clearly self-conscious. It was perhaps the first time in his life that he felt something close to hatred for someone. Myra had visited him as if in a dream and he knew that the chances of another visit were very remote. He wanted to make the best of it, and to avoid simple errors, but Saint Peter interfered. Yet he was innocent. And, sadly, in his lackluster way he couldn't understand how his actions were annoying and thoroughly unfunny. Since the events at Booby Trap, Monty had carefully kept his distance from Saint Peter. But his efforts could only achieve so much, and he was incensed by this truth.

Myra had settled for a salad and a glass of apple juice. Most people were still eating when she whispered in Monty's ears that she had to leave soon. Monty welcomed any excuse to leave though he wasn't quite done with his own meal. When they got up, Myra threw out a general "thank you, nice meeting you all" greeting as she waved at everyone. They acknowledged, almost like a chorus. The two were still pushing their chairs aside when, from the corner of his eyes, Monty saw how Saint Peter began to rise too. In his frantic effort he pushed his chair over and bumped into a neighbor who was lifting a glass of something to her lips. The dark liquid spilled all over her sweatshirt and she looked hard at Saint Peter. But he was too preoccupied with seeking Myra and Monty's attention. He cared little about apologizing and less about realizing that he had done something wrong.

With the stupid smile on Saint Peter's face, Monty knew that he was headed in their direction. Surely, before their final exit, Myra and Monty owed him a few minutes of uninterrupted attention. That was how the gigolo's mind worked. It would be another opportunity for him to squeeze Myra's palm, maybe throw a few more mischievous winks at Monty. Monty sensed it all and pretended that Saint Peter didn't exist. He pushed the door open for Myra as if to hurry her out. They escaped.

She had left her pocketbook in his room and they returned there for her to pick it up. Before she headed on out, she expressed her gratitude.

"Thank you so much, Monty. I had a great time."

He knew that she was being well mannered and, for that reason, didn't believe her. Maybe it was an okay time, good at best, but not great. He thought about apologizing for Saint Peter's antics, but decided to leave it alone. He couldn't really talk anyway. Again, he had lapsed into a state of near muteness, the result of uncertainty and some anxiety. He was afraid of losing her and yet in her presence he lost all composure.

"Thank you for coming." For now, it was all he could say.

"You're welcome, can I have a hug?"

Myra's request defied past family rules that denied close, personal contact with him. It didn't matter; her visit had already broken those rules anyway, and blatantly too. She held out her arms and he reached out to receive her. In spite of his drooping tummy, she was able to wrap her arms around him. For her it was supposed to be a quick, light hug and she began to let go once it was accomplished. But he wouldn't let go. In fact, he tightened his hold. Myra's hug had been light, but it came with a power that overwhelmed him. It was the power of her softness, of her breath, of her scent. And like he had done years back before he was sent away from the Orphanage at Ireland, he held on as if she alone could be his sustenance, as if he was pleading that she stay forever. The unexpected had taken place more than once that evening and her touch evoked the possibility of more unexpected things. If it worked, she would stay a little longer. Better still, she would stay on in his life for all eternity. On TV, many relationships had been inspired by a daring move. Why couldn't his move pay off too? In truth Monty had degenerated into a transient world of fantasy, only that this time he wasn't alone. One could say that it was more than a world of fantasy; it was more like a chaotic state of rash lunacy. When she realized what was happening, she became nervous and began to push. But the harder she pushed, the more pressure he applied until her face reddened. She knew that she was in for a battle and it was one that she was losing. If she was going to find victory, she had to look to another strategy. First, she decided to re-compose herself. Then she began to call his name repeatedly. It was a whisper, but it was frenzied and carried strength.

"Monty, Monty, Monty, Monty, Monty . . . "

When the whisper became louder, he was thrust back to reality. He let go instantly and, instantly too, his mind was cluttered with thoughts about what he had just done and why he had done it. He had made a permanent error and he knew it. If he had been fed some exotic love potion, no matter how much, it was still one of the most reckless things he had done. Like other members of her family, Myra had looked on a lot of Monty's atypical behavior patterns with sympathy. They were, after all, the result of some childhood disorder. But she judged his action that evening as calculated.

She looked at him once and her eyes couldn't have peered any deeper. For the first time, Monty couldn't find beauty in those eyes. He wanted to believe that they communicated agitation and nothing more. Actually he saw a lot more in there but looked away, wanting to refuse that such angelic eyes could store those things.

More from habit than anything else, she straightened her hair, turned, and walked through the door with swift, regimented steps. He walked her out of the room and down the hallway, barely keeping up with her. When they reached the exit door at the end of the hallway, she turned and faced him for the last time. He was scared though he looked straight in her eyes. Actually it wasn't courage. It was the effect of the poorly lit hallway. He had to look extra hard to see well. She managed a smile though she spoke sternly, and with her arms folded just above her stomach.

"Monty, I'm not sure how to put this, but maybe you should know something about Madison. So many things count as rape in this state and you could be thrown in jail for any of them. Be careful how you push your luck with ladies out there. Okay?"

With that she opened the door and disappeared into the darkness. Her words hadn't made much sense to him, and he would merely add them to his list of things to be understood. He was devastated.

...

She continued to show up in his dream world, but in a short time she increasingly became more of a blur and less of a possibility come-to-life. And as she receded, so did the warm feeling that flared up in his heart and inched its way downward. Part of it was caused by fear. Part was caused by accepting the stupidity in hoping, and the absurdity of drooling over someone who at least didn't respect you, and who at most hated you.

Because of Myra, his desire to visit with the Kennedys died considerably. But when he did visit, she acted as always and without any indication that the events of that evening had taken place. Her calm and refusal to show resentment, at least not openly, allowed him some ease. It also produced deep remorse, the type that subdued him even as it caused him to love her more.

Lamentation

When he couldn't re-create his private cravings in private dream worlds, a lost emptiness began to revisit him. It was not caused by the dream itself, but by its substance. Any craving that wasn't completely dead shriveled to the point of near lifeless and wasn't worth pursuing.

Myra continued to reduce and transform into a haze, an obscurity whose outline was theorized. When he fell after Dorothy let go from high up, he didn't bother to scream anymore, and came to accept his fall as another typical journey back to his reality. And when he, in turn, let go of Dorothy, it wasn't so much that she struggled loose as it used to happen, it was more like he released a burden. And though he came shuttling down soon after she let go, it wasn't a deliberate flight down in the bid to save the one who had taken with her a piece of his heart. That is how it was at first. Now it was more like a destined fall that didn't matter anymore. He accepted and shrugged off the fall. And if it didn't happen he didn't care either.

While he was losing major actors and episodes of his fantasy world, his desire to learn about himself and the factors that produced him was ignited. The flames blazed and soon they raged, and there was no indication that they were going to subside. So, he formed doctrines to explain or assess most of the things he couldn't resolve.

While he had convinced himself about his normal, if not good, looks, he was still forced to contemplate the things that distinguished him. After all, the constant gazes had not ceased; there had to be a reason for them, and a reason to search them out.

He began to wonder more and more about the people who shared his attributes to various degrees. Where did they come from? Did they emerge from experiences that compared with his? If not, why not? For those who seemed to place much better than he did in society, where did they discover the secret that they exploited. What was it that shaped them to fit more snugly into a world that he still found as unfriendly as it was friendly?

He began to read books, though he didn't read many. Those with accompanying, colorful pictures attracted him the most. They were available in Madison's Central Library on Main Street, and in the two or three secondhand bookstores on State Street. He valued the secondhand bookstores with the same passion that he valued Goodwill. He read or simply looked at books that spoke to and about people that reminded him of himself. They talked about Africa, India, Mexico, and the Arab world. They talked about the aboriginal worlds scattered randomly from place-to-place, and which brought together the modern and the ancestral. They rediscovered within the Americas, Holland, and England, ethnicities that he connected with for reasons that weren't clear.

The Bible wasn't like any of those books that centered on a unified subject. But that is why its inspiration was unmatched. In it there was something that identified with all of Monty's experiences and concerns. When his interest in himself became definite and bore the decision to search until an answer was found, he was refreshed by the knowledge of victory that always succeeded pain. It was a motif most forcefully realized in the essence of the godhead known as Christ.

But most of all he invented, first, a world that breathed life into him, and then a smaller world within, one complete with a father and mother. They were vivid and yet he could never quite make them out. He always returned from his reverie without specific answers, but with his dissatisfaction came a determination not just to inquire some more, but to find.

...

When he first heard the sounds, he thought his dreams had come to life. They came at night, and sometimes during the early hours of the morning. And yet they didn't go away when he half woke up and hung there like he sometimes did for several minutes, at some intermediary zone where he wasn't quite awake or asleep. Neither did they stop when he woke up fully and alert. Only then did he realize that they were not part of his dream world; they were real and came from the room next door.

Beatrice was a shy lady in whom several worlds met. Though she was officially Native American, she must have been a mixture of at least three racial backgrounds. Of a dark yellow shade and with full, black hair that reached below her shoulders, her beauty shone through in spite of her droopy, almost always teary eyes, the result of some rare ailment. The ailment might have been as mental as it was physical, and the reason for her slurry speech. Many times her manner of speech brought back memories of Dorothy.

Her nightly sobs unfolded like a dirge, and were rendered in uneven rhythmic tones and pitches. The sequence was fairly similar and began with disconnected, monosyllabic hums, the only part of the lamentation that was monotone. And then it shifted to a piercing wail that rose and fell in a manner that wasn't necessarily ordered. This was the part that frightened Monty the most. For that reason, he welcomed the next stage even though it suggested derangement more than the other stages. Beatrice would actually begin to utter recognizable words, except that they were meaningless and laced with surges of hard breathing. They sounded urgent and always seemed to demand, from Monty's standpoint, that some form of aggression be done to her. Monty was confused. Finally came the loud howl and then normalcy returned. Surely someone else must have heard, but because no one said anything, Monty was deterred from saying anything, at least not right away.

But he felt terribly sorry and concerned for Beatrice. He was sure that whatever her sickness was, it was responsible for the disturbance from her room in the dead of night. Maybe she needed help. Maybe she was dying. He was worried for her, but he didn't say anything just yet.

Talk Show

An interview on a discussion show organized by PBS, the Public Broadcasting Service? The Consulate was not aware of the extent of Monty's popularity. In the past his photo had shown up in one or two of the local papers, accompanied by a short piece on the young man who possessed what had to be a natural and divine gift. But an invitation to appear on PBS? And it wasn't just an invitation by PBS at Madison; it was by PBS all the way in Milwaukee. How was it that he was known in Milwaukee? The Consulate refused to grant permission, but PBS was persistent.

It was a TV station that relied heavily on sympathetic gifts and donations. To secure such benevolence, it had to steer from the tradition of more dogmatic stations. It unearthed images, people, views, and stories that wouldn't be seen or heard elsewhere. A lot of its themes were culled from American society, but it also reached into the most remote and nameless corners of the world and dug up information that often appealed to the heart and solicited compassion, even alarm. The geographies, histories, cultures, and rites of people from faraway, if not mythic, places were brought to life, examined, or romanticized. Diseases, both from the past and present, and those not yet proven to exist, were studied and displayed. It exposed degrees of poverty, mourned and decried the alienation of women and other subcultures, introduced the arts and literatures of non-mainstream America, and promoted formal education. The family was supposed to gain tremendously from the station, and while it had a hard time defining the family within the context of liberal America, it produced *family* shows that featured what was supposed to be in the best interest of mom, dad, the kids, and anything in between. Cartoon and puppet shows played along with pro-family topics. They targeted children though their contents were sometimes more adult than anything else.

Featuring the flute-playing talent of a young, dark-skinned man was strategic and in the best interest of PBS. For one, the talent was inexplicable and violated expected standards. The hero was an American, but he was also a first generation refugee from a distant land. He would be promoted. His talent would be promoted. And there would be some entry into his original homeland, another opportunity to bring the existence and lifestyle of an exotic place to America. A show like this would confirm the station's concern for those on the periphery, the unrecognized and even the downtrodden. It would prove its desire to inform rather than make profit like the other major stations, those that corrupted the mind with deodorized filth.

PBS pressed on, each time responding to the Consulate's polite refusal with a letter or delegate that stressed its mission to enlighten and liberate. When the Consulate finally agreed-- actually it was more like it gave in--, it demanded a number of conditions that had to be met. The demand came in the form of a long document that was to be signed and notarized by PBS. There were to be no questions about Monty's parents. There were to be no questions about his decision to come to the United States, or how he was relocated. There were to be no questions about race. There were to be no questions about his job with the Church or anything that alluded to his earnings. Father Smith had to accompany him to the show. PBS complied.

Two weeks before the show, Father Smith met with him either at the Cathedral or at the Co-op, and almost on a daily basis, to coach him. He instructed Monty on what to wear that evening and how to comport himself. Questions were to be answered precisely and information was not to be volunteered.

"They will ask you why you love to play the flute so much, and where you acquired your talent. Say it's all from God, nothing more…. Look straight at the person interviewing you…. When the program comes on, smile. Smile at the camera whenever it's focused on you. It will be easy to tell; it will be pointing straight at you. Smile…. Sit up straight…. If you sneeze or cough, cover your mouth with a handkerchief. Make sure you bring one with you.... They will ask you to play. Don't play more than two songs. Decide on what you'll play well before hand. When you are done, bow and return to your seat while your audience is still clapping. They will clap for you; talk show audiences always clap.... But above all, please, please don't answer any question if you are not sure of the answer. Please! That's why I'll be there, to answer such questions. Under no circumstance should you talk about things you are not asked about. If a question is inappropriate, you know, like if they ask you about anything that has nothing to do with you or flute playing, leave it alone. I'll point out that it's inappropriate. Okay?"

Monty was virtually attacked with instructions. He always sat quietly through Father Smith's training sessions, nodding his head in acceptance of each rule. He was the perfect student who accepted the instructor's words as sacred. They were not to be interrupted or challenged.

The routine, religious and repetitive, was all about protecting the Church and advancing its charitable reputation. Monty knew it. Whatever risks it was taking, the Consulate was essentially worry-free. This ward, after all, had constantly proven to be compliant and unobtrusive.

...

PBS had done a good job advertising the forthcoming interview with Monty who it described as "one of the most recent wonders to grace Wisconsin." It was able to spice up its ad with a short clip showing Monty at work. With the permission of the Church, the clip had been secured from one Sunday morning mass at Lourdes Cathedral when he performed a solo. PBS had brought its equipment into the Cathedral. For a very short take it looked like a large amount of equipment. Its crew didn't spend a long time there but it was a nuisance the short time it was there. Regular Church goers were glad when they left.

191

That evening Monty had a large viewing audience. Those Kennedys who were at home all watched together. Myra wasn't at home. Monty would never know whether she watched or not. He believed she didn't and he never asked. There were Consulate officials who were assigned to watch the interview. Their assessment would determine the method of allowing or disallowing similar interviews in the future.

The show was titled "Unearthing Our Hidden Talents" and featured "Monty Monty." The studio setup resembled that of a typical talk show except that the main players were already seated when the show began. They were not required to make a grand entry after a flamboyant introduction by the host.

Monty had faced enough large audiences, so the studio audience didn't bother him. It was good that he couldn't see the thousands who watched from home. His only inconvenience, and it was a first-time test, lay in the fact that most of the time he wouldn't be playing for this audience. He would be talking, something he didn't do particularly well.

A series of well-placed words were used to introduce Monty. He was identified as an icon, a phenomenon, and a miracle on two legs. A short history of his involvement with the flute was traced from when he was at the Center to when he won the coveted trophy at the Institute. Some mention was made of other forums when he played, including as choir member and for bands and theatrical troupes. His job with the Church was hinted at, but only hinted at.

While his introduction was not as flamboyant, Father Smith was lauded as special counselor whose guidance contributed in no small measure to Monty's quest for perfection.

As rehearsed, Monty and Father Smith nodded and smiled lightly during and right after they were introduced. They sat upstage on plush looking leather seats that shone. On his laps Monty carried his most prized treasure, the silver box that housed his flute. Whenever he thought a camera was on him, he smiled broadly, showing his teeth, so large they looked like ivory nuggets. At least they were white. The artificiality was all too apparent and became an unlikely source of comic relief. Because it had been carefully directed, the studio audience repressed its giggles. But non-studio viewers were not so inhibited, especially as most of them had never seen him before. For those who had, it was usually from a distance, maybe on a stage with lighting that revealed a part of him, or in a newspaper page where his traits were either dulled or remade. Seeing him up-close triggered reactions that were anything from astonishment to curiosity to disappointment to hatred to pity to mockery. Whatever they were, they increased interest since they tried to work out the incredible link between the face and the art form.

The questions were fairly simple and he answered them without straining himself. It was just as the Consulate would have wanted it. At the early stages of the interview he relaxed and discarded the vestiges of uncertainty that he had come with.

"So, your name is Monty. Not your everyday name, but it's a nice name. Welcome to the show, Monty."

"Thank you." Slight grin.

"And, Father Smith, you are welcome too. We hear you're on your way to becoming a bishop. Congratulations. You have our best wishes."

"Thank you." Slight grin too as he nodded his head once or twice. The audience clapped as they were required to.

"So, Monty, what got you started with the flute?"

"It was the guidance of God."

"Hmm! The guidance of God. And what has kept you going and getting better?"

"The Lord shows me what to do. Father Smith and everyone at Church also help me a lot."

"Isn't it just wonderful that you get so much encouragement and support?"

"Yes, it is."

The host paused here before going on. He opened his mouth but produced no sound for a brief interval, during which he squinted his eyes.

"Now, if you don't mind, I'd like to go back to your name again. It is a little fascinating. Where did you get the name? Does it have a meaning?"

Father Smith knew that Monty had no response to the question and jumped in without hesitation. His role was to stave off embarrassment, more so for the Church than for Monty.

Monty hadn't even done the standard, uneasy, not-sure-what-to-answer shift on his seat when the priest began to speak.

"Well, actually, it's a name that was given him in his original native land. That is, em, in the tropics or, you could say, off the coast of West Africa...."

"Anywhere in particular?" The host goaded him on.

"To be more specific, em, areas around Cape Toria or, em, Beuvera, depending on how you see things. The name probably has some cultural meaning; most names from there have a meaning."

The host sensed some discomfort with the subject and left it alone. But Father Smith's revelation stirred in Monty a yearning to learn more. It dawned on him that the things he was ignorant of were many and far more crucial than he had ever known. His yearning was a baptismal reaching out for that brand of knowledge that, more than teach, would protect him from the artificial sense of direction that came with ignorance. Without knowing it, Father Smith had said things that would have a lasting impact on the young man he counseled. For the first time in Monty's life he was not only aware that his roots stretched back to a region that had something to do with one or all of three places--the coast of West Africa, Cape Toria, Beuvera--, he was going to act on that awareness. As yet he had no idea as to where the places were or what they consisted of either physically or socially. If more of his counselors and teachers knew the details of his background, maybe they would have mistakenly blurted out something. But only the very few who worked closely with him knew, and they faithfully protected the secret like a jealous lover watching over a once-in-a-lifetime soul mate. Too bad he couldn't recall how when he was much younger the

Joneses had talked much more than they were supposed to, and generated a number of exaggerations about Monty and his past. Even if he could recall, like too many fellow Americans he would have conjured Africa as a monolithic culture, something like a single, large nation, and he wouldn't have bothered to know more. The longer he had lived in America, the more he embraced the general concept of being a part of a hemisphere that comprised a population of immigrants and their descendants. The past, even when respected and loved, was often eclipsed by the supremacy of the here and now. Now that he had a more specific indication that his beginnings, even if tied to a far-off place, were of some consequence, another confusion set in. Was it a place called Cape Toria or a place called Beuvera or a place called West Africa? The realization and uncertainty angered him as much as it humiliated him. But he maintained his artificial grin.

Otherwise, the interview was without incident and made progress until the host invited Monty to give a demonstration. They clapped as he made his way to the end of the stage that was raised a little higher and on which a microphone had been mounted. This was the easiest part for Monty. His flute-playing skills had advanced to a level where he now played with little effort and spellbinding ease. When he was done he bowed and returned to his seat. From when he finished up until a few minutes after he sat down, the people went wild. They temporarily discarded all civility and didn't applaud simply because they were required to. They had been affected deeply and wanted to show it. What should have been a customary standing ovation transformed into the type of hyperactive reaction accorded a European soccer team after it scores a decisive goal. On the outside, among the external audiences, most of the emotions, even those that were hateful and intolerant, were reborn in a renewed spirit of awe, appreciation, and noble disbelief.

"Unbelievable Monty, unbelievable. Can we have another round of applause?"

195

The place erupted a second time, then quiet returned and, with it, feigned etiquette.

"It's been so nice having you here with us this evening, Monty. We are so glad you came too, Father Smith. We've had a very nice and enlightening evening. But before we leave, I'd like to ask you one more question if that's okay with you, Monty."

"Okay."

"Look, tell us some more about your place of birth. And I'm sure the people want to hear something about your family back in … is it Africa? Cape Toria? Or, Father Smith, did you say…"

"Beuvera," Father Smith interjected. He knew to jump in again, and did just that. "Like I had said, Monty is originally from the tropics, you could say the area around West Africa … Cape Toria or Beuvera, em … you know, from the southern part. But he's now an American like you and me."

The more he spoke, the more the priest became defensive. Close observation would have also shown that he was becoming irritated.

"Actually he became a citizen two years ago. His family may be an extended family like it happens in a lot of cultures of the world. Of course one day he'll probably visit, just like people of Jamaican background want to visit Jamaica, and, you know, Jewish Americans keep visiting Israel. But his heart and soul belong to his country, America. We all, directly or indirectly, come from somewhere else; that's an indisputable fact. We're all like Monty and we love America."

Once again, the host sensed discomfort and knew to leave the subject as it was. Monty had been his usual introverted self so far, quiet and obedient. So when he spoke, he startled the host and Father Smith almost fell off his seat. It was bad enough that Monty dared to speak when he hadn't been asked a question, but even more disturbing was what he said.

"It may also be good to say something more about who my parents are and the name of the town where I was born."

Father Smith started to glare at him but then remembered that they were on TV and pulled back. His grin faded fast and a clear sign of agitation quickly overtook the little that was left. For that moment he concluded that Monty was mean. No, that he was plain evil. He took in a deep breath as if to pacify himself, then explained.

"Well, I didn't really go into that because ... there's so much to say about his family. I don't think we have the time.... Maybe we'll talk about it some more during another show. Okay, Monty?" He threw his right arm over Monty's shoulders as he ended his response, really a detour, with a political laugh. "Ha, ha, ha!"

The laugh was sinfully false and lacked any mirth. No one else laughed, not even the audience that normally would as a sense of duty. There was nothing he had said that came close to being funny. He felt betrayed. Monty had been defiant, but even more serious was that Father Smith had failed the Church and its Consulate. They held him responsible for ensuring an acceptable interview and he had guaranteed nothing less. He had become one of many who had misjudged what, on the surface, looked like an impressionable Monty.

"Thank you so much for coming to the show, Monty. I wish you the best in your musical career. And to you, Father Smith, good luck in doing the work of the good Lord. Good night everybody."

As the host walked over to shake their hands a camera zoomed in on Monty and he obliged with a loud smile. It was more real than the rest because now he felt a sense of accomplishment. Father Smith also smiled, but it was too faint and almost blanked out by the redness that had now taken over most of his face. The audience, as if refined, was on its feet clapping graciously.

...

Father Smith said nothing on the hour drive back from Milwaukee. He turned the radio on so that everything else was silenced. It was a station that played rock music. Monty said nothing too. When Father Smith's Toyota pulled up in front of the Co-op Monty said a quick "thank you" and was about to hop out when the Brother's voice halted him. It was characteristically small and soft, and yet it was severe.

"You know you were not supposed to say anything except you were asked. Why did you ask about your parents?"

Monty's response was a stare that Father Smith wasn't familiar with. At a loss for a counter-move, he looked away from Monty and took a breather before he continued. His conscience began to inform him that his question was quite senseless. How could he restrain anyone's desire to learn the secrets about him or herself? But he couldn't stop here because he didn't want to appear indecisive and weak.

"You know, Monty, what you did was shameful and very bad. Learn to obey directions, okay? Learn that simple lesson as a good Catholic…."

He now talked because he thought he had to. He wasn't quite sure what his message was or, if any, how rational it was. His anger had reduced because in his heart he questioned his right to anger. Monty's response was simple and lazy.

"Okay."

In all the years he had known Father Smith, this was the only time the counselor had been mad at him. And all because he had dared to inquire about something that was so intimate even if so alien to him? As he made his way down the hallway to his room, he vowed to be more resolute than ever.

Good that he was clueless about information on him provided the Joneses and Kennedys years before. Good that he was clueless about information on him provided those counselors and teachers who worked most intimately with him. They were delivered as if classified, and mostly treated that way. If he knew, he would be very resentful. Except of course there was a way to appease him, to convince him that while others deserved to know about him, he didn't.

The next time he walked into a secondhand bookstore, he searched hard until he found two books, one on Cape Toria and one on West Africa. They had a lot of colorful pictures.

...

In subsequent days to come, local papers reported on the show and one or two underscored what came across as the obscurity surrounding the great flute player's past. It didn't bother Monty, not even after co-workers and co-members of the Co-op approached him on the issue. There was finality to the way he stated that it was not an issue he wanted to address, and they knew better than to ask again. He knew that he had embarrassed the Church, not out of malice, but as a step toward getting answers. If nothing else, he would begin to receive attention, serious attention.

Those who watched the show on behalf of the Consulate were satisfied with everything, except Monty's mention of his unknown parents and place of birth. Their views, along with those of officials who watched the show out of interest, was part of the reason for the letters the Consulate sent PBS and Father Smith. While it didn't threaten a lawsuit, the letter to PBS accused the station of breaking its promise. Monty was not supposed to be asked about his parents. The station replied in carefree fashion, noting that Monty was not asked about his parents. His family maybe, but not his parents. The letter to Father Smith, short of chastising him, expressed regret at his poor handling of Monty during the interview. In response, a flustered Father Smith reminded the Consulate that his training did not equip him to prevent people from inquiring about their parents and birthplaces. The letter was not apologetic or insulting, but it was firm and brought temporary closure to the matter.

Still Sobbing

The noises were still coming from Beatrice's room almost every night. Monty ignored them as best he could. No one had yet said anything, so he kept his mouth shut. Then there was the night when she terrified him the most. Just as she was making the loud howl before silence returned, he heard a loud bang. Something had certainly struck something. Then something fairly large, like a table, crashed to the floor. Following immediately were the sounds of other less heavy things hitting the floor. The commotion was a fantastic addition to the habitual sounds. What was going on? Was she being attacked? Maybe she had lost her mind to the point of inflicting injury on herself. In that case she was probably demon-possessed and in dire need of the type of exorcism for which the Church was famous. Whatever it was, he wouldn't forgive himself if the nocturnal events in her room resulted in grave injury, even death. He decided to speak out.

Before going to work the next morning he stopped by at Mr. McPherson's office and described, at great length, the series of strange sounds that came from Beatrice's room at night. It was behind closed doors and the supervisor either listened intently, slowly nodding his head from time-to-time, or scribbled something on a notepad. Before Monty walked out, Mr. McPherson thanked him for his observation and concern.

...

That evening when he returned from work there was an air of tension at the Co-op. A small group stood near the entrance talking excitedly in low tones. Emotions were strong, whether they caused laughter, compassion, or wonder. Inside, and along the hallway that led to his room, another group chatted with the same fervor.

It was not long before Monty learned how a team of Consulate officials and local cops had been in the building earlier that day. They came to carry out some investigation and walked back and forth between Saint Peter and Beatrice's room. Voices were heard and they occasionally got very loud, suggesting confrontation, accusation, and disagreement. Clearly, an infraction of some sort had taken place. It must have been conclusive because later that afternoon Saint Peter and Beatrice were ejected from the Co-op. They weren't simply tossed and abandoned since they were still the Church's responsibility. A white mini van had been arranged for them. On its sides were written in black, "Offices of the Catholic Consulate." Not long after the van arrived, they were whisked off in it, together with their belongings. More than likely the two would be relocated and given the opportunity of fresh living standards as prescribed by the church. Depending on why they were taken away, they would probably be separated.

That same night Mr. McPherson handed out a document to each member of the Co-op. It was actually a copy of the "Rules and Regulations" sheet that they were given the first day they were admitted into the place. Two areas were highlighted--the part that stated that guests of the opposite sex could not spend the night at the Co-op, and the part that prohibited members from spending the night with each other, whether they were of the opposite sex or not.

Monty didn't quite get the significance of redistributing the document and highlighting specific portions. Not until the next day or two when he learned from dinner and careless discussions that Saint Peter had been a frequent nighttime guest at Beatrice's room. Only then did it occur to him that the sounds he was hearing did not come from pain or the effect of any sickness. They were sounds of rapture, albeit errant and illicit rapture. And the extra noise that last night was merely an instance of such rapture getting out of control.

He felt very guilty. Saint Peter could be very irritable but Monty still liked a lot about him. He was happy to regulate contact with him but he had no intention of having him thrown out of the Co-op. To make things worse, Beatrice had been ejected too. He hated himself even though he had confided in Mr. McPherson in hopes of protecting her. Then he became insecure, believing that other members would blame him, maybe ostracize him. But they didn't know that he had anything to with revealing Saint Peter and Beatrice's liaison. Even if they did, they would have concentrated more on the juicy subplots within the drama. Like the ability of the lovebirds to keep their romance a secret. Within a few days they even forgot about the two former members.

But Monty was haunted by a stubborn guilt. It added weight, unbearable weight, to the load he carried by himself. Not long after, he too desired to get out of the Co-op even though he had no plans for a new destination.

Dorothy Again!

Monty welcomed the opportunity to be alone. For him, alone didn't imply loneliness; it was an opportunity to search for elusive answers and to console himself. But loneliness crept in after the departure of Saint Peter and Beatrice. It came with a feeling of abandonment, perhaps the type that accompanied Beatrice and Saint Peter when they were sent away. Still weighed down to the point of almost being crushed by guilt for their removal, he began to pine away.

More and more solitary, he drifted from fellow Co-op members and Church workers who were aware of the futility of trying to ask questions whenever he was moody. His was a hushed type of seclusion, but it carried power and erected a wall between him and everything on the other side. His anger, his irritation, his frustration could all be discerned, sometimes felt, even when he didn't say or act out anything.

The lonelier he became, the more he longed to leave the Co-op. But more than escaping the Co-op, he anticipated a place unlike the limbo that he had existed in practically all his life. He wasn't sure what to look to, but he guessed that it would be away from Madison and the Co-op, perhaps away from this land where, in all its attempted kindness, he still couldn't quite settle in. Wherever he went, it had to be more than a physical relocation; it also had to reorganize his total psyche and insight so that even if he started all over again it would be a refreshing start. Maybe that place that Father Smith had mentioned during the interview was the place to go; the place called Cape Toria, which, he had found out, was actually in West Africa. It would be much different from the United States, and mixed in with its tangible differences would probably be those abstract differences that could enrich pieces of his life and bring them back together. The one or two books he had read on Cape Toria and the pictures he had seen could not have provided enough details about the country, but they engendered images that were more concrete

205

than illusionary. References to Beuvera were little and cited the nation as nonexistent; it was a former, recalcitrant experiment that had tried but failed to break away from Cape Toria for reasons that weren't explained fully. The images sparked interest and along with interest came fear and uncertainty that fiercely contested his yearning for painless contentment. His departure from the Co-op would entail big risks no matter where he headed on to, as long as the move foresaw major changes. He knew it but he also knew that without sacrifice he would continue to live and relive a cycle that was bare and without trust.

Monty's seclusion shifted from unconscious to conscious. It really shouldn't have been of any consequence; his personality, after all, was naturally aloof. But the more he withdrew, the more he discharged an air of hostility that either avoided others or begged to be avoided. He had opened up to and embraced the quality of divine and mundane tolerance that was part of Church tradition. Now he closed up to the same tradition. Those who observed his change didn't despise him; they simply allowed him to dictate when and how they interacted with him. To approach him with questions and solutions wasn't an option. When he didn't open up, chances were he didn't want to share his reasons for not opening up. If he didn't want to share, the issue was best left alone. It was an unwritten rule, but one well known and obeyed.

...

It was different when a young lady walked up to him after one Sunday morning mass and introduced herself as Dorothy. The name immediately weakened him and transported him back in time to the splendor of his relationship with his first best friend. He wanted to see that first Dorothy and began to reinvent her in the lady that stood before him. But his creation clashed with his recent promise to move further away from illusions in a bid to reach and grasp new possibilities.

Dorothy lived near campus on Johnson Street. She didn't work with the Church but she attended mass and benediction frequently, and not just on Sundays. Once or twice a week she also worshiped during early morning mass. She was probably a little older than Monty and worked as secretary in one of the departments on campus. She was down-to-earth and not very pretty in that biased, cover-page magazine sense. But with her sheer poise and self-confidence came a semblance of authority that couldn't be forged by any fabrication of beauty. It was an attitude that favored Monty who was in terrible need of the reassurance that comes with confidence.

But it wasn't her character or poise that first attracted him to her, it was her name.

"Hi there, Monty? Nice to meet you. My name is Dorothy."

She extended her hand and he received it respectfully. Before she continued, there was a short interval during which he took her in.

"I just want to let you know that I enjoy service much more because of you. I'm sure you've heard this many times, but you are exceptional with that flute."

"Thank you."

"I'm curious to know what your inspiration is. Do you ever teach people how to play?"

"I have never."

"Maybe you should. I've got to be leaving soon but do you mind if we talk about this some more?"

"No problem."

They exchanged numbers.

Eventually it just wasn't her name; he began to appreciate her sincerity and unpretentious elegance. She couldn't have been desperate for company and she had to be aware of the attention they received, mostly subtle and sometimes more than simple observation. There were those, after all, who cursed under their breaths at what they thought was an anomaly.

Her grace brought out a beauty that was hidden until you got close to her. She was petite but symmetrical, and not much taller than him. She kept her red hair short, letting her freckles stand out some more. He thought she had one of the best smiles.

His skills with the flute had drawn her to him. But with time she valued him for what she perceived as his strength and resolute spirit. Like Saint Peter, she obtained fairly substantial information about him before she abandoned questions that he refused to answer. From what she learned, she was able to assess him from an angle that very few were able to. He was alone in spite of his job, his gifts, and any support from the Church. He was a survivor, sad and hopeful. He was versatile, aspiring, and, no matter what his disposition seemed to say, he was kind on the inside. His confidence level vacillated, but that was understandable.

At first their meetings centered on the flute. They discussed it and he played both songs she requested and those he felt like playing. Sometimes he played when she visited him in his room, but mostly they met by the lake behind the University's Memorial Hall when it wasn't cold. He played for her and taught her as best he could. She became so engrossed to the point of buying her own flute.

Then they began to do coffee. They also watched an occasional movie. She didn't play a lot of board games, but the one or two she knew was enough for them to spend some time playing. When he learned that she played tennis, he was glad to go out with her to the courts beside the University's Southeast Recreation Facility. It had been a long time since he played and he was no match for her, but he hadn't lost the competitive zeal encouraged by the Kennedys, and he summoned it. There was no victory for him but their games were always spirited and, more than a simple workout, they had fun.

He didn't fantasize about this Dorothy, and Myra had taught him to keep his distance when there was no reason not to. He was afraid of disappointment and abandonment because of the first Dorothy, and Myra had scared him from trying to get physically or emotionally close to anyone. The punitive reaction to Beatrice and Saint Peter's romance, the grief that must have followed, and the remorseful feelings on his part, confirmed the need to be cynical about that type of intimacy. He and this Dorothy were affectionate yet they remained formal and subconsciously agreed on an invisible line that neither one of them crossed. He never felt as strongly for her as he had for the first Dorothy, but maybe it was because he resisted the desire.

Even when he taught her to use the flute, he knew that he held back. To share the much he knew and felt, he would have to get closer to her the same way a good teacher networks closely with his or her students. But because he panicked at the thought of getting close, he held back and taught as if from a distance.

Yet they were close, for he wished not to lose her. In his heart he did, but he kept it there.

Dorothy taught him that his strategy of a radical detachment from everyone and everything served no purpose. He had problems, but to ostracize himself and lose potential guidance was hardly the solution.

At first he enjoyed her company. In time he needed her.

War Songs

The Consulate refused to allow him to play with *Shekere*, one of Madison's recent musical sensations.   Comprising mostly African immigrants and a few Wisconsinites, the band played a brand of music called African *high-life* on which a vibrant *rock* beat was interposed.

Students flocked to anything alien and unfamiliar. Whenever *Shekere* played, whether it was indoors or outdoors by the lake, a huge crowd gathered to watch, dance, and frolic. There was never enough room for the crowd or enough performance time.   Once the band sounded its first beat, the people lost whatever sanity they came with.   Mostly students, they did what they considered to be African tribal dances, really a mixture of invented antics with an offbeat metallic rock frenzy. For those who received extra motivation from alcohol and marijuana, the frenzy was either slowed to an incantational pace or raised to a fierce trance state.   They sweated hard, they yelled, sometimes for no reason, they stepped on each other's toes, and they bumped into each other.   Curse words were exchanged freely and, though it was rare, a few punches could be thrown. But even punches couldn't take away from the fun they had. Whenever *Shekere* closed for the night, there was a lot of sorrow.

The Consulate associated the band with debauchery and would have nothing to do with it.   Besides, it hadn't quite recovered from the talk show and was more cautious about getting involved with what it doubted.   When *Shekere* invited Monty to play flute backup and a solo by way of a letter through the Consulate, the Consulate's response was swift and stern. Under no circumstance was Monty to be seen with any of the band members, let alone play with them.   As always, a copy of the denial letter was sent to Monty.

Monty read the letter with joy.   His joy had nothing to do with the Consulate's decision.   Here was another opportunity for him to aggravate someone. Too bad it was the only way he knew to get attention. He tore the letter and tossed it into his little, green trashcan.

About a week after he received the letter, he was rehearsing with the band. Bandleader Cornelius was indecisive when Monty showed up at their popular rehearsal studio on State Street. If the Consulate had changed its decision, he wasn't aware of it. He welcomed Monty but inquired about the Consulate's stand. Monty calmly pointed out that he wasn't there under the auspices of the Consulate; he came as an independent performer. While his response wasn't logical, Cornelius was itching for an excuse to have him perform with the band. So, he decided to believe Monty, at least for the time they would work together.

"I have come because I want to play with you. I like your band."

"That's great," Cornelius remarked, feigning what came across as no excitement. "But what about your organization?"

"Oh, this is just my decision. I just want to have more experience as a musician. They don't have anything to do with this."

Cornelius wanted him to play with the band. His contribution, no matter how minor, would embellish its style, making it more exclusive than it already was. More exclusive meant more notice. More notice guaranteed more money. Cornelius jumped at the opportunity. Scared of a lawsuit from the Consulate, he hurriedly drafted a memo that cited Monty as making the decision alone, willingly and without any pressure or undue persuasion, to play with *Shekere* during selected performances. The document underscored *Shekere's* innocence as a free spirited band that valued and supported the discovery and exhibition of talent by anyone, regardless of race, gender, nationality, ethnicity, religion, or sexual preference. In the event that Monty's involvement with the band resulted in any problem, the group exonerated itself beforehand and regretted that Monty would handle such dispute by himself and in a manner he thought best. The document was signed by Monty and Cornelius, notarized, and a copy forwarded to the Consulate.

Officials at the Consulate raged at Monty's insolence and obvious ingratitude. To make a decision on the matter, they had to circle a bureaucratic process that was unnecessarily long. Before they were done, Monty infuriated them some more by performing at least twice with *Shekere*.

True, his presence spiced up the music of *Shekere* and rejuvenated its reputation. After his first appearance with the group, the news spread. During his second appearance, the turnout increased dramatically. For those who had heard about him but not seen him up close or in performance, it was their chance to do so. Those who had seen him play before were glad to have another chance.

Father Smith didn't feel like delivering the Consulate's letter. After his last penal session with Monty, he contemplated his reasons for chastising the refugee. He contemplated until he was remorseful. Because of the lack of simple justification, he felt foolish. This time, though the charge was more concrete, he couldn't endorse the Consulate's tactics. Its initial error was the failure to assess Monty's sudden assertive and subversive behavior. Father Smith suspected that it had something to do with his desire to know and re-identify with a past that was as ambiguous as it was dismal. But he kept his analysis to himself, hoping that someone else would be chosen to run these errands. They were becoming a little too depressing for him.

Monty read the letter. Short of cursing him out, it was vehement and condemned his affiliations with a band he had been denied performance for or with, and whose style either flaunted decadence or encouraged it. It was unbecoming for a Christian man of his standing, an imminent member of the Cathedral's choir. Couldn't he see how *Shekere's* music countered the sacred musical tradition that he was a part of? Under no circumstance was he to play with *Shekere* again. If he disobeyed a second time, he would be summarily disciplined as thought fit by the Consulate. The letter finally warned that

Shekere would face legal action should he ever be seen with the group again. A copy of the letter was sent to the band.

After Monty read the letter, Father Smith gave a short sermon on the need for him to desist from such daring behavior. Much unlike him, he avoided eye contact with Monty. He wasn't keen on giving the sermon and was glad to end it as quickly as possible. Monty listened patiently, but it was deceptive and Father Smith was aware. He knew not to take Monty for granted anymore, or to draw conclusions based on his mannerisms. A nearly inaudible "thank you" was Monty's response to the sermon.

His job done, Father Smith exited fast and without ceremony. He knew that his visit, sermon, and the letter were quite meaningless to Monty and, again, he felt like a fool. He had wasted his time and so had the Consulate. Monty wasn't done and Father Smith knew it. Clearly, he was on a journey and would not stop, look back, or retrace his steps until he arrived at a final destination, wherever that would be. Instead of sharing his views on Monty with Consulate officials, Father Smith decided he would let them find out for themselves. For one, he didn't want to go through the annoying, sometimes humiliating, experience of trying to get them to listen.

Indeed Monty wasn't yet done.

...

When the notorious Boyz R Us hard rock band from Milwaukee visited Madison, he didn't wait for them to invite him. Perhaps they didn't plan to, so he put a plan into motion. He went after them. That the group lodged at the Howard Johnson Hotel off of Highway 95 was an open secret. The group didn't want it to be public knowledge but it was, thanks to regular and journalistic gossip.

He wrote a short letter and sealed it in an envelope addressed BOYZ ROCKBAND. Then he took it to the hotel and dropped it off with the receptionist. He introduced himself in the letter, expressed his desire to play with the band, and left his phone number just in case. The next day after he returned from work, he received a call from Short Stuff, the lead vocalist.

Their conversation centered on proof that Monty was indeed Monty, the guy who dazzled people with his flute. Monty's only proof was "I am the one, try me and see." His words carried little conviction but Short Stuff decided to "try him and see." He arranged a meeting with Monty over the phone. The meeting was for that same night. If he were the one, the meeting would be well worth it. If he were a fraud, he wouldn't be a threat to five men in the bar of a hotel, two of whom were hefty.

As he made his way to Howard Johnson right after the *M* bus dropped him almost in front of it, he wondered at his boldness. For a moment even he couldn't believe what he was doing. He had actually come out at night to meet with a group of men whom he knew nothing about. Either he was committed in his quest to move on or he was going crazy.

True to Short Stuff's word, they were waiting for him at the bar on the first level. Even in the dim light he could see how they looked like a collection of abstract art. The stench of cigarette smoke hit him hard when he arrived their table. They were drinking too.

They all wore black leather jackets and pants, and long black boots dotted with shiny metals. Their outfits were also dotted with bright silver and gold-looking metal objects, including short chains that hung from different places.

Each one colored his hair differently. There was one whose hair displayed a motley of colors, was fan-shaped, and stood out like a peacock's tail. Their faces were also painted with a variety of colors and designs, and one had smeared his lips with very dark lipstick. It was only after he spent some time with them that he observed how their tongues had been colored too. And then there were tattoos, lots and lots of tattoos. On their necks, arms, and faces. They must have also had them on parts not visible to Monty. The tattoos were of many things. Of women's names, of flowers, of animals, of faces, and of naked women.

But the only thing that troubled Monty was the piercing. They stuck pins above their eyes, through their tongues, and through their noses. To say nothing of the numerous gold earrings that lined their ears.

From street posters Monty knew what to expect, but no replicas could compare with actually meeting the band members. He was dumbfounded for about 30 seconds during which he regarded them as closely as the lights would allow him.

Their behavior contrasted with their appearance. Soon after Monty made his way to their table, Short Stuff rose to welcome him. Monty wondered why he was called *Short Stuff* since he was well over six feet and towered over him.

"Ah, you must be the great flute player, huh? Welcome man, welcome."

He gave Monty a handshake and proceeded to introduce him to all the band members. They all shook his hand. But their names were either too weird, too long, or too difficult to remember. *Short Stuff* came closest to being normal, and was the only name he remembered. He relaxed within a short time because they were very nice. Although he politely refused the beer or liquor they offered him, he was glad to have a virgin Margarita for the first time in his life.

They told him what they had heard or read about his mastery of the flute. If it was true that a number of groups had shown interest in him, surely he was good. When they asked him about his inspiration and his ability to play by ear, his answers were fairly constant. He credited God and the Catholic Church. They thought his answers were "cool" since they also saw themselves as spiritual people. He hoped they wouldn't ask him about his family and past. They didn't.

Before they discussed his playing with the band, they beat about the bush a little and talked about Madison. Their opinions varied and they described the city as old-fashioned, nice, boring, and awesome. They had already performed once and had two shows to go in the area. His role would be largely improvisational. If he could do what they heard, then he would

216

be able to accompany their winding, multi-rhythmic tempo with a high-pitched medley that blended in nicely. Since a specific beat would not be sustained, he didn't have to worry about losing track; it hardly ever happened. There would be a break or two during which he would slow things down with solo performances. Rehearsal times and venue were worked out and agreed upon, including the amount he would earn.

Boyz R Us didn't expose its enthusiasm that night. A band that relied heavily on the bizarre, using Monty was to its advantage. Monty would appear in the midst of all the madness and radiance, looking different in every possible way. He would be a misnomer and yet his being out of place would favor the band greatly. It would raise its status as weird and unpredictable, the qualities that attracted it to thousands of young people. And so it was.

...

Monty was a sight on stage. His best attempt at being a nonconformist was wearing a pair of tight, black jeans and a red T-shirt that had *The Badgers* written in bold white on the front and back. It was in a bid to fit in with the radical persona of Boyz R Us. The jeans exaggerated his bowlegs and the T-shirt was stretched to the limit by his distended tummy, so that you couldn't see his belt from the front. His bright yellow socks didn't match anything, and it wasn't meant to. He was being "cool," which was one of the favorite concepts and pursuits of the band members. It was the first and last time he would do anything this ridiculous.

Audience members went through phases in their reaction. They were confused, not sure whether Monty was actually on stage to play with the band. Then they doubted. When it was obvious that Monty was indeed part of the show, their acceptance of him was mixed with amazement. Those who had seen or heard about him strained to ensure that their eyes were not deceiving them. Others tried to rationalize his being up there. Then they found humor in his presence. But most of all, and especially when the show began with Monty playing along, they were thrilled and, again, overpowered by the band's imagination, one that always caught them by surprise. This was the main reason why he was there and the band was very happy with the effect. It added to their reputation as unruly in an entertaining way. With the reputation came fame and infamy. With fame and infamy came praise and condemnation. With praise and condemnation came more attention. With more attention came more money.

Monty couldn't recognize a structure to the songs and music on stage, or the activities that took place on and off stage, though he tried to. The phenomena were alien to him. While as a flute player he was not rigid in his style or choices, whatever he decided on adhered to a particular sequence or related sequence, until he changed to something else. But here the songs climbed in pitch and fell without warning. Sometimes they were rendered in the form of meaningless words that transformed into a drone that lasted too long. The music was an accumulation of too many impatient sounds that struggled to be heard; Monty didn't even try to make sense of it. But somehow he managed to sustain tunes that penetrated everything and stood out because he played into a microphone specially provided him. It was as if his melodies sidestepped everything, resounding above and beyond what could easily be described as mayhem. This admixture of soothing, sometimes soft, yet dynamic flute music with hard rock instrumentation fascinated the fans. They hadn't experienced it before now. It was a deviation that worked out well and everyone was at least contented. And then there were those intervals when Monty played alone, providing much needed solace and rest, but only for a brief moment before the place exploded again.

Dancing among band members came in the form of bodily and facial distortions. They jumped around, rolled around on the floor, and ran all over the stage. Sometimes a band member lost it all and smashed his guitar on stage and the crowd cheered and cried for more. A lot of guitars were smashed that night. There were a lot of spares too. Now and then a band member dived into the crowd. He was immediately caught by a sea of waiting hands, hoisted above numerous heads, and passed around in that way until he was returned to the stage.

The audience often passed around a small cylindrical object too. Smoke oozed from one end of the object and gave off a smell that Monty was a little familiar with. It reminded him of Saint Peter's room for some reason. When the object was handed to you, you took a long drag, inhaled deeply, and then blew out the smoke. If Monty were closer to the people, he would have seen how the object turned their eyes red. He would have also remembered how Saint Peter's eyes were sometimes that color.

Audience response came in the form of screams and loud obscene utterances aimed at no one in particular. Dancing came in the form of any type of body movement and disorderly antics that were supposed to imitate the performers. Fans ran around, pranced around, and rolled on the floor too. Monty was bothered when a fistfight broke out in a section of the crowd. He was more bothered by the ovation from people who stood close by, some of whom would eventually join the fracas. Within a short time that section of the crowd was involved in a free-for-all, punching, biting, wrestling, and tearing. A few young ladies even joined in. Monty came to realize that such exchange of blows was a common audience reaction; it was their way of participating more intimately in the show, and of showing their appreciation for a great show. It was an indication of how lively and successful the show truly was.

Monty couldn't keep still. He normally played his flute with very limited motion. But this wasn't a normal show and there was too much activity for him to stay still. So he danced if what he did could be called dancing. He didn't do the monkey strut for which he was famous as a child. Perhaps he wouldn't have been able to. It was a long time and maybe he had forgotten to do the steps. So he did something else. He squirmed and went into intermittent spasms as if he itched all over. One moment he looked like a dying earthworm, the next moment he looked like he was about to go into an epileptic fit. Compared to the dances on and offstage, his was not elaborate, but it was peculiar and there were those who noticed and laughed. But it wasn't mockery; it was an expression of joy for a show that carried so much originality and inspired so much innovation.

He appeared twice with the group. During his second appearance the crowd swelled with people who wanted to see this special addition to Boyz R Us.

...

The fans loved him. Some non-fans who knew him thought he had made an interesting excursion into another musical experience. Others believed he was in great need of psychiatric help.

Dorothy had been disturbed when he confided in her about his plans to appear with Boyz R Us. She wanted him to broaden his horizon and explore all possibilities that made sense. To her Boyz R Us made no sense. She had attended his performances with *Shekere* and had even bought him dinner to congratulate him for doing a fine job. All she said when he told her about the rock band was "I don't know, Monty, I don't know." She let him know her misgivings without saying too much or being forceful. She was his friend and wanted to be as supportive as possible. For that reason she didn't want to belittle or dismiss his plans. When it was clear that he had made up his mind, she left the matter alone. She knew that persuading him to see differently was useless. Instead she prayed fervently for him and begged the Virgin Mary to send her angels to protect him.

Local newspapers carried the story. Most praised the band for taking the risk to experiment beyond what was thought to be practical. Monty's skills were perceived on an even higher plane. No one was known to have shifted that abruptly from church altar to hard rock stage, and to adjust so perfectly. More conservative dailies thrashed the show as nothing but an exploitation of Monty's talent. He was only an exhibit, a cheap sideshow that would increase audience attendance and bring in more money. It was a shame that a man who played for the Church would change sides so recklessly. Whatever amount he was paid, he had stooped too low, from church altar to satanic stage of hard rock. He should never have been seen there. One conservative paper said that on stage he looked like an ugly, fat toad in heat. The only difference was that a toad knew to stay in its habitat.

But Monty's business with the band had little to do with money. And the band had not dragged him in; he had essentially imposed himself on it.

Officials at the Consulate fumed when they read the papers. They had heard and had enough and decided to take swift, decisive action. Father Smith was calm; none of this surprised him.

Philip U. Effiong

Crossroads

He hated to have to be there, yet he was relieved. He was Monty's chief counselor, even mentor in some ways, so he couldn't escape the process. As he raved silently, Father Smith, his eyes now set on becoming a full-fledged bishop, also foresaw an end to a conflict that wasn't getting any less spectacular. He had no clue what the turn out would be, which didn't matter since it was not what he cared about. That it would soon be over was his only concern. Once the case was either closed or transferred to some faraway place, a sense of lost peace would return and he would pursue the final stages leading up to his ordination without diversion or uncertainty.

The Consulate's subsidiary office was located in a tall building about a block away from the imposing, white Capitol building. Downtown Madison bordered the upper end of State Street and was home to a number of important government offices. Monty remembered the day a huge crowd gathered in front of the Capitol. Every now and then a speaker walked up to one of the three mounted microphones and made an elaborate speech, to which the crowed either clapped or yelled in approval. Before the crowd dispersed, a few men wearing long feathers held down by headbands, hammered out a monotonous beat from four heavy-looking drums. As follow-up to the beat, they let out a continuous howl broken erratically by what sounded like a smothered chant. Monty didn't understand the song and neither did majority of the people. But it didn't matter. A section danced around the drummers and the drums, others danced and clapped from a distance, while the rest, like Monty, just watched. It didn't take long for Monty to learn that the gathering was organized by sympathizers and supporters of the rights of Native Americans to spearfish. Recently there had been an outcry, even violent protests, against their spearfishing season. Monty couldn't understand how something so commonplace could generate such political novelty.

There was the middle-aged man who sat on the Capitol steps one cold afternoon, and though he wore gloves, a coat, a woolen hat, boots, and a scarf wrapped around his neck, he shivered noticeably. Maybe it was because most of what he had on was old and worn, and therefore unable to fully serve their original purpose. Beside him, and supported by one hand, was a huge sign that read, "IF I AM RESPONSIBLE ENOUGH TO WORK AND GIVE MONEY FOR MY KIDS, WHY CAN'T I SEE THEM?" As he walked by on his way to a coffee date with Dorothy, Monty read the sign but couldn't make anything of it. There was no way for him to discern the suppressed chicanery and pitiful drama that revolved around another institution that ironically called itself Family Court, too powerful for its own good. On his way back from the coffee date, the man was still there, still shivering and neglected, but relentless. The cold had become more brutal so that he locked his fingers together and leaned his chin into them. The sign lay on the steps beside him. Under the growing darkness, the words were barely visible. Monty felt sorry for him, but even worse that he couldn't reach out and do something.

...

When Father Smith handed him the Consulate's letter about two weeks before, he received it with as much indifference as he could muster. He had expected it so it came as no surprise. Communication between both of them was kept to a minimum and they liked it that way. Father Smith was eager to leave as quickly as possible and Monty had nothing important to address.

The letter was filled with rage and rebuked Monty's audacity and ingratitude. It suspended his job with the Church until the matter at hand was well taken care of. After evaluating his steady fall from grace as a good Christian music maker who, "for thirty pieces," now chose to "betray his faith," he was summoned to the Consulate office. He noted the date and time, tore up the letter, and tossed it into his trashcan.

That morning Father Smith knocked on his door at around 9:00 a.m. His appointment with Consulate officials was at 10:00 a.m. They walked down to the office together, barely speaking to each other. It was a strange and abrupt twist in a relationship that had otherwise been cordial and marked by moderate conversation at least. Monty had expected such nuances and mentally prepared himself for them. He hadn't foreseen a smooth ride when he decided on a radical quest for another world that he as yet didn't know but trusted.

The conference room and main lounge of the Consulate subsidiary office was exquisite and made more so by its white tone. Everything was either white, cream white, or whitish, including the soft, leather couch that Monty and Father Smith shared in the living room section. At the other end was a long table covered with white cloth, and around which were arranged several white chairs. Monty refused all offers of coffee, cookies, juice, or fruit. Everyone else nibbled on or drank something. The Consul, a wise-looking reverend mother from Ireland, was there. So were her secretary, a bishop, and two officials in black suits that contrasted with the domineering white.

No one asked him why he defied orders from the Consulate. No one asked him why he performed with Boyz R Us. No one seemed to be interested in why he suddenly transformed from dutiful and compliant to stubborn and recalcitrant. Father Smith thought he knew why. In his heart he also objected to the Consulate's method of handling the case. But he didn't say anything. He wasn't about to face the rigors of convincing the Consulate that his analysis was valid. The whole thing had drained him and he decided not to stress himself anymore, even if it meant the difference between justice and the lack thereof. His prayer was for it to be over with, regardless of what it took or what decisions were made. In the end justice would probably not be served. The truth was sad and his hopes were selfish, but in the end at least normalcy and some sanity would be reached.

The Consulate had determined that Monty committed an unpardonable offense. Simple. He had been warned after he performed with *Shekere*, so there was no excuse. There would be no room, too, for defense or explanation. He would not be judged any more or less than he had already been judged. And since his defiance came across as planned and methodical, a probable case of mental imbalance was also thrown out. Years back it may have counted, but not now.

Monty was viewed as a ward, an exemplary ward of the Church in fact, who had, for reasons best known to him, turned his back on the Institution that had lifted and preserved him from the day he was born. The Church all but owned him in other words. For him to now challenge it was incomprehensible, let alone acceptable. No, there would be no room for him to defend or explain himself. And while Father Smith's conscience constantly urged him to speak up on behalf of Monty, he swallowed the urge. Disgusting though the entire experience was to him, the only solution he envisaged was one that would permit him to pursue his career and thrust him into another line of responsibility that wouldn't require him to counsel anyone devoid of a sense of self.

The session was formally opened by a short prayer led by the bishop whose disposition displayed both the stern and the benign. After recounting everything Monty already knew, essentially a repetition of the last letter sent to him, the Consul concluded by announcing what he actually hoped would be the ultimate decision.

"As our regulations require, the penalty for dangerous, unruly, or unusual behavior is to send the dependent concerned to an environment that is considered appropriate and rehabilitating. Do you understand?" When she asked the question, she stared right at Monty. Monty stared right back but didn't say anything. The stare hit Mother O'Colonel and careful observation would have shown that she reeled back slightly. In a few seconds she gathered herself, during which she took a sip from her glass of orange juice.

"We have decided to send you," she continued, but before she could go any further he cut her off. The interruption was as annoying as when he raised further interest in his past at the PBS interview. Attempts at intimidating him and putting him in his place had obviously failed.

"Can I say something?"

"No you can't, especially since I am not done yet. You should know better than to interrupt me."

"But I have something to say."

"Well, you can't say it, especially since I'm not done yet. And I know that you understand me perfectly."

No one else spoke, but the tension began to build at tremendous speed and they all felt it. The fall had arrived with a cold that projected a bitter winter. That day in particular was very cold and the heat in the room was on moderate, which was just right. That is, up until the tension began to mount and then it was as if the heat had been set at 120 degrees. With the stuffy feeling came a stillness and a craving for fresh air and water. The stillness was overpowering such that all breathing seemed to have stopped. Although everyone stared at the other person, it appeared more like they stared through each other without seeing anything. It was a blank expression with confusion written all over it. Up until this point the Consul had been taking careful, royal sips from her glass of juice. Suddenly she downed everything and after she placed the glass back on the side stool to her left, she raised her head to reveal a face that was clearly agitated and bloodshot. She began to tremble all over.

"You will be relocated to …" but again he cut her off.

"I will not go there."

"I beg your pardon! You've not even allowed me to tell you where we've decided to send you, young man."

"If it's anywhere in America I don't want to go there."

"And since when did you decide where we place you, eh? I'll have you know that I've had enough of your interruptions and obnoxious, rude behavior. We are in charge of you and we'll continue to be in charge of you, whether you like it or not! That means we'll make decisions that you'll have to obey and you'll have no choice but to obey. Understand?"

"Are you going to be in charge of me until I die?"

"If that's what it takes, yes!" Mother O'Colonel was virtually screaming and Monty had never seen a redder face. His calm caught their attention. It was unreal, in a sense spooky.

"I don't want to go there."

"Young man, don't you think you've caused enough problems?" It was one of the men in a black suit.

"No!" Monty's "no" was emphatic and halted the man briefly but he didn't want to accept defeat and decided to engage Monty some more.

"Well I'll let you know that you have. And you should be grateful for all that the Church has done for you, not bite the hand that has fed you. Show some gratitude." The Consul took over.

"Yes, show some gratitude even if you are incapable of showing respect. What were you when the Church picked you from misery, from nothing and gave you the opportunity to have a life? What were you?"

Monty's calm concealed the hurt that her words caused him. Otherwise, she may have stopped there. Since he acted so undaunted, she pressed on.

"Nothing! Do you hear me sir? Nothing! Without us you'd be nothing! Invisible, not even dirt. Nothing! D'you hear me!"

"Maybe we should calm down a little." It was the other man in black. His words carried an appeasing touch that everyone needed, especially the Consul who was visibly shaken as if beyond repair. She would have preferred if everyone didn't notice how her breathing had become faster and heavier. To hide the fact would have been futile, so she didn't bother. The tension and imaginary heat stayed, but the fury was gradually replaced by quiet so that heartbeats could almost be heard. After a moment, during which everyone seemed to retire momentarily into a private place of refuge, Mother O'Colonel spoke again. Her words were broken by tremendous, short heaves, a sign that she was fighting heard to normalize her breathing. And she still trembled all over.

"It is important, Monty (*short heaves*) for you to understand that in the case of extreme violations, which your insubordinate behavior (*short heaves*) may soon add up to, extreme penalties may be required (*short heaves*). In your case that would (*short heaves*) be a revocation of your citizenship based on our case and request (*short heaves*) and your subsequent deportation to your (*short heaves*) place of birth or wherever we want you deported. This country has enough criminals and will be glad to get rid of (*short heaves*) anything that is a potential threat to (*short heaves*) safety and decency."

"That's what I want, send me back." His words, especially since they were delivered with astonishing calm, caused another wave of consternation that came with its own brand of discomfort. But his calm was a camouflage. He burned on the inside with hurt. The Consul's words had ignited a flame in him and the heat continued to eat away at everything that was inside of him. For the first time in a long while there was motion and people shifted uncomfortably on their seats. They looked at each other, and not simply to confirm that the other person was still there. They gave each other questioning looks. There was no other way to voice their mystification.

"There you go again, interrupting. Haven't you learned yet? You will have no say in deciding where we send you." This time the Consul's words weren't as forceful and they were expressed more out of necessity to speak than to communicate.

It was here that Father Smith caved in. All along he had held back from saying anything though the pressure to speak out increased with each rise in heat, anxiety, and resentment. Each time he had fought back, hoping and waiting for the confrontation to end so that he could leave and get away from it all. But when Monty asked to be deported, he couldn't fight back anymore. He knew that it was his chance to help the refugee, to create an option so that he could escape the labyrinth that was his life, to help him seek out something else even if it didn't necessarily come with all the gratification he longed for. Besides, the whole thing would still end anyway, especially if his intervention was of any use. It was his chance to do what he resisted all along, and without going through annoying formalities. If he didn't speak out now, he would be a coward. He would never forgive himself. He spoke out.

"Em, may I say something, Honorable Mother O'Colonel."

"Yes you may, Father Smith."

"I understand that what Monty has done is despicable and his behavior this morning has been, em, careless, maybe poor. But I honestly believe he should be sent back."

"What?" the Consul interjected. "Are you suggesting that we grant him his wish? I think that would really be encouraging unruly behavior and would most certainly trivialize our desire to discourage disobedience and rebellion. Don't you think?"

"Mother O'Colonel, I'm certainly not defending irresponsible behavior. But think about it, while Monty has interrupted you today, he hasn't used foul language, or cursed you out, or been overtly confrontational."

"Really? Oh, now you're saying it was okay for him to interrupt me!"

"Not at all, Mother. But, let's think about it, what other options did he have? How else could he have expressed himself? I mean, we never gave him the opportunity to tell us why he is suddenly behaving differently. It's not in his nature; there has to be a reason. For all the years we've known him, he has been the very opposite of what we now know him to be. He has never had the chance to defend himself."

"Well, I guess we're guilty of being unfair to him. After all we've done for him all these years. You really think his behavior deserves a defense or an explanation? You think it deserves our understanding?"

"What I'm saying, as a counselor, is that there is always a reason for a spectacular change in behavior. Before drawing conclusions and reacting to such change, it is always best to first understand the basis for the change. Maybe we haven't done that."

"Really?"

"Really." The more he spoke, the more Father Smith became confident and forthright. "Do we really expect that at some point a grown man would not inquire about his background, his birthplace, his parents, exactly who he is? This is not the first time we've had to deal with a problem like this. Think about it. That's what Monty's recent, sometimes outrageous, and rebellious behavior has been all about. He has had no other method of inquiring, of asking questions, of expressing his feelings or his loneliness or his pain."

"Wow. Good talk Father Smith, I'm surprised you're not a lawyer." The Consul's remark was in a bid to constantly present herself as being in charge and, therefore, unswayed by the counselor. Her carefree stance was fake though, and deep down the core of what Father Smith said had touched her such that she began to look upon Monty with some compassion. But she decided to camouflage her reconsideration of everything. She thought she had to.

"Maybe it is worth thinking about what Father Smith has said." For the first time the heavily bearded, South African bishop spoke.

"Perhaps, perhaps," the Consul agreed uncharacteristically, nodding her head in the process. Her face had let go of a lot of its red, her trembling had ceased, and her breathing was almost back to normal.

Father Smith saw another opening and jumped in.

"It would be good to think about these things. It would be. And I think it would be best to send him back to his home of origin, not deport him. Let him keep his American citizenship. I know he is grateful to the Church for everything. He shows it by working hard for the Church and obeying all Church laws. How can he not love the Church? If he continues to work for the Church, as I believe he will, it would be best to allow him to travel freely. Let him keep his citizenship, please. He should be allowed to explore as much as he can about himself and his past. But he should also be allowed the privilege of free travel and free work for the Church."

"Okay Attorney Smith, ha, ha, ha. I think we've all heard enough." The Consul's attempt at infusing humor into what almost became a disaster was another strategy, though it failed, of appearing in control. In reality she had no desire to pursue anything else other than Father Smith's requests. She was weary and prepared to see an end to the matter, but hidden even deeper was a yearning to apologize for some of the things spoken under frustration. Which was not to be since her position, in order not to lose its prestige and exhibition of preeminence, was one that spurned any hints of guilt or suggestions of regret. As much as she wouldn't have wanted it to be known, when she spoke again her voice betrayed her sense of relief.

"I believe we all know what standard procedure demands whenever a case of this nature hints at indecision or conflicting opinions. We'll all have to come to an agreement; otherwise majority will have to rule. We are going to put it to vote. Monty, will you please step out for a minute. We'll call you back when we are done."

Preoccupied for a while with each other, the Consulate officials had diverted attention from Monty, the main reason why they were there. During that time Monty remained silent, his head bowed. When they refocused on him, they realized the truth that he hadn't been as silent as he looked. His shudders had been tight and hardly detectable. Now, when they concentrated on him again, he couldn't hide the tears. Father Smith noticed and decided to escort him out to the corridor himself. He returned, only to be challenged by the Consul again; it didn't matter that a relaxed mood had almost been restored.

"You do know, Father Smith, that Consulate policies demand that dependents be detached from their macabre pasts. Wouldn't we be going against this policy if we send Monty back to his place of birth?"

"I don't think so. For one, that policy best serves the interest of children. Monty is a man. His progress also shows great potential. Isn't it true that not long from now the Church may very well grant him complete autonomy? And then what? Are we going to continue to make choices on his behalf?"

Mother O'Colonel had heard all that needed to be heard and Father Smith knew that no other questions were forthcoming. He leaned back on the couch and took in a deep breath, really a sigh of relief. For one who had planned to stay mute, he had said a lot and couldn't believe it himself. But even more unbelievable for him at this time was his original plan not to speak out. He was satisfied with his effort, no matter the outcome. He was glad that he had spoken out. He had done his best which is all that counted.

The Consul's voice interrupted his reflection and brought him back to the room. "We will now go ahead and agree on three proposals concerning Monty, after which, by vote, we will make a final decision on his relocation and redeployment."

...

Father Smith informed Monty when they were done, and escorted him back into the room. The Consul didn't follow any particular protocol before reading out the final decision of the committee. It was unofficial and would be made official after a letter was sent to Monty and a copy sent to the Consulate headquarters in New York.

Monty would be sent back to West Africa at the end of the year; that is, in about three months. He would go under the auspices of the Catholic Church, which would plan and ascertain the trip. He would also travel as an American citizen. The Church would also authorize his pursuit of any career and his employment on any level, within or outside the Church. His trip was not final, meaning that he could return to the United States when it was considered suitable or necessary. Until such a time when his maturation and mental state were assessed as fit for complete autonomy, he would remain a ward of and/or affiliated to the Church. For the time being his job with the Church would remain terminated since his recent acts of defiance disqualified him from Church employment and were bound to set a bad precedent if he was reemployed right away

When they dispersed the businesslike ambience at the beginning remained though all tensions had eased off. There were no handshakes, "thank yous," or salutations. The Consul officially dismissed the session and that was that.

On his way back to the Co-op Monty sighted Father Smith about a block ahead. He called out to him and when the counselor spun around Monty ran up to meet him.

"All I want to say is thank you. Thank you so much Father Smith."

They shook hands before Father Smith leaned over and pat him a few times on his back. The tears welled up in both their eyes.

The meeting had lasted about four hours. Monty was twenty-nine years old.

The Ribbon

He had never been this isolated and yet he wasn't quite alone. For the three months leading up to his departure, he was mostly by himself, except for the times he spent with Dorothy. They had grown closer and acted as if life was incomplete without the other, yet they still enforced limits when it came to intimacy. All socializing with co-workers and colleagues at the Cathedral became a thing of the past and even with co-members of the Co-op interaction was distant and ceremonious. It barely went beyond a courteous "hi" in the corridor or bathroom, or beyond greetings and exchanges that were merely part of mealtime etiquette.

Yet being alone, strangely enough, did not lead to regret and despair. He found strength, not in his flute this time, but in the knowledge that change was inevitable, whether it was change for the better or not. He couldn't know for sure, but he knew that he had worked against accepting and adjusting to a situation, and instead had pursued the possibility of something more substantial than what he was expected to be used to. He was apprehensive at the thought of the new direction he was headed and yet he was excited by the anticipation of difference. The thought offered more hope than the acceptance of a stagnant, even if sheltered world that went around in cycles.

Since he had been *relieved* of his position at Our Lady of Lourdes Cathedral--that was how the letter from the Consulate put it--, it changed things a little bit. His stipends were less but at least he didn't work for them. Under Consulate directives he was also required to close his bank account. While he didn't have to, he was strongly advised, in a manner that almost came off as an order, not to touch his savings. Together with a traveling allowance, the money would come in handy during his trip. He wasn't to expect a huge allowance, the more reason why he was forewarned to leave the money alone.

235

He didn't stop attending mass and benediction at the Cathedral. Neither did he slow down on his daily, sacred routines of Bible reading and prayers as especially stressed upon by Father Murphy. He usually sat at the back of the Church and drew glances from people who were used to seeing him up on the altar playing his flute, reaching deep into and firing up the soul of the congregation. But Monty had dealt with stares practically all his life and so ignored the sneaky stares very easily. He didn't even have to stare back to counter a stare that was too long and too direct. Because it was God's house, the lookers conducted themselves with careful discretion that had to be occasionally fake. Monty had also come to associate playing at the Cathedral with payment, so he didn't offer to and he wasn't asked to.

His infamous performance with Boyz R Us was well known and while no one approached him on the subject, their stares were accompanied by perceptions that varied greatly. Some sympathized with him and commended his courage at testing another space that he was barred from in principle. They missed the passion that he brought to services. Others denounced his violation of an unwritten code that separated him from the world of the likes of Boyz R Us, and were insulted by his continued attendance of services at the Cathedral. Within this group there were those who had been disappointed after he worked with *Shekere*. But they were prepared to forgive and reaccept him into his consecrated role; after all, *Shekere* wasn't that sinful in its attitude and entertainment style. Compared to Boyz R Us, the band was actually mild and tolerable. Not Boyz R Us. Its seditious styles reached a height that was comparable to demonic. And yet there were those who didn't care. These ones missed him too. But no one said anything to him on the subject. When he was approached, it was in deference to him as the finest flute player around, and ended with a few words of salutation. "Hi there Monty." "Good to see you again." Physical contact did not go past a handshake or a pat on the shoulder.

The few times he visited the Kennedy home before his departure, he felt the discomfort from their end. While he had to adjust to this new trend, he felt no discomfort from his end. They remained politely formal and more detached than usual. It wasn't anything malicious, just a sudden realization that in all these years they had not really come to know him, and buried inside of him was much more of a complex character than they would ever know. They knew not to make any more assumptions about him because he could spring a surprise from nowhere and without the slightest warning. Maybe not scared of him, they began to grow defensive and weary. What would the other *him* that they couldn't see come up with? And what would the results be? Was it safe to have him around? No, their discomfort wasn't anything spiteful, just a sudden concern, one that required extra attention as it did extra caution and distance. They had a standard and class to preserve after all, and only wanted the assurance that they weren't going to be threatened by one who had come to be stranger rather than more familiar. They sought the assurance from behind a make-believe wall that they found necessary to erect.

But none of the Kennedys monitored him as closely as Myra, though she also remained the most detached. It was impossible to know how concerned she was, being that she never seemed to bother about his presence or absence. She was the most detached when it came to Monty, but she had also been the only one to have an encounter with him that was frightening and puzzling. None of them knew, so none of them could decode the worries that were veiled behind what came across as indifference. And like everyone else, no one confronted him with the matter of Boyz R Us.

···

Thai Menu was on the outskirts of Campus and served some of the finest Thai meals. At 4:00 p.m. it was already dark outside, a sure sign that winter was steadily taking over. The light was dim so that the darkness on the outside appeared to have carried its influence to the inside. There were a few people in there and this added to the dullness of the reddish hue, one that brought back a fleeting memory of Red Red News. The round table was appropriate as it could sit only two. Dorothy sat across from him; she was treating. In about a week Monty would be leaving and this was a farewell dinner. Even at their last dinner their relationship was still one of discretion. They were still eager for each other's company, yet once together they withdrew even as they reached out, careful not to cross that very thin line that separated affection from wild intimacy. She would miss him, perhaps more than he would miss her. For while she was losing something that had become an important part of her ordinary life, he was looking forward to adding a lot more that would quite easily overshadow his loss of her. They each wanted to express how much they would miss the other person, but the passion that would otherwise have been let loose was contained by the self-consciousness that controlled their friendship.

"I hope you have a nice trip Monty, you will be missed by a lot of us."

"Thank you, I will miss a lot of people too."

"Oh, I'm so glad you taught me how to play the flute. I'll continue to practice and learn after you leave."

"That would be nice. One day you will become a great player. I pray you do."

"Ha, I don't know about that. No matter how much I know, I don't think I'll ever be like you."

"Don't say that, don't. Everything is possible. With God everything is possible."

"Well, thank you, I hope your prediction is true."

They ate and drank mostly in silence. A comment was thrown in every now and then, and they looked at each other from time to time, careful not to gaze.

"So, are you excited about going to Africa?"

"Yes, a little bit."

"Are you sure you'll ever come back?"

"Maybe."

"Do you know much about the place?"

"A little bit."

"You know, since I learned about your trip, I read a few things about Africa. Interesting place."

"Hmm." He nodded, his eyebrows slightly raised, an indication that he half thought it was interesting that she read about Africa because of him, and an indication that he wondered about the purpose of her doing so.

There was some more little conversation. They weren't in the habit of talking much, as trusting and as free as they were with each another. And even if they typically talked more, they still wouldn't have been able to. The curried sauce was very spicy and she handled it much better than he did. His eyes watered and his nose ran constantly. Embarrassed, he downed glass after glass of water and orange juice, and visited the bathroom twice. But the food tasted good and they both enjoyed it.

After she paid the bill and he thanked her, she looked into his eyes, perhaps longer than she ever had and with more affection than she had ever expressed.

"Well, this is the last meal we'll be having together, I'm glad you could make it."

"I'm glad, I enjoyed it."

"I have something for you, something to remember me by."

Monty didn't understand. Whenever he had received anything from her, it was expected, like Christmas and birthday cards. He had also learned to give her cards because she first gave him. But whatever it was she was going to give him at the restaurant was unexpected. Somewhat baffled, he looked back at her with a half smile that seemed to suggest suspicion more than it did curiosity, and waited patiently.

"It's a souvenir."

He didn't know what the word meant, which sparked his interest some more. But he continued to wait patiently. She

239

reached into her pocketbook and removed a red ribbon. A tiny replica of a shinning silver flute was tied to one end.

"Keep this, Monty. It will always remind you of me. It will always bring you good luck."

"Thank you." He received it graciously, not sure what to do with it, and lay it on the table in front of him. Looking down at it, he was forced to reflect on the truth that he was going to miss a number of things, places, events, and people. Not a whole lot, but the little he would miss would cause him some sadness and his departure would not necessarily be an all-thrilling adventure into a new future. While it was a bad time to think about any of the people he would miss, that is exactly what he began to do. It was easy to recall the first Dorothy because she was his first friend, and the lady who now sat across from him was Dorothy too. Maybe he would remember this Dorothy, but he wanted to remember the first Dorothy more, partly because their friendship ended abruptly and with unanswered questions that remained unanswered. For that reason he formed a picture of what he remembered of her and placed her in the seat across from him. When he looked closely at her and realized that she wasn't there, he shook his head, uttering the words under his breath, "but you are not Dorothy."

"What! What was that?"

Dorothy's words awakened him from his daydream and he struggled to find an answer.

"Oh, nothing, em, I-I-I I'm sorry. I guess I must be a little sleepy. . . . My mind began to wonder off. I think we should leave. I'm probably sleepy. Thank you very much."

They walked back most of the way, their conversation still careful and scanty. Before they parted and headed in different directions, they hugged like they always did. It was brief and loose, except that she rubbed him a few times on his shoulder. Before she could decide whether to go an extra mile and give him a final squeeze and a farewell peck on his cheek, he separated himself with finality. As he did so, he also snatched her ability to make or not make the choice.

"Good night, Monty, thank you for a good evening."

"Good night, Dorothy. Thank you."

Her voice had begun to quiver and she walked off quickly so that he wouldn't notice the tears. Before she disappeared completely, she began to weep. He didn't notice. But he observed her form until she disappeared into the blackness. He thought she bore a beauty that manifested itself only after she was well known. But almost as soon as the thought came, he dismissed it. It was a pattern that he had faced several times before, and had therefore gotten used to it.

Just before he arrived the Co-op he sighted a large public trashcan and an idea came before he walked past it. He stopped, removed the ribbon from his pocket, untied the little flute, and threw the ribbon into the trashcan. He thought the little flute was cute and slipped it back in his pocket before heading straight for the Co-op. The old building stood as if brooding, hardly visible under poor street lighting.

Flight

Monty soared. Few days leading up to his departure, he dreamed dreams of flying. They were fresh and unadulterated. He flew and flew, and when he reached the stars he danced among them, sharing music from his flute. Among the stars the brilliance was outstanding and pierced him, but he pierced it too, finding a story without searching too hard. It was a story that only the stars could fashion and shape, and with each subplot a sparkle unfolded, floating with him across a vastness whose darkness was contained. It was a story that he understood and held on to in his dream, leaving behind its meaning and existence only when he woke up. He could never remember or retell it on this side of reality, but it didn't matter because it didn't belong to this side. It belonged to the other side where he was transported in sleep, and each time he was going to sleep he looked forward to the story, the music, and the dance among stars that could not stop laughing.

When he soared, the words of an ancient prophet always sounded in his ears and continued until they materialized and became visible, mingling with the stars too and filling any area that would otherwise have been void.   With simple direction from his *Daily Devotion* text, he sampled a little bit of his black Bible every day, and kept a covenant he had made long ago. With each step the scriptures provided one more source of inspiration that wasn't too obvious, and one of its promises matched the storyline of his dream. Isaiah had given it at a time that, perhaps, would never be relived, and yet it was timeless and timely.

... but those who hope in the Lord will renew their strength.
They will soar on wings like eagles;
they will run and not grow weary,
they will walk and not be faint.

In spite of all the beautiful words of the prophecy, each time it was the words, *they will soar on wings like eagles* that jumped out at him and echoed up there over and over again. And because he invited no one else into his dream, he enjoyed the liberty of spending as much time there as he wished to, and of avoiding distractions that brought him guilt and regret. He enjoyed the liberty of entering as deep as he desired, and of searching as far as he could.

At their sendoff for him, unusually modest for a celebration at the Kennedy mansion, the discomfort didn't go away, and it was still from their end. The meal comprised an elegant spread, but nothing extravagant. He would typically have been asked to play his flute, but not this time. Events that evening were clearly stipulated and strictly complied with, almost to the point of being stiff and stuffy. But the Kennedys maintained their good sense of diplomacy. They smiled when they were supposed to and shook hands when they were supposed to. They hugged when they were moved to and proposed a toast when they thought it was the right time. And they told him things that were expected to be told a soon-to-be traveler.

"Have a safe trip."

"Don't forget to write."

"I'm sure Africa will be interesting."

"Are we going to see you on National Geographic? Ha, ha, ha. Just kidding."

"When you come back, don't forget to stop by."

"Hey, send us pictures, okay."

He responded with light nods and a grin that didn't go deeper than the skin of his face. After all these years it was still unique, his grin that is, but they had learned to get used to it.

Grandma Kennedy sat in a corner throughout, on a settee that seemed to have been specially made for her. Though she didn't need it when she sat, she didn't let go of her walking stick. Except for when she slowly moved her mouth from side-to-side as if she chewed on something, a grin was stamped to her face. It was scanty but large enough to show some of her false teeth.

With Great-Grandma Kennedy it was slightly different. Monty had to be escorted to her basement room to say goodbye. She lay on her bed throughout the visit, her eyes, even behind a pair of thick glasses, showed a milky white that almost concealed her gray pupils. A few white whiskers were sticking out of a lump at the side of her jaw. If she wasn't more than a hundred, she was in her nineties, her late nineties; but from all indications, death, that hooded shadow, that uninvited guest, was hovering nearby. Her well wishes and blessings came in the form of inaudible, monosyllabic whispers or an occasional grunt.

Whatever their discomfort and caution, they were all there, including Myra, and he was very grateful. In his eyes she had faded from those times when he longed for her attention, to the present when he suppressed the remnants of his longing and replaced them with concealed remorse and unease. But he was thankful that they were all there, and when Mrs. Kennedy, now walking with the aid of a walking stick, the result of some bone surgery, handed him the white envelope, he was extra thankful. In the past they would have asked him to open the envelope, but they allowed him to do with it as he pleased. He didn't open it until he returned to his room, and was stunned by the number of dollar bills it carried.

He thanked them sincerely for the envelope, the meal, and everything else that he could recall. He thanked them over and over again before he left. As he sat in the bus on his way back to the Co-op, the Kennedys began to shrink in his mind's eye. Not that he would ever forget them, but they began to retreat to where he thought they belonged. It was an exclusive domain that he had been introduced to and even allowed into, but he had long come to know that it was one that he didn't belong to. As they diminished, he, in turn, looked forward to rediscovering another domain that he would meet with more naturally. And yet a part of them didn't quite recede with the rest. It was Centaur. When Monty remembered him, it was with great compassion that isolated the drinker from other Kennedys and everything about them. It moved him to miss Centaur all over again.

...

Except for a few lines of well wishes and farewell, especially in the dinning area, other Co-op members were largely indifferent to his departure. The coming-and-going of members was fairly common and so his going did not grab significant attention. On the day he vacated his room, as his luggage was being loaded into the Consul mini van, a caretaker was already assessing and preparing the room for a new occupant.

Aside from Consul officials, the only one who showed sincere concern for him on the day he left was Dorothy. He hadn't expected to see her and though he wasn't surprised he was appreciative. The night before she had called to check on him and to ask if he needed help with anything. She was actually looking for an excuse to stop by but he didn't take a hint and insisted that he didn't need anything. The next morning her arrival was timely as he was about to board the mini van. He gave her a big smile and thanked her for coming. She wished him everything beautiful under the sun and then they hugged in their customary way. The trashcan into which had thrown the red ribbon stood only a few yards from them, silent and innocent. A few days back the ribbon along with other contents of the trashcan were emptied into a garbage truck by impatient garbage men. He turned one last time as the van drove off and looked, and sure enough she was still standing there in her black jeans and black winter coat, on her face a sober look that spelt resignation. She waved mechanically from behind a frame that seemed to droop more and more each time it reduced, until it disappeared completely. He was touched and waved back, hoping that she saw his last gesture of recognition. In a few seconds he was back to a normal sitting position and looking ahead, reaching for a future that would never have to be left behind.

Father Smith, now close to becoming Bishop Smith, accompanied him to Chicago's O'Hare Airport along with a Consulate official whose winter coat covered most of him, and a shy, petite reverend sister whose parents had migrated to Canada from Trinidad. She was a Consulate official too. Their interaction was mostly businesslike, so there was little time for pleasantries and relaxation. They helped him check in. Except that the blue suitcase he had come to the U.S. with was slightly faded in one or two places, he had taken good care of it all these years. Now it wasn't just that suitcase. He was going to travel with two more, larger and more sophisticated; they were both white, made of real leather, and easily dragged around because they had wheels. He held on carefully to the rectangular box that held his flute. Its lock was still damaged from being flung across their dormitory room by Theo that fateful day, and the small dent it suffered when it landed was there too. The defects were minor though and obscured by the loud shine maintained over the years by tender care and plain love.

Though he had only vague memories of the airport through which he had come into the U.S. about 19 years back, its sheer magnitude and hustle brought back initial feelings of being diminished more than he had already been diminished by a trip and life-change that he had dreaded. It brought back the innocent fear that added to his confusion and yet he struggled and managed to look ahead for a future less callous and less complicated.

Because they were Consul workers, they were allowed to accompany him past the security post that preceded the gate where he would finally board the huge 747 owned by Sabena Airlines. Conversation was light during the period of wait, about an hour or so. They went over final instructions on his itinerary--where he was going to make each stop, what he was expected to do each time, and who would be meeting with him.

When boarding for his flight was announced, he quickly checked to make sure his blue passport, flight ticket, and boarding pass were in his left breast pocket. It would be his first flight since he arrived into the waiting arms of the Joneses many years ago, but he was ready for it, and not just mentally. Father Smith and others had coached him well. There was a brief moment during which fear inched in. He reminded himself that he was actually leaving. The day had finally come and it wasn't one of those dreams when he returned to the tangible, sometimes consciously, after spending time in a halfway house. Was he actually going to a place that had answers to secrets that could remold and redirect him? What if the place only added another load to what he already carried? Would it be real, providing him some sort of baptism, or would it be another myth that raised hopes of a glorious world that never existed? He waved off the thoughts though they were persistent, and turned to face his escorts.

The reverend sister wished him God's blessings as she shook his hand. The official in the long winter coat also shook his hand and wished him well. Then he and Father Smith hugged each other. They simply reached out and grabbed each other; it was unplanned but soothing.

"God bless you, Monty. I'll be praying for you. Have a safe trip and write as soon as you can."

"I will. Thank you for everything. I will miss you." Monty's words to Father Smith were sincere. They both did well in holding back the tears.

Before he headed down the mini tunnel leading to the mighty silver machine, he turned one last time and they were still there, their individual expressions very different and therefore difficult to read. He waved and they waved back. Then he made his final turn and continued toward the plane, not looking back again.

...

Unfamiliarity can turn the simple task of fastening a seat belt into a challenge. But for Monty it was more so because of anxiety, not just at the thought of flying at the mercy of the huge machine, but at the tangled expectation of things to come. Still he settled in nicely for one who was flying for the first time as an adult, and alone too. His heart moved further up his chest when the plane sped down the runway, but when it lifted off his heart did the opposite, separating itself from him. He unconsciously grabbed his chair and anything else that was close by, including the elderly lady who sat beside him.

"Excuse me young man."

"Oh, I'm sorry." He realized what he was doing and withdrew his hand. The higher the plane lifted, the more his heart seemed to fall further away from him, to say nothing of the beats it missed. He dared to look out of the window and was fascinated by the speed at which everything below seemed to shrink. His stare brought a sense of confidence and relaxation, but he lost it all when a slight shudder caused an airhostess to stumble. The initial nervousness came back and he couldn't look out anymore, at least not right away.

Monty felt trapped, as if he was in a coffin that held many corpses at once. It was an uncomfortable sensation and while he was careful not to grab the old lady again, he clutched the hand rests on each side of him. A fiery ray pierced the window as if donated by the thick orange glow in the distant horizon, the byproduct of a carefree sun. He pulled down the shade and with the semi darkness came a semblance of calm. But he didn't escape the torment of the silver coffin until he dozed off, and only then was he temporarily rescued.

Monty

Child of half-moon is he,
Monty, descending from the womb, all soaked up and breathless.

From sunrise to sundown, lamentations and eulogies for him,
A song for each broken season, a song for each prophetic dream.

At the dead of night, before wolves begin their howl,
Monty, finding a flicker of light--red flame, mother of formless
shapes.

Silhouettes without form is his dance, melody of flute along his
way.
Blood trail to keep track in silence, melody of flute by his side.

Monty, in dark flight, falling from the womb defiled--
Man-child cutting his way through, out of child skin.

Flesh torn up at rebirth to show the man slicing through
With power, obdurate and frail, to reenter man skin.

Child of half-moon is he, crowded in by promises given and
taken back,
Crowded in by words that weigh too much.

At the passage where all roads meet,
Monty, making funeral songs of joy.

At the entrance to the oracle,
Monty, waiting for a sign from echoes of a foreign tongue.

In his hands, the secret of dream, flying and flying, only to let go
(At the footstool of the real), to dream again and again.

Philip U. Effiong

Monty, nameless and formless, losing faith in the rainbow,
At one end a full moon waiting to be seen.

He is emerging, all soaked up and breathless, to breathe again,
          to descend, to ascend;
He is emerging, raw flesh created before the soul.

If only the wind will blow his way, if only...

Monty, child of half-light, acolyte of dying flames;
Monty, buried in the mystery of the flute, raised by the mystique
of the flute.

At fetal position, tucked inward,
Monty, if only the wind will blow his way, if only.

Trapped

He was tired. He was tired of many things. The mental attacks and the flight depleted his natural strength and whatever was left of his resolve to go on.

From Chicago his first stop was Ontario, Canada. The plane took a one-hour breather there and he didn't have to dismount for any reason. And then there was the long flight to Brussels, filled with the usual dread, fascination, thoughts, and partial disorientation.

At Brussels, Secretary to the Catholic Consul was on hand to meet him with an assistant who held up a sign that read MONTY MONTY. The secretary, an exceptionally young-looking Bulgarian redhead, spoke English with an accent foreign to Monty. He was all business and carried out his job briskly, confirming that Monty was fine, that his papers were in order, and that he knew what to do next. A firm handshake concluded their meeting and the redhead disappeared. During the six-hour wait at the airport, Monty wandered around a little, but slept on a secluded corner most of the time. When he didn't use his flute box as a pillow, he clutched the silver container tight, especially in deep sleep. He was not interested in the over-priced merchandize sold in mini markets scattered all over the place, neither was he interested in meeting strangers who spoke an unknown language and/or with an unknown accent. And though, as an American citizen, he enjoyed the liberty of wandering out of the airport and into the city if he wished to, he wasn't interested. But he did take advantage of the free soda and sandwich given once to Sabena Airline passengers at any of the fast food places. They made sure you didn't come back for more by stamping your ticket with a dark blue message that they must have all understood.

The plane he boarded at Brussels, also a 747, was the last one he boarded, though it made one stop at Freetown, Liberia. A nun and priest met with him on the plane at Freetown as it took

253

its two-hour break, their identity cards hanging from their necks by long, silver chains. He was expecting the priest, not the nun, not that it mattered. Yet she did most of the talking, again inquiring about his comfort and needs, and making sure that he was doing well. He was doing well, well enough at least. The man, sporting a bulky afro lined with streaks of gray, said little and communicated mostly with his eyes and an occasional nod. Like the secretary at Brussels, they were all business too and, once done, left as ceremoniously as they had come. The plane departed a little after two hours, its next stop was his final stop, Aegus, Cape Toria.

He was on this flight when Grandma Kennedy passed unexpectedly in her sleep, but he wouldn't know until months later. Death was on a mission it seemed, for Great-Grandma Kennedy died two months later. Like she had done many times before, she had cheated what should have been the natural balance and left only after Grandma left. Everyone thought it was going to be the other way round. Also, because she put up a fight, she didn't die in her sleep but had to be taken to the hospital. After a week of defiance and miracles, she gave in, having already begun to shrink before her ghost decided that the body was no longer capable of providing a home.

He was tired and sore, but he was glad too. Not because he envisaged a happy future, but because he was finally going to confront whatever it was going to be, head-on. Whatever the outcome, he was glad that the time was here at last.

He slept a lot and when he did he visited his latest dream a few times. He still soared except that now the vastness of his galaxy was not altogether limitless. It began to show boundaries, jagged shadowy boundaries that the stars couldn't touch. He still flew but with the boundaries he checked himself, reduced his distance, and slowed his flight. But he still soared.

He learned a lot about air travel. Not to the point of rejecting fear completely, though he acquired a level of confidence that kept coming and going. It couldn't stay because each time he thought he was content, the plane teased him. It would vibrate, sometimes violently, rock suddenly, or lose height with one short, unexpected drop, and his heart would jump out of his chest. He learned that airplane toilets behaved differently than home toilets, and sometimes had to be flushed more than once to truly get rid of everything. He learned not to push buttons out of curiosity, but not before an attendant walked up to him and asked him what he wanted. Realizing his blunder, he looked up at the man and said "nothing" in the must unassuming voice. Hours of training in civility prevented the man from yelling at him. Instead, without saying more, he took one look at Monty, tightened his lips, then turned and walked off, his anger having been transferred to his military steps. Monty learned not to order drinks by pointing at them when he didn't know their names. He had ordered a small bottle of red wine that way and drank it fast because he thought it was a soda or some type of juice. Before he understood that it contained alcohol, a lot of alcohol, it was too late. Though he slept well, he first went into a slight stupor during which his head and everything around him spun. He woke up hours later, sick and light-headed. He had to visit the bathroom, and not just to move his bowels.

He was tired, very tired. He was not here or there. He was happy and frustrated, hopeful yet weak in faith. He was the child of half-moon, forcing his rebirth so that he could be one with light, complete light, not one that was shaded; a full-moon with thousands of stars as acolytes. After the proverbial storm he would wait on a rainbow with colors that couldn't all be made out. He would look for one that came with its own wind, and with the wind a pair of wings that he could borrow whenever he felt the need to.

Descent

The plane banked. When it did, its nose began to point downward. And yet it seemed to fight with a power that tried to hold it back. Whether the strain was real or imagined, Monty felt it; he felt a pressure that resisted the huge coffin. Perhaps the strain was a manifestation of his knowledge that they had entered an atmosphere that was different and peculiar. It wasn't the plane's first entry into Africa's space, but it was its first entry into the actual realm that would change his life forever. Instinctively he knew and for that reason the pressure that assaulted him came with such force that it assaulted the plane too. The machine summoned all its inconceivable strength but it still had to push extra hard, nose downward, against the pressure that defied it, almost convincing it to turn back.

Although West Africa was in the midst of its cool harmattan season, the period that brought in a dry wind that cracked the skin and required the use of a lot of Vaseline, it was very warm compared to America's Midwest. But over this final frontier, and though the air-conditioning was working well, a surging heat seemed to penetrate everything and besiege both mind and body. Monty's mindset foreshadowed an eerie walk where he would be home in principle, and yet, perhaps, more of a stranger than he had ever been. His consolation was that such sense of alienation didn't necessarily have to be cause for depravation, failure, and unacceptance.

The plane was in descent. Each step of the way it brought him closer to what he was made to believe was his birthplace, his ancestry. It was the place that was supposed to expose him as it revealed the unknown or the untold to him. It was his place of descent. After they descended, he hoped to climb up again, and without reservations. As quickly as things had shrunk during liftoff at Chicago, they now enlarged. Trees, people, cars, roads, buildings, and partially sizzling corrugated roofs that gave off the impression of rainbow colors, the effect of sunrays that

257

pounded on and bounced off of them. Even from up there he knew that he was steadily making his way into a world unlike any he had ever been to before. He remembered Father Murphy's teachings on fear and said a short prayer for confidence and the ability to adjust, clenching his teeth as he did so. On the plane's final entry, as everything zoomed by with such terrific speed, so did transient, sometimes obscure, memories of Madison, the Joneses, both Dorothys, the Kennedys, Myra, Theo, Father Smith, Mr. Ranjid, Saint Peter and events surrounding his flute. They were implanted in the things that zoomed by and, with the same speed, came and went with them. A tremendous jolt brought him back to the present and caused him to grab his armrests. The descent was complete.

Where All Roads Meet

Freetown was the stopping point for many of the travelers who disembarked the airline and made room for new passengers. Most of the people on the flight from Freetown were West Africans, in fact Cape Torians. The fact had caught Monty's attention; not so much that they were West Africans for he had little knowledge of what West Africans looked like, but that almost all of them shared features similar to his. There must have been people from other continents on that flight, but they were few and quite overshadowed. At no time in his life had he been in a group where the dominant physical trait was like what he was in the midst of. And yet he stood out. Not because he didn't qualify as stereotypically attractive, for the results of Third World living and eating actually produced strong features that sometimes came across as odd in a good number of the Africans. It was his complexion. While it was dark it displayed a rare shade, at least for this part of the world, which bordered on grayish when closely observed. It was the type of dark that one expected of a dark Indian or Australian aborigine or Moor. And his hair, though curly, easily stood out in comparison to the tinier tight knots, as if painted on, that covered the heads of other West African men. Of course the West African women on the flight didn't count in this regard, since perming, coloring, and stretching by heat had transformed theirs in ways that made it impossible to determine originals.

Anyone conversant with the geography of the land would have guessed that his lineage stretched as far as the extreme north where Islamic-Arabic influence produced such exceptional traits over several generations. But he was short and northerners were known to be tall. There was the possibility that many worlds met in him. Maybe the results of his gory birth were more severe and permanent than would ever be ascertained. But this possibility would not be guessed at, not yet at least, and so, even before the plane landed, he was already marked as different. It wasn't the type of mocking and distasteful scrutiny that he had known most of his life, it was observation that concluded he was either part or fully foreign, but one that aroused too much attention nonetheless. For West Africans, people who subconsciously believed they were the only ones who wore dark skin, it was always intriguing to be faced with the possibility that they, in fact, were not the only ones.

...

He joined the long queue of travelers that trickled from the aircraft. Otherwise, he had no clue where he was headed. The signs were few and not always clear in their directions. In the airport he was again fascinated by the concentration of people who possessed features close to his, all within one area and in a large number. There were much more of them than there were in the plane. He expected that there would even be more on the outside.

Once in the airport building the smell hit him. It wasn't necessarily a bad smell; it was just unlike any other smell he remembered. The central air-conditioning needed to be increased some; either that or it was faulty. He had long taken off his coat, even before they made it to Freetown. Now he felt like taking off more. It was hot. He noticed, too, that technology was far less than what he was used to. There were hardly any screens propped up high for travelers, family members, or loved ones to confirm departing and arriving flights. There weren't too many computers. There were few escalators and among the few a good number were lifeless. Whenever a voice sounded over the public address system, he knew that what he heard was delivered in English, but he had to strain to understand. Like a faithful warrior he stood his ground and fought off all remorseful thoughts that tried to creep in.

"Ahh! You must be Montee Montee." A voice, only a few feet away, surprised him when he reached the bottom of one of the lifeless escalators. The man did not hold up a large sign that announced, *MONTY MONTY*, neither did he have an assistant for that purpose. He was by himself and never lost his broad smile, showing an impressive set of very white teeth. Half amused and half pleased with the way the man pronounced his name, Monty nodded his head and veered in the man's direction. He guessed right that the man was Mr. Ben Ubi, the man who he had been told would meet him at Aegus International Airport. He was administrative assistant at the Catholic Consulate office in Aegus city, the country's chief commercial center that accommodated a teeming population of over 5,000,000. But how did he recognize Monty? Someone must have described him well, maybe sent a picture ahead of him. It wasn't important though, and Monty left the thought alone. Attached to a long silver chain that hung around the man's neck was a laminated nametag with the words, Mr. Benson Ubi, Administrative Assistant, Catholic Consulate. But why did the man wear a black three-piece suit? He had to be cooking under the agonizing dry heat. What people did just to be professional!

"Yes, I am Monty."

Mr. Ubi offered his hand and Monty received it in a stiff handshake.

"And I am Benson Ubi, but please feel free to call me Ben. You are welcome, I hope you had a good trip."

"I did, but I am a little tired."

"Sorry, but don't worry, we will soon give you a place to rest."

Monty wondered why Ben apologized. The trip had taken its toll on him, but it wasn't the officer's fault. With time he would learn that English in this part of the world, because it was spoken alongside numerous other local languages, comprised a unique handling of diction and jargon that was unlike anything he had ever heard. The public address system had already hinted at this linguistic quality, but he would face a lot more of it outside the airport.

"Can I carry your box for you?" Ben continued to be as hospitable as he was expected to be, and reached for the silver box that protected the flute.

"Oh no, don't worry." Monty declined courteously and with a smile, but behind it all there was almost an agitated reaction, a suggestion that he could trust no one with the flute.

In a short time Monty was exposed to idiosyncrasies that went beyond idiomatic expressions and with each exposure he learned something new. They came to within about four long lines of people. Obviously some of them had been on line before his flight came in. At the top of two queues the signs read *VISITORS* while at the top of the others the signs read *CITIZENS ONLY*. Both signs were raised high for all to see. Grabbing Monty by his free arm, Mr. Ubi escorted him to the top of one of the *visitors* queues and lifted his name tag once they arrived at the large desk behind which two uniformed women and one uniformed man sat. Monty noticed the glares from people who stood nearby, not just on this queue but on others too, and who obviously had already been waiting long and still had very long to wait. A few words were thrown their way, and though he didn't understand them because they were either spoken in a local language or Cape Toria's special variation of English, he knew that they were unfriendly. Mr. Ubi understood but ignored them; it was a hostile recurrence that didn't surprise him anymore. Monty didn't know how lucky he was not to have understood. Most of the verbal attack wasn't merely directed at the fact that they were cutting in front of so many people; it was directed more at his face and stature. Little was said between Mr. Ubi and the uniformed people before and when Monty's passport was stamped.

Before they walked past the desk, the uniformed man looked up solemnly at Monty and said, "*Oga* sir, we are hungry O!" Mr. Ubi knew that Monty couldn't figure out what the man meant and interceded on his behalf.

"He's with me. Don't worry; you know I'll be back. I will take care of you as usual. Ha, ha, ha, ha, ha!" Then he grabbed Monty's arm and led him on.

Monty still didn't understand and grinned either in embarrassment or in confusion. He would come to learn that to get around and to get what was rightly yours didn't always happen because you were entitled to anything. Whether you were entitled or not, an unwritten code demanded that in order to receive you had to give a little *kola*. Usually offered as a symbol of hospitality to guests, the word *kola nut* was also used in key situations to represent the demand for or offer of bribe. Such euphemistic usage must have sugarcoated and shifted attention from what in reality was growing into a serious, national epidemic, and provided the guilty with a sense of not being liable.

After retrieving Monty's suitcases, they headed on to the final security checkpoint before leaving the building. At the gate, the initial checkpoint drama was acted out as Mr. Ubi again took Monty to the top of a long queue and held up his nametag once he arrived there. Again, there were glares and protests not well masked, and while Mr. Ubi understood and ignored them, Monty recognized but didn't understand them. Before the uniformed man began to open and dig into Monty's suitcases, Mr. Ubi winked at him and he left the luggage alone, unchecked. A Consulate Peugeot 505 waited for them outside the building. An elderly man sat in the driver's seat. His head was covered in gray except for the little patch in the middle, a sign that he had started to go bald. Mr. Ubi simply referred to him as *driver* and he, in turn, addressed Mr. Ubi as *sir,* which he pronounced *sa.* Just before they drove off, a figure emerged at the window where Mr. Ubi sat. It was the uniformed man at the last security post, the one who had suddenly decided not to go through Monty's suitcases. Mr. Ubi matter-of-factly held something out and the man received it quickly, then disappeared as mysteriously as he appeared. With time Monty would understand.

...

The sun was not shining as brightly as it had a few hours back, but it was bright enough to show the things and events that passed by. For one, there were much more people to see, and, like he had suspected, he was seeing a huge number whose features matched his. It was not always a perfect match, but it was close enough. Never before had he pictured the scenario that now unfolded before him. But more captivating than witnessing the people was witnessing the habits that guaranteed survival for them.

Monty was sleepy but couldn't go to sleep, and even if he could he wouldn't dare. He was kept awake and alert by the hysteria that was acted out all around them. It was pervasive and therefore infectious, and beat anything Monty had heard or imagined about Los Angeles or New York. There were few traffic lights and stop signs, and where they existed they received little respect. For those intersections that enjoyed the supervision of policemen, their authority also received little recognition and to prove it they were sometimes almost run over by overzealous drivers in a big hurry. Monty periodically clutched his seat or shut his eyes when he was sure that they would either slam into another vehicle or person, or be slammed into by another vehicle. Mr. Ubi, relaxed in a manner that was baffling, observed Monty each time he reacted nervously.

"Ah, Montee, there is nothing to be afraid of. This is Aegus driving. It is normal. We will get there in one piece. I promise you. Ha, ha, ha, ha!"

But Monty didn't find anything funny, especially since the driver was also impervious to what looked like a gamble with death. Erstwhile quiet and reserved, he had come to life, weaving in and out of traffic like a snake on the run, escaping collisions by the skin of his teeth. Rather than detach himself from the recklessness, he conformed to and indulged in it almost to the point of being euphoric. But it was the only way to survive the chaos, to temporarily shed all sanity and become one with the insanity, embracing it without any thought for the risk of doing so. And all around it seemed to be the assumed attitude--to transform potential danger into frenzied play, one that too often turned bloody, even fatal.

Peace hardly returned and when it did it didn't last. If it wasn't broken by a near collision it was broken by the impact of the car as it hit a pothole the size of a backyard fishpond. Each time they were briefly tossed off their seats and Monty held on for dear life. But Mr. Ubi and the driver remained impassive, unimpressed by whatever size the hazard came in.

Since impatience was a major reason for the chaos, curse words were hurled all over the place, sometimes for no apparent reason. The driver got involved every now and then, either cursing someone out or cursing out the person's parents. Or else he exchanged words with a pedestrian who he almost ran over, or with another driver with whom he just missed crashing into. Either way the other party was ready to stand his or her ground and fire back.

"God punish you."
"God punish your mama and papa."
"Your mother."
"Your father."
"Your head is not correct."
"Come on shut up your mouth."
"Idiot!"
"Bastard!"

At one intersection impatience had caused the inevitable and a bus and car met head on. A crowd began to gather as two men argued furiously over whose fault it was. From the uniform one of the spectators wore, Monty guessed that he was a policeman and couldn't understand the man's indifference. Before they made it past the intersection, he noticed how one of the men, totally outraged, decided to throw a punch. The crowd cheered. Before they were well past the intersection, he caught a glimpse of one of the men being raised high above the other one's shoulders. The crowd cheered louder.

Monty observed the numerous yellow cars that looked like cabs, and that seemed to be many more than the non-yellow cars. He also observed that several primordial-looking, dilapidated lorries were also yellow. They must have been overcrowded as people hung casually by their open doors, either ignorant of or unconcerned about the dangers of doing so. There were a lot Volkswagen buses too in different colors, and he noticed they stopped many times, and each time a young man or boy would stick his head out of a window and scream something repeatedly in a local language or in Cape Toria's musical alternative to English. People then practically dropped out of the bus; it was amazing how many it could contain. Sometimes they were not done coming out when others would start struggling to enter. The confusion caused the archetypal curse words to be thrown and exchanged, and sometimes along with them a few punches. The confusion wasn't always settled before the bus began to move on.

Perhaps one day Monty would learn about the dilemma of transportation in Aegus, and the challenges, maybe horrors, of relying on public transportation. There were those who avoided the torture by simple walking, and they were many. Monty had never seen so many people walking all at once, and a good number didn't wear shoes. For some that did, the shoes were so worn and disfigured; they might as well have been barefoot. Even during Madison's most beautiful summer days only a few people could be found going anywhere on foot. At best they walked around the Farmers Market, but only first driving there in their cars. Or they walked around some footpath in a park, but, again, only after first getting there in their cars. Here they didn't first drive to a spot before walking. They walked all the way though some of the distances they covered were short. But some were long, very long, and stretched for miles. As if the agony was not severe enough, some carried things on their heads as they walked. Monty had never seen people carry things on their heads. It was mostly women, and along with their loads, some

266

of them also had children strapped to their backs by means of a loincloth. Monty had never seen that either.

There were hawkers by the roadside and in spots that were not originally marked for that purpose. They sold everything from clothing to foodstuff. Some of them were cooking what they were about to sell in low, coal stoves heated with charcoal. When the flames got low, they fanned them with simple fans made from palm fronds. The more he observed, the more he saw things he had never seen before.

There were the exotic hairstyles and fashions. The men still wore natural short cuts except for a few large Afros that stood out, but it was the women who proved to be creative in this area. Aside from those who had permed and stretched with hot combs, which wasn't new to Monty, ingenuity was by far apparent in the artistic designs that must have taken hours to accomplish. The cornrows, the braids, and plaited style resulting in pointed strands held that way by special black thread, came in very impressive varieties and Monty admired them. Ordinary western-type dressing was intermingled with ethnic designs. Both men and women adorned distinct styles of flowing robes that were anything from dull to plain to flowery to bright, from expensive to not so expensive to recognizably poor. Whatever the caliber, they were beautiful. The women also tied loincloths and wore blouses that aimed at matching colors. Another style among the men came in the form of baggy pants and heavy shirts made from light, local material that perfectly suited the weather. Some of the things that attracted Monty were therefore not tied to the havoc on the roads, and they were interesting. He already had too much to say in the letters he would write to Father Smith.

Speed was a natural reason for Monty's discomfort. It had long brought a terror that wrapped him like a protective hen sitting on its eggs. And yet slowing down didn't bring any consolation. Whenever traffic forced them to slow down to foot race pace, they met with a barrage of mobile hawkers who tried to sell them anything from boom boxes to clothing to foodstuff to umbrellas to laptops to TV's to wigs to stationery to telephones to watches to you-name-it. The list was endless. As long as it could be carried, they had it. A good number of them were children and their tactics were aggressive, sometimes ruthless. They chased you down and tried to compel you to buy by thrusting whatever it was through your window. And then they offered you prices that they steadily reduced if you showed no interest. It could easily come down to an 80 percent drop from the initial offer. Known to be very stubborn, they only gave up when there was room for you to speed off. And if you did, their curse words pursued you until you were out of hearing range. But nothing would upset the calm that Mr. Ubi and the driver assumed from the start.

...

And yet not too far from, and sometimes alongside, those who trekked many miles, who fought and scratched their way into public transportation, who carried loads on their heads, who hawked along the roadside and made pennies a day, there were the intimidating skyscrapers and expensive cars. There were the western-style restaurants that sold Italian and American foods, and even one or two McDonalds, small but indicative of an encroaching flamboyance. There were the tall banks and prominent supermarkets that took up too much space, pushing other petty traders to inadequate corners. There were the reserved, suburban areas that could be sighted from the highways, some on hilltops, with their grandiose fenced-in homes and imported cars. They were not always far from a slum covered with wretched zinc homes, giant piles of filth, stenches so caustic that they sliced through your nostrils, disease, hunger, and death.

As the sun sank down further, it enlarged the contrast because the more affluent areas turned on their lights before complete darkness spread its cloak, a reminder that that they too were there in the midst of so much madness and poverty. It was also in hopes of monitoring the thieves that sneaked in from the slums under the cover of dark. Already dwarfed by their magnificence, the more modest and wretched homes were drowned out by the glitter once the rich began to turn on their lights. Though humbled, they were prepared to wait for more darkness before they turned on their lights. That way, they saved money. Either that or they had no power supply. For those who did, the blackouts were so frequent anyway; it wouldn't have really mattered if they didn't have any power supply.

Sometimes the affluence was so dominant that it altered the face of everything, not just homes and cars. Driving became a means of getting from one place to another, not a means of letting wild emotions loose. Human encounters became more civil and roads were roads, not war zones. When the affluence was far away from the more modest and poor, public transportation was less valued and therefore fewer, and the walkers as well as load and baby carriers decreased, as did the roadside hawkers. The air became more breathable and the smell was mostly natural, not the unusual admixture of pressure and waste.

So it was when they arrived Venus Island where the Catholic Consulate was located; it was as if they entered a new country. But it wasn't a new country, just another territory, and a variation of what was not too far behind. The fresh air poured in and with an extra force generated by the persistent surge of a sea whose bridge they were crossing. The sun had sunk some more so that shapes dimmed some more too, taking on the form of three-dimensional shadows. In the growing darkness the brilliance of the lights became louder and completely displaced the insanity that they had just escaped from. The contrast was as fascinating as it was disturbing, and the realization hit him again. Yes, some of the things that amazed him were not tied to the havoc on the roads. There was a lot more to this world than that segment, and until they were all encountered or stumbled upon and understood, no conclusions could be drawn. One thing was for sure; it wasn't boring over here. And before he would, if ever, make inroads into other behavioral and physical parts of Aegus, the little he had seen was enough to teach him that it was a place where all roads met. How true. From the bestial to the compassionate, from the fiendish to the sanctified, from the rustic to the sophisticated, they all met here. From the primitive to the contemporary, from the African to the European, from the industrial to the underdeveloped, they all met here. From the wealthy to the destitute, from the African to the American, from the obnoxious to the saintly, from the living to the dead, they all met here at this crossroad created artificially by ambitious colonizers.

As at the airport, he had to defend himself against guilt and skepticism, against regret and fear. But he was also one whose life had been plagued by these assaults. So he put on his armor, reminding himself that judgment could not be arrived at after a single trip from the airport and into a city. Besides, there were the likes of Venus Island, now a phenomenon that balanced things out with its radiance, reintroducing hope. No, he had worked too hard and taken too many chances to come this far. He wouldn't give up. If all else failed, he would return to his other home, the United States. But for now he couldn't dwell on that easy way out. He would search hard with whatever resources that were left at his disposal; he would dig deep until he would find answers that wouldn't necessarily improve anything. They would be answers nonetheless and, as far as he was concerned, answers were synonymous with victory if not growth. But first, he must learn and adjust.

...

It was past work hours but the security guard at the Consulate gate recognized, first, the car, and then Mr. Ubi, and let them into the compound. It was decorated richly with flowers that were apparent even in areas not well lit by the security lights. For a few years after the War the consulate had not been allowed to exist in the country, being that the Catholic

Church had come to the aid of Beuvera--that section of the country that had tried to secede. Now defunct, Beuvera had not only lost the war but had come to understand that when you lost, your ideals and concept of justice went down with you.

Mr. Ubi escorted Monty to the guestroom where he would be spending two nights. The guard and driver hauled his luggage up to the second floor where the room was located. Monty had wanted to help them but Mr. Ubi would have none of it. Here, the distinction between the powerful and the powerless was very clearly defined and strictly complied with. In spite of the fact, Monty held tight to his silver box.

Mr. Ubi gave him final instructions for the day. Since he must have been tired, he would be allowed to take a bath and rest. But first, he was served a meal that was delivered to his room by one of the servants. It was spaghetti covered generously with spaghetti sauce. He was lucky. Food would not always be this familiar. But while it was familiar, it was also the spiciest thing he had ever eaten. He had to request for drinking water though he had already been served a tall glass of Pepsi. The water was served in a pitcher, which was good because he needed more than a glassful. Mr. Ubi left after Monty was done with his meal, and after he made sure that Monty had everything he needed.

"See you tomorrow Montee. Nice to meet you."

"Thank you Ben, good to meet you too. Good night."

They shook hands and Mr. Ubi left.

The room was not plush, but it was self-sufficient and comfortable. Indigenous masks hanging from the wall, an aesthetic departure from the western-styled furnishing, confirmed the combination of worlds that had shaped Aegus. After taking a shower, Monty lay down on his bed and decided to watch TV. There weren't that many channels to watch and they all shut down by midnight. It didn't matter anyway, since he didn't care about anything that was showing. He couldn't anticipate what to expect in the coming days, though he still believed in the promise that he would ultimately soar, so his mind remained blank in that area. Since he had nothing to anticipate, and since he had abandoned most habitual dreams in the United States, he had nothing to dream about. So, with the power of jetlag, he dozed of and slept soundly throughout the night, not dreaming once. It had been a long time since he slept without dreaming.

One More Bridge

A knock on his door woke him up.   With the chain still hooked
on, he opened the door slightly and peered through.   An elderly
man, slightly bent, immediately spoke out.

"Good morning sa!   Mista Ubi say your breakfast will be
ready in thirty minutes.   He will be waiting for you in the
dinning room, first floor."

Monty wasn't used to the veneration, but he was grateful.
"Thank you, I will soon be down there."

"Okay, sa!   Thank you sa!"   Getting used to the veneration
was going to be tough.

He was ready and in the dinning room somewhere between
thirty and thirty-five minutes.   It wasn't yet 10:00 a.m. and he
had already learned his first lesson for the day.   In this world,
thirty minutes didn't necessarily mean thirty minutes.   His meal
didn't arrived for another thirty minutes and Mr. Ubi arrived an
hour later, after he was done eating.

"Ah, Montee.   Good morning.   I hope you slept well."   His
smile was still broad and his teeth were still impressive.

"Good morning.   Yes I did, thank you."

They shook hands.

"Is everything alright?"

"Sure."

"Well, I am a little late, so I won't have breakfast.   Did you
have something to eat?"

"Yes, I did."

Again, Monty had been lucky.   He had recognized the bowl
of oatmeal, two slices of toast, a cup of tea, and a boiled egg.
The thick, Carnation milk in a small jug was new to him though.
Carnation milk was sold in the United States, but he had never
had to use it for oatmeal or tea, or anything else for that matter.
The cubes of sugar tasted like sugar.   But he had always used
granulated sugar.

"Good. Your meeting with the Consul is at noon. You remember? I told you last night."

Monty nodded.

"We should be heading on down there."

"No problem."

They didn't have far to walk. The Consul's office was in another section of the building, on the ground floor. Because the Consul was meeting with someone, they had to wait in an area specially designated for that purpose. A heavyset woman sat behind an empty desk with a distant look in her eyes. She looked as if she had been forced to sit there at gunpoint. After some fifteen or so minutes a short, round man in flowing robs emerged from the office. The way he huffed and puffed, and with an obvious frown on his face, it was either he had problems breathing or he had come with needs that weren't met. He took one look at Monty and Mr. Ubi as if he had something to say to them, then turned and walked off with quick, deliberate steps. The heavyset woman addressed Mr. Ubi.

"You can go in, sa."

On the door a sign read in bold, gold prints, *REV. FATHER DARIUSZ BOCHENSKI, CONSUL GENERAL.* The office was almost a replica of the subsidiary office in Madison; everything about it was either white or whitish. A Polish priest sat behind an enormous, stylish desk made of the finest wood but covered with a black top made of material that Monty couldn't make out. With an accent like none that Monty had ever heard, he rose and welcomed them, extending his hand as he did so. They shook hands.

"Mr. Monty Monty, very good to see you. I have been looking forward to meeting you. It is my pleasure. You are welcome."

"Thank you, good to see you too."

"And you, Benson, how is everything."

"So, so. I can't complain. Everything is great."

"Well, Monty, we have heard so much about you."

Monty wasn't sure if the disclosure was as in a compliment or if it implied bad news. But he was consoled by the Consul's next words.

"We sure hope you will get to play your flute for us one of these days, eh?"

"Oh, I'll be glad to."

Reference to his flute reminded him that he had left it in his room. Stories of people losing their belongings in hotel and guestrooms struck him and his heart skipped a few beats. But his mind couldn't afford to wander off now. So, summoning enough restraint, he brought it back, but its return was not sufficient. He had to summon enough faith to reassure himself that his *best friend* would still be there when he got back to his room. Whether he meant to or not, he was forced to put the concern aside when Father Buchenski's voice demanded his attention.

"Do sit down."

"Thank you," Mr. Ubi and Monty responded almost simultaneously.

"Well, Monty, I'm not going to waste your time, I'll go straight to the point. I have been made aware of certain developments while you were in the United States, and the Church has deliberated extensively on your situation. We have decided to send you to the south tomorrow, to meet with Father Brendan. He has been here for many years and knows a lot about a lot of things concerning the Church in this part of the world. He also seems to know everything about everyone. Ha, ha, ha, ha, ha. He is truly a wise man and we respect him a lot. When you meet him, I'm sure he will be able to answer a lot of your questions and tell you things that only he can tell you. We hope he will be able to help you in many ways."

Monty and Mr. Ubi listened carefully. Though the air was serene, it was heavy and slightly unnerving. They were all aware that the Consul's words and the events that would ensue on account of them were going to have an inalienable and constant impact on the rest of Monty's life, for better or for

275

worse. It was a sober turning point that weakened Monty and yet he found strength in it, and with the strength the valor to subdue anything that could prevent him from reaching the very end. Monty's emotions were strong, so strong that Mr. Ubi and the Consul must have felt it, for they, too, became sober. In their eyes it was either pity for him that came through or a realization of their limitations, for in truth they could do only so much for him. As if to make up for the fact, their demeanor hinted at a desire to do more, maybe just as little as reaching out and hugging or comforting him, but formality checked such sentimentality.

"Mr. Ubi will give you all relevant information about your trip to the south, who you will be meeting, and where you will be staying. Any questions?"

Compared to the meeting at the subsidiary Consulate office in Madison, this one was uneventful and friendly, and Monty was glad. But it did pack as much energy as that one, albeit energy embedded in expectation and hesitation, not conflict.

Neither Monty nor Mr. Ubi had any questions. They shook hands and exchanged compliments with the Consul before leaving. The meeting hadn't lasted as long as Monty thought it would.

...

The rest of the day was without incident. Monty spent most of it in his room, peering out of his window every once in a while. There wasn't much to see and so he ventured out one time and walked around the compound. It was beautiful and neat, and must have taken extra, diligent effort to keep the flowers alive. After all, most plants had either lost most of their leaves or dried up because of the effect of the harmattan. Where they still had leaves, the leaves had lost most of their green, displaying a yellowish or brown effect. Through the main gate he observed people walking or driving by, otherwise there was little activity outside the Consulate building and the little was nothing sensational.

Mr. Ubi called a couple of times to check on him and to make sure that he was okay. During the early evening he stopped by to give him details of his travel the next day. Once he was done, he left after a handshake, a smile, and a greeting.

For a while Monty was bored and almost fell back on the comfort of his daydreams and meditations. With the resolve that dissension had taught him, he resisted the temptation and reaffirmed his decision to displace the past and its icons with new discoveries that would re-channel everything. A thought immediately came to him and he wondered why it hadn't come earlier. He brought the silver box out of the corner of the closet where it lay and removed the flute that it protected. He played to himself, something he hadn't really done before. The times he had played alone in the past, he wasn't his own primary audience; he mostly played for the sake of practice. Now he played for himself and it dawned on him that he could do for himself what he had done for others. He could revive his own spirits, lift himself to subliminal heights, and tell himself stories with plots and sub-plots that altered what was inadequate. He could find solace and certainty, laughter and excitement, and breathe life back into what appeared sterile and stale. He took a break when his dinner of roasted potatoes and chicken were served. Otherwise, he didn't stop playing until he was ready to go to bed.

That night, though the dream was not as domineering as it used to be, and though it didn't last as long as it used to, he found it. He found it deliberately and savored the thrill of dancing among stars and of making music with them. And because the prophet Isaiah's promises were at the nucleus of the dream back then, they reverberated again and propelled him higher until he soared on *wings like eagles*, neither growing *weary* nor *faint*. So it was until he departed the dream and slept without witnessing pictures of any kind. But his mind, even when it didn't conjure pictures to guarantee his wishes, was

277

secured by the majesty of a dream that had come across as more tangible and less illusory.

Sunray On Glass

If he could, he would have liked to know about a woman called Dorothy with a speech problem, who had defeated an aneurysmal attack not long after she graduated from the Special Training Center. She went on to get a degree in Criminal Justice and worked as a lawyer's assistant. But whether she would be victorious in her most recent battle or not, no one could tell. She pined away under the weight of the battle, the struggle over who would keep her two sons, and, after all said and done, whether she would survive a ruthless husband whose bestiality had multiplied her disabilities, so that a speech problem was a small thing.

He would have shaken his head at the thought of a lady called Betty, who had aged too fast and had begun to dry up because it was hectic, not necessarily to hop from one club to the other and dance naked and half-naked, but to give yourself freely to all types in order to secure your job. This and the fact that she was also eaten into by cigarettes, hard liquor, and powders sniffed generously to prevent memory. She had vowed to get married, for, in her mind, a good husband was the only gateway out of the debauched cycle that defined progress for her.

If he could, he would have been saddened by, but would have pretended, even to himself, not to be saddened by the marriage of a gorgeous woman and soon-to-be surgeon called Myra, whose wedding had comprised all the extravagance that one would expect at a very special Kennedy event. And yet he would have rejoiced for her, for he still cared deep, deep inside and wanted nothing more than her happiness.

He would have been happy to know that a brown angel called Mr. Ranjid, with a thick beard now mixed generously with gray, had been appointed Consul General at the Catholic Consulate in New Delhi, India. There, with his English wife and three children, he exercised his powers with efficiency, the outcome of many years of sincere and devoted work.

If he could, he would have been consoled to know that a man who preferred to be called Saint Peter had proven a point by marrying an introverted woman called Beatrice. In so doing, he was telling the world that a sex liaison with a fellow co-op member didn't necessarily imply a lustful exploitation of cohabitation; it could very well mean that love, authentic and powerful, was the driving force, not cheap sex.

If, like sunray on a piece of glass, these stories bounced back at him, he would have known and cared; he would have known and either shaken his head or smiled back at them. But he didn't know because around him sunrays didn't hit pieces of glass.

Fragments

They were at the local airport, not the international airport through which Monty had arrived. But the overall scene and events were about the same, even more rowdy. Avoiding overextended and disorderly lines of passengers trying to get boarding passes, Mr. Ubi asked Monty to wait for him while he walked into an inner room. Before he returned, Monty observed, less in disbelief and more in awe, as would-be travelers yelled at each other and airline agents, pushed and bumped each other to secure spots in long queues that didn't start or end anywhere, and very nearly came to blows. As if the chaos was closing in on him, even enticing him, he was almost as amused as he was bemused by everything, a clear shift from what his reaction would have been a day or two before.

Soon Mr. Ubi returned with a boarding pass and two men who took Monty's luggage through the same room from which they had come. Before the men left, Mr. Ubi passed something to one of them. It was just like he had done that first day before they drove from the international airport, when a man showed up at his side of the car. The transaction was becoming familiar, but Monty was yet to fully understand.

The flight was delayed for two hours during which Mr. Ubi and Monty sat in a lounge where videos of American professional wrestling were shown. The TV was so old; termites could easily have been living in it. It was an opportunity for Mr. Ubi to chug down bottle after bottle of *Star* beer. The more he drank, the louder he became, the more he talked about Aegus women, the more he laughed at his own vulgar jokes, the redder his eyes became, and the more his breath reeked. His beer-drinking persona reminded Monty of Saint Peter and for a fleeting moment he wondered what had become of him. Monty didn't drink beer but he drank too much Sprite until he had to use the restroom. Mr. Ubi pointed to where it was. He knew because he had already been there a few times.

Monty almost toppled over from the force with which the pungence hit him at the entrance. All the urinals were full and overflowing and so were all the toilet bowls--they were overflowing too, and not only with liquids but also solids that were bloated and disintegrating because they had soaked up too much water with time. Hundreds of Black flies, robust and arrogant, feasted excitedly and without modesty. How they managed to stay in flight was a mystery. It's not as if he had never seen big flies before, but these gave new meaning to the word *big*. When they flew, they hovered as if they came from another planet. He had to swipe away those that buzzed around him or those that sought to settle on his head and shoulders and take a break that way. He was stunned when a man walked in and casually unzipped his pants and pissed on the floor. No wonder the floor was wet and slimy. The man's actions were despicable but they also motivated Monty. He would have loved to hold *it* in and return to his seat because the smell was unbearable and tiptoeing on that wet floor required too much patience. But what options would he have had if he held *it* in? Better he did it here on the floor than in his pants. He unzipped them and, just like the man who had left because he was done, relieved himself. Eager to escape the sludge, he hardly zipped up his pants before he did so. How did Ben make a number of trips there and back, looking normal each time? Perhaps it was just another thing that he would come to understand.

...

His flight was finally announced and there was a rush to the aircraft out on the tarmac. It had just arrived from somewhere. Though a stagger was noticeable in his steps, Mr. Ubi did his thing. He took Monty to the top of the queue that had bottle necked at the stairway leading into the two-engine jet. On arrival, he waved his nametag at the flight attendant that was checking boarding passes. The man immediately created an opening for Monty to pass through, and had to shove a few people in the process. They complained, both those who were and who weren't shoved, because they didn't appreciate the privilege accorded someone who looked as ordinary as they did. As before, Monty recognized the disapproval though he didn't know what was said, which was good because he truly didn't want to know. Ordinarily Mr. Ubi wouldn't care, but spurred on by the power of alcohol he ordered them to *shut up* otherwise he would make sure that they didn't board the plane. It worked and they obeyed. Mr. Ubi gave Monty a hurried handshake and wished him the best.

"Stay in touch and remember to write." His breath was foul but Monty managed not to show his revulsion. He even manufactured a smile.

"Okay, thank you for everything."

Before Monty boarded the plane, Mr. Ubi turned and walked off. His sway was slight but visible nonetheless.

In the fuselage, a lanky man in a yellow French suit was sitting in seat *13A*, the seat specified on Monty's boarding pass.

"Excuse me sir, I think this is my seat."

The man's response was offhand and straight to the point. "You can seat anywhere." As quickly as he had looked up at Monty, he looked away as if Monty was never really there.

Monty had seen enough to know that unassigned sitting on an airline, in spite of what a boarding pass said, merely conformed to a trend that was rampant and loaded with surprises. Smart enough not to consider the option of argument, he walked to an empty seat and sat down, carefully placing his silver box under the seat in front of him. No one challenged him for sitting there. And then he prayed. He prayed fervently in silence because he was concerned. With all that he saw and encountered, what were the chances that the plane was in any shape to move, let alone fly?

He had good reasons to pray. Turbulence in the air turned out to be only one among other threats, and when he looked back at his trip from the United States, it was child's play compared to the challenges of that flight from Aegus to Nucourt. It all began before the plane budged. More boarding passes must have been issued than there were seats. At least thirty minutes were spent trying to resolve the problem. It was never resolved. Monty was glad that he boarded the plane as early as he did. Boarding passes had been duplicated, sometimes triplicated, and since seat numbers did not necessarily indicate where you sat, finding an empty seat was achieved on a first come basis. About fifteen raging men and women, some with children, stood at the entrance and on the aisle, all speaking at once and frantically waving now worthless tickets and boarding passes. They were, after all, on the verge of being cheated out of a trip and money. As usual Monty didn't understand what they said but to know that their words were filled with venom he didn't have to. They yelled and cursed at no one in particular, and if their words were meant for the administrative staff, the ground crew of White Vulture Airlines, none of the staff was there to suffer the onslaught. They must have known because the more they ranted and screamed at something, the more their frustrations enlarged, as if with the knowledge that their words, in spite of the appearance of potency, were in fact feeble. The closest thing to the administrative staff was the flight attendants and pilots. Sometimes the disgruntled mob, still fuming at peak level, turned on them sporadically, spewing every acrimony and obscenity that they could seek out or invent. Perhaps used to the commotion, the indifference of the attendants was as puzzling as the insensitivity Mr. Ubi and *driver* had shown toward incidents that alarmed Monty. The pilots never came out of the cockpit which, for them, was a safe haven until things came to normal, or at least close to normal, on the outside. The otherwise potential passengers were finally forced out by a small band of soldiers and policemen who stormed the aircraft and threatened them with rifles and long whips made from cowhide. Such brisk and crude intervention must have been expected because everyone else watched with that all too familiar indifference. The last of the indignant mob was hustled out and, with her, the hopes of a trip or a refund.

Monty had already come to the conclusion that he would meet frequently with people and incidents bizarre beyond comprehension. But he was also cautious about judging anything as bizarre. All his life he had been made to be conscious of and ponder over the meaning of existing outside of those things categorized as okay. While he had perceived himself and others whom he had been grouped with in those training grounds as okay, he had been compelled to feel and sometimes react to the looks and comments that suggested something else. Instead of break him, his experience equipped him at an early stage with resistant and survival tactics that were mental and direct, and later, spiritual. And aside from hardening him and furnishing him with a rare endurance instinct, he had acquired a strong sense of sympathy and patience too. It was time for him to put to practice the things that life had taught him. He was ready to meet with and deal with anything.

He did hold his breath when the angry yet hopeful passengers were removed from the craft. No matter how prepared he was for things that were as scary as they were meaningless, they still confounded him. The fuselage door was soon shot and the formal preliminaries that preceded most flights were hurriedly carried out.

The plane vibrated with such force that he hadn't thought possible, swayed and bounced around. He was jittery because the disturbance happened too often and when it didn't the smoothness soon turned into a mind game. Whenever he thought he could relax and afford not to be anxious, they began again. Sometimes the vessel lost so much height in one swift fall that Monty was so sure it would slam into the earth, but proving to be more obstinate than it looked, it never did. Each time it seemed like it would, it invoked reserved power from somewhere and began a slow and strenuous, yet steady climb. The fall always caused Monty's heart to jump out of his chest. That's why he was grateful that the craft never gave in, and that it lifted to the point where he could meet with and recover his heart, even if it was pounding too hard and too fast when he did.

And yet, but not surprisingly, everyone else seemed so relaxed. He was learning.

It was on this flight that he first tasted food that was completely unfamiliar. Indeed some grocery and ethnic stores in Madison sold plantains. But Monty had never been exposed to them and therefore had no reason to experiment with them himself. On the now infamous flight they were served fried and with scrambled eggs. He peeked at others to see how they ate it and imitated them. Though he could handle the taste, he would have liked some ketchup on the golden-brown slices. It was also too peppery for him and he had to ask an attendant for water after he downed his can of Pepsi. The lady gladly served him a tall glass of water but when he asked for another she gave him a cold look that clearly told him not to send her on any more errands.

It had been a ninety-minute flight that seemed more like a ninety-day flight. Monty gave a great sigh of relief and unconsciously made a sign of the cross when they touched down at Nucourt.

As had been the case at Aegus airport, he was also received here and not just by one person. A young lady, a nun in training, and a short, elderly Irish sister must have also been given good descriptions of him or sent his photograph. Once he walked into the main building from the tarmac, they called out to him.

"Hi there. Monty?" The reverend sister was all smiles, which brought out the pink of her plump cheeks.

"Yes, I am Monty."

She stretched her hand and they shook hands. They must have been waiting for a long time since his flight from Aegus had been delayed.

"You are welcome to Nucourt. I am Sister Rosalind Sweeney and this is Rachel Tarka. She is in fact originally from Nucourt."

"Good to meet you."

"Good to meet you too, sir." Rachel responded and curtseyed as she received his hand. Her shy smile was unmistakable. Though her method of reverence was new to him, no one would have been able to tell from his reaction.

Because it was a small, local airport, they didn't have to deal with many people, long queues, or security checks. After retrieving his luggage, they loaded it into a Volkswagen van with the help of a man who sister Sweeney introduced as Matthew, but whom Rachel called *driver*. On the sides of the van, in bold, black prints, were the words, *CATHOLIC MISSION STATION, KALA.*

...

The four-hour drive to Kala was largely uneventful depending on how you see things. There were miles and miles of undivided two-lane highways. Unlike at Aegus, not too many people were walking on the sides of the roads, but there were a few, some with full baskets on their heads, and some selling mainly foodstuff in hurriedly erected makeshift stalls.

Once or twice they stopped to buy something to snack on, and Monty admired the way Sweeney spoke a native language with ease. *If she could learn and adjust, why couldn't he?* She inspired him without realizing it. He had eaten roasted corn and coconuts before, but not together as a combination snack. It was also the first time he ate corn roasted like the ones Sister Sweeney bought. Their husks were removed after which they were placed on red-hot coals until they turned to a crispy dark brown and hardened. When he chewed them they made a crunchy sound and didn't taste like corn he had eaten in Madison. He recognized mangoes because he had seen them in grocery stores at Madison, but he had never eaten them. Peanuts were packaged in small cone-shaped packets made from ordinary paper. Monty was fascinated by the dexterity with which the seller peeled them, tossed them in the air, and blew off the husks before putting them in the pre-assembled packets. He was glad that Sister Sweeney didn't buy what looked like dried up fish and meat hanging from low poles by fiber cords. When they didn't drive by those stalls at lightning speed, he noticed that the meat wasn't always dried up; sometimes it was an animal killed not too long before, the blood still visible--whether wet or dry--from a fatal wound.

Except to buy snacks, they also stopped to fill up the van's tank. Here no one trusted you to fill up your tank by yourself. There was always an attendant on hand, and he or she always expected a little *kola* after receiving payment for filling up your tank. In some cases the gas pumps were so archaic and were operated by a device that looked like a huge see-through jar sitting on a contraption from which a hose was connected. The attendant would push down repeatedly on a lever until the liquid showed up in and filled up the jar. And then the lever was released so that it drained from the jar into the tank in which the hose had been inserted. Monty was learning.

But for the most part they saw few people, few vehicles and motorbikes, and few cyclists. For the most part both sides of the long, thin, sometimes winding road was bounded by thick bushes populated mainly by palm trees. Monty had heard of palm trees growing in parts of the United States but he had never seen any before now. With time he would also learn about the side roads that led into many villages carefully hidden behind the bushes.

Not a lot of homes were visible and the few that were displayed a simplicity that distinguished such rural areas from the likes of cosmopolitan Aegus. Most of them were brick homes and often too close to the road, but then there were those red, mud homes with roofs made of palm fronds. Monty gazed and thoroughly took in those things that he had never seen before. The few books he had read had talked about the mud homes among other things, and even shown pictures, but reading and seeing pictures could not arouse the emotions that came with seeing the real thing.

Once in a while they passed through small towns that weren't as empty as the highway, though they didn't exhibit the vibrance of Aegus. They contained more people, more roadside hawkers, more walkers, and more methods of transportation than the rural areas surrounding most of the highway. Traffic was also heavier but except for a few stops at intersections, some of which had policemen controlling the traffic, it didn't come close to the clogged traffic of Aegus roads. And while activities were richer, they, too, were drab compared to the rush of daily Aegus life.

The highways weren't as busy as Aegus roads, but sometimes they felt as dangerous. There were too many potholes and too often they crashed into them. At speeds in excess of seventy-five the impact was always severe and though it was brief, they were rocked wildly. Without the potholes, the speeds were enough to scare Monty to death. He couldn't understand the logic in driving so fast on roads that were so narrow, so winding in areas, and so full of potholes. Whenever Matthew overtook another vehicle, Monty looked away, expecting the worst. Whenever a car overtaking another came face to face with their van, he looked away, sure that a collision would bring their trip to an early finish. Sometimes they had to swerve wildly to escape a collision. Sometimes other vehicles had to swerve wildly to avoid them. There were those times when oncoming traffic loomed in the shape of a large lorry. Because the roads were so narrow, there wasn't always enough room for both vehicles and one of them had to make room for the other. Naturally, the lorry never gave in. When Matthew veered off the road, sometimes he nearly slammed into a pedestrian or roadside stall. As Monty expected, Beatrice, Matthew, and Sister Sweeney didn't allow any of this to ruin their peace.

But what Monty would remember most about the trip was not the roadside vendors or potholes or near accidents. It was the sheer embarrassment that came with his desire to use the bathroom. And it just wasn't to pee; obviously the new foods he had been eating had begun to cause some havoc in his stomach. He felt a warmth that began to spread and soon he needed to let loose the extra gas that built up in there. With the warmth came an occasional rumbling and soon he realized that he had to release a lot more than gas. As if Sister Sweeney read his thoughts, she let Matthew know that she had to *ease* herself. Monty was relieved and expected that they would stop at the next modern gas station. But that was not to be. Matthew found a quiet area that looked desolate except for the bush and the sounds of birds and other small creatures. He cleared there and Monty was puzzled since there was no indication of life, let alone a gas station. Then Sister Sweeney and Beatrice climbed out of the van and headed into the surrounding bush. Matthew climbed out too but hardly stepped into the bush when he unzipped his pants. Soon a long, yellowish jet shot out from between his legs. This time Monty understood and, almost trembling, began to wander into the bush, carefully picking his way through trees and branches, and carefully stepping over shrubs, rocks, and waste. When he thought he had gone deep enough, he unzipped his pants and guessed right that he had to squat. In seconds he was emptying himself of a watery mound that had tormented him for too long. When he was done he was faced with another dilemma. How would he wipe himself? His instincts told him to grab some leaves. Washing his hands was another issue, but he refused to consider his options since he had none. Instead he concerned himself more with returning to the van safely. When he got there, they were all sitting inside waiting for him. His complexion could conceal the fact that he blushed tremendously, but his face couldn't hide his embarrassment. This time, instead of anticipate their indifference, he hoped for it. He got his wish.

Otherwise, yes, the trip could be seen as uneventful. Conversation was little and simple, but it existed. Most of it centered on him, his life in the United States, his mastery of the flute, his trip from the United States to Cape Toria, what he thought about Cape Toria, and how much he looked forward to his trip to Kala. He welcomed thoughts of his impending experience at Kala as he used them to block out aspects of their drive that didn't console or uplift.

...

Exhausted but relieved, they arrived Kala. Though it was early evening, it was sunny enough to reveal a town that had made miraculous progress since after the War. It wasn't a bustling city like Aegus, but it wasn't small. Of all the towns they had passed on their way here, this was the largest and busiest. Commercial activity was high and the roads, though not crowded, were filled with people who walked, carried, drove, cycled, and traded. If there was an urgency about them, it was either not obvious or checked by a civility that seemed to come naturally. Somewhat of a mini Aegus, Kala contained the activities, patterns, and fashions of Aegus, but in a quantity that was smaller, more tolerable, and therefore sane.

Sunset Hotel. The name was ambiguous as pine trees that gave off a canopied effect surrounded the yellow building. Though they had shed a lot of their leaves, they still shielded the hotel from sunlight. Perhaps being yellow was what qualified it as *sunset*. It was a four-story hotel and Monty later observed how it didn't have elevators. But first he noticed how the parking lot could have been larger, and could have had marked out parking spaces. And while its trees provided a composure that only nature could bring, some work still needed to be done on its gardens. The flowerbeds had caked and were cracking because of the dry season. It was normal for plants and flowers to lose their leaves and even dry up a bit, but sterility of this kind was a little excessive, even for the season. A scanty arrangement of shriveled flower stems mingled with browning weeds that also encircled the beds, an indication that not enough attention had been given to gardening.

His room was tidy and ordinary, and sustained a jaded effect because the color of everything--bedspread, blanket, chair, towels, and curtains--was pale. If they weren't grayish or bluish they were brownish or plain red. While the walls were white, they were shaded by the prevailing dullness. But the room had everything he needed and that was all that really mattered.

Sister Sweeney and Rachel decided to have dinner with him before they left, but it wasn't just to keep him company. Sister Sweeney used the opportunity to brief him on his visit with Father Brendan the next day. The meeting would take place at the Kala War Museum, what was once a secret airstrip from which the Catholic Church sneaked out Beuverian refugees, and to which it received food, medical and relief supplies for war victims. They had dinner in the small, quaint dinning area on the first floor.

For the second time, Monty ate what looked and tasted outlandish and somewhere in his psyche, repressed and held within, he thought it was a risk, but maybe it was one worth taking. It was what the hotel served all its guests and customers that late evening. There was no menu to make choices that satisfied personal tastes. In one bowl was a sauce made from green vegetables and melon, and laced with pieces of beef. Another plate contained what looked like a mound of mashed potatoes except that it was thicker and harder than mashed potatoes. It was, in fact, the result of yams pounded with long pestles in large, hollowed, wooden mortars. They weren't the yams Monty was used to in the United States. These were yams larger than any human head and sometimes as much as three feet long. Their skins were thick and rough, more like the bark from matured trees than the skin of an average American root crop. After they said grace, Sister Sweeney leaned toward Monty and said, almost in a whisper, "I'm sure you've never had anything like this before, but, trust me, *foofoo* is delicious. If you would prefer, though, I'd be glad to see if I can get you some toast and eggs."

"Oh, thank you very much, but I'm sure I'll be fine." It was one of the few times Monty feigned contentment.

He understood the purpose of the large bowl of water when Sister Sweeney and Rachel washed their palms in it before they began to eat. They cut pieces from the *foofoo*, which they rolled into Ping-Pong sized balls, dipped them into the sauce, and put them in their mouths. They worked into the meal like they relished it so that well before he tasted it he found it tasty. But he didn't observe closely enough otherwise he might have observed that they didn't chew; they swallowed everything whole.

When it came to being daring and adventurous, even Monty had his limits. He requested cutlery and Sister Sweeney chided him playfully and with a smirk that guaranteed she was being facetious.

"Oh, Monty, that is sacrilegious. *Foofoo* must be eaten with your fingers alone; otherwise, it doesn't taste the same. It doesn't taste good any other way."

But to the people of Cape Toria, Sister Sweeny's concept was taken seriously and conceded to in that manner. Not convinced, and unwilling to always conform too easily and too rashly, Monty responded with a grin that could have meant any of several things. He ate with a knife and fork and chewed because he didn't know not too. Even if he knew, he would have still chewed because it would have been too radical for him. It didn't taste too good, but it wasn't because he ate with a knife and fork. It was because he chewed.

That night Monty took a bath with cold water because, try as hard as he did, he couldn't cause the faucet marked *H* to produce hot water. Next morning, though the harmattan cold was still nothing compared to Madison's cold, it was enough to desire a warm bath. Down at the lobby he found a woman sitting behind a counter. She had prominent saggy eyes that gave her a lackluster, half asleep look. After he presented his lack of hot water plight, she promised, in words that fell out as sluggishly as she looked, to bring hot water up to his room. He wasn't sure how she would accomplish the task, but he chose to have faith in her. Not long after he returned to his room he heard a knock on his door and opened it to see the woman standing there, as if she had sleepwalked from the lobby. She handed him a metal pail half filled with hot water and must have noticed his bewilderment as she went on to explain. He was to add cold water to the hot water until it reached a temperature he preferred.

In spite of her explanation, he didn't quite understand but would rather figure things out than be irritated further by her lethargic attitude. He pretended to understand so that she would leave.

Standing the pail in the bathtub, he added cold water until the temperature was just right. Then, using his palms, he scooped the water on to his body and bathed that way. What he didn't realize is that he had done the right thing and washed himself as was common in many Cape Torian homes. But since he lacked the experience and skill of indigenous Cape Torians, a good amount of the water ended up on the floor.

Memories

The spot was still there after some thirty or so years, the spot where, with a rusty blade, Sister Doherty had separated him from his mother when she cut the bloodied placenta. The holes broken open by explosives were now covered up and the red, dusty road coated with black tar. But the spot was still there, now carpeted by shrubs and short grasses waiting for the rainy season to come before they reclaimed their luscious green. The spot was still there, and still some two hundred yards from the white buildings that were once a refugee camp, a black and brown and ashy wasteland.

The walls displayed the brilliant white that used to be before the War displaced them with cracked and dented walls, stained and dismal. And they stood tall and strong again, so strong so that they didn't chip away, not even when the sun was at its angriest. They were white again, bright white, on the inside and outside. The walls represented one among three primary schools in Kala. They were proud and full of praise, bringing honor to a town that had stopped probing the twentieth century since it had arrived there and was still making inroads.

The crumbling sensation and crumbling spirits within the walls had been taken over by an exhilaration that planned to stay. Since the walls didn't crumble anymore, neither did the spirits or strengths that they molded, held, and preserved. And for that reason the walls didn't welcome certain things and took quick authority over them when they ventured in. The gray, the ugly scars from one end to the next, smudges of pus and blood and vomit and forgotten grime, lively rats and sophisticated roaches--they were eliminated and barred because a sensation that wasn't crumbling was also selective in what it met and welcomed. When laughter now echoed and re-echoed from those walls, they didn't go dry.

Even in dry season, and even on the outside, leafless trees and gardens emphasized a loathing for filth and the filthy.

Because the walls contained a fervor for purity, sickness, misery and death were sent away before they could unfold and multiply. They were the same walls, now restored, where Monty was delivered but not born.

With purity came the obsession with health and the inhabitants of the walls now looked full and content. With good health came the desire to be active, not simply stare until your eyes got tired of staring. They ate when they were outside the walls and they ate when they were within them, and because they ate, there was no reason to be still. There was no reason not to laugh. They ate real, sufficient food, not make-do meals of cats and snakes and dogs. And since they didn't have to fight for or with their meals, they didn't have to soak themselves in their own blood or in the blood of animals in an orgiastic battle for a bite.

Little ones didn't have to manufacture milk by tearing at their mothers' depleted breasts; they were well fed long before they entered those walls, and when they were in there they were fed well too. And mothers didn't have to swallow the pain for the sake of their infants because when they fed them with their breasts the breasts were loaded and even had reserves stored up.

Death did not have a place here; it had to retire to where it belonged and only showed up when it was meant to, and away from the walls. There was no need to dig up emergency, shallow graves behind the walls, and for that reason there wasn't the fear of a rodent or dog nibbling on a skull or arm that had been unearthed by a slight rain or by chickens scratching for food. There was no need to suffer the stench of buried and unburied corpses. There was no need for the howling lamentations that didn't last because of the lack of energy. There was no need to steal from the backs of the dead.

The walls, now confident and tall, shielded its occupants and won their trust. They were alive, really alive, not replicas of what the living should be. Their flesh had substance and didn't hang thin from their bones, almost transparent, decaying and sometimes bloating inexplicably. Inside the walls you could find people, not skeletal zombies pretending to be people. They were the same walls within which Monty was delivered but not born.

So much had been lost within those walls. No, not lives. The stench had been lost since the walls were rebuilt. The stench from black and yellow teeth, and from gums neglected. The stench from sores and blood and pus. The kids didn't run around with their heads covered in boils that grew and spread fast. And without the boils, there was no need for a loving mother to force her child's head between her knees so that she could burst them between her thumbs. There was no need to practice a cure that didn't heal.

There wasn't any irrational scattering of excrement within, outside, beside, or on the walls. Not by infants or toddlers, not by boys, girls, men, or women, and not by adults whose ability to reason had been stolen by the inanity of war. There wasn't the visible flow of menstrual streams that couldn't be hidden by rags because there were no more rags, or by leaves because they itched and stung and left bruises and rashes.

There was no need for flies so large they frightened children, there was no need for the stench, there was no need to give birth.

...

They were the same walls, once ominous and hunched, where Monty wasn't born. There was no need for forced romantic escapades in the dead of night and with emergency lovers totally unknown. There was no need for the gropings under the protection of dark, where the proof of masculinity, of femininity, of humanity was fabricated in an eerie play that was more disturbing than it was gratifying. There was no need for the agony, the weeping, the pleadings, the screams, and the loss of consciousness. There was no need for the shame that came with sunrise and the denial, the pretense, the refusal to admit out loud or reminisce over the truth of their carnal game, really a bestial gamble, the night before. There was no need for a resented pregnancy that mostly ended in miscarriage or death at

297

birth, snatching the lives, or what remained of the lives, of mother and child. There was no need for rape and sex, so terrifying and painful for the giver and receiver. There was no need for telltale signs at sunrise, spurts of dried-up sperm and blood, putrid and losing their original color.

Because their foundation was solid, the walls repelled dilapidation. There was, therefore, no need to seek regeneration in folklore, in song, in dance, or in music that revealed their frailties because they were limited in how much they could regenerate. There was no need, in dance, to expose their broken down silhouettes in advanced state of disintegration. There was no need, therefore, for the miracle of a stoic and persistent pregnancy that lasted its full term, gnawing away at a mother's insides--not so much her tissues and blood, but their remains--, and eating away at a soul in dire hopes of freedom from the secular.

In truth, the Hand of God had formed Monty before he was placed in the womb, but the womb should not have been barren and cruel. For nine months he need not have grappled with a womb that rejected him, starting him out on a journey of resistance that would continue even when he came out. He should never have had to emerge half-dead and half-human, squashed up beyond recognition, nameless. He should never have had to come by way of a father with too many faces, who had vanished into a mystery, dark and untold. He should never have had to take his first two hundred-yard trip when mother and child transformed into little more than a red orb held together by the umbilical cord and dragged by it. She should never have had to crawl and writhe, and he should never have had to be dragged.

They were the same walls, but with a new face, the walls where he had been delivered but not born. He was born some two hundred yards away. He was meant to be but he was not meant to travel the way he did, not inside or outside the womb. He was not meant to travel empty-handed, but he was also not meant to haul a load that made breathing difficult.

His mother should never have had to end her journey suddenly, for when she did everything inside her ceased too. She should never have had to stop forever, her eyes wide open and showing a ghostly white upon which flies buzzed, settled, and fed freely. Her prayers had been answered at last, but she should never have had to say that prayer.

...

Sister Sweeney, Rachel, and Monty were on their way to the Kala War Museum where Monty would be meeting with Father Brendan. They had no clue that they were repeating a journey Monty had taken his first day on earth, albeit the instrument of travel, the quality of things, and the purpose of the trip were different. They drove in Sister Sweeney's white Volkswagen Beetle and on the way passed by places and sites that recounted Monty's genesis, but they didn't know. Even Father Brendan who knew a lot wouldn't have known. No one knew about the spot though they drove past it, the spot where he had been severed from his mother forever. They passed by the beautiful, bright walls of the primary school, the walls within which he had been delivered but not born. But they didn't know.

And far behind the walls on the other side, the bushes were still there; they had not been cleared and nothing had been built in them yet. It was where the federal troops had dug out a huge moat, an emergency, public cemetery that didn't have the grace of more standard burial grounds. Here, the bodies of Beuvera's civilian and military dead were dumped. In spite of how large it was, the moat was overcrowded back then. Hunters and farmers now walked by and on top of the site, but they didn't know. Lack of vegetation and a raised surface once isolated it, but the surface had since flattened out and was covered by grass, weed, and shrubs. When the planting season arrived, farmers would plant on top of it because they did not know. Otherwise, they knew to revere the home of the dead. There were those who knew at the time but in thirty years their number had dwindled and the few who still knew preferred to leave a sad past alone. So they said little, if anything.

Among the numerous bones and skulls that lay there, intertwined as if fighting for space, the bones of a young woman had begun to break and disintegrate. Her dauntless efforts at keeping her baby alive were a lesson in fortitude, and a major reason why her bones were now locked forever in a deserted tomb. If the bones of Monty's mother could cry out to her son, maybe they wouldn't have. After all, he wouldn't hear.

They arrived a side road and turned into it. Once the road-- not much wider than a footpath--that led to what used to be the secret airstrip from which Monty was airlifted many years back, it had since been tarred and widened, and freed of rocks and potholes.

Homecoming

At first Cape Toria had deplored the Catholic Church and its *insolent* efforts at providing relief to a devastated Beuvera. She even accused the Church of supplying the Beuverian army with weapons, which wasn't true. Catholic churches weren't closed down in Cape Toria, but all Catholic convents, seminaries, Consulate and subsidiary Consulate offices, as well as all mission stations, were shut down and disbanded. Catholic hospitals and schools were seized by the federal government and given new names that omitted the word *Catholic*.

Then Cape Toria began to show a change of heart. It began when she realized that the Church wielded a lot of power and could influence her sale of crude oil to Italy. Even then she stood her ground for a while, exuding the type of pride that held no substance. At first Italy merely looked to more sources of oil trade, not necessarily abandoning Cape Toria. But the more her sellers increased in number, the more Cape Toria faded into the background. Things soon became unbearable and Cape Toria took the hint, quickly swallowing her pride without shame. In her panic she systematically reversed her position on the Church, for she new better than to be completely shunned by Italy before she did so. First, she returned all Catholic schools and hospitals to the Church, funded the reopening of seminaries and convents, and encouraged the reestablishment of mission stations and a Consulate with subsidiary offices. Then, at the request of the Church, she granted permission to convert the former secret airstrip at Kala to a war museum. It was a tough request to grant since Cape Toria would have preferred not to flaunt her war atrocities. But the power of oil money prevailed over ideals and over the humiliation of being exposed. *Were millions in profit worth losing over the possible impact of a museum?* Cape Toria didn't think so.

...

When Cape Toria extended a hand of *friendship* to the Church, Father Brendan began to contemplate his return to a land he was bonded to in ways that could not be easily explained. His charitable nature agreed well with the Church's insistence on distributing aid, but more than that was the warmth and laughter of people who were apparently content not to have much, a virtue only equaled by their tradition of hospitality. Even when the War seemed to have crushed whatever was left of their lives and minds, and reduced them to a state of wretchedness that couldn't easily be recaptured, not even in great poetry, they were able to tell stories and make music, song and dance. When they reached thus into the great reservoir of their folklore, what they made was deeply emotional in spite of being weak, for they had to be weak.

And then, because the people seemed to be in close commune with the natural, he too received sustenance from nature. It was as if they had welcomed industrial growth with caution, careful to reap from whatever it offered without allowing it to encroach more than was necessary, and setting it apart from a natural realm that was idolized. More than the sustenance of nature, and in spite of mosquitoes and malaria, the landscape was beautiful and the weather mostly moderate. If it ever got too hot it never got too humid, and there was almost always a surge of evening cool breeze, and sometimes cool rain, to offset the heat. The water was clear and cool, whether it dropped as rain, flowed in a river or stream, or was fetched from a deep, local well. Nature was friendly and generous, handing out food whenever the people sowed in the right way and at the right time; it all depended on how they treated her. Father Brendan cuddled up to her because she was never too busy or too tired to receive him. She had earned the right to be trusted.

The elderly priest, now in his late seventies, had returned to Ireland after the War, unable to cope with the hostility toward the Church. When he left Cape Toria, his desire to continue as priest waned fast and after trying without success to feel as useful as he was in Cape Toria, he decided to stop lying to himself. Using his arthritic condition as an excuse, he entered his resignation and it was accepted. Still living in Gallway when he learned about Cape Toria's revived *love* for the Church, he wept at the opportunity to return to the land he loved dearly. To leave had been tough and his heart had ached when he was compelled to. Yet he was not sure if the hostility had not been too ingrained, whereby safety and the liberty to function could not be guaranteed.

The permission to convert the airstrip to a museum motivated him more than anything else. His decision to come out of retirement and return came easily after that. He would not retire again, but would die while serving, and willed his pension to the Church. His stay after twenty years was relatively peaceful and his old age couldn't have been spent better. He worked at the Mission Station as one of its supervisors. Built where the former Catholic Medical Center once stood, the Station served as health center, mini mental institute, and temporary abode for the destitute and homeless. He also said mass at Kala's St. Joseph's Church, but was perhaps most honored to have been nominated second Curator of the Museum. He did the things he loved to do and thought his payment was more than enough. It came in the form of monthly stipends, the love of his job, gratitude from the people, and solace from the land. Unknown to many, he had planned to live the rest of his days in Kala.

...

After Consulate officials appraised Monty's case, their conclusions led them to Father Brendan, former Director of Supplies at the Kala airstrip. He was well known for his methodical handling of airlift operations; his success at keeping them hidden from federal troops until the War ended. When Father Brendan was approached in person by a Consulate delegate who gave him details about the altercation with Monty at Madison, he was not disappointed, just a little dazed. He had never forgotten about Monty, the child who was like a bloodied mouse when he received him into his arms. How could he forget him? He was the one who named him *Monty* after all. The long periods he spent thinking about him began to shrink when he began to doubt that he would ever see Monty again. War and post-war conditions had interfered with communication concerning Monty. Soon after he was taken away, news about the child was piecemeal and not always verifiable. Then there was no news about him. The trend, after all, was to lose touch with the children not long after they were rescued. There were simply too many of them to keep track of their progress or regression. And it was out of the question to request that special attention be placed on one.

Before Monty's departure that night, Father Brendan had predicted that one day they would meet again. The prediction had been sincere but it wasn't easy to trust it when he heard nothing substantial after ten, twenty, and more years. The delegate was a reminder that faith was rewarded when it was least expected. He brought other news about Monty concerning his educational progress and, most incredible of all, about the icon he had become because of his outstanding abilities with a flute. Father Brendan was moved in ways that were not simply profound; they, in fact, could not be measured. He was overpowered but he was very pleased. If he could do anything to help Monty's situation, he would be very happy. If it meant making sacrifices, he was willing. Of all the refugees that passed through the airstrip, none had won his heart like Monty. None had been as frail. None had been so more dead than alive. And yet none had demonstrated the same degree of courage and perseverance. From the day he took Monty in his arms, he felt attached to him. And after so many years of separation, the sense of attachment had not declined. The thought of seeing his hero after so long brought tears to Father Brendan's eyes.

The delegate was happy to inform the Consulate that Father Brendan was ready to help. The agreement was sealed by an official document sent to the priest by the Consulate. He read it, signed it, kept a copy and sent the original back to the Consulate office at Aegus.

Weeks leading up to his arrival, Father Brendan spent hours in reflection. He imagined what Monty would look like, his mannerisms, his perceptions, his spirituality. On the day in question, he arrived the Museum earlier than usual. He was restless, drank more coffee than usual, and paced around more frequently and more quickly than he normally did. When it came close to the time he expected them to arrive, he kept peeking out the main door and window, hoping to see Sister Sweeney's Beetle. Finally he walked out on to the porch and remained there, pacing occasionally, a mug of black coffee in his right palm, and muttering something to himself. He only broke his meditation when he returned a greeting from a visitor walking in or leaving, and it was only for a moment. In his other hand he carried a soaked handkerchief, soaked because he constantly wiped the sweat as it ran down his forehead and through his wrinkled face. His heart was beating as fast and as hard as Monty's was. He finished the coffee, placed the mug at the base of one of the window frames, and continued to pace and mutter.

...

A large, white sign was mounted right before two small, elegant gates and displayed the words, in thick black, *KALA WAR MUSEUM*. Smaller prints publicized visitation days and times. Monty had been calm during the drive, but once they reached the gates his heart began to pound harder and faster. He didn't know where this visit to the Museum and his meeting with Father Brendan would lead to, but he knew that that they would bring closure to some of the most personal things he had pondered most of his life. They would also bring him into contact with highly sensitive truths that he may not have been prepared for. He knew and he was uneasy, but he wasn't about to retrace his steps after coming this far. In telling him about their trip to the Museum and visit with Father Brendan, Sister Sweeney either didn't know how his situation tied in with the trip and visit, or simply refused to furnish him with hints or information. But he would rather have it the way it was--to receive the entire package at once rather than be told things in bits and pieces and without completion.

They drove through the gates. Immediately to the right was a small cabin, slightly larger than an outhouse. It was where a security guard stayed from when the place was closed at night, until it was reopened in the morning. They had arrived what used to be a clearing with a single runway, now a huge fenced-in area, now open to all, and exhibiting a degree of maintenance and organization that wasn't there during the War. On the other side of the walled fence was a rich forest area, except for a few buildings that had been erected since the War ended. Within the fence were trees, mostly palm, mango, and oak, sparsely planted alongside the fence. More centrally located were a few more trees, smaller trees like the orange and guava. Flowers of every kind and of every color were strategically planted around the main building and at various areas of the compound, especially around and within the lawns on both sides of what used to be the single runway. Even in the midst of the ravages of harmattan, it was obvious they were very well maintained.

Because the runway had become part of the Museum, it was virtually left untouched except for a routine uprooting of weeds and grasses from its surface, particularly during the rainy season. For that reason it was riddled with bumps, potholes, and rough edges that had multiplied since after the War. From this angle it was impossible to see the two-propeller plane that stood to the rear as if indifferent to all that took place within the compound, and a graveyard that stressed its own innocence. The building hadn't necessarily been rebuilt, but had been upgraded significantly with a new roof, new doors and windows, and furnishing as was expected in a museum. It had also been repainted.

Sister Sweeney steered her car into the parking lot situated in front of the building and on the other side of the historic runway. By the time they all climbed out, Father Brendan was standing before them, tall and impressively firm for a man his age, notwithstanding the amount of wrinkles that crisscrossed his arms and face, and even though his white robe covered most of him. Sister Sweeney did the introductions.

"Good morning Father Brendan. Good to see you again."

"Hi there Rosalind."

"And, of course you know Rachel."

"Well, hello Rachel."

"Good morning Father Brendan." She curtseyed.

All along the priest had been avoiding direct contact with Monty's eyes. Monty was excited and a little unnerved, but with the priest it was something else. His anticipations, as unsettling as they were, soon transformed into emotions so high they began to show. The more pronounced, the more they aroused a sense of apprehension that was really more an expression of gratification than it was nervousness. It was becoming tense, very tense, and everything began to stand still. When Sister Sweeney introduced them, Father Brendan had to build up the courage to look directly at Monty for the first time.

"Monty, would you like to meet father Brendan. Father Brendan, Monty."

Finally their eyes met and Father Brendan's mouth half opened and froze before the rest of him went into temporary paralysis. All his life people had looked at Monty's build as something not too symmetrical, something awkward. But from what the priest recalled of him that fateful night when Sister Doherty, half-dead, brought him to the airstrip, he thought that Monty had grown into a regal and courageous specimen of manhood. He reached for his glasses and removed them. Monty had no knowledge of him, but when he looked into his light brown eyes he felt a connection to him, a connection that seemed to gather strength with each passing moment. With Father Brendan it was different. Because he had known Monty, it was more difficult for him. He was eager to reunite with the man whom he, among others, had given the opportunity to live. But the success of his handwork was not his main concern that afternoon. It certainly brought its own variety of joy, but beyond the joy was the intricacy of reentering the young man's life, of adjusting to the spectacular truth that Monty had survived and grown, of unraveling and assessing the knowledge of who he had become, and of determining, if necessary, the type of relationship they would establish from where they had left off almost thirty years back.

Either from age or from delirium, Father Brendan began to breathe heavily as he reached out with both arms, his movement careful and mechanical. Monty understood and reached out too even though he held his silver box in his right hand. It was a light hug and in seconds they let each other go. Then, without warning, the old priest lunged forward and grabbed him a second time. Monty tightened his grip on his box so it wouldn't fall. He reeled slightly then steadied himself, partly because the priest's hold was solid. This time, Father Brendan wasn't looking for a mutual embrace, he was vigorously going after something that he took as a part of himself, something he had once cuddled and revitalized as if it was of his own flesh and blood, something he hoped to reclaim. He had helped safeguard Monty's birth, now he would help to baptize him. They were all taken aback by his speed and energy; they thought he might topple over and land on his face. But he didn't. He grabbed Monty and steadily squeezed tighter and tighter. He was powerful. It was only when he began to tremble in short bursts that they realized he was weeping like a baby.

Ordinarily Monty would have been embarrassed, maybe a little bothered, but he felt the power and sincerity behind Father Brendan's love. And though he was confused about why the stranger reacted so fervently, he was deeply moved and very appreciative. The hug was deliberate and meant to impart the feelings it imparted. Then just as suddenly as he had lunged at Monty, Father Brendan released him though he still clutched his shoulders, and they stood there staring at each other, both breathing heavily. Monty was still overwhelmed and now quite demure, but he looked back at the priest, he looked back because the tall figure that stood in front of him began to become familiar. It wasn't the familiarity that comes with knowing, maybe growing up with someone else; it was the familiarity that only affection, undiluted and freely given, can inspire and sustain, even when separated by years and miles.

"Monty, Monty, Monty." Father Brendan repeated the name in a voice that was hoarse but loud. "I knew I would see you again, I prayed for it with all my heart. Hardly a day went by that I didn't think of you. Or pray for you. Monty." The tears still poured from his eyes and he didn't even try to dry them.

Monty was now sure that the priest knew him perhaps better and more intimately than anyone else he had ever met. No one had ever expressed such fervent interest in him. His bewilderment began to fade, not because he began to recognize Father Brendan, but because he recognized the need to remain relaxed in the presence of one who knew him well and whose adoration had not worn under the influence of time and activity. They stood there as in the high point of a dramatic act, staring at each other, Father Brendan weeping, his fingers still holding tight to Monty's shoulders as he tried to recognize him all over again. And Monty, shedding his perplexity, but perplexed nonetheless, looked forward to the things that this strange man would reveal.

Sister Sweeney and Rachel had taken in everything, overcome by the awesome expression of raw sentiments. For the most part they stood there solemnly, barely moving, their eyes all teary, their faces storing a glow because in reality this was a time of gladness. Sister Sweeney knew that both men had best be left alone to sort out everything they needed to sort out.

"Come on, Rachel, let's go see if there's anything new in the museum. See you later Father Brendan and Monty." They responded with light nods. The women headed for the main entrance.

Baptism

Father Brendan took Monty on an incredible journey. It was the most hazy and hallowed he had ever been on, and yet it introduced clarity and understanding to many things. He told Monty how Sister Doherty, his long time friend and co-worker, had delivered him that night, the front of her robe mostly covered by a large patch of red. He guessed that she was shot either before she discovered him, or after. Either way, she held on to life for Monty's sake, dying soon after she handed him over. Father Brendan didn't hold back on the truth, but he tried to hold back on brutal details. So, while he told Monty that he was fragile and smaller than usual, he didn't tell him that he was like a rodent soaked in blood, the umbilical cord still dangling from his abdomen like a butchered worm. It was covered in red too and rough in the edges, an indication that it had been cut with a tool not too sharp. When the priest had received Monty, he didn't feel anything until he almost tightened his fingers; that is how tiny the infant was. But he held back and skipped the fact.

He guessed that Monty was born in one of the refugee camps just before federal troops had stormed the town and razed it, but he couldn't say which one for sure. His mother must have died either at birth or by enemy fire. He hated to tell Monty certain truths but thought it was best to; after all, his homecoming was more about revelation than anything else. He could water down cruel details but he couldn't withhold what he knew and what he visualized. He hated to tell Monty that in those days it was more common to die than rejoice after childbirth. If child and mother didn't leave together, one of them almost certainly did. Rather than tell him that in those days sex was defined by a pervasive, unruly atmosphere of spontaneity and survival by any means, and thus produced children--the ones who survived childbirth--without known fathers, he suggested that his father had probably taken off in self-defense when the enemy arrived. Back then when a father was identified there were always conflicts in opinion, so, it was hard to be certain if the one pointed to was indeed the one.

Monty knew that if he had been found soon after birth, he couldn't ignore the trials of being nursed in the womb during such times of scarcity and death. If there was uncertainty about his father being in the vicinity when all this happened, there was no doubt about his mother being there. She had supplied him with the lifeblood that still flowed through his veins and sacrificed herself to give him a chance at life. For how else was it that she died while he lived? Even if subconsciously, she had allowed him to drain her completely, sucking away at the little she really didn't have.

But his mother wasn't the only heroine--unsung thus far-- whom he would later sing of. Alongside, and even more poignant, was the self-sacrifice of the total stranger linked to him only by the unselfish rush to bring him warmth and life. The reference to her bloodstained robe inspired thoughts, though brief, of that Arm of the Godhead called Christ the Messiah. The sacrifice, especially of blood, of life for another, had to be the greatest sacrifice of all, and yet Monty felt a sense of dissatisfaction, the inability to resolve the relation between death and the restoration of life. Why did it have to be that way? He was grateful to Sister Doherty as he was for his own mother. But more than gratitude, he felt sorry for her. If she had allowed him to go, his would have been a minor, unknown loss, easily forgotten. Who would have had the time to care about anything as inconsequential as a miserable, lifeless bundle whose origins could not be traced? At least Sister Doherty was known, was useful, and had put in so much to get to where she was. It was a lot and shouldn't have all been snatched away by one gunshot.

Father Brendan told him about the efforts, frantic and with very humble tools, to prevent every breath from being the infant's last. He told him about how evil the effort looked, for the tubes that were passed through the infant's skin were almost as large as its limbs, and the many needles that were used to transport life ingredients into its body looked more like deadly weapons than carriers of life-saving liquids. Most were pierced through the child's skull for it was virtually impossible to find veins in its near transparent skin, withered and still withering away. The infant, like Christ and Sister Doherty, had to shed blood and feel severe pain in order to rediscover life. It lost blood that ordinarily looked little, but is was a lot for one who was so tiny and who contained a tiny quantity of blood to begin with. And though it could hardly squeal or writhe to express pain, it felt but endured ruthless pain. In light of such therapeutic torment, it is a wonder that it came out victorious. For this reason, Father Brendan admired its gallant spirit, and knew that if it survived this first step, the same spirit would take it through anything else. His vision had come to pass.

Father Brendan told him about his exit by way of a two-propeller plane. He was the only one, except for his escort, because his situation was too urgent and couldn't wait for more refugees to be taken in before the flight to where there was more aid. He couldn't believe that so much was given to give him back his life. For the first time he felt important, not the importance that comes with performing a role--like playing a flute with inexplicable talent--, it was the importance that came with just being a creation, an art piece direct from God's Hand. He felt accepted, not tolerated, viewed as human, not an exotic curiosity. He was embraced for being himself, not because he could do or not do certain things, and not because he looked or did not look a certain way. He was honored and felt a self-confidence that came without strain. He didn't have to fight or beg for it. It was free and natural and he was grateful to those who gave it back to him, who made him know that it was there for him to accept and that no one could take it away from him. He was grateful to all the people and to the Church that equipped them and sent them out. He hoped that the Consulate didn't still think he was unappreciative; that would be terrible! He wanted them to know that squaring off with them as he had done was not an act of cowardly snobbery. It was a necessary move that he believed would redefine him so that when he served

313

the Church or anyone else, he would serve with the type of vigor that comes with conviction and the knowledge that you come with a meaningful amount of self-worth. He would serve, not as a dependent who had to follow instructions, but as a man who gave himself because he felt strongly about giving. If they didn't realize it yet, soon they would.

The kind, aging priest told him how he named him Monty unceremoniously. When Monty asked him why he chose the name, he had no precise answer. The name had just fallen out of his lips. Even if it was because the day was a Monday, the indirect reference to the day must have been an unconscious choice. Unlike most Cape Torian names, the name seemed to have no meaning. But in its own personal way it did have a meaning; it just wasn't obvious. Either that or it was too complex to decode. On one level its origins incorporated the savagery caused by greed and the self-centered craving to dominate. But above all, and within the context of the war saga, it embodied every reason to survive and to go on living.

When Father Brendan informed him that his escort on his flight out had died, Monty felt sorrow again and accorded the man the Christ-like prestige he accorded the women before him-- his mother and Sister Doherty. He hadn't only given up everything for Monty, he had given up everything for the sake of hundreds before and after Monty. Whether the plane had crashed or had been shot down by enemy fire was never determined. Either way, the man and fifteen or so refugees sank quietly down the Atlantic after hitting the water with a tremendous bang that sent out mighty balls of orange and red flames. Their glow was so bright, they lighted the water for miles around even after the old plane and its occupants went down quietly.

···

Up until now the early stages of his growing up were jagged and murky. With Father Brendan's revelation he was able to tie *a lot of things together, even if not everything. He remembered life at the Joneses fairly vividly. The Orphanage at Ireland materialized in spurts that were often fuzzy because his memory, especially of that time and at that time, were impinged upon by the cruelties that preceded and followed his birth. But he was able to tie the knots where they needed to be tied--his birth, his preservation, his removal from danger, Ireland, the U.S. and everything else. More than ever before in his life, he felt wanted, no, needed. He felt like he belonged to a culture that didn't seem to exist but really did, one where belonging meant being human and having the potential to live, and where everything else mattered but didn't determine the extent to which you were taken in. More than ever before, he felt like he belonged without having to prove that he needed to belong. Chains were broken all around him and he felt light and refreshed. He felt like living all over again.*

...

Father Brendan began to disclose things soon after Rachel and Sister Sweeney walked into the building. His trip with Monty took them from the parking lot to the porch to the main indoor area of the Museum. This section displayed many framed pictures hanging from the white walls. They were mostly of the War from the standpoint of Beuvera. There were pictures of bodies, dead and half-dead, tortured, shot, raped or starved. There were pictures of refugee camps and the people they tried to shelter. It was astonishing how some of the refugees posed for the pictures, even managing a ghostly smile. They had been plundered, and not only in the flesh. It was possible, if you concentrated, to see through and inside those emaciated bodies, and to recognize that their minds were as broken as their bodies. Monty knew that any of the women--starving, half naked, and stark naked--could be his mother, but it was a thought he would dwell on later. For now he was going to listen carefully to

Father Brendan and to deal with other things of interest at another time.

There were pictures of armored cars, both those that were federally owned--actually gifts from England--and those produced from Cape Torian ingenuity. The latter were inferior because they were built from inferior materials, but they were also evidence of how desperation was partner to creativity.

There were pictures of triumphant federal troops on the day Beuvera surrendered. There were pictures that recorded the ceremony of surrender, showing Beuvera's Second-in-Command signing relevant documents. Of course the Beuverian leader wasn't there; he had taken off--his tail between his legs--once it was obvious that more resistance was futile.

Showcases held Beuverian military boots, hats, uniforms, bullets, empty bullet and cannon shells, defused grenades, rifles made from pipes, and one even displayed one of the many bombs Beuvera had manufactured. To the right and left were doors that led to halls carrying more exhibits, while a staircase led to a second floor.

They chose a secluded corner away from the visitors. It took only a few quick glances for Monty to take in a lot and yet he still listened intently to Father Brendan. He decided that he would come back later and take his time to see everything. For now, not even the impressive, sad details of the War that crowded him would distract him from the knowledge that the old priest imparted. As if Father Brendan read his thoughts, he paused, leaned toward Monty's ears and lowered his voice.

"Don't worry, you'll have all the time in the world to go around and see everything. But come, this is not all. Follow me."

Monty obeyed and followed father Brendan through a back door. The compound was larger than Monty had originally thought it was, all fenced in. About thirty feet away and toward one end of the building was an aircraft that had seen many, many days. The two-propeller plane stood behind a small sign that read, **Model Catholic Relief Plane**, and had been well kept even though it had lost its main door, most of its windows, and most of its blades. Its front tire was still okay in spite of a few bruises here and there, though the two beneath both wings were in shreds and had rotted considerably. Because its white paint had peeled off in most places, it began to look more like a home fit for the small lizards that ran around as well as in and out of it, and less like a craft fit for human transportation. It had earned its spot as part of the Museum and was allowed to deteriorate as it pleased. A mini stairway leaned against its side, an indication that Museum visitors sometimes climbed in to look at its emptiness. It must have been the ambiance in there, one that was spooky, because, as it preserved the courage and compassion that inspired airlift operations, it also preserved the inaudible screams of those whose lives had been distorted forever because they were products of a war of psychosis and greed. It had to be the mood, the stillness, otherwise there was nothing to see there except a resounding void and a cockpit that had given in to all kinds of agents of wear and tear. After flying several missions, one day the craft refused to budge. No matter what the most experienced pilots, technicians, and engineers did, it refused to stir, at best letting out an occasional croak. It had every reason to be tired and seemed to respond to insensitive overuse with a mind of its own. Like its other brothers and sisters who had flown many missions faithfully, and with mediocre maintenance, it was a miracle that it hadn't given up before now.

At the other end, and further off, was an area that was clearly marked off and appeared to tell a personal story in its solitude. This, too, was a part of the Museum and maintained a somber effect that was sublime yet lamentable. Located in front of low, sparse undergrowth, but decorated within with flowers and a well-trimmed lawn, the area was dotted with white crosses planted at the head of slightly raised mounds. Nailed to each cross was a label, most of which carried the words, Unknown Victim of War, R.I.P. A few did spell out the name of a known victim, like the one at the head of Sister Doherty's burial place. When Father Brendan pointed it out to him, Monty lowered his head as he grieved some more for the heroine who lay beneath, and all for his sake. But with his grief came an ironic sense of joy, for, except for Father Brendan, this was the closest he would get to one of the major players from his past.

Father Brendan informed him that this was also one of two gravesites that may have been the final resting place for his mother. The other was less known and more hidden, situated within bushes some distance behind the conspicuous white walls of a primary school that couldn't be missed. He withheld the truth that the latter was a single, unmarked and communal tomb that occupied a fairly large area, and yet had little room for the number of dead it contained. It was therefore congested with corpses twisted, squeezed, and piled on top of each other in order to manufacture space.

"One more thing, Monty." He looked up; his trend of thought was interrupted by the priest's words. "Look closely, Monty, behind the tree over there."

The tree, even without most of its leaves, had numerous branches and an umbrella-type shape that partially hid the car. In spite of the prevalence of rust and fading colors, it was easy to see that it had more than one color by which it could be identified, the result of being patched and re-patched, of being built and rebuilt. It stood on its wheels, its tires having been long lost to vandalism and age. None of its windows were there, but its front windshield, except for a major crack, had withstood the test of time and everything it came with. Rodents and lizards played a hide and seek game, running around, on top of, into, and out of the Volkswagen Beetle. Monty understood before Father Brendan pointed to Sister Doherty's car, the one that had started him on the second leg of his journey. Transfixed, he gazed at the car as if he would bore a hole right through it. Father Brendan felt the energy and noticed how he began to tremble. When he began to weep, the old priest knew to leave him alone and allow him the time to have everything sink in.

"I'll be waiting for you in the building, okay?" He didn't wait for Monty's response before he walked off.

Divination

If fire could burn through and expose the mystique of nightfall, perhaps he would have foreseen the nomadic travels of an ageing flute player, not the sporadic wanderings of a mind lost without calculation or creativity. If he could, he would have witnessed a constant, kinetic response to duty, an emotional and divine repayment to a Church body, one that had prepared him for a task that rebuilt as it tested the most delicate extremes of human patience. He would have witnessed the only calling that made sense in the midst of many others.

He would have seen a man who had still not added an inch in height since his thirteenth birthday, but whose expansion everywhere else was offset by a sagging that produced an artificial loss of weight. Whose skin had begun to take on a tattooed quality, really streaks carved in by much travel, and much, much sacrificial work. Whose crown of dark, curly hair and bushy, Old Testament beard were invaded by threads of gray that didn't curl like the rest. Whose outstanding build and poise were not completely free of curiosity, but had long been overtaken by recognition of his fierce allegiance to, and immersion in work.

He would have seen happiness as never before. For what prevailed on the outside, especially if you didn't know him well, would have been a serious lie about what lay within. His elation, his fascination at working for the Church, at helping to lift, to exhume, to resurrect, just as it had been done to and for him many years before, and all to God's glory.

He would have not seen a Bishop, or Father, or Brother, or anything like that, and not even the mass server he had trained to be. Neither would he have seen a ward of the Church, for the man had since been raised to a higher plane and thus recognized, many years back, once it was confirmed that his mental capacity was so equipped. If the man remained within that space, therefore, it was because he chose to. He didn't occupy any of those standard offices, which was good because like an unofficial ambassador, a troubadour extraordinaire, he operated within a greater sphere of freedom and freewill though his responsibilities were as taxing.

If he could, he would have seen America as home of the ageing flute player, though the man traveled a lot. Like an anxious minstrel he was always on the move, and this time when he flew it wasn't the romanticized flight of repetitive dreams. And when he made music it was with the same treasured flute he had owned since he was fifteen. As he traveled and played it was also obvious that he severed people, events, and remnants of his past when they were not likely to offer anything of substance.

If only fire could burn through to what oracles safeguarded, Monty would have understood that of all that changed, the man's dexterity with a flute had not, except that it had improved to the point where full appreciation was impossible. And he would have been satisfied with the truth. With his too-busy schedule, the man would get tired of many things, but he would never get tired of playing. He would never get tired of doing sideshows at the Museum and he would never get tired of playing at hundreds of church ceremonies and services. He would never get tired of playing at mental facilities to soothe feelings and brains that had wandered off without control or direction, often lost. And at home where he always left a small family spellbound, he would never be too busy to play. Not for himself he would never get tired of playing, and not for his mother whose grave home had long been overrun by homes and small businesses.

True, he wouldn't hold any of those prestigious offices, but neither was he your everyday flute player. Embedded in the outpouring of his music would be, among other great things, an inspiration that assisted and counseled in health facilities, homeless shelters, and schools that tackled special needs.

If he could, he would have seen that the box was the same, though rust had eaten into it, beginning from where it had suffered a slight dent that afternoon when Theo had run amok at the Institute and hurled it across the room. The lock, victim of the same rampage, was still broken. But the flute, as healthy and as stunning as ever, remained pure, as if untouched. It would always remind him of that Biblical teaching that advocated and extolled inner purity over outer decay. It would always remind him of himself. And tucked in a corner of the box so that it kept the flute company for many years and until the day he would pass on, was the tiny replica of a shinning silver flute that had initially come with a red ribbon. It was the same one given to him by the second Dorothy many years back, even as he carefully put her love in check.

It would have been tough for him to see and accept his assignment as Coordinator of the Museum--still kept good as new-- though it would be his most prized assignment. Next to the position of Assistant Curator, it would have been tough to deal with because he would have loved to work for and with Father Brendan. But he couldn't because the priest had since passed on and his tombstone lay almost lost among others that dotted a section behind the main building.

If only time could be squeezed and bottled, maybe he would have seen a growing fondness for Cape Toria, Kala in particular. It wouldn't be like home for those raised and nurtured there, but he wouldn't stay away for long periods and it wouldn't just be for reasons of upholding the Church's long tradition of charity. It was home in a real, ancestral sense, and the people were his people by the same token. But, above all, he wouldn't want to feel like he was abandoning his mother even though there was no room to lay a flower on her grave home.

If only the drapes could be lifted to reveal the other side, maybe he would have seen the woman who was once a Reverend Sister, but who had risked taking off her hood in order to express warmth toward him without reservation. As her affections for him grew, so did his for her, and with a certitude and peace that he had never known in his dealings with anyone of the opposite sex. She would finally remove her grayish hood so that she would marry him and give him two children.

If, around him, drops of sunray hit glass, maybe they would have dropped hints too. But he would have to wait because they didn't. And since fire could still not burn through the secrets of nightfall, things would only unfold when the time came.

Wayfarer

All vestiges of torment and regret were gone and he felt free. He had every reason to laugh, to climb higher, to fly, and to make new songs. This was not the time to throw everything away, certainly not after many had given up themselves so that he could be himself. This was not the time to dwell endlessly on questions, whether there were hopes for answers or not. The answers he received on this day were sufficient to answer other questions. He was standing, and standing tall. He could easily have been one of those beneath a raised mound of mud that had hardened because of the harmattan, or one of those whose bones were bent and folded because of cramped up space in a common grave. But he wasn't. He was standing, standing tall because there was a small world, almost drowned out by the real one, where people lived to bless others at any price. He was the wayfarer who had come full circle, enlightened and lucky to have arrived. But his arrival didn't mean he had reached his journey's end; it only meant that from now on his path would be different and equipped with a new set of road signs. He hadn't decided on his direction but he knew that it, too, would be different, more desirable, and more specific.

In his moment of ritual cleansing, the words of the great prophet echoed in his head again, but it wasn't as in a dream-like ecstasy where hope was seen but not touched. The words came with a force that would propel him higher and higher until the limit would not just be the sky and its elements, but as many skies as could be reached on many horizons. And with the words of the prophet came other words of spiritual insight that could make no sense in the flesh, words that spurred him on too and that taught him to release any counter intuition and leave it behind. *Was he not greater than the birds of the air?* And, for those who would continue to gloat at him, openly and in silence, *wasn't a table about to be prepared for him right before them?* Perhaps the table had always been there, well laid out and

323

extravagant, but he hadn't been able to see or eat from it. His eyes had to be opened first, his faith kindled, and his arms unleashed by the courage to reach out and take.

He was thankful to the Church and those who served in it selflessly, and to its source, the God that could remake continuity where it seemed to end. Whatever he would do and wherever he would go, whether within Cape Toria or beyond, and even if it took him back to the U.S., he would remain attached to the Church. *If, as his black Bible taught him, everything was possible with faith in God, then what were the chances that he could become a priest?* There could actually be more chances than there weren't. And even if it wasn't to the point of becoming a priest, he could investigate other openings, not only within the Church, but also within the institutions, organizations, and facilities it possessed. He would investigate within Cape Toria and far beyond, within the U.S. and places where he wasn't called *citizen*. If he had gotten this far when he wasn't expected to make it past the day of his birth, then he was prepared to sacrifice all without feeling like he lost everything. Until the day when God planned to call him, not an earlier date that would have been a blunder resulting from human sadism, he would embrace the Church and rummage hard until he found people buried in mud. Immersing everything he came with, he would reach far inside and pick them out, not stopping until he was completely done. Then he would raise them until the sun found and caressed their faces.

...

From inside the building they heard the tune. It was new and different from every tune they had ever heard. It was hard to explain how, but it was new and different. For people like Father Brendan and Sister Sweeney who had learned about his precious gift, they thought right that it came from him. They, with Rachel, had been studying an artistic piece on blood and torture when the tune wafted in, first through one window and then through other windows and doors. Father Brendan was the first to raise his head and head in the direction of the door that led out to the back. As if in obedience to a power that drove the three of them, the two ladies followed. The effect was contagious and soon a few visitors to the Museum, like acolytes in a funeral procession, headed in the same direction too; on their foreheads faint wrinkles asked many questions.

It was not like any tune they had ever heard from any instrument, let alone a flute. The way it built up then dropped suddenly without losing balance or solidity, the way so many subplots seemed to be written into one very moving story and in so few words, the way it hit its listeners as a dirge and panegyric all at once; it was unreal. The way so many pitch and tonal levels could be achieved didn't seem to make sense and yet it made so much sense. And though it wasn't for them, it soon arrested its uninvited listeners and held them captive. Once they chose to listen, there was no escape.

As he played, Monty pointed his silver flute in the direction of the burial ground that doubled up as an exhibit, and, with a prudence that could barely be detected, pointed it in the direction of where Father Brendan had indicated the other gravesite. The one that was a distance off and somewhere behind the tall, white walls. He wondered there and back, but only he understood his deliberate oscillation. It was in memory of his mother and, for now, he lost consciousness of anything else that would otherwise have mattered. He lost consciousness of anything else, living and unliving, within him and outside of him. Though he couldn't remember his mother in flesh, Father Brendan had exhumed her spirit and he had come to know and receive it. He played in memory of her and to her glory. He would play for others at another time; for now he would exhume and eulogize his mother alone. It was unusual for him to title the tunes he created, even though he could reach into his head and extract them from his rich repertoire of tunes whenever he felt like it. But this one he titled. He didn't title it before he started to play;

325

the title crept in as he raised his mother in elegy and adulation. He called it, *if only the wind would blow her way, if only....*

About the Author

The fifth child of Major General Philip Effiong and Josephine Effiong, Philip Uko Effiong was born in Kaduna, northern Nigeria, on November 5, 1960. He began his preschool education in Lagos, Nigeria, and finished his primary education in Enugu, Nigeria, where his family relocated after the Nigerian-Biafran Civil War in 1970. He attended secondary school at Holy Family College (High School) in Abak, southeastern Nigeria, and later received his university education at the University of Calabar, also in southeastern Nigeria, where he earned B.A. (Hons) and M.A. degrees in English and literature. In 1988 Philip Effiong was awarded a Fulbright Scholarship to pursue a Ph.D. in Theatre and Drama at the University of Wisconsin at Madison. He received his doctorate in 1994.

Philip Effiong has taught English, writing, drama, literature and cultural studies at the University of Calabar, the University of Wisconsin at Madison, the University of Tennessee at Martin, the University of Delaware at Newark, and Lincoln University in Pennsylvania.

Philip Effiong has also published a number of articles in literary journals and magazines, including twenty entries in the 1996 *Dictionary of Twentieth Century Culture* and a recent article in the 1998 summer issue of *African American Review*. His poems can be found in the following poetry collections: *Bean witch* 13 (1996); *Bean Switch* 12 (1995); *Whispers in the Wind,* Vol. 3 (1989); *My Heart Sings* (1989); *Voices on the Wind,* Vol. 2, (1989); and *Poetic Voices of America* (1989). His work of poetry, *Solitude,* is yet to be published. His dissertation, *In Search of a Model for African-American Drama: The Example of Lorraine Hansberry, Amiri Baraka, and Ntozake Shange*, has been accepted for publication by University Press of America, and should be in print later this year (2000). In 1998

Philip Effiong completed his first novel, *Give Me Words, I'll Fly*.

Also in 1998, Philip Effiong made a dramatic change from university teaching to computer programming, and currently works with Automatic Data Processing (ADP) in Rockville, Maryland, as a Senior Programmer Analyst. However, he continues to dedicate a lot of his time to writing.

Printed in the United States
6305

9 780759 608733